Totally Bound Publishing books by Jaime Samms and Sarah Masters:

The Dreaming
Tools of Justice
Tools of Change

I0598046

The Dreaming

TOOLS OF CHANGE

JAIME SAMMS and
SARAH MASTERS

Tools of Change
ISBN # 978-1-78430-647-2
©Copyright Jaime Samms and Sarah Masters 2015
Cover Art by Posh Gosh ©Copyright June 2015
Interior text design by Claire Siemaszkiewicz
Totally Bound Publishing

TOOLS OF CHANGE

Dedication

For Sarah — for being the brilliant writing partner and
friend that she is, and applauding my forays into the
dark with her (and holding my hand so I don't freak
the…heck…out, and for Stacey B., because she so gets
what it's all about to be dance mom, writer and
everything else and still keep on smiling. You inspire
me, baby!) — Jaime

Lova ya, Jaime — Sarah xxx

Chapter One

I'm a jerk. A goddamn fucking jerk.

Daniel sighed. Loud. Long. It felt like his lungs were going to collapse the way he arched his back and caved his stomach. As though he'd never breathe in again. And if he didn't, right now he couldn't give much of a shit. He'd fucked up, and a fuck-up wasn't someone he wanted to be. Couldn't be. At the time...well, he thought he'd been doing the right thing—thought he'd still had everything under control—but last night, everything had changed.

And then some.

He'd been the one to call the shots in his relationship with Jase. The twink was submissive in many ways, allowing Daniel to direct where they went, what they did and for how long. It wasn't as if Daniel had meant it to happen like that either. It just had—the way some relationships do—the way things form a pattern without your knowledge until it's too late. It was too late now, Daniel knew that as surely as he knew he'd get up off his bed in a minute and take a shower, and he could kick himself for not spotting the signs.

Fuck, he'd loved Jase—still did—but his little blond guy had moved on. Found someone else. And who could blame him? Daniel hadn't been supportive enough of those weird-arsed dreams Jase had been having. Didn't believe, like Jase did, that the dreams seemed too real *not* to be real.

Who the hell dreams real stuff? Who the fuck watches people die then sees the dead guy's story on the news a couple of days later?

It freaked Daniel the hell out, and he'd concentrated on how it made *him* feel, rather than being a support to Jase. Was Jase a freak? Was he one of those psychic people? Was he—God forbid—in on the murders? Could Daniel cope with that? In the midst of it all, he reckoned he couldn't, thought he'd go mental every time Jase woke in a sweat, gripping Daniel's arm so tight his nails sometimes drew blood. But then the morning always came, with Jase back to normal, going about his life as he'd always done. And Daniel had taken it for granted that Jase would always be there. Until that one morning when Daniel had spoken out, had ridiculed Jase. What kind of partner did that to someone he claimed to love, eh?

A bastard partner, that's who.

"So," he'd said as Jase sat up in bed beside him, "you had another one of your *real* dreams last night. It's got to stop. I can't go on like this much longer."

Jase had let his mouth drop open, and he'd widened his eyes—eyes full of hurt and incomprehension. "It's got to stop? I wish it fucking would! And *you* can't go on like this much longer?" He'd scrubbed his head, the sound of hair shifting against his fingers kind of obscene right then. "How the fuck d'you think I feel? I'm the one having the dreams. I'm the one struggling to make them stop and not being able to. I see shit,

Dan. See people being killed. Feel every stab, every bullet ripping through them. Through me." He'd laughed, a dry chuckle that had nothing to do with mirth and everything to do with incredulousness. "Yeah, I'd say you had it pretty damn easy only hearing about it."

It was the first time Daniel had seen Jase angry and it hadn't sat well. It had bugged the shit out of him, to be honest. The usually calm twink had ruffled feathers, and Daniel wasn't quite sure how to handle that. Daniel didn't like being at a loss, not knowing what to do, how to fix every situation. Reminded him too much of how he used to be when... But *that* morning he'd struggled to come to terms with Jase acting like he had.

Jase had gotten out of bed, shoulders hunched, arse presented to Daniel, and totally out of context, Daniel had had the urge to follow him and fondle that arse until Jase submitted, forgot the idea of his dreams being real. Daniel had wanted the anger gone, wanted to take away the rigidity in Jase's muscles, and in the past his hands *had* smoothed hurt away. He'd touched Jase with care, made him forget.

More than anyone ever did for me.

Liar. Jase did the same for you and you know it.

Fuck off.

Daniel remembered that morning with such startling clarity it was like he was living it all over again. He saw the tic flickering beneath Jase's left eye as his lover turned slightly to bend down and pick up the jeans he'd left on the floor the previous night. He saw Jase slide the denims up his legs, button them with slim fingers. And he saw the resentment in Jase's features as he turned to face Daniel fully, eyes watery, mouth quivering.

"You know what?" Jase had spat. "I don't need this fucking shit. You don't care about me, only your goddamn self. It's all about you, always has been, and *I* can't go on like *this* much longer. I can't help the dreams, can't help it that I know inside me they're real. Can't explain it either, and if you're honest—and let's face it, you always are, no matter how much it hurts me—you think I'm nuts." He'd bunched his hands into fists by his side then unclenched them again, like he worked his fingers over imaginary piano keys. "Look, we're done. We both know it. We're only together because of the fucking rent—for this place, for somewhere to live. I don't need this crap."

Fear—real fear—had gone through Daniel then, and he'd leaped from the bed to stand before Jase, suddenly apprehensive about touching him, for his hands to work their magic. But he'd reached out anyway, and Jase had lifted his arms, shoving Daniel in the chest.

That push had said more than Jase ever could. And it hurt. Not in the painful way of hand against flesh, the sting of skin on skin, but the other way. The one Daniel didn't like to dwell on too often because it meant he was weak. Meant he cared.

"No, it won't work this time," Jase had said. "You can't support me in this—it's not in your nature. It's better I go on by myself. Cope with the dreams myself. We'll sort this place out, give up the tenancy and go our own way. If you don't understand what I'm going through—don't even seem to *want* to understand—then our relationship isn't worth shit anyway, right?"

What Jase had said struck deep, burned more than the shove. Daniel, usually so forthcoming with the right words, silver-tongued and assured, having taught himself to be a different person to the one he was years ago, had been stumped for something to say. That Jase had come out of himself like that had shocked the shit out of Daniel. The bathroom door slamming, the lock being snapped across in annoyance, was the last time he'd seen Jase while they'd been a couple.

Daniel had left their apartment, waiting until Jase made his way to work before returning to gather his stuff. He'd put half the rent and utility bill money on the sideboard in the kitchen—a sideboard they'd fucked against in happier times—and had gone straight out to find the dump he currently lived in.

Christ, if he'd only taken a step away and looked at the bigger picture back then, he wouldn't be sitting here now in this crummy, one-room-plus-a-bathroom joint with roaches crawling up the damp beige walls. He wouldn't open the shabby, holey brown curtains and see a red-brick wall as his view, stained from the weather and multiple hues of birds' shit. He wouldn't look down to the alley below and see arced piss stains from the local hobos or men having been out on a bender, too lazy to wait.

He wouldn't be aching like a bitch—the kind of ache that left him numb from the inside out. Loneliness, that's what it was—all-out loneliness and regret, scoffing him whole. Before long it'd get rid of him all together if he wasn't careful, chewed up and spat out, the unpalatable bastard that he was.

Yeah, he knew he'd been wrong, but how the hell was he supposed to make it all better now? How did he learn to care more, to show it more without constantly battling with feelings that it wasn't right? Oh, he knew why he couldn't fully let go and tell Jase how he felt, to even admit it properly to himself, but he wasn't ready to explain that. Yet.

But you'll have to fucking learn to. He won't take you back if he thinks you're like you were before.

"Dickhead," he muttered, thinking a stream of other nasty names for himself. There was no one else to say them to him, no one to make him feel a worthless piece of shit.

No one to say the things he'd heard virtually his whole life.

Yeah, yeah, feel even sorrier for yourself. Dredge it all up, arsehole.

He shook himself, shrugged the memories away about...that. If he thought about the past, his childhood, it led to thinking about another 'that'. God, he'd drifted from one abuse to another, hadn't he? What a prick.

Shut up. I don't want to be a prick. Can't. Got to prove I'm not.

He shrugged again, concentrated on what he needed to focus on now. The past could wait. He'd analyze it one day. Just not today.

So he'd finally thought about the day he'd moved out of their apartment—the one they'd shared for two years, seven months and four days. The one they'd fucked in, laughed in, argued in. The one Jase had started dreaming in. The memories... Christ, they were other demons who ate Daniel alive, and here he was, messed up with no way of sorting himself out without acknowledging every other damn hurt he'd ever felt.

He'd followed Jase ever since he'd left, discreet distances between them, just so he could get a glimpse every day of what he'd lost. He was punishing himself—yeah, he was doing a good job of that all right. But on the days he didn't see Jase, he went a bit nuts. Like he had to see him in order to get through his long hours. And they *were* long—drawn-out bastards that made a pact with time to go slow, be agonizing. Taunting him for being such a selfish jerk. A game show with the host gleefully patting the loser on the back and saying, "Come and see what you could've won." Rubbing it in. Salt in the goddamn wounds.

Daniel shook his head, breathing stuttered, and pushed up off the bed. 'They' said time healed all wounds, that hindsight was a wonderful thing, that there were plenty more fish in the sea. Hindsight could go fuck itself, and he didn't want any other bloody fish. He wanted Jase back, and if what he'd seen last night was to be believed, he'd have a long wait.

What the hell have I done? What the fuck do I do now?

He went into his bathroom, a small affair that had just about enough room to hold a tub, sink and toilet. The wall tiles, grout stained with mold and God knew what else, needed a good scrub, as did the bath, with its outline of a slim limescale mountain at the far end by the taps—taps that dripped constantly no matter how tight he shut them off. But what was the point? There wasn't a point to anything these days. Daniel went to work—that damn demoralizing cell phone factory driving him more mental by the hour, sought out Jase after—yeah, just to spy on what he was up to—then returned home to wallow on his bed. It was all he had left to do. No energy to do anything else.

You need to get the energy. To do something. Anything.

In the tub, he washed all over, mind not on the task but on where he should go next. Last night came to mind… The worst of his life, he reckoned. Beat the abuse hands down—and he shuddered at the recollection. It was bad enough that Jase had moved in with some older guy—one Daniel had later found out was an ex-cop P.I. named Barry Whittaker—and made Daniel think Jase had gone for a father-figure type, but to then realize this Barry was a fag whose partner had also moved in? Shit, he'd thought all sorts. Were they a trio? Did they all fuck nightly in the same bed? What? What the hell was going on? But finding out that wasn't the case proved even worse. Jase wasn't fucking them. They weren't fucking him. No, from the looks of it, Jase had been taken under that Barry dude's wing, given time to get used to his new life.

And Jase had gotten used to it all right. Last night...

Shit. Stop thinking about it. You messed up. It's over. Really over.

Daniel splashed water over his face, the heat of it meshing with the hot sting of tears on his cheeks. What, he was crying now? Of all the goddamn things he'd done in his life, crying wasn't meant to be one of them. He'd cried enough for a thousand people in the privacy of his bedroom, got caught a few times by his old man who'd told him it was weak—a useless activity that just showed how gay Daniel was.

'I can just about tolerate the fact you're gay, Daniel. Just. But a crying faggot? No. No way.'

Daniel clenched his teeth until pain shot through his gums.

Please, fuck off. Just...just go away.

"Jase has met another man." There. He'd said it. Said the one thing he didn't think he could in order to push out the other hurts.

His old man would have a field day with this, knowing Daniel hurt so much.

"Jase has found another man and doesn't need me anymore."

His father would taunt him, say he couldn't even get being gay right.

"Jase is over me enough to be happy with someone else."

His father would have a right old laugh about this crap.

Fuck you, Dad, and the scabby donkey you rode in on.

The guy Jase had left the club with looked similar to Daniel, what with his craggy features — lived-in skin, Daniel liked to say — and dark hair that reached his shoulders. Funny, that. Was it significant? Did it mean Daniel was still on Jase's mind? Or did it just tell Daniel that Jase had a certain type?

I don't fucking know.

Daniel had followed them to a swanky address, his stomach bottoming out as Jase and the guy entered a posh place with a curving, brick-paved driveway. The house, all white façade and large windows, a roof that *so* didn't leak like his did and a mahogany front door with leaded panes, screamed money. How could he compete with that?

He let out a ragged sigh and rinsed off. Got out of the bath and scrubbed his skin dry with the only towel he owned, a ratty blue effort that had lost its fluff. He scrubbed until it hurt, the pain still not enough to eclipse that of the other kind. He ran the towel over his shaggy hair, as black as the gaping hole inside him, and strode out of the bathroom with a new sense of purpose. Thinking wasn't all that bad, then. Sorting through the muddle his thoughts had become had its benefits. He'd do something. Just had to think of what it was, that was all.

While dressing — a pair of dark jeans and a red polo top that had long since given up any pretense of looking new — he thought so hard about his next move that his head hurt. He huffed out a laugh.

Might as well have a hurting head to go along with everything else.

God, he felt sorry for himself, didn't he?

'Goddamn emotional faggot, Daniel. Never thought any son of mine would be so...so fucking wet.'

"Jesus Christ, just piss off, yeah?" he told the chilly air, running shaking fingers through his hair in lieu of a brush. "Sort yourself out. Think. *Think!*"

He lifted his duvet — the cover in need of a visit to the washing machine — shook it out then let it fall back onto the mattress in a semblance of the bed being made. Ignoring his pillow, still proudly bearing the indent of his head — *one head, not two. Sucks, fucking sucks* — he sat on the bed and pulled on his socks then his boots. Fuck work today. He'd call in sick. Fuck everything except his need to sort something out.

After shirking on his black jacket, he grabbed up his keys, stuffed them in his pocket, and left his shithole of a place. Out on the residential street void of people, he strode with his head down, half-seeing the gritty path beneath him, mind on a million things. After a time of walking, he lifted his head and found himself...there. The house Jase now lived in stood on the opposite side of the street, the second car gone from the drive, leaving the ex-cop's ugly green clunker parked at an angle by itself. Daniel glanced at his watch. Nine-thirty on a Friday morning.

Fuck.

He pulled his cell phone out, quickly rang work, adding a croak to his voice when he told the receptionist he was too sick to come in. *What's up, Mr. Priestly?* Tonsillitis, he reckoned. *You'd better get to the doctor, Mr. Priestly.* Yeah, he'd better visit the doctor, get it sorted. *Will you be in Monday?* He thought so, depended on how things went over the weekend.

Call ended, he stared across the street again, knowing Jase would have already left for work. A shadow inside the house drifted past the large window at the front, and Daniel matched it to the times he'd seen that shadow before.

The ex-cop's.

He was a P.I., right? He looked for people. Looked *into* people.

Daniel had Jase's new guy's address branded into his mind. He had a credit card he could draw from, one he kept for emergencies. Enough to pay a retainer. The barest of background checks, at least.

That was it. What he'd been waiting for. The answer. That something, that *anything* he could do to end the pain.

He crossed the street. Stood at the front door. Lifted his hand.

And knocked.

Chapter Two

Jason glanced at his watch. The black leather strap stood out sharp against his pale skin, seeming too expensive to be on his wrist and failing to hide the bruises. He gave the wrist a light rub. It didn't hurt that much. He hadn't exactly noticed when he'd acquired them, only discovered them in the shower this morning. He couldn't help but think Dan had never left a mark on his skin. Always went on about how gorgeous, how delicate his nude body was. Always careful not to leave bruises, even when he was being his usual strong, almost overbearing self.

Hadn't stopped the asshole leaving bruises on his heart, though, had it?

Jason pursed his lips and tried to ignore that much greater pain.

After a minute, he glanced at his watch again, not having actually registered the time on the first go-round.

Five after nine.

Late.

He studied the expansive kitchen. He was meant to have the place looking like he'd never been here. Karrick had been quite clear about that. And Karrick didn't seem the type of guy you discounted. When he said jump, you didn't even waste time asking how high. You jumped — and hoped you got it right.

Jason was rather proud of himself that he'd gotten it mostly right last night. It had been fun. Very unlike nights with Daniel. Karrick's control was absolute, whereas Daniel's just seemed desperate. Karrick wanted control for the sake of it. Daniel needed to control something because he couldn't control everything.

And it had been easy for Jason to allow Daniel control in bed because it meant he hadn't needed to worry so much about what he couldn't dictate. Like dreams.

"Fuck." He rubbed his fingers under his twitching left eye and frowned. As if he could rub Daniel out of his head. Not likely, however hard he tried. Even letting this Karrick stranger take him home and fuck him hadn't pounded his ex out of his brain.

Carefully, Jason pulled his thoughts back to what he was doing. Not that wiping down the counters and replacing his breakfast dishes in the cupboards required that much concentration.

Satisfied he'd gotten everything back the way it had been, he left the pristine room and wandered out into the hallway. Karrick had told him to wait for him in the foyer after he'd eaten, said he'd drive him to work, but he was beginning to worry the man was going to take too long with the phone call that had drawn him off into his study at the end of the hall.

Jase was meant to go and see Barry Whittaker today and put in some hours at the ex-cop's P.I. shop, and normally, Barry wasn't one to begrudge a few minutes on the clock here or there. Jason had had some pretty horrible nights when the dreams had kept him from sleeping. Barry never questioned when Jase said he'd had a rough, sleepless night. Jason didn't think this kind of rough and sleepless qualified as an excuse to swan in to work whenever he felt like it, though.

Determined he was not going to put himself in the position of having to lie to his boss and friend, Jason made his way down the plush-carpeted hallway to Karrick's office door.

"He isn't an issue. He's just a kid. A good fuck."

He heard annoyance in Karrick's voice, clipped tones telling him the older man was not happy about the conversation he was having. Jason lowered his hand from where he'd raised it to knock.

"Oh, calm the fuck down. I'll keep him if I want. He isn't any of your concern. Trust me...he won't interfere."

There was a pause and a heavy sigh from Karrick.

"Of course I can take care of him. If the need arises, but it won't arise because he doesn't have any idea what's really going on, and there's no reason for him to. He's a good boy. No need to worry."

Heat seared Jason's cheeks. Was Karrick talking about him like that? Like a possession? Or a well-mannered house pet? Once more he glanced at the gold-faced watch around his wrist.

Karrick had offered it to him two days ago as a loan, teasing Jason when he'd been late to Karrick's office with his lunch delivery for the third time in a row. As much as Jason loved working for Barry, it just wasn't enough to pay his rent now that he was living on his own. He couldn't have stayed living with Barry and Tag forever, after all. So he'd been forced to take another part-time job working at a lunch deli on the days he wasn't at Barry's office filing papers and cooking meals for Barry and Tag—the two were as hopeless in the kitchen as a one-wheeled cart without a horse—and part of his new job entailed delivering lunches to the posh offices across the street from the little diner.

Well, one of his most regular clients had quickly become Karrick Evens, a handsome, obviously very powerful man whose flirting had gone straight to Jason's head. When Karrick had laughingly offered Jason the watch right off his wrist, he'd also offered him something more substantial than flirting.

A date.

That date had led here, last night, and almost immediately to Karrick's bed. Almost immediately to the bruises as well, but Jason had felt a sort of satisfaction at the roughness, at the firm handling. In some ways, Karrick was a lot like Daniel. Not just in looks, but in the way he took such a dominant role, and Jason liked that. It made him feel safe.

And there was Daniel again, seeping into his thoughts like cancer. Daniel, who didn't believe in him, in his dreams, in anything that was really important. But who could make him feel safe and wanted with just a touch. Daniel, who didn't want to feel anything himself, but who could reach inside Jason and soothe every hurting thing just by wrapping his arms around him and telling him it would be okay.

Except it hadn't been. Because in the end, Dan had said, essentially, "You're a freak" one too many times. It was too hard for the man to put himself out there and believe when Jason most needed him to. Even at the last, when he'd resorted to tempting Dan's baser instincts, showing off his arse and half hoping for, half dreading, the touch that would take all the harsh words and ill feelings away.

Only that touch had never come, and Jason had returned home to an empty apartment. An empty life. Now, he thought bruises without any kind of emotional attachment might still be preferable to that emptiness. Not even Barry could help him fill that emptiness with all the understanding in the world.

* * * *

"You're late!" Barry's voice rumbled out from the kitchen, followed by a clatter of dishes and a string of mild cussing.

"What are you doing, Barry?" Jase leaned in the doorway to the kitchen, arms folded over his chest, a slight smirk on his face as he watched Barry fumble with the unopened vacuum pack of coffee.

"Making coffee, because my office boy is *late*," Barry grumbled.

"Oh, for the love of all that is good and decent, please don't." Jase gave up his post to hurry across the shiny linoleum tiles to Barry's side. "I know you're mad, but please, *please* don't make me drink your coffee as punishment." He eased the package from Barry's grasp and reached in front of him for the basket, already overfilled with fresh grounds.

"Oh, woe is poor, fucking you." Barry shuffled back to give him room.

Pausing in his task, Jase gave Barry a quick but careful once-over. His shirt was buttoned crookedly and he hadn't shaved. There were dark circles under eyes that held too much of the black left over from the Dreaming.

"Want to tell me about it?" Jase asked quietly, turning his gaze to the coffee.

Barry didn't like close scrutiny—Jase knew that—but the man looked in need of a good night's sleep and a friendly ear—probably in that order. But Jase also knew Barry wouldn't sleep without Tag around. Since Tag was out of town attending training, Jase could only offer the latter.

"What's to talk about?" Barry asked. "I had a bad dream."

Jase snorted.

"Not enough details," Barry said after a minute passed with only the sounds of the water running and Jase's puttering. "Never enough details. Not going to be able to save this one."

"We can't save them all, Barry. You know that." It twisted Jase inside out to remind his mentor of this fact. But it was true. Sometimes, even the Dreams came too late to do any good.

"That doesn't make it okay!"

The anger in Barry's voice ripped a new hole in Jase's heart.

"I know." Jase couldn't say anything else. This wasn't an argument. More like another litany of useless, brick-wall facts they continued to crash into, headlong and at speed, night after fucking night.

God. He missed Daniel. He missed the touch, the hands and the crooning that took all this shit away, if only for a short time.

Turning to face Barry, he offered the only thing he could. "Give me all the details you do have." Action was about the only thing that could appease Barry right now, he knew. Once Tag was back, it would get better again. "I'll run down every lead I can find. I'll talk to Leyton. I can set up a meeting. You just tell me what you know and we'll go from there."

"I really should..." Barry bit his lip.

"Should what?"

"A client. We got a client." He shook himself and straightened. "Simple stuff, really. Just a background check. That's all he could afford, but..."

"You want me to do it?"

"No." Barry smiled, and if it wasn't his usual, bright grin, it was an expression less haunted than the one he'd been wearing for days. "No. I will. It'll do me some good to think about something else. But you're right. I'll tell you the dream, then you can start running down details." Again, Barry gave himself a tiny shake. "Right. Good. Let's go."

Chapter Three

Karrick had dropped Jason off at Barry's place then returned home. Yeah, he'd told the boy he'd be going into work too, but what he didn't know wouldn't hurt him. He chuckled at that. Fuck, the boy didn't know the half of it.

On his bed, he crossed his hands over his chest and closed his eyes. He found this position the best one to make him relax and fall into the Dreamstate which took him to his master. As he allowed his body to grow heavy, he thought about what he had to do. His master, Morland, had been adamant that Karrick follow instructions to the letter, and he had—so far. He'd picked Jason up after watching him for several days. Easy as anything to get the needy little prick into his bed. Easy as anything to get the needy little prick to expect a long-term relationship too. Giving him the watch had seen to that. Telling him he wanted to dominate his arse for a long time to come had cemented it.

He'd known Jason was a sub from the minute he'd laid eyes on him. Small in stature, the boy—for that's what he looked like—was as fair-haired as it was possible to be without the aid of dye. Karrick's watch hung loose on Jason's wrist—he'd promised to have a few more holes added sometime in the future, got to give them something to look forward to—and Jason's arse wasn't as meaty as Karrick normally liked, but hey, a job was a job.

And getting a good fuck while he was working only sweetened the pot.

Morland had expressed concern that the other Dreamer master, Rivald, was set to rule them all. Morland had yet to have it confirmed, but his suspicion had watered the roots of unruly panic-weeds and Karrick's master was getting antsy. Rivald, according to Morland, was a master who, although tough, was somewhat friendly toward those working for him. Tools, they were called. Karrick didn't like that term. He was no fucking Tool. But if it meant being in on the biggest usurping Dreamers had ever seen, he'd keep his mouth shut on that. Morland wanted the ultimate master position for himself, and Karrick had no doubt in his mind that Morland would achieve it.

Unless Karrick got there first.

One of the other Tools posed a problem, though. Everyone else—Barry, Jason and Jessica, some young woman who'd joined one of Rivald's teams—had discovered they were Dreamers only recently. They'd naturally assumed what they'd been seeing while they slept were nightmares, until the problem guy, Leyton, had alerted them that wasn't the case.

Leyton, some scar-faced freak who, like Karrick, killed killers before they had a chance to snuff out too many lives themselves, was that problem guy. That Tool. He was one messed-up son of a bitch, a man

Karrick didn't relish meeting, but in order to help Morland, he had a strong feeling he'd come face-to-face with Leyton all the same. Leyton was Karrick's equivalent—the link to their Dream masters, the person who kept the other Dreamers under their command in line.

He thought about his Tools and smiled. One of them, Graham, had telephoned earlier, asking questions he had no business asking. Why did he think he had a right to give advice on what Karrick was doing? Graham knew how the pecking order worked Morland instructed Karrick, Karrick instructed Graham and the others.

Graham might need a short, sharp lesson in obedience if he carried on the way he had this morning.

Karrick's body grew heavier, and he felt the beautiful tug of Dream sleep calling him—a sleep unlike the usual. As he faded from this world into the next, he smiled and embraced the feeling of belonging that cocooned him during these times.

A cave stood in the distance, one he'd always wanted to go inside but had never dared. No, it belonged to Rivald, and any Tool just walking in wasn't welcome. Besides, Karrick would be seriously reprimanded if he walked into a domain not belonging to his master. He sighed, spying the carvings on the inner walls just inside the opening, like Egyptian hieroglyphs, telling the story of Rivald's reign as a master so far. Karrick wanted to see if that tale was as impressive as Morland's—or better. If he were honest, he had a suspicion Rivald was the stronger of the two masters. Of course, he had to shield those kinds of thoughts. Masters could read minds at any time, appear in the real world at any moment, and it wouldn't do for Morland to think Karrick wasn't trustworthy.

Karrick let out a soft chuckle. He wasn't trustworthy — far from it — but he played the game well. Morland had no idea, just like Jason...

He drifted away from Rivald's cave and moved toward another, some few hundred feet away. This entrance wasn't as large as Rivald's, and Karrick had to bend double to fit through the archway. Once inside, however, he stood upright and stared at the carvings on the walls. Morland had a good story, a sound basis for him being the one to rule them all, each chapter of his master life highlighted by the wavering flames in free-standing sconces dotted around the perimeter.

What Karrick wouldn't give to become a master...

As he wandered through another archway opposite then down a claustrophobic tunnel, he wondered why the hierarchy even had to change. It had worked well for years, Rivald and Morland each guiding their individual teams, taking their instructions from some higher being Karrick had never laid eyes on, had only heard things about. He'd been told by Graham — and wasn't sure if he ought to believe him, either — that the amount of Dreamers in the real world was increasing, which meant *more* masters were required instead of just the two.

So where had Morland got the idea he was in with a chance of being the only one? How could one master lead so many different teams all over the world?

He hated to admit it, but Graham might well be right.

Karrick came to the end of the tunnel and turned right into a well-lit space, a room-like area that held a couple of hard-backed chairs and a coffee table. This was where he was to sit until Morland was ready for him. The dust in this cave always got to him, and he cleared his throat then swallowed to try to ease the aridity. It didn't work, so he walked over to the far wall and placed his hand over a smooth, square piece of rock about a meter square. It slid out of the wall a couple of inches then lit up blue, showing a panel of buttons, each with a picture on them. He jabbed a finger on the drink button and summoned the image of a cool glass of cola into his mind.

Turning to look over his shoulder, he was pleased to see a pint glass full of his required drink fizzing on the coffee table.

He had to love this place.

Karrick sat and drank deeply, keeping his thoughts light now he was so close to Morland. He filled his head with visuals he thought his master might like to see — Morland taking Rivald's position, Karrick kneeling at Morland's feet as his master sat on the much-talked-about throne in Rivald's cave. Karrick doing Morland's bidding.

Oh, yeah, he knew how to play the game all right.

* * * *

Morland had kept him waiting thirty minutes so far. Karrick's throat was dry again, the respite the cola had given him long gone, and he rose to order another. He held his anger in check, irked at the fact he had to do as he was told but his master didn't. Wasn't them all working together, on time and in sync, what kept the Tools in line and the real world safe from harm? Okay, they didn't always catch killers in time — there were kinks in the chain that prevented them knowing who a killer was immediately sometimes — but they damn sure found them in the end and dealt with them in the only way the killers understood — by killing them too. Tools didn't always interpret the information fast enough, but given time, they'd learn to push their Dreams to reveal what they needed to know faster. Despite Rivald's latest team being relatively new, from what Karrick had observed, they worked well together and got the job done.

Then there was Jason to consider, the 'youngest' member of that team. Youngest in age and experience. He was just now learning who and what he was, and if Barry didn't keep him in line, the boy could royally fuck things up. Which was where Karrick came in. He'd be a delicious distraction, infiltrating Jason's dreams himself if he had to, putting false knowledge into his mind so Barry and Leyton didn't know where the hell to turn and what the fuck was happening.

Karrick had to watch he didn't attract Rivald's attention, though. He didn't much fancy being on the receiving end of that horned bastard's wrath. Still, Morland had promised to protect him, and he had to believe that.

"You may come to me now."

Morland's voice brought Karrick out of his thoughts, and he stood, waiting for the fake wall to open, giving him access to his master's domain. The rock shimmered. A crack appeared from ceiling to floor, parting like a watery curtain to form a crevasse through which Karrick could enter. He did so, hearing the rock close behind him, and stood staring at Morland resting on his side on a gold-colored velvet chaise.

"Sorry to have kept you," Morland said, tucking stray curls of black hair behind his ears. "I was in a Dreamer meeting with my master. We have some important things to discuss. Please, sit."

Karrick sat on an Edwardian chair at the end of the chaise and stared at Morland. His master was a peculiar mix of creatures, not horned with goat feet like Rivald, but a fucked-up version of a human being. Oh, he had a human body, albeit with lion paws as feet, but the skin on his face resembled a tree trunk, all roughness and gouged-out lines, his nose a knothole of bark. And that skin, the same, green-gray hue of years' old, molding trees, looked hard to the touch.

Karrick suppressed a shiver.

"My master has told me some disturbing news, Karrick. Unless you can up your quota" — he cleared his throat — "and beat Leyton's impressive killing results, then the sole Mastership will most likely go to Rivald. His results far outshine mine — Leyton's results far outshine *yours* — and something must be done to remedy this."

"I thought we had this in hand, Master."

"So did I, but it seems we have less time than I thought."

"But it takes patience to infiltrate a Tool group. Jason isn't going to introduce me to the others any time soon. I need a few weeks to have him eating more out of my hand than he is already. Barry has the boy thinking he has a right to his own opinion, therefore I'm finding it tougher to tell Jason otherwise."

Morland waved a dismissive hand, fingernails similar to dog claws. "That may be the case, but I do not think we have the amount of time you need. Your Tools need to understand their dreams sooner, find the killers in swift order, not sit about for days trying to decipher what they have been shown. They have a unique gift, and from where I am sitting, they are squandering it."

From where you're lounging, more like.

"I shall pretend I did not hear that, Karrick. I understand this will put you under a lot of pressure, so your outburst has been forgiven."

Karrick brought a shutter down on his thoughts before he revealed exactly what he thought of his master. He had the urge to get up, leave the cave and seek out Rivald, telling him everything. But that wouldn't be wise—not if Karrick's plan to take Morland's position was to happen.

"So, what do I have to do?" Karrick asked, staring at a long strand of hair growing out of Morland's navel.

"That, dear boy, is what I am about to tell you."

* * * *

Daniel had waited two days for Barry Whittaker to get in touch and the silence was almost killing him. He'd visited the guy, been inside the house, walked the floors Jase had walked, and shit, he swore he could smell him everywhere.

Or maybe that had just been wishful thinking. Jase did have his own place now, didn't he? Daniel couldn't decide if that was better or worse than him living with Whittaker.

Barry had told him with great honesty that he might not find anything out for days. Although Daniel had only requested a simple background check, the P.I. insinuated he had things on the go he might have to attend to at a moment's notice, shoving Daniel's request further down the ex-cop's to-do list. At the time, Daniel had nodded, eager to hand over his money, grateful Barry had said he'd help him at all. But now?

God, it was hard going.

He'd tailed Jase again since visiting Barry. Shouldn't have, really, because the journey always ended up at that new bloke's place with Jase and his man disappearing inside. This morning, though, as Daniel had waited outside the man's house he'd noticed a dark bruise on Jase's wrist as his former lover had gotten into the car.

The sight had pained him. Brought it home that Jase was a sub for this guy, doing all the things he used to do for Daniel. Oh, it was all well and good *thinking* you knew your ex was fucking someone else, but when you saw the proof, when you knew another hand had stroked their cock, other lips had kissed their mouth...

It hurt.

Daniel had walked in the direction of Barry's home and office, the car with Jase in it long gone. He'd telephoned in sick again—Monday morning had come around pretty damn quick—and reached his destination a little after nine forty-five. He sat behind a bush to watch the house, hoping to see Jase's silhouette as he did whatever the fuck he did inside there.

Instead, Jase left the house with Barry. They appeared in a hurry and got into the car, speeding off down the road with a squeal of tires.

What the fuck was going on?

With nothing to do but wait it out, Daniel sat on the damp ground and hoped the homeowner whose bush he occupied didn't spot him. This was an okay place for him to hide for a little while, but it stood to reason he'd be caught sooner or later.

An hour passed. Daniel yawned, wondering if he'd gone loopy. He'd turned into one of those mad stalker exes, but he couldn't help it. He missed Jase so badly, and if all he could manage was to apologize just so

Jase knew Daniel hadn't meant to be so goddamn selfish. He'd take that and try to move on.

Although that would be painful as hell.

He closed his eyes, bent his legs and rested his forehead on his knees. He stayed like that for a short time, keeping an ear out for the sound of Barry's car, but the street was silent apart from chattering birds. He almost nodded off so snapped his head up and opened his eyes.

Jase's new bloke stared at him through the leaves, head cocked to one side. His lips spread in a wide, unnerving grin. "What are you doing in there, Daniel?"

Chapter Four

"We have to hurry up!" Jase bounced in place in the passenger seat of Barry's car. "Come on. Come on," he muttered under his breath as Barry slowed to let a mother pushing a stroller cross at the walk.

"Jase, you know this is probably a wild goose chase, right? The Dreams..." He shook his head. "They don't work like this."

"Mine do." Jase clenched then unclenched his fists. "I know what I saw. We can still stop it."

"Here." Barry handed him his cell. "It's still ringing. Just tell Tag what's going on."

"So he can fret from halfway across the country?" Jase shook his head but put the phone to his ear.

"Just in case something happens to us."

It was Barry's turn to mutter to himself. Jase felt for the man. Barry had tried contacting Tag twice, but the phone had cut him off before he'd gotten to his partner's voicemail both times. He'd even tried thinking his way through to Leyton but failed.

Jase suspected lack of sleep had muddled Barry's head and made contacting the other members of their team difficult in the past few days. Barry said all he got when he tried lately was an odd sort of static, like his radar was skewed or the tuner knocked off the station.

As yet, Jase's abilities hadn't progressed to the level of the other team members'. He was beginning to wonder if they ever would.

"Tag." Jase spoke into the phone the second it went to voicemail. "We've got a lead. Going to check it out. It's…" He peered at the watch dangling from his wrist and squinted at the fogged-over surface. "Shit. Morning. Monday morning. We got this guy, Tag, before Leyton could this time —" The phone clicked and a mechanical female voice told him the customer he was trying to reach was away from his phone. "No fucking shit." Irritated, Jase snapped the device closed then tossed it onto the dash. "Piece of shit cell. Twenty-first century, Barry. Get a fucking smart phone already."

Once more, Jase glanced at his watch, but he must have left it on when he'd showered or something because tiny droplets of water clung to the inside surface of the crystal and obscured the position of the hands.

A queasy twist cornered a bit of fear in his gut as he wondered if Karrick would be pissed at him if he'd destroyed the watch.

"Where'd you get that?" Barry asked, sparing a bit of attention from the traffic to indicate the new jewelry on Jase's wrist.

"Just…" Jase shrugged and covered it with his other hand, also hiding the bruises. "This guy."

"This guy." Barry tipped his head and fixed a skeptical look on Jase for a second. "And was it before or after he gifted you with those bruises that he gave you the bling?"

"What are you? My father?"

"Friend." Barry returned his attention to the task of driving. "I'm your friend, Jason. Sue the fuck out of me for giving a shit."

Jase pulled in a sharp breath then let it out again. "It's nothing." He scrubbed at the marks, as if he could get them off, smudges of charcoal-colored evidence of something he shouldn't have to be ashamed of.

"Not my business what you get up to in bed with blokes, Jason, but…"

"But what?" He shot for belligerent but landed somewhere between pathetic and petulant.

"Nothing." Barry tightened his fingers on the steering wheel and shook his head. "Forget it."

"Whatever." Jase directed his glare out of the passenger window, continuing to trace over the more tender marks with his fingertips.

Outside, his old neighborhood staggered by around the stop-and-go traffic. Barry inched the car along, and Jase's former building, where he'd shared the apartment with Daniel, came into view. His gut turned over. He moved his fingers faster on his wrist. He couldn't stop his gaze drifting upwards to the bay window that faced out to the street below from their old living room.

A ghost of foggy darkness drifted in front of the building. Jase stopped breathing for a second or two. He rubbed frantically at his wrist, leaving a burn behind.

"Stop the car." He reached for the door handle. "Barry, stop the car!"

"What?"

"Stop!" The Dream he'd detailed to Barry less than a half hour ago that had led them out here trickled through his head. He could see the details change as it scrolled through his memory like a movie trailer. The street sign in his dream came into focus as dark fog drifted over it and away. "Here, Twenty-Ninth," he whispered. Not Ninth. "Fuck!"

"That's here." Barry swerved from the lane up onto the curb then threw the car into park. "But where here?"

"There." Jase pointed up to the window of his old apartment. A ghost of a figure passed behind the sheer curtains. He knew the silhouette. "Dan..."

He knew it couldn't possibly be. Knew Dan had moved out, too, to some smaller, rat-infested shithole, but the shadow was him. Then it was gone, dissipating in a rain of sharp shards that pierced Jase's mind and left him screaming in agony, rocking and holding the sides of his head, his brow bouncing off the dash.

"Jase!"

Barry gripped his shoulders, held him back from ramming his brains out. Jase felt the grip but couldn't react. Only the glass slivers of his false dream mattered as they sliced through him.

"Jason!"

"Fuck..." He moaned and sagged against Barry, the pain beginning to fade.

"What was that?"

Jase shook his head. Tremors ran through him, tightening his muscles into knots. "I have to..." He couldn't catch his breath. "Have to..."

"What, Jase, have to what?"

Barry smoothed his hand down Jase's back now, and Jase gripped a fold of the P.I.'s shirt.

"Find him."

"Who?" Barry asked.

He could feel Barry trying to pry him upright, to see into his eyes.

"Who do you have to find? Daniel? Jase, did Daniel give you those bruises?"

"No!" Jase tore himself free of Barry's grip. "No. Dan wouldn't..." His head swam as he moved and fumbled again for the door handle. "I have to find him." After getting the door open, he toppled out, almost on his knees before he found his feet then pelted off down the street, back the way they had come.

He didn't know where he was going. The world, shrouded behind a gray mist of confusion, passed in jagged snatches of dulled color and frightened faces. People scattered out of his way.

He knew only that he had been brought here, to this place, the one place he'd ever felt...right...for a reason, and it wasn't a good one. The knife-edge of pain had eased, but his muscles still cramped and made him stagger. Behind him, Barry hollered down the street. He ignored the shouting, turned the corner and let his instincts guide him.

The car drive had been long, Barry taking the easiest route through the busy city streets from Barry's house to the downtown core. Jase knew the streets like the back of his own hand, and he dodged down an alley which spat him out across from a park. He jumped a bench and a flower planter, leaving behind the barking of a yappy little dog. He crossed a path, dodged a wading pool then lurched through a sandbox. Grit flew up into his hair and down the back of his shirt, but he kept running.

The watch on his wrist banged against the bones and the band spun. He lifted his arm, clutching it to his chest, terrified he'd lose the thing, even while he fixated on the ghostly figure in his mind of his ex-lover disintegrating before his eyes. The band of the watch dug into his wrist, the buckle like molten metal cutting into flesh.

"No."

He refused to believe the Dream meant anything. Barry had been right. They didn't work that way. He'd been too literal and he'd missed something.

His feet hit pavement on the far side of the park. His breath burned hot, liquid fire running through his lungs, but he pushed on, letting the fading pull of the dream guide him down another alley and out to another street and there, he skidded to a stop. Every breath scorched his throat, his legs cramped and his knees shook and threatened to give out on him.

Back where they'd started. His flight had led him right back to Barry's street. He shuffled off the sidewalk into the gravel on the side of the narrow road. Three houses on Barry's side of the street passed as he dragged himself toward *something*. Two houses on the far side of the street sat with empty driveways, then the duplex closest to Barry's and he was at Barry's house. Like a giant hand guided him, he turned, back to Barry's house, and stared at the empty lot across the street, at the tall cedars lining the deserted yard.

His imagination showed him a few tendrils of fog curling along the sidewalk. It had to be his imagination. The fog snaked and twisted through the low branches of the cedars, disappearing behind their screen. He blinked. A dust mote and a swirling flurry of cigarette butts and gum wrappers skittered along with a soft plunk and crackle he shouldn't have been able to hear from that distance.

Like someone was trying to make it too real, a movie effect conjured for his benefit.

"Jason?"

The soft purr of his name snapped him out of the surreal moment and he looked up. Right into Karrick's deep, incredibly dark eyes, still shrouded behind a pall of smoke and shadow Jase couldn't blink away.

"K—" His voice broke.

"What are you doing here?" Karrick reached for him, taking a firm grip around his wrist, big hand covering the welts left by the watch bracelet.

Jase winced. "I—"

He twisted his hand, but Karrick held on, his gaze turning slightly frigid.

"I was... I thought there was someone," Jase said, though who he'd been looking for slipped from his memory like a bad Dream.

"Who?" Karrick spread a patch of warmth over his shivering by placing his other hand at the small of Jason's back.

Jase glanced around, then at Karrick, and got caught up in the dark, forbidding glare. "I—" The Dream he'd chased across the city faded, dissipated—a wet, sticky sensation gloaming onto the last dregs of it and dragging it all away. "What? I...don't know." He relaxed, tension running out of him, and shook his head. "Doesn't matter. What are *you* doing here?" A smile played over his lips.

"Business." Maybe Karrick's gaze darted to the tall cedars across the street. Maybe he hadn't, for a second, taken his eye from Jase's. "But I'm done with that for the time being. Come." He lowered Jase's hand, although he didn't relinquish his hold. "We have the afternoon off. What say we spend it together?"

"Sure." Jase fell into step beside him and let Karrick lead him off to a car on the corner. He got in, buckled his belt and smiled at his lover. "Your place?"

"Insatiable creature, you are, Jason." But Karrick smiled and started the engine then smoothly guided the car from the curb.

A drab, green sedan passed them on the corner, traveling fast in the opposite direction, and a twinge of doubt twigged at the edges of Jase's mind.

Karrick reached for his hand across the seat and squeezed his fingers. "Relax, cherub. We have the entire afternoon to ourselves."

* * * *

In his car, Karrick studied the young man at his side. There was a wild light in his eyes. Eyes that were darker around the edges than they should be, a deeper shade of steely gray overtaking the pale blue. Karrick frowned. Manipulating a Dream was dangerous, even in a seasoned Dreamer. Messing with one so young and untried was downright idiotic. Speculation was rampant that some of the very killers they took down were failed, twisted, malformed Dreamers listening to the half-heard whispers in their heads.

What choice had he had, though? He'd had to deal with his young lover's ex somehow. He had no wish to kill innocents, but Daniel Priestly was becoming a nuisance.

The question was, how had Rivald known anything about it? And on such short notice? How had he contacted Jason so quickly? How the *hell* did he know? Karrick had been forced to manipulate Jason's vision on the fly, and he'd very nearly shattered the boy's mind.

"You all right?" he asked quietly, letting the concern filter through. It didn't matter if the kid thought it was genuinely for him. That could only help.

"Headache," Jason mumbled.

Karrick reached over and laid a hand on Jason's trembling thigh. "We'll soon take care of that."

"Mmm." Jason nodded but kept his head bowed.

"Want to tell me what happened?" Karrick asked.

Jason shook his head.

"You're bleeding." Karrick touched a finger to the skin just above the welts on Jason's wrist. "Who did that?"

"No one." Jason tugged his hand out of reach. "I just..." He shrugged.

"You look like you've seen a ghost, Jason," Karrick said, keeping one eye on the road and one on Jason.

The blond snapped his head up and stared over at him, eyes big and round in his pale face. The dark was dissipating, finally, and now he just appeared scared.

Scared played right into Karrick's hands.

"What?" Jason's voice quavered.

A tiny twitch beneath his left eye drew Karrick's attention and he had to resist the urge to smooth it into stillness.

"Relax, cherub. Whatever it is, it can't hurt you now. I can protect you." He reached again, and this time, Jason offered his hand and Karrick laced their fingers together. "You're safe with me, Jason. Just relax."

The rest of the ride home was blessedly short, and Jason was as pliable as putty in his hands as he took him inside, undressed him then carefully, thoroughly, scrubbed his small body clean in the shower. By the time he was kneeling at Karrick's feet, naked, his hands tied securely in a soft scarf and laying in his lap, Jason was the picture of perfect, obedient calm.

"Such a beautiful thing," Karrick said, caressing the fair skin of Jason's cheek.

Jason gazed up at him, silent. Finally, the blues of his eyes were pure again, almost luminescent, and Karrick smiled.

"Lovely lips." Karrick caressed those, too, and stroked his own hard cock.

Jason darted his gaze to that movement for a split second before bringing it back to Karrick's face.

"You want that?" Karrick asked.

He dragged the wet tip of his cock over Jason's cheek, stopping just at the corner of his lips. A sticky trail glistened against skin blushed to a perfect, pale pink.

Jason nodded and licked his lips.

"Good."

Karrick let his hand drift back to Jason's hair and touched his cock to those pretty lips. Force didn't have to be all about rough and hard. He slid his cock into Jason's eager mouth, curled his fingers into his hair and made it very clear he was in charge of how fast and how far Jason took him.

Jason blinked up at him, and Karrick felt a surge of gratification at the sight of those pale blue eyes and perfect lips, the complete trust. This was his.

He pushed deep.

Jason tried to stop only once.

Karrick tightened his grip on Jason's hair and smiled at the way his cock strangled the yelp of pain as he pushed in farther and studied Jason's reaction. He panicked, of course, Karrick's cock cutting off his airway.

Jason flared his nostrils, widened his eyes, and still Karrick held him in place.

"Relax, cherub."

Jason twitched, his posture stiff. His eyes watered, but at last, he gave in and Karrick felt him melt into proper submission.

"That's it, cherub."

He touched Jason's cheek and began to pump his hips, pushing deep once more, picking up speed, thrusting until Jason's tears spilled and Jason was huffing noisily trying to keep up.

When Jason glanced up, a pleading look in his eyes, Karrick relented and pulled clear.

"Get up." Karrick kept his voice low, but the power was not mitigated by the soft tone.

Jason didn't hesitate, nor did he balk when Karrick took his tied hands and raised them, catching the cloth holding them over an ornamented hook hanging from the iron bed frame above.

Karrick was gratified to see the boy's cock hard and jutting out in front of him, and his gaze soft. Whatever plane Jason was on, he clearly liked it there. Stepping back, Karrick admired his trophy. All pale skin and flushed need, Jason had to lift up onto his toes to keep all his weight from pulling at his shoulders. It was the perfect place to keep him, if he ever got out of line. It was tempting. He was lovely, and to have the convenience of flogging him or fucking him whenever Karrick wanted...

He shook himself, dragging his thoughts back to this moment. He had wandered to his wardrobe for lube and slathered some on his cock, using lazy gestures that commanded Jason's full attention.

"Mine," he whispered in Jason's ear, stepping close, stopping right against Jason's back, cock in hand.

He wrapped both big hands around Jason's slender waist and used that grip to hold the smaller man in place, allowing him to claim what was his. Jason's cry rang out, rugged and broken as Karrick forced the stretch necessary to take his cock.

"That hurt?" he asked.

Jason whimpered, bobbing his head in assent, chest heaving, lungs working to catch his breath.

Karrick moved part way out then pushed back in deeper, listening to the sounds while he pumped, feeling the heat rise on Jason's skin. If it was pain, it couldn't be all bad pain, because Jason didn't ask him to stop. His cock never flagged once, although his entire body shook and his voice grew hoarse.

When it seemed like the pain had fully dissipated and was turning to pleasure, Karrick shifted his grip, sliding his hands up and trusting Jason to keep himself in place. Karrick strayed his fingers over tight nipples then pinched, hard, until Jason's voice rose and he thrust his hips back and bowed his head.

"Painful?" Karrick slipped a thumb over one tiny bud.

Jason shivered. "Yes," he hissed.

"Do it again?" Karrick licked at a bit of sweat rolling lazily down Jason's back.

Silence.

Karrick stilled.

"Again?" Karrick asked, letting a twist of anger bend the word.

"Again." Jason's consent was barely audible.

Was he ashamed of the way he wanted it? Karrick couldn't tell. But he reveled in the surrender, in the way Jason clearly ached for him to move again, tension humming through every taut muscle and his breath coming in short, sharp gasps. All that power.

Karrick held it over Jason, could do anything, and he knew it. They both did.

Yet there was no fear in Jason when he asked, "Again. Please."

Karrick obliged, letting out the pent-up energy he would normally have spent by killing Daniel. He pinched that nipple, hammered his cock hard into Jason, no mercy. He'd spent all the mercy he had in not killing when he'd had the chance. It was a new, frightening thing to realize Jason *wanted* what every other one of Karrick's marks had feared.

Jason's voice rose and fell on waves of rushing adrenaline until his voice was rougher and his words garbled.

"Once more." Karrick pulled Jason's body back tight against his, snapping his hips forward and burying himself deep. He snuck one hand up to wrap it loosely around Jason's throat. Continued the torture on his nipple with his other.

Jason dropped his head back onto Karrick's shoulder. His entire body went still, rigid, and he came, not with a shout but with the softest of whimpers.

Jason's Adam's apple bobbed beneath Karrick's palm, and he felt the tight squeeze of that slim, perfect body around his cock. His own orgasm washed over him and he flattened his hands, pressing Jason to his chest, holding him there as his release pumped out.

Jason melted into him, every muscle going as lax as it had a moment ago been rigid. If Karrick let him go, he knew the boy wouldn't be able to hold himself up. Carefully, he lifted him then removed the ties from the hook so he could lower Jason to the bed. He untied him, preparing to get himself to the bathroom and cleaned up, but Jason's eyelids flickered and he looked up.

Karrick didn't recognize the expression on the young man's face. He did know, in that moment when Jason had given over control of everything, including his pain, Karrick had felt something flutter somewhere inside. He'd ignored it, fucked it out in hard thrusts and invested every touch to Jason's body with it, knowing he could never let it linger inside himself.

He half-expected some sort of dreamy smile aimed at him.

Jason watched him, face devoid of expression, gaze fixed on him, tracking Karrick's every motion.

Karrick propped one knee on the bed. "Come on," he said gruffly, needing Jason to move, to break the spell of watchfulness. "Get up." He peeled the covers back and shooed Jason up to put his head on the pillows.

They both crawled in and Jason shuffled close to curl against him. Karrick allowed the snuggling, letting Jason rest his head on Karrick's shoulder. He wrapped an arm around Jason's slight frame.

In a few minutes, they were both still and comfortable.

Jason said nothing, and Karrick deliberately kept his mind off whatever had just happened. Kept his mind off that *something*.

Jason had always known certain things about himself. Physical sensation, intense enough, took everything else away for a while. Pain didn't have to be bad. He'd known this a long time, and he'd very quickly let Dan in on that fact.

A smile crept over Jason's face. Dan. Dan, who had a hot wax fetish that had satisfied them both in that regard.

But Karrick wasn't Dan. And this pain had been something else. Frightening. Perfect. And like a drug he *knew* was going to be bad for him. A drug he knew he'd come back for.

Somewhere in the back of his mind, he was aware that the afternoon with Karrick had obliterated something important. Something he cared about.

Mentally, he cataloged all the little sensations left over from Karrick's touch. He was still exploring them when he fell asleep.

Chapter Five

Daniel blinked up at a perfect, clear blue sky. Grass tickled his palms and sun shimmered into his eyes.

"Wha—?"

He lay still for a while, aware of an overwhelming lethargy and stiffness in his body. His brain staggered through the memories of what he'd done and where he'd been until it finally brought him current to the last thing he remembered.

Jase's new lover. Jase's new lover with the black eyes and the voice like cold fog and empty spaces.

Daniel groaned and rolled to his feet, testing his wobbling legs carefully before he pushed through the hedges and stepped out into the street.

Across the road, Barry's car sat crookedly in his drive.

"Not going to happen," Daniel muttered, clenching his fists and stalking across the street and up the drive. "Damned if I'm walking away from this shit."

He knocked on the front door, waiting with his hands on his hips. This man, this Karrick guy, whatever he'd done to him, was not going to get his claws into Jase.

The door flew open just as Daniel lifted a fist to knock again.

"Jase!" Barry backed up a step, glancing over him and the porch beyond in a vague sort of way before he spoke again. "Oh. You. Sorry. Not done yet. You'll have to come back another time."

He was already swinging the door shut and turning away before Daniel had a chance to speak.

"Wait!" Daniel put out a hand and hurried into the house. "Wait. What about Jase? Where is he?"

Barry spun around. "How do you know Jase, exactly?" His dark eyes blazed. "Who the hell are you?"

Daniel pushed back the sting of realizing two years together hadn't been enough for Jase to tell even his closest friends who he was. Had their relationship already been so shaky when Jase met Barry that Daniel hadn't warranted even a passing mention?

"We have to talk," Daniel said quietly. "I think Jase is in a lot of trouble."

Barry sighed and closed the door. "Come through to my office."

Daniel followed, sitting in the same black leather chair he'd occupied the last time he'd been here. Barry didn't sit opposite him, instead stood in front of the voile-draped window, looking outside. The man's back was rigid beneath a black pullover, as though he suppressed the need to pace or do something constructive. Daniel knew all about how that felt, but he was still weary, baffled over what the hell had happened out there in that bush.

"So," Barry said, voice tight. "Get on with it. And it'd better be good, otherwise you're out of here. I don't have time to waste."

Daniel took a deep breath and stared out the window too, seeing nothing but the images in his mind. "That guy I asked you to check out for me…"

"Karrick Evens, yes. What about him?"

"Jase has been seeing him."

Barry spun to face Daniel, pressing his hands to the desk and leaning forward, his fingertips going white. "What?"

"They met recently. Jase has been going to his place—staying there the night. It's him who hurt Jase, gave him bruises on his wrists." Daniel tapped his hands on his knees, nervous beneath the P.I.'s frightening glare.

Barry frowned. "And just how do *you* know Jason?"

"I was… I was his boyfriend before…before he came to stay with you."

"Ah. You're *that* Dan? How did it end—and why?" Barry cocked his head as if waiting to catch Daniel out in a lie.

"Not well. I moved out. I wasn't… Jase kept having these nightmares, and I wasn't supportive. I didn't understand. He said… Fuck, this is going to sound nuts."

"I doubt it. Go on." Barry sat in his chair and propped his elbows on the desk, lacing his fingers in front of his chin.

"All right." Daniel took a deep breath, sick that he was about to divulge Jason's secrets. But Barry had said he wouldn't be surprised, so it was okay to talk about it, right? They both cared about Jase, and it was all for the good. "He said the dreams were showing him things. Killings. And…shit, they appeared on the fucking news after he'd dreamed about them. At one point I thought—"

"He was the killer?"

"Yes."

"Understandable. I'd think the same in your position. If it makes you feel better, my partner thought the same as you over my dreams. And?"

Barry has those dreams too? "We split. But I couldn't stand being apart from him so, uh, I tracked him." Daniel felt all kinds of bastard, like some freaky weirdo stalker. "It isn't how you think. I wanted to make sure he was okay. I…um, I missed him. Still do."

Barry nodded. "Continue." He drew a notepad toward him then began jotting.

Daniel breathed a sigh of relief that he was being taken seriously. It wasn't something that happened very often in his life. He'd always known he was a waste of space and time, just like his old man had told him. Jase had been the first to tell him otherwise, and now Jase's friend acted like Dan wasn't a complete freak… But he needed to get a move on so Barry could do something about finding Jase, making sure he was safe.

"So after Jase met that guy," Daniel said, "I came to you. Then this morning, I dropped by here, saw you both going out. I hung around for a bit, hoping to catch sight of Jase when you got back because…well, just because, but that Karrick guy, he… Shit, he caught me hiding in the bushes across the street."

Barry lifted his head, pen poised over the pad. "What happened?"

"He did something to me."

"What?"

"I don't know. He asked me what I was doing there, then his eyes went funny and I fell back, wanting to just go to sleep, you know?"

"His eyes went funny how?" Barry frowned again, the ridges in his brow deep.

"They did this thing. I swear to you I'm not mucking about, but they went black. Totally fucking black."

"Shit!" Barry stood, scraping his chair backwards. "Shit!"

Reflexively, Daniel flinched, shrinking back into the chair and half lifting an arm as Barry held up a hand. But all he did was poise it there in the air between them, palm out and say, "This is going to look fucking weird, so just indulge me, all right? I have to think. I have to contact someone, and you need to sit there quietly while I do it."

"Sure. I won't listen in on your call." He felt ten times a fool for the way he'd cowered but Barry hadn't seemed to notice so he straightened again and tried to ease his breathing back to normal.

"Uh, it isn't a phone call. I can't explain it now, but just shut up and wait a few minutes."

Daniel didn't know what the fuck to think. Was this Barry some nutcase or what? He stared at the P.I., who sat behind his desk and leaned back in his chair. He closed his eyes, pressed his fingertips to his temples, his lips in a blanched tight line. Barry frowned, and those lips of his disappeared as he curved them over his teeth.

What the hell?

Barry opened his eyes, blinked a few times and stared at Daniel.

With black irises.

"Holy shit! You're like him!" Daniel jumped up, ready to bolt the hell out of there and go home, go anywhere but be near this nutter. He reached the door and gripped the handle.

"Wait!" Barry said.

Daniel turned to see Barry had remained in his seat.

"I'll explain everything," Barry said, "but first you've got to understand. I am *not* like him. Yes, our eyes go black—and Jesus, I *know* how weird that looks—but I swear to you it isn't how it seems. Jase is also like him, like me, but me and Jase fight for the same side. I don't know about Karrick. I've had a hell of a time tracking down anything about him past two years ago."

Daniel gripped the door handle but didn't turn it. "So...what did you just do?"

A sigh bled out of Barry and he slumped slightly. "Nothing. Tried to contact someone..." He shook his head. "Difficult to explain. All you need to know is that it didn't work. It isn't working at all." This last bit seemed to be said to himself, without his being aware he'd said it out loud.

Daniel tightened his grip on the door handle, his hand sweaty. "How do you know that? You said when I got here you hadn't done the check on Karrick yet."

"Hadn't finished it yet, actually." Barry motioned toward the empty chair. "Please, sit down. Please, for Jase. I need you to be calm and listen without running out on me. God knows I realize this is going to sound fucking insane to you—it all did to me at first—but if you want me to help Jase, you *have* to stay here so we can find him together."

Wary, and leaving the door open so he had instant exit access, Daniel retook his seat. "Jesus, this is freaky as fuck. What the hell is going on? Who are you? *What* are you?" He shook, unable to comprehend how

Barry's eyes had gone black and were now their normal brown.

"I am who I said I am, except..." Barry sighed. "There are things in force you're not aware of. Things that happen. The general public have no idea... What they see on the news every day really isn't how it goes down most of the time. The Dreams, they tell us things, and we act on them to prevent innocent people being killed. Sometimes it doesn't work. We get there too late to save the victims, but we always find the killers."

Daniel's stomach rolled over. "Karrick's a killer?"

It took Barry a moment to answer, as though he was unsure how much to tell Daniel. "Of a kind, yes, although he doesn't kill like your average murderer. I doubt very much he'll kill Jase, so take that stricken look off your face."

"What? So he kills differently? Like, he has a good reason or something? That's just mental. Like you guys have watched too much bloody *Dexter*."

A slight twitch lifted one corner of Barry's mouth. "It sounds it, yes, I agree, but... It's complicated. We operate as a team known as Tools."

"Tools?" Daniel had the absurd urge to laugh.

"Unfortunate name, but there you go. Tools are a group of people who are Dreamers."

"Like Jase?"

"Yes. We Dream, and we help our Tool Master to find killers."

"And I'm meant to accept this shit as if we're just discussing the weather, right? Okay, I'll play along. So then what happens?"

"The Tool Master kills them. Karrick is a Tool Master, but I'd like to stress I'm not one of his Tools. I have a different master, one I wish I didn't have to deal with because Leyton is… Well, never mind about him."

Confused and also struggling to process the information, Daniel scrubbed a hand through his hair. If this Karrick was a killer, what did he want with Jase? Had they met through a Dreamer party or something? "So, you said you and Jase are the same. What does that mean? He works for Karrick?" The idea twisted a tight knot of fear deep into Daniel's gut, somehow seeming worse than Jason sleeping with the older man.

"I don't know. Just now, when my eyes…changed, I was trying to find out. I was trying to contact my own Tool Master, Leyton. Unsuccessfully. I'm sorry I can't answer your question about Jason right now, but believe me, I intend on finding out. I'm not keen on the idea of him being mixed up with a guy who doesn't seem to have a past any more than you are."

Daniel barked out nervous laughter. "Oh, fuck right off. No way! You didn't call this Tool Master or —"

"No, I speak to Leyton in my head." He frowned. "Usually."

Barry had said it so matter-of-factly Daniel was hard pressed to disbelieve him. Yet, he couldn't believe him, could he? No one spoke to people in their damn heads.

Did they?

Daniel stood. "Look, much as I'd like to believe your crazy little story, I can't. I need to find Jase, and if you won't help me, I'll go to the police."

"No! Don't do that." Barry rose, holding both hands up in a placating gesture. "Please. Look, come into the kitchen, have some coffee or whatever. I'll explain some more, but I'm telling you, if you care about Jase, you'll damn well listen, whether you believe me once

I'm finished or not. Finding him is important, because if Karrick is planning to use him to..."

Daniel sucked in a breath, dithering on whether to indulge this guy and drink his coffee or run for the hills. "Fuck. One coffee, but you get that black-eye thing again? I'm gone."

* * * *

Karrick dozed, Jason fast asleep beside him. He really ought to check in with Morland but couldn't be bothered. He was spent, all his vigor used up in fucking the dainty little piece in his arms. His cock stirred as thoughts of him taking Jase the way he had filled his mind, and he smiled at the fact he'd *find* the vigor for another fuck if the chance presented itself.

"I am saddened you cannot be bothered."

Karrick nearly sat bolt upright at the sound of Morland's voice. His master had come to see *him*, had read his damn thoughts. Karrick glanced around, trying to work out where his master was but failed to spot any telling fog.

"Yes, I *have* come to see you and I *did* hear your thoughts, but we cannot discuss that now. I would have thought, despite your interaction with young Jason there, you would have known the importance of checking in with me often at this difficult time."

Karrick didn't reply, worrying that if he did Jason would feel the reverberations of his voice and stir.

"Then get out of the bed and talk to me elsewhere!" Morland said.

Karrick obeyed. He extracted himself from beneath Jason's arm strewn across his belly then slung on a pair of jeans. If Morland was still in the room, Karrick failed to give a shit his cock was on display. Morland never worried that his intrusive visits sometimes came at inconvenient times. As far as he was concerned, if he needed to speak to Karrick he would, dick on show or not.

Karrick left the bedroom, closing the door softly behind him. With a bit of luck Jason would still sleep, the after-effects of Karrick invading his mind taking away his energy. He went into the kitchen to pour coffee from his percolator. He'd added cream and sugar by the time Morland spoke again.

"Jason's old friend is going to pose a problem."

"I dealt with him." Karrick fought back a surge of annoyance. "He won't give us any trouble now."

"Oh, but he will. He already has."

"What?" Karrick spun from facing the work surface, coffee spilling over his hand. "Fuck, that burns."

"Hot coffee tends to. Now, whatever you did to Daniel was not enough. He woke, completely aware of what you had done."

"So I'll do it again, totally wipe his mind. Kill him if I have to."

"No, we do not operate that way, you know that. We do not kill innocent people unless it is absolutely necessary."

Karrick sighed. "So what has he done?"

"He has gone to see Barry. Told him everything."

"Shit."

"And, in turn, Barry has given Daniel information he really should not have."

Karrick jammed a hand into his hair. "Do you want me to collect Daniel and keep him out of the way until this is all over?"

"That might be a good idea. However, I cannot see Barry allowing the young man out of his sight now, can you?"

Karrick scratched his head then took a sip of coffee. "No, but I can manage it."

"I know you can, but they are on their way over here. Now."

"What?" Karrick frowned, anger beginning a slow boil inside him.

He should have offed the little bastard. He'd known he was trouble the minute he'd laid eyes on him.

"Yes, it is as I said. You have Jason in there and the other two will be here shortly. I suggest you do not open the door. Wait for a more opportune time to deal with Daniel. I will monitor the situation, but please, do *not* feel you cannot be bothered to check in with me more often. I have a complete Mastership to win, and if you cannot do your job properly and help me succeed, I will have to think about speaking to Graham. I am sure he would be a willing Tool Master."

Karrick held back a retort. He sipped his coffee in silence, blanking his thoughts until he felt Morland had definitely gone.

The first thought to enter his head after that made him smile at the prospect of doing something he had always been forbidden to do. Killing innocent people.

But Graham didn't count, did he? He was a Dreamer, so perhaps, if Karrick got found out as being his killer, he could get by scot-free on that little technicality.

Chapter Six

Three streets from their destination, Barry slowed, crossing a large bridge. "Shit."

Fog roiled up, slicking the road under his car tires, and he slowed to a crawl.

"This is the weirdest bridge in the city," Daniel muttered at his side. "Always foggy."

Barry glanced at him, curious. He didn't think it was any weirder than anything else in a strange city. And it really wasn't foggy like this all the time, but the fact Daniel seemed to associate the fog with the area had him concerned. Right now, though, he knew this fog was not a normal occurrence—not the way it had moved to roll in delicate curls and tendrils over his car bonnet and around the windshield wipers.

He pulled the car to the side of the road just on the far side of the bridge and put it in park.

"Why are we stopping?" Daniel asked. "I thought we were going to this Karrick's place—"

"Shh." Barry held up a hand and watched as the fog slithered around to wrap under his door handle. "Shit,

shit, shit." He turned the engine off. "This is going to suck. Stay here."

"What?" Daniel looked slightly panicked now. "Why?"

"Because I told you to." He yanked the car keys from the ignition then got out. "Lock the doors." He slammed his and waited until Daniel had leaned over to press the button down.

Without thinking too much about what he was doing, Barry followed the tails of fog down the hill toward the riverbank. Half of him expected to find a body at the end of the trail, even though this was not the way things usually worked, but he also knew much of what usually worked just wasn't right now. Not with Tag gone. He had never expected his lover to be such an integral part of the equation, but evidently, after closely working with him to interpret what the Dreams had told him, it had been next to impossible to do his job without Tag, his police captain lover. Barry didn't like the implications that held for Jase and this erstwhile boyfriend of his.

"Daniel is so not ready for this shit," he muttered, thinking of the pale face, the wide eyes under that shock of dark hair and the look of fear on the younger man's features. "This will fuck him up."

But it was what it was. Daniel would either deal or he wouldn't, and at some point maybe become a part of the Team—or a mess for the Team to clean up. He hoped it would not be the latter. But Jase was a good kid, and as uncertain as he seemed now, Barry sensed a good heart in Daniel. He just hoped their feelings for one another could live through the shitstorm of the Dreams. He knew first-hand how that was not foregone. The year and a half apart from Tag might be a long time ago now, but he remembered the hell of being alone inside the nightmares. He knew how the reality of the Dream's 'gifts' drove wedges between people, turned them away from one another, broke even strong relationships. And he and Tag loved each other deeply.

Mist curled in a sickly, loving sort of way around his wrists and ankles, exerting a tiny, unsettling amount of pressure for him to move forward again.

"What are you going to show me?" Barry asked the fog. He'd long ago decided he didn't care if people looked at him funny when he talked to himself. They could think he was crazy. From the outside, he was. No one deserved to have to know any more than that. In fact, the world was probably better off not knowing. "What is it, Lassie?" he asked as the fog tugged him along a little faster now. "Did Timmy fall down the well? Again?"

The creek itself came into view and Barry braced himself. Dead was one thing. Bloated, water-soaked bodies went beyond simply dead into stomach-churning gore. He hated attending water dumps and drownings.

Please don't let there be a body.

All he found was a shoe and a set of car keys. One black leather dress shoe and a set of Toyota car keys — if he remembered the logo correctly — almost lost in the grass beside the shoe.

"How is this any better than a Dream?" he asked the air. "And a shitty, cryptic Dream as vague as the ones I had when I was Jason's age? You're going to have give me more to go on. Or better yet, figure out what's fucking with my reception and fix it."

Around him, the trees swayed and he shivered. There was no wind. He stepped back only to find a clammy wall of mist behind him. A tendril of it slithered up his spine and wiggled behind his ear. Goosebumps rose on his flesh and he shuddered, not liking the way his body responded to that chilly, unreal touch.

"Enough of that shit," he growled, swiping at the side of his head. "That's Tag's and only Tag's right, so stop with the touching. You got something to say, say it, or fuck the hell off." Furious, he whirled and fought to get back up the hill.

"Wait."

A shadowy form coalesced in the air before him, trapping him again between the creek and the climb to safety.

"Rivald, you're creeping me the hell out. You stay on your own side of the frickin' veil, asshole. Touch me like that again and I swear to God..." He curled a lip in revulsion and clamped his mind shut, slashing an arm through the foggy vision before him. The mist whorled at his touch, dripping like rain back to the earth. "I'm not a broken mess anymore. Tag and I have done a lot of work. Come a long way. You don't own me. I do this because it needs doing. Because I choose to now. You have something to say to me, say it and let me get on. I have a lost friend to find and you're wasting my time."

The mist bubbled at his feet and the tree branches stirred above him, groaning and whispering in the stillness. He sensed impatience and...fear? When had Rivald ever exhibited fear?

"What's going on?" Cautiously, Barry opened his mind a fraction, feeling rather proud of himself that he finally had this much control, even with Tag on the other side of the country. He'd pay for it in exhaustion later, but at least he could control his own emotions in the moment this way.

"Open your mind to me, Barry."

"Oh, Jes-us. Rivald, calm down." Barry clutched the sides of his head. "You trying to split my brain open?"

"I apologize."

The intensity of the communication eased somewhat and Barry let his hands fall back to his sides.

"The issue has become rather urgent, and I could not reach you in that miserable little house –"

"You mean my *home*?" Barry snorted. "Of course you couldn't. Because it *is* my home. Sacred space. Deal with it."

"You haven't been checking in with Leyton, Barry."

"Because I haven't been able to." Barry frowned, the idea of confessing his difficulties to the ethereal being making him uncomfortable. "All I get is static. I figured he was laying low. Even really good murderers get sloppy occasionally, after all, and you can't constantly bail him out – not if the way I feel after blocking you out for a little while is anything to go by." He crossed his arms over his chest. "Come to think about it, you've been pretty much off the grid yourself since I left the Force and things calmed down. Why?"

"Not yours to question."

Rivald sounded irritated and Barry smirked.

"I'm right, aren't I? All that interference over Lorelie and Jessica took it out of you, didn't it?"

"Mind your place, Barry."

A gale of such force blasted through Barry's mind it almost felled him and he had to clap his hands over his ears. Not that it did anything to keep Rivald out. But he'd practiced and practiced, and he had the imaginary 'shields' in his head half closed when the bastard finally relented.

"All right."

The pressure eased significantly and Barry straightened.

"I do not have the time" – there was a distinct pause and a tiny breath of what would have been a sigh if Rivald wasn't a pile of mist and disembodied thoughts – *"or the energy to fight with you. It seems pointless to deny that yes, I have limitations. No one and nothing is invincible. My recovery from that…experience has been slower than I might have liked, but you as a team have been doing an exemplary job. For that I thank you."*

"So what's the problem now?" Barry asked, thinking it wise to keep his amazement at the admission and the approval, to himself.

"Now, a shift in the 'veil', as you called it, is occurring. It is a precarious time. Your own experiences with your abilities in Tag's absence are proof that things are shifting. Teams will disband during this period and reform. For my part, I would prefer that I keep my core players. You are all extremely effective and believe it or not, a change for the better may be on the horizon for your plane, if things continue as they are. I want to see that happen, Barry. My ties to your world are not so very distant that I do not remember what it was like to live in an environment where fear lurked around every corner. I would prefer your existence to have more light than that, and I believe we can achieve it. If we work together. If we trust one another."

"Trust." Barry gazed at the fog still swirling around his calves. "You're fucking with me, aren't you?"

"I assure you, I am not."

"So what is it you want from me that you couldn't tell me through Leyton? Or those bloody Dreams? If this is so hard for you – so taxing, why are you doing it?"

"Because we both know Leyton has trust issues. He does his job, but the bond he and I once shared is not what it was

before Jessica. During the coming months of upheaval, I fear he may… I fear for him."

"You want me to believe you give a rat's ass about us?"

A soft chuckle wound through Barry, rolling the fog a little farther up his legs. He stepped back.

"Leyton is fragile, Barry. A boy still, in many ways. Surely you can see that."

Barry snorted. But one tiny corner of his brain would not let him deny what Rivald said.

"I want to protect him, Barry. As I said, he is fragile."

"In a deadly, slit-your-throat-and-pry-out-your-teeth-with-pliers sort of way, yeah, I get it."

"It is natural at times like these for teams to divide and drift into new formations. Sometimes, that is for the best, but sometimes not. I believe Leyton would be one of those prone to drift. I highly doubt he would find another team willing to work with him as ours does. He would be lost. I would prefer — "

"To protect him. I said I get it." And he did get it. He also got the stomach-churning understanding that Rivald wasn't alone in that desire. Much as the Killer of their group creeped Barry the hell out, Leyton *was* fragile. And if he drifted away from them, as Rivald seemed to think he would, or even, perhaps thought he already was, who would replace him? "Better the devil you know," Barry muttered.

"Indeed. And believe me, Barry, there are plenty of devils out there you want no acquaintance with."

That was not something Barry had any trouble agreeing with. "So what is it you think I can do about any of this, given that until Tag gets back, I'm pretty much useless?"

"Enjoy the holiday, Barry. Find the boy. He is key. We need him for Leyton's sake. And beware. There is another team operating in our territory. Unusual, but not unheard

of. I anticipate difficulties, so do not expect to be able to work with them. Find the owner of the shoe and car keys. All I can tell you is that he is a Dreamer and his name is Graham. His Tool Master has betrayed him, and I fear the rogue may have the power to tear our little family apart if left to his own devices. I would not have that."

"And you're telling me all this because Leyton can't be trusted?"

"Because he is a devout disciple of his craft, Barry. Intrigue does not suit him. It so rarely agrees with Killers, however, I fear the leader of this interloping team might be a better hand at it than our Leyton. We want to keep our boy focused on his strengths. Do what you can with the Dreams I send you. I know they are not of the best quality just now, but it is all we have to work with until your lover returns or you find the boy, Jason — or this Graham. Perhaps he can be persuaded."

"You know this is way more shit than I signed on for," Barry pointed out.

"It will not last forever. Just until the instability passes and then we can go back to business as usual. Perhaps with a few new members added to our team."

"Oh goodie. Back to your regularly scheduled nightmares, Barry," he mumbled to himself. "Fabulous."

Rivald's dry chuckle followed Barry back to the creek edge. Crouching to take a few pictures of the shoe and the keys with his phone, Barry heaved a sigh and dialed his former police partner, Jeremy Ross's private number. Since today was Ross's day off, it made more sense to talk to him first. Ross was already an old hand at sorting out which bits of Dreamer business to bring to the attention of authorities and which to make disappear. They were lucky to have such an ally in the department. There was no use alerting the police on a missing person Barry couldn't identify, and who no one, as far as he was aware, knew was missing yet.

By the time he got back to his car, poor Daniel was crouched in the passenger seat in a huddled, frightened ball.

"What the hell happened?" Daniel demanded the minute Barry opened his door. "What took you so long? Where did you go? Is Jase down there? Is that why you made me stay here? Is he…dead?"

That last word came out in such a small, miserable squeak Barry felt ashamed of himself for making the kid wait so long.

"Nothing happened. Much." He didn't think it the best time to go into the details. Daniel was barely coming to terms with the idea that any of this was real. "I had to…chat with someone. I was beside the creek—no, Jase is not down there. I had you stay here because I didn't know what I would find and I didn't want to put you in danger. And no, as far as I can tell, Jason is not dead. And I intend on making sure it stays that way. We'll find him."

He glared out of the window at the now clear surroundings. "I don't know everything, Daniel, but I have a hunch and I've learned to follow them. Jase is in trouble, and it's going to be hard to convince him of that, I think. But I'll try. I don't like this Karrick person he's with. I have a bad feeling about him."

"I want him back," Daniel said quietly. "I should never have let him go, and I'm sorry I did. I'll make it up to him. But I want him back."

Barry turned into the face of Daniel's determination and found the young man meeting his gaze, unflinching and intense.

"He's mine, see?" Daniel said. "And I want him back."

Shades of Tag all over. How many times had Tag whispered that declaration over and over in their bed each time he hauled Barry out of the blackest mire?

"We'll find him," Barry assured the kid. "We'll find him."

Barry turned again to gaze out of his window. He waited for Ross, wishing he had a better plan.

Chapter Seven

Leyton sat in the driver's seat of his old VW camper van, drumming his fingers on the steering wheel. He wasn't feeling quite right. Hadn't for some time. Something off was going on, something out of his control and by God, he hated that. Not knowing what was occurring did a number on him, sent him off-kilter, away to that place where everything was alien, nothing familiar.

Like he didn't belong.

He ought to be used to that feeling, what with being brought up the way he had been by an insane mother who thought nothing of wrenching his teeth out every time he'd done something she hadn't liked. Then being recruited as a Tool Master, sent out to kill people before they killed someone else. He didn't mind that, the culling. It was something he'd been born to do anyway, something he enjoyed, so being paid to bump people off was a bonus. That and an assurance he'd never be caught. His master, Rivald, was there to scour away any mistakes — fingerprints if

Leyton had been careless enough not to use gloves, stray hairs that had fallen on or around the victim.

He stared out at the trees ahead where he'd once again parked in a woodland clearing. It was his favorite place to be, amongst the tree trunks and foliage. It gave good cover, made him feel safe. Undetected. Still, no amount of forestry would stop him being found by Rivald. His master contacted him through Dreams and often arrived beside him without warning, first as dense fog then as his horned-beast self, dishing out orders for Leyton's next assignment. But Rivald had been difficult to contact lately, as though he was preventing Leyton from speaking with him. No amount of lying on his narrow bunk in the back of his van and closing his eyes so he entered the Dreamstate allowed Leyton to reach the man who had become a constant in his life.

What had happened? Were the Dreamers on a break, was that it, and no one had thought to tell him? They all knew how Leyton was, how he needed to kill often, to assuage the burn inside him that forced him out into the night—or day—and murder someone. And that burn flared hot, a relentless searing that seemed to raze his insides and leave him hollow if he didn't follow his instincts. The burn refused to go away, and if he couldn't find a person to kill, he resorted to animals. Oh, he knew full well how most of society would frown at that if he admitted to grabbing a stray dog off the street and snapping its neck, but they didn't understand.

Couldn't understand.

Neither could his fellow Dreamers.

And where was Barry? Why couldn't Leyton contact him either? Leyton was a Tool Master, should be able to get hold of his Tools without any trouble, but his attempts to reach Barry and Jessica had also proved fruitless.

"You don't like feeling this way, do you, little bastard?"

Leyton sighed. He heard his mother's disembodied voice all too often, had thought a short while back he'd gotten rid of her for good, but here she was again, plaguing his mind with her chalk-on-a-blackboard voice, her pitch and nasal twang churning his gut. He clenched his jaw, irritated that she could make herself heard when it seemed no one else could.

"Fuck off," he said. "I've told you before, you're not welcome here. I don't need you. I hate you and you ought to realize when you're not wanted."

"But where would I go, fuckface? And who would I torment if I didn't have you?"

He decided it would be better to ignore her. He ran his tongue over his new teeth, dentures he'd paid a dentist to create out of teeth he'd wrenched from his victims' mouths. He looked up at the rear-view mirror and smiled, spreading his lips so hard they hurt. Admired how the dentist had made the teeth match as though he'd been born with them—as though they belonged in his mouth.

"You ought to hope that dentist doesn't report you," Mother said.

Leyton didn't have to hope anything. The man who had skillfully crafted his pearly whites had taken the huge sum of money for his work and made it clear he wasn't about to tell anyone a damn thing. A threat to his life saw to that.

A muffled sob came from the back of his van but he ignored that as well. The man he'd captured was prone to whimpering. It got on his nerves, and that was another thing that wasn't right. Normally, Leyton reveled in their cries, their pleas to be set free, but this time he gained no pleasure in hearing those sounds.

Funny how such a brawny, big-mouthed fellow had been reduced to a quivering wreck once he realized Leyton meant business, though. When Leyton had found himself outside a pub and they'd gotten talking, the man—introducing himself as Graham—said he might have a job for Leyton if his intuition about him was correct.

"What intuition is that then?" Leyton had asked.

"Well, I sense you like the darkness. You know, real darkness."

Leyton had been intrigued and hoped he'd stumbled upon a man who would readily spill his sole reason for living, tell him all his deepest secrets so Leyton could determine whether the man needed killing or not.

Graham had, to a degree, hinting he enjoyed 'the chase' as he'd put it, leaving Leyton to take that as he saw fit. Leyton chose to believe the man was a killer and asked him if he fancied an after-hour's tipple back at his van. The man had agreed, and here they were, Graham trussed up with a sock stuffed in his mouth. Leyton had taken a detour and put Graham's shoe and car keys down by the creek, sending out a message with all his powers for Barry to go and find them, to know they were on a mission. And now Leyton was wondering how the hell they'd arrived here, and where his instructions had come from.

Who they had come from.

Had Barry received his message?

Before he'd bumped into Graham, Leyton had suffered a blinding headache, one similar to the pain Rivald inflicted when Leyton or anyone under his command weren't doing as they'd been told. As the headache had receded, Leyton had experienced the burn, that all-encompassing blaze that pushed him toward the pub and to strike up a conversation with Graham, who'd smoked a cigarette while leaning casually against the pub wall. Rivald hadn't spoken as he usually did. He hadn't given him a name, a location and a place to discard the body. Hadn't give him chills down his spine when he'd approached Graham, letting him know he'd met the correct target. All he'd known was that Graham needed getting rid of, as though someone had dumped that knowledge into his head like a fly tipper with a heavy refuse sack down an abandoned alleyway.

Now, Graham said something that sounded like "Please, I can help you" but Leyton wasn't sure. He gunned the engine and sighed as he drove out of the clearing, knowing he needed to make contact with his Tools — with Rivald — so he could take the next step. Yes, he could just kill this Graham man now, get rid of his corpse and await further instructions, but although Leyton was essentially a bad man who just wanted to make the burn go away, he didn't want to do anything that would jeopardize their team's arrangement. Getting caught would be an end to his ability to release the burn. There was no killing people in jail without the fear of getting caught.

He took corners sharply on purpose so Graham was flung from one side of the van to the other on several occasions. It gave the man something to really whimper about. After traveling for about ten minutes, Leyton drew up outside an apartment block and killed the engine, wishing he was killing something else entirely. He shifted around so he could stare into the rear, one arm resting across the back of his seat. Graham was hunched in the far corner next to the slim wardrobe, the toe end of the sock flapping from his mouth like an errant black tongue.

"I do not know why you are here," Leyton said, "but I know you are important and that there is a reason I met you. Although I would love nothing more than to slice your neck and watch you bleed to death, I must consult with someone first. I need to make sure I'm doing the correct thing. However, do not think if I'm told I have the wrong person, I won't kill you. I may well use you for sport." He sighed. "It seems such a long time since I killed a *person*."

Graham widened his eyes and snorted. Snot spewed out of his nostrils and Leyton fought back the urge to heave.

"I realize you are quite frightened, but really, was there any need for that?" Leyton frowned and held himself in check. "I have to visit with someone now, so if you don't mind, I'll be tying you to the bed legs so you can't escape." He climbed over the seats and into the back, ferreting beneath his bed for his coil of rope and tool pouch, which contained knives and the instruments he needed to perform his job. The latter he placed on the passenger seat, out of Graham's reach, then used the rope to bind the man in place.

Graham mumbled, shaking his head from side to side. Another influx of information came then, unceremoniously thrown into Leyton's head as if text messages that had been stalled in arriving. One after the other the images came, of Leyton stabbing Graham until the inside of the van was claret, of Leyton out of breath, exultant that he'd been able to sate his needs.

Leyton shook his head. "No, not until I know who sent the message." *And never in his own van. That didn't make the least bit of sense.* He stared at Graham for a few heartbeats. "Who?"

Graham, his back resting against the side of the bed, his arms out either side of him, wrists tied to the metal bed poles, narrowed his eyes.

"Look," Leyton said to the invisible image dumper, "it's all very well showing me what I have to do, but if you don't reveal yourself, I simply cannot move forward on this mission. I am not comfortable with how these messages are being relayed — and I know it isn't you, Rivald." He stood and planted his hands on his hips. "Who are you? Who do you work for?"

He glanced down at Graham, who stared back at him with a light of realization in his eyes, as though he understood why Leyton appeared to be talking to himself. How could that be? How the devil could this Graham fellow know Leyton heard voices? How was it he seemed okay with that?

Leyton kneeled. Wrenched the sock from Graham's mouth. The man attempted to speak, but his lips were dry and, Leyton suspected, his tongue was too, preventing him uttering anything coherent. Although Leyton wanted to meet with one of his Tools and try to figure this mess out, the pull to hear what Graham had to say tugged him harder. He stood and took a step to his sink unit, turning on the tap so a steady stream of water came out from a contraption he'd rigged up a long time ago, housed in the cupboard beneath. He filled a plastic beaker — he wasn't fool enough to use a glass with a victim — then shut the tap off. Faced Graham again.

"Now, if I give you a drink, you had better have something interesting and worthwhile to say, otherwise I will be forced to act upon any urges that take me over. I suspect you understand what I mean. If I hear anything remotely like you pleading to be set free, I won't meet with my associate and things will go rather wrong for you. Sooner than I had intended, anyway. Can you give me your assurance you will comply with my wishes?"

Graham nodded and eyed the beaker.

He's very thirsty then. Leyton almost chuckled at that. He hunkered down and held the beaker to Graham's lips, amazed at how quickly the man guzzled the liquid, annoyed at the slurping sounds he made. Graham turned his face away and gasped, pink-cheeked, struggling to catch his breath. His inability to speak to Leyton immediately annoyed him. Time was of the essence here!

"Stop dilly-dallying and say what you have to say," Leyton snapped, rising so he towered over the man.

Graham stared up at him. "Don't kill me. Please, don't kill me!"

Leyton gritted his dentures. "Deary me. How irritating. Why is it that when I give people a chance, they always, always mess it up? Why can't they just do as they are told, hmm? Why do they *always* have to plead for their life?" He thumped himself on the thigh, frustrated at being lied to, at being taken for a fool.

Simple orders. Nothing too complicated. Yet none of them have ever been able to follow them.

"I didn't mean for that to come out." Graham panted, going to raise his arm then realizing it was held fast by rope. "I just needed to let you know you *mustn't* kill me. It's important that you don't. *I'm* important. More so than you might believe, although I have a feeling you'll know exactly what I am when I tell you."

Leyton laughed. "What, you're important to your wife? Your children? Your mother? Do you think I care about things like that? I'll have you know I have a job to do, orders to follow, and regardless of who might get hurt by me obeying those orders, I do as I'm told. Unlike you, who thought nothing of ignoring my instructions and blurting out the one thing that grates on my nerves more than anything else you could have said. Please don't kill me," he mimicked. "It's almost as bad as, 'Please, I won't tell anyone. Just let me go!'"

Graham gave up trying to free his hand and slumped, his shoulders sagging. "I know who's filtering you information. Orders."

How on earth could that be possible? Leyton frowned. "Go on."

Graham huffed out a breath, as though he was defeated, as though he knew that Leyton was coming to the end of his tether and Graham might be coming to the end of his life. "I'm a Dreamer too."

Now that surprised Leyton. He knew other Dreamers existed, but not in this city. As far as he'd been aware, the only Dreamers in these parts were those he was Tool Master of. Barry, Jessica and the new recruit, Jason, a kid Barry had promised to nurture until the young man was at a level where he could be trusted — where his dreams and visions could be trusted. If this Graham was one of their kind, that might mean he was a man who dreamed and acted by himself — not something advisable, as Leyton knew from experience. He'd been one such man himself until Rivald had entered his Dream one night and had taken him in hand.

"Who do you work for?" Leyton demanded, pacing as well as he was able in the small space, mind working overtime as he tried to process what he'd learned.

"I'm really not at liberty to say." Graham shrugged.

At least he's sticking to protocol. "Let me put it another way, then. Do you work alone?"

"No."

"Do you work for my master?" *Would I even know if he did? With no contact from Rivald, how am I to know if new recruits have been acquired?*

"No."

"How do you know that for sure? How do you know who I work for?" *I'm not at liberty to tell that information either.* Although now that he thought about it, he had said Rivald's name out loud. Before he'd known Graham was also a Dreamer. To a regular person, the name wouldn't have meant a thing.

"Because Rivald isn't my master." And there it was. Rivald would not be happy Leyton had revealed him to another Dreamer. "Someone else is," Graham was saying, and Leyton forced himself to concentrate. "Someone who isn't working wholly for the good. And I can hear what you're thinking, you should know that."

Leyton shut his mind off so the man didn't poke into thoughts he had no business knowing. Like those about Lorelei, a woman he'd thought was Jessica, the female promised to him by Mother if he'd just do as he was told and kill, kill, kill. Sadly, Lorelei turned out to be another Dreamer, a woman gone rogue, who'd broken from Rivald's group and ran amok until Leyton had seen to her, killed her. He'd been crushed, discovering there was no happy ending for him, no happy ever after with a wife and two children as he'd been promised. No future except killing and being a Tool Master. He still held a torch for Jessica, though, a woman he had saved from another killer. She had turned out to be a Dreamer too, and Rivald used her as feminine bait to ensnare killers for Leyton to cull.

Such a delicious, nasty web we all weave...

"Yes, we do," Graham said, "but it serves a purpose, one I'm sure you're fully aware of."

Leyton inwardly cursed at letting his mind block slip. He made a snap decision. "I must meet with one of my Tools before we discuss this further. You will remain here until I come back—not that you can get away. If you're gone when I return, I'll know you've contacted your master or another Dreamer from whatever faction you belong to, but rest assured, I will find you again."

"I'm not going anywhere," Graham said.

"No?" Leyton cocked his head. "Why ever not?"

"Because I need your help."

Chapter Eight

Jessica was bored. There was only so much shopping a girl could do while pretending she was Barry's personal assistant, a job that wouldn't pay the kind of wages that allowed her to buy whatever she wanted, whenever she wanted it. Being a Dreamer meant money arrived regularly — untraceable money sent from Rivald. How he got it or where he got it from she didn't want to know. Barry struggled with the same thing, knowing their bank accounts were invisible except to them. She'd long stopped trying to work out how she could go to an ATM and withdraw money from an account that only existed in the Dreamworld. She had thousands stashed away, and since being bait a while ago after Leyton had rescued her from a killer, she hadn't done a damn thing to earn it.

It seemed just by being a Dreamer, you were entitled to cash.

She stretched out on her sofa and recalled the last meeting she'd had with her mother. How she'd lied and made out her job with Barry was the best thing since sliced bread, how she enjoyed the filing and typing, making him coffee. Being normal. Gradually easing herself into everyday life after her face had been splashed across the front of every newspaper and filled TV screens—the young woman who had been abducted, missing without a trace. And at first she *had* been abducted—by a killer Leyton called Charles—a man who had murdered her boyfriend, Cal, and had then come after her. Leyton had arrived to kill Charles and took her back to his camper van, insisting she was some woman named Lorelei who had been promised to him.

She'd been afraid of him then, freaked the fuck out by his weirdness, the very air that surrounded him, but ultimately, when his dream had been crushed, she had felt sorrow for the abused little boy he'd been and the confused, tortured man he now was. Although he still gave her the creeps, she tolerated him. Finding out she was a Dreamer and that a whole other world existed had taken some getting used to, and to be honest, she still hadn't gotten a proper handle on that.

Communications had gone silent. She still met with Barry at his house, though, really did do some filing and making coffee, but for the most part the new recruit, Jase, did the lion's share of office run-around. Leyton hadn't infiltrated Jessica's normal dreams or spoken to her inside her mind, giving her a heads-up on her next job. Not that she was complaining. She didn't relish being bait for killers, dressing up to the nines in clothes that made her uncomfortable and look like a prostitute. Going out to clubs and bars, Rivald in her head telling her where to go, making her body go where he wanted. She'd hated it the last time he'd done that, orchestrating her movements, clamping her mouth closed so she couldn't speak. Only allowing her to talk when she'd reached her destination and snared the attention of some pervert who wanted to fuck her down an alley then stab the life out of her.

She shuddered, got off the sofa then wandered into her kitchen to get a cold drink. Earlier that morning she'd shopped until she'd wanted to drop. Dumped her purchases on her bed and hadn't had the energy or desire to unpack them. That was something, wasn't it? To not want to take each item out of the bags and pore over what she'd chosen? To no longer be excited that the dress or bag she'd coveted for so long now belonged to her.

There's something seriously wrong with this shit. With my life. I have no dreams – not even the weird kind – no ambition. It's all been taken away by this other-world crap.

She sighed, knowing it was useless to complain about it. She was in this for the long haul now, knew too much to ever leave and was in no doubt that Rivald would hunt her down if she ever decided to break free. Or send the creepy Leyton after her. Besides, she couldn't let Barry down. Or Tag. They'd been good to her.

She sipped cola from a can and wondered how Barry was faring with Tag out of town. She wanted what they had, a relationship where they were equals who fitted together just so. Yeah, they had their ups and downs, but that only made them stronger. Would she ever have a bond with someone like that? How could she even contemplate meeting a guy with the life she now led? How would she explain the money? How would she explain going out at odd hours, all tarted up like she was on the pull?

She couldn't.

Who would have thought she'd long to have Leyton contact her with an assignment? Who knew boredom would push her into *wanting* to put on those hideous clothes and enter a bar showing a bit of tit and leg?

She returned to the living room and flopped on her sofa again. Rested with her eyes closed, attempting to enter that Dreamstate, the place where she could get hold of Rivald and ask the million questions pistoning inside her brain. She practiced every day but hadn't yet mastered the art. Leyton had said a while back it would come in time, if she relaxed and didn't push it, and he would know. She'd seen him lie down and close his eyes a couple of times and go to Rivald's cave.

"It's all so fucking weird," she muttered, snapping her eyes open, frustrated as hell. "I can't fucking do it. May as well not bother."

The jangle of the two-tone doorbell startled her and she sat up quickly. Who the fuck could that be? Only those in the know knew where she lived. She wasn't expecting any parcels, and had made sure she remained aloof with neighbors so as not to encourage any friendships. Giving out a cup of sugar or whatever led to intimacy—something she couldn't risk.

She strode across her living room and out into the short hallway where doors led to her bathroom and bedrooms. The front door, solid with only a peephole to blot the shiny expanse of wood, appeared to rattle in its frame as though someone was beating on it with the side of their fist. An angry someone. Her stomach contracted and she sidled to the door with her back to the wall, hands splayed either side of her. Peering through the peephole, she saw the startling image of a convex eye and leaped back, biting off the urge to scream. Heart beating too fast, she lifted one hand to her chest and told herself to calm the fuck down.

Going into meltdown mode wouldn't help the situation. She could ignore the door or call Barry, so there was no need to get so riled up, was there?

Instinct told her otherwise. Something was wrong. She shifted to the left and leaned against the wall, taking a moment to steady her ragged breathing. It felt as though something was tugging inside her head, like her ability to receive incoming thought messages from the other Dreamers was broken. Or that someone was trying to warn her of danger but they weren't quite able to push past whatever barrier was in her mind.

She moved to the door, the bell tones slicing through the air again, setting her nerves further on edge. Her pulse thudded, the sound loud in her ears. She reached out a shaking hand to brace herself on the door then leaned forward to stare through the peephole again.

The owner of the eye had stepped back and she got a clear view of him. Leyton stared as though he could see through the wood, his expression one of irritation tinged with worry. God, the last thing she needed was him coming in here going on about how she could be his Lorelei if she only tried a bit harder. That he could love her if she'd let him. She didn't *want* to love him or have him love her, had made that as clear as she could without going a step too far and hurting his feelings.

She still wasn't sure of him. Didn't know if an outright, spiteful rejection from her would tip him over the edge.

"Do you have a job for me?" she asked loudly, still reticent to let him in.

"Oh, thank goodness you're in. I need you," he said.

Oh, fuck... "You do? What, as bait?"

"No. I only wish that were so. Do you not think it odd we haven't had any assignments lately?" he asked, his voice low. "I need to discuss this turn of events with you. Please let me in."

She sighed. "Leyton, you know that's not a good idea. We agreed that you'd only contact me through thought."

She watched him move closer to the door then glance from side to side. "Don't you think I've tried that already?"

Jessica closed her eyes and rested her forehead on the door. The wood was cold, soothing. If he was having trouble communicating like she was, he had a point. Barry had said maybe the killers out there were on strike, which rendered them, as Dreamers, unneeded. They'd laughed about that, but now, after so long with no contact via thoughts or a personal visit from Rivald, Jessica had to admit something was off. She let out a breath, annoyed that once again she had to do something she didn't want to, and dragged open the door. Stepped back so Leyton could enter.

"Come through to the living room," she said, "but don't get comfortable. You're not staying."

She sat on a chair so he couldn't seat himself beside her. He took the sofa.

"I can't stay. I have someone in my van," he said.

"Oh, fuck." Chills sped up and down her spine. "Did you *have* to tell me that? Do I *have* to know these things when I haven't been used as a lure to get them there? Please, keep that shit to yourself. It's hard enough knowing what you do without you rubbing it in."

Leyton jerked forward, perching on the edge of his seat. "That's the thing. I wouldn't have told you, only...there's been a development."

She closed her eyes momentarily then opened them to stare at the ceiling. "What?"

"I wanted to...needed to...do what I do, and I got this information, but it wasn't how Rivald usually delivers it. What I mean is, I somehow know it wasn't from him."

"What do you mean? Another voice told you to do whatever the fuck you've done? Like, are you telling me you're not only insane to want to kill before you were a Dreamer, but that you also hear *other* voices? I already know you hear your mother, but are you telling me there's someone else now?"

"Yes, except it isn't a voice. It's more a dump of information."

Jesus fucking Christ, give me strength. She clenched her hands into fists. "What's happened?"

"I went to this pub, just knew I had to go, you understand, and met with this fellow..."

Fellow. He tries to sound so refined all the time. "And?"

"I took him back to my van, knew he needed sorting out."

"Right..."

"Except...except he says he's a Dreamer."

"What?" She whipped her attention from the ceiling to him. "How the fuck is that possible and we don't know him? Has he only just come into his abilities, is that what you're saying?"

"I only wish that was the case, my dear. He works for another master."

Jessica went cold and lifted her hands to rub the tops of her arms. "Stop. Don't say anything else. I can't fucking deal with this crap. It's nuts! I didn't want it, *still* don't want it! There's stuff going on here that would make anyone go mental. Go and see Rivald. Do that thing you do when you go to sleep. Or take your crap to Barry. This isn't anything to do with me."

Leyton looked crestfallen. "Oh. I thought you would know what to do. That you would help me. I thought we might become friends eventually, that I could turn to you in situations like this."

"No," she said, harder than she'd intended. "You know how it is. How you felt. We must remain as colleagues. Friendship just isn't in the cards, all right?"

"I realize that, but Barry won't want me bothering him with this."

"Are you fucking *kidding* me?"

"Oh, Lord, your swearing really doesn't becom—"

"Fuck my swearing. You have some guy in your van, someone you intended to kill, and he's another damn Dreamer who works for someone else. *Are* there other Dreamers in this city apart from us? How come we weren't told about it if there is? How come no one's got hold of us? How come we have no jobs to do when a city this size is usually teeming with psychopaths out there murdering people left, right and center? Isn't that all a bit weird to you?"

Leyton nodded slowly. "It is strange, but do you know what's stranger?"

She pushed out a breath, annoyed beyond measure. "No, but you're going to bloody tell me, right?"

He nodded. "He has no problem reading my thoughts, but I can't read his. It's as though my communication channel's been blocked."

"Yours and mine both. I never hear a damn thing these days. Thought it was because I'm relatively new to this crap." She gnawed at a hangnail. "We need to go to Barry, see if Rivald's got hold of him, see if we're all in the same boat. If we are then that's fine. We'll just take it we're not needed at the moment and enjoy spending our money and our free time as we see fit."

"That would be nice, but what about my burn?" He twiddled his thumbs and stared at her with a pained expression. "I can't just ignore it."

Chapter Nine

Jase stretched, cat-like, crisp sheets delicious against his skin. Various parts of him ached in that way that reminded him he was still alive. And that he'd slept for hours on end without a single Dream.

"Well, well, well." Karrick's voice carried in a crooning baritone across the room that was already dipping into shades of night.

Jase sat up.

"Oh, don't bother getting out of bed, cherub," Karrick said, rising from where he'd been lounging by the window. He was dressed in a long, silky purple and gold robe and a condom.

"Just gotta piss," Jase informed him, swinging his feet toward the floor.

"So hold it."

Karrick grabbed his wrist, twisting expertly, and the next thing Jase knew, he was flat on his face on the bed, legs half hanging off the edge and his wrist pinned at his back.

"Nmmf." He sputtered, getting a mouthful of sheets and mattress for his efforts.

Karrick hauled on him, drawing him up and demanding he get his knees under him.

Jase struggled to comply as his shoulder creaked with the pressure, and Karrick hammered bruises into his arse with the flat of his hand for the delay.

"Lemme go," Jase muttered.

He fought for the leverage he needed to get even one knee up just as Karrick knocked him back onto his stomach with another blow to his backside. The sting brought tears to his eyes and he tried to pull free.

Karrick laughed, lifted Jase's head by the hair until his neck ached, then licked a path up the side of Jason's cheek, taking the salty tear away with him.

"Knees, cherub," he whispered, his voice no more than a deadly flat whisper. "I grow impatient."

A very cold pulse in Jase's gut convinced him to try harder to do as he was told, despite the pain of pulled hair and strained muscles. He managed to push himself to his knees and widen the distance between them when Karrick nudged at his thighs roughly with his own knee.

"Better," Karrick said, though there was no warmth of praise in his voice. Just cold satisfaction as he pushed Jase's face into the comforter and spread his arse cheeks.

The pain and stretch of being filled by a hard, implacable cock, the way eased only by the scant pre-lube on the condom, finally broke Jase's voice free. He keened, a horrible, gut-wrenching sound even he didn't recognize as coming from his own body.

Karrick pumped him hard, one hand in his hair and the other still holding the back of his wrist at that painful, awkward angle against his spine. Hair parted from Jase's scalp and the muscles in his neck wrenched as he struggled to turn his head enough to breathe. For long, silent moments he was sure Karrick was going to fuck him until he was dead, his lungs bursting, his arse raw, and the rest of him bruised and battered.

This was not the same sensual, half-pleasurable pain he'd experienced the last time. This was raw and brutal — and terrifying.

Karrick's thrusting and his grip got harder, more implacable as he neared his goal, and in the end, Jase's face was mashed so thoroughly into the bedding he could no longer draw air. Black spots shrouded his vision, and his brain whirled into a darkened tunnel where fog and the imagined image of his own personal, horned demon lurked.

"Stay calm."

It was almost like that vision spoke to him — or thought at him. He held onto the idea of it, not bothering to contemplate how it could be the less frightening thing to deal with, when he associated it with so many horrible night terrors.

"Let me protect you," it seemed to whisper to his heart. *"Stay close to me, and he won't take you."*

So he did, because he could not bear the pain in his body anymore, could not breathe, could feel the fire in lungs deprived of air, and the heavy, distant pounding against his body. It was too much, and the company, the life-long familiarity of the creature in his sub-conscious was infinitely preferable to dying alone. He was so close to passing out, he didn't even feel Karrick reach his orgasm or realize he had been released until he was rolling him over.

Jase blinked up through the haze of tears and fear, clinging to the demon in his head, the one he knew from dreams as far back as he could remember, and heaved air into his racked body. Eventually, he managed to focus on Karrick.

The man stared down at him, a blaze of something darkly glittering and far more dangerous than a rough fuck in his eyes. Something warm and wet splashed onto Jase's belly. Jase glanced at the condom that had landed there and for a moment was mesmerized by the sight of Karrick's jizz oozing thickly down into his belly button.

"Get cleaned up," Karrick snarled. "Don't piss on my bed. I have work to do."

He ambled away, still wearing just his gown, wide open and flowing out behind him as he headed for the door.

"Karrick!" Jase swept the condom and the mess off himself and struggled to sitting.

Karrick stopped, turned, the edge of Jason's world visible in his dire expression. "What did you call me?"

"Karrick," Jase said again. "Your name."

Karrick's head tilted slightly, as though he was listening to something in the far distance. "For you, I don't have a name," he said coldly, his gaze finally coming back to Jase. "You have no need to address me. So long as you do as you're told, you should be safe enough." He cupped Jase's cheek in one gentle hand. "You are...very pretty."

Jase twitched his lips into a half-hearted smile. "Thank you."

Still gentle, Karrick touched his thumb to Jase's lips and an anticipatory smile ghosted across his face. "For later, I think." He bent, kissed Jase, a soft, sweet kiss, then stood. "Shower. Eat. You'll be needing your strength."

All Jase could do was nod. Until Karrick left the room, he didn't dare give any indication he'd be anything other than pliable.

Once Karrick had gone, Jase got shakily to his feet, went to the door and listened. He heard the retreat of him down the stairs and a moment later, the creak of his office door then the definitive sound of it closing.

Relieved, he scurried as fast as his wobbling legs allowed to find his clothing. He searched the entire room, under the bed, behind the door, everywhere, and continued on to the bathroom but found not a stitch. Even the door to Karrick's extensive walk-in closet was locked. Jase rattled the offending doorknob and cursed.

"Looking for something?"

Karrick's voice, just a few feet behind him, made Jase jump, a startled yelp escaping him before he could stop it.

"Clothes," he said hastily, glancing around for something to cover himself with and finding nothing. He crossed his hands in front of himself.

Karrick smiled, the expression kind, soft even. "No need, cherub," he admonished, walking slowly forward until he could carefully shift Jase's hands from their position. "You have nothing you need to hide."

"Where are my clothes?"

"No need," Karrick said again. "It's just us. I like looking at you." He smiled again, and it was like the cruel man of just moments before had never been. "It's just us. No reason for modesty. Come. Let's get you clean."

The man's mood swings were giving Jase whiplash. He stood his ground.

"I thought you had work to do."

"Nothing that can't wait. Come along."

"Go with him," the voice in his head told him. *"Comply. I won't be far away should you have need."*

Jase almost snorted at that thought. What would his imaginary friend, horned nightmare or not, be able to do if Karrick went crazy and tried to snuff-fuck him again?

But naked, alone and with Karrick between him and the bedroom door, he had little choice but to comply. At least for the time being.

* * * *

Karrick took slow, methodical care to bathe Jase with every ounce of gentleness and propriety he could muster. The boy seemed terrified. Fresh bruises bloomed on his backside, his wrist, and he moved his left arm gingerly.

Clearly, some line had been crossed. Several, if Jason's demeanor meant anything. The trouble was, Karrick had only a very vague recollection of the past half hour. Obviously, rough sex had been involved. Jason gave off not-so-subtle signs any attentions more intimate than a soapy cloth trailed over his skin were not welcome. Karrick let him have his way. Until he recalled just exactly what had transpired, he preferred to keep Jason at least compliant.

All he did remember with any clarity was sitting in the chair by the window watching his new lover sleep, seeing him wake, and admiring the way his young, supple body flowed into those languid stretches on the bed. Then a red-hot sheet of agony had sliced through his mind, and much of the next half hour came to him in maddeningly short and useless snippets.

The next distinct memory was of sitting at his desk, in his robe, wondering how he'd got there. Every time he delved into the vague heat of the foggy memories in between, that blanket of fiery pain reasserted itself and Karrick felt the murderous rage of his Killer rise.

He had spent long, frustrating years learning to control that rage. To let it out only on a very short leash, and only when absolutely necessary to do his duty. He never let it have free rein over his better judgment. That was how murderers got caught, and Karrick was not going to get caught. He had far too much to do.

Now was not a good time to be losing his mind.

Pressing his fingertips to his temples, he closed his eyes and let the soft patter of hot water fall across his back in soothing waves.

"Are you all right?" Jason asked, voice tentative but solicitous.

"Yes, cherub. Fine." Karrick steeled himself for the brightness of the bathroom's white tile surfaces and smiled down at the slender youth. "You're quite timid this evening." He tilted his head. "Not at all the sly, greedy boy I had last night."

Jason visibly paled. "What would you like from me?" he asked softly.

Karrick cupped Jason's face in one hand and lifted it to the light. Jason stretched up onto his toes to allow the grip to remain. But he trembled and braced, as though expecting violence beyond the pleasurable pain he'd received as he'd hung from Karrick's bed last night.

"Perhaps just your company tonight, eh?" Karrick said at last, releasing him.

"Yes." Jason nodded, too eager to agree to the tame suggestion. "Yes, of course." He slipped the shower door open. "I'll get you a towel."

Karrick nodded absently, turning back to the hot spray as Jason stepped out of the enclosure.

But some slash of instinct reached out. Moved Karrick of its own volition, and he grabbed the boy's wrist just before he'd stepped out of reach.

"Where are you going?"

"A-a towel," Jason stammered. "To get you a towel, like I said." He twisted his hand, turning his whole body on the other side of Karrick's immovable grip. "Please. You're hurting me."

"You like pain," Karrick growled, hearing the words, the harshness of his own voice, like the saying of them was an action outside his own directive. "You will, by the time I'm done with you. You'll beg. And beg. Endlessly. You'll see."

"Please." Jason whimpered and twisted, the bones in his wrist grinding, on the verge of snapping as he pitted his entire diminutive frame against the strength Karrick didn't quite understand himself.

Holding the tiny creature was no effort. Breaking him in half would be easy.

Karrick shook himself. "Go."

He shoved, and Jason stumbled back, hitting a shelf of toiletries as he lost his footing. The metal edge of the shelf dug into the soft flesh just below Jason's ribs and a tear of blood welled then trickled down his side.

Pulling the coppery scent into him with flared nostrils, Karrick felt the signs, the break in reasoning, the splintering of self as the rage clawed up through his careful restraints.

"Go!" he shouted. "Get out!"

He slammed the shower door closed with a reverberating crash and seconds later, the frantic pattering of bare feet across the bedroom carpet told him Jason was on the run.

The rage snarled to get free, to join the chase and bring down that scared little rabbit. Karrick gripped the towel bars on the shower door and the wall opposite and held on for dear life. Jason's life. He could not kill the boy. Not yet. But oh, how that raging beast in him wanted blood. Wanted to destroy anything its jailer even thought to hold precious.

"You. Don't get to win," he snarled at it. "I'm in charge. You won't touch him."

"*Already have.*"

The clarity of that rage-filled, taunting thought was horrifying.

"What happened?" Karrick wondered. "Why don't I remember?" He could recall every kill. Every drop of blood shed by his own hand, every torturous, sadistic sexual predation he'd turned back on the degenerates he'd hunted down and dispatched. So why couldn't he remember this?

"*You have to calm down, Karrick.*"

"Morland?"

"*Your beast has been busy tonight. You frightened that boy half to death.*"

"What happened?"

"*Vague is better, I think. He's gone now. Stole your trench coat from the hall closet. It is safe to come out.*"

Shaking and furious, Karrick stepped from the shower and stood dripping on his bathroom floor as the indistinct image of his master hovered in the shower's mist before him.

"That's never happened before," Karrick said, staring at the few drops of blood Jason had left behind. "I've never blacked out like that. Not ever."

"It is a stressful time," Morland pointed out. *"Disturbances in the veil make what we do...precarious. We have spoken of the shifts in loyalties. The dangers. Especially for your ilk. Killers are fragile creatures. Prone to breaking."*

There was a hushed pause. Even the steam in the air stilled and hung motionless.

"The veil is tattered. Floating like streamers in the wind. Take care it does not tangle you up, Karrick. There is no telling what might happen to a Killer who gets caught in the rags of the veil. Carelessness. Thoughtlessness. Madness. One soul or another to knit the veil back together, Karrick. To keep its secrets. Its prisoners."

"What are you talking about?"

A chill radiated through the air like a cold grin.

"What do you think holds our worlds apart, Karrick? Magic? Souls of the innocent for warp. Souls of the damned for weft. And those who fit nowhere else to weave the pattern."

Morland, apparently, was also losing his mind.

The mist around Karrick abruptly chilled and dropped out of the air, landing in sticky, clammy dampness on his skin and splatting in wet slicks across the floor. The spots of blood blurred and mingled, turning pink and thin and disappearing altogether.

He was alone.

* * * *

Jase cinched the coat belt tight around his waist and hurried through the darker places toward Barry's house. He kept to the shadows and the quiet streets, not daring to let his barefoot, disheveled and damp state be seen. He just wanted to get to where it was safe, with as little delay as he could manage.

He was practically running by the time he reached Barry's desolate street, ignoring the sharp gravel on the side of the road that dug into his soles. The house stood, a cheerful spot of light in the darkness at the end, and he dashed forward, relief flooding him.

The porch light was on, the door unlocked. He burst into the house and slammed the door, locking it behind him then leaning on it to catch his breath.

"What the hell?" Barry's voice cut through Jase's heavy breathing.

Jase looked up. A slim, hesitant figure appeared in the hallway behind Barry, and for a moment, Jase thought he had to be hallucinating.

"Dan?"

"Jase!"

Dan shoved past Barry and grabbed Jase up in strong arms, cradling him close. "Where have you been? What happened to you?"

Jase groaned, feeling the ache in his sore shoulder and the sharp twinge in his wrist where he thought maybe he'd broken something after all.

"Dan," he whispered again, too grateful for the supporting arms to even remember to be mad that the guy had left him, even though Jase had been the one to instigate their split.

"I'm here," Dan promised. "I'm here, and I'm not leaving. Come on."

It took little coaxing for Jase to allow his ex to lead him through the house to the living room and the soft, welcoming leather of the couch.

It took far more cajoling, hot beverages and warm clothes to get his story out. Barry sat in frigid, seemingly horrified, silence as Jase spoke. Dan moved ever closer until Jase was whispering out the final horror in broken sentences loud enough that he thought only Dan could hear.

"You're safe now." Dan pulled him close and Jase curled up, nearly in his lap.

"Don't leave," Jase mumbled. Exhaustion was plowing him under fast. "Don't..." He held onto Dan's shirt and tried to get closer.

"Won't."

The darkness that folded over him was full of voices and horned demons and promised nightmares he wouldn't understand. At least, this time, one of the voices was Dan's, whispering protections and secret vows over him he couldn't hear but that seemed to weave a web of comfort as the Dreams started.

Chapter Ten

"Here he is," Leyton said, inordinately proud of showing Graham to Jessica, despite his confusion as to why he'd taken him. He grinned, wanting her to be pleased with him, to know her opinion mattered.

They stood in Leyton's van, the side door closed, and stared down at Graham, who stared back with a glimmer of hope in his eyes, that sock hanging out of his mouth again.

Please tell me I did a good thing. Tell me bringing Graham here was wise.

"Oh, fucking hell," Jessica said, lifting one hand up to rest it on her chin, her other arm across her middle. "What if he isn't a Dreamer? What if it's just a coincidence he used that word? What if he's just some innocent man?"

She scowled at Leyton, two firm lines between her eyebrows showing her displeasure, her confusion and inability to fully accept the world she now lived in. She still had hope, he saw that—hope that this wasn't happening, that her life hadn't been turned upside down forever.

Something sank inside him.

"Who else but a Dreamer would know the term?" Leyton asked, his voice harsh, more from him hurting at her reaction than anything else. Piousness rose inside him then, and before he could fight it down he said, "You're rather silly to think otherwise."

She narrowed her eyes at him, clearly fighting her own battle. "A Dreamer could make him say things, get inside his head. And those ropes look like they're cutting into his wrists. Couldn't you have been a bit kinder? Just in case? If he isn't a Dreamer and we let him go, we're in all kinds of shit if he opens his mouth."

"Stop deluding yourself," Leyton snapped. "He *is* a Dreamer. You need to accept that. How else can he read my mind?"

She clamped her mouth closed then hunkered down in front of Graham. Leyton's gut clenched.

"Keep away from him," Leyton said. "I don't want you to get hurt."

"Hurt?" she asked, looking at Leyton over her shoulder. "Are you fucking kidding me? He's trussed up. How the hell is he going to hurt me?"

"I thought..." Leyton had thought Jessica might lean forward, that Graham would headbutt her. "It's best you keep away. He might turn violent."

"So would I if I were him," Jessica muttered.

Graham frowned and mumbled, the sock end flapping against his chin.

Jessica turned from Leyton to face Graham and removed the sock from his mouth. "Do you need a drink?"

Graham nodded, and Jessica glared up at Leyton again. Leyton sighed, swiveling to the sink then filling the beaker with water. He'd have to get the canister refilled soon. Perhaps he'd do that once Jessica had gone back home. The mundane task of buying water would give him time to think on what to do next. What to do with Graham.

"You're far too caring," Leyton said, choosing to forget he'd given in to his softer side earlier too and had allowed Graham a drink. After all, the man had needed one in order to give Leyton the information he'd required. Maybe he would offer more information now. He handed the beaker to Jessica, wanting to hold the cup to Graham's lips himself, but knew she'd throw him one of her looks. The kind that said she could manage, thankyouverymuch, so back off.

Jessica let Graham drink, and Leyton watched her face to see if the slurping noises affected her as much as they did him. She had an expression of pity on her face, not the annoyance Leyton knew was on his. Why did he get so upset about such things as loud drinking or eating? Perhaps his strict upbringing had something to do with it. Mother scolding him for eating with his mouth open had ended with a tooth removal once — and a slap to the side of his head that had resulted in him seeing stars. Yes, that was it. *She* had ingrained this loathing in him. He made a mental note to try to be more tolerant in the future. If it meant going against something *she* disliked, it would be worth it.

"Are you all right?" Jessica asked Graham, lowering the beaker.

The man nodded, swallowing, and tipped his head back, closing his eyes. "Throat's sore."

"I expect it is. Your wrists too," Jessica said, moving to touch his arm.

"*Don't* untie him!" Leyton said, panic spiking, a sharp spear in his belly.

Jessica stood and rammed one hand on her hip. "I wasn't *going* to, all right? Jesus!" She poked Leyton in the chest. "I was just going to... Oh, what the hell does it matter *what* I was going to do? You need to take him to Barry's. He'll be able to sort this out."

"Me?" Leyton had thought Jessica would want to go with him.

"Yes, you! I can't bloody drive, can I, and even if I could, getting him out of this van while it's parked outside my place isn't going to happen. I have neighbors, people who have no clue that we're like we are, obviously. If they see us carting some man around with his wrists tied and a fucking sock in his mouth... D'you get the picture?"

Leyton did — with startling clarity and more than a pinch of upset that Jessica was being so...so *mean*. He nodded. "So you do not wish to come with me to speak with Barry about our blocked minds? I rather would have thought you would."

She pursed her lips and eyed the ceiling for a moment, then leveled her gaze on his face. He loved her so much and she had no idea — and if she did, she didn't care.

"Can't care, Leyton. Who would want to care for someone like you?" Mother said.

"Go away!" he said, fisting his hands.

"Oh, I'll go away all right," Jessica said, reaching a hand out to open the van door.

"Not you. Please, I didn't mean you..." He felt sick to his stomach that she'd gotten the wrong idea. He wanted her to go to Barry's with him. Needed some company while his head was in such a mess. She'd take his mind off his loss of control.

"Your mother," she stated, dropping her hand to her side.

"Yes." He glanced at Graham then back to her. "Will you please come with me?" He was aware of how he sounded, that his voice held a pleading edge. Normally he wouldn't want her to know how he felt, but at the moment...he *needed* her close.

She considered his question for a second or two then huffed out a long sigh. "All right." She raised both hands. "All right, I'll bloody well come with you."

* * * *

Jessica wondered, not for the first time, how she got herself into these situations. She sat in the passenger seat of Leyton's van, on their way to Barry's. Yes, Leyton had had a point in her visiting Barry with him, to find out what the hell was going on with their heads, but not like this. Not with a man in the back. Without Rivald's intervention, him seemingly unable to contact them now, would his powers in preventing the police from pulling them over if they had a mind to even work? Did he know what they were doing now? Maybe he could see them but just couldn't contact them in their heads or in person.

"Do you think the link between worlds has been compromised?" she asked Leyton, turning to look at him. "I mean, if there's another Tool Master that this Graham works for... D'you see what I mean?"

Leyton flexed his jaw muscles and took a sharp right turn. Jessica was thrown against his side, and a thud from the back indicated Graham hadn't fared very well either. She pulled herself off him, trying not to shudder, and gripped the handle on the door in case she was forced into him again.

"I have thought about this," Leyton said. "If another band of Dreamers are here from either another part of the country or, God forbid, from another realm..." He swallowed, his Adam's apple bobbing erratically. "This could account for our problem. I have not heard from Rivald in a long time. I tried to ignore my burn, but it has got to the point where I feel it is directing me instead of me directing it. I have no idea whether I selected Graham because I was told to somehow or because the burn wanted it to be so. I am confused."

She wondered if he was a little frightened too. She knew enough about his childhood to realize that without being told what to do, without someone steering Leyton on the right track—if killing was, indeed, the right track—he might be feeling vulnerable.

"Look," she said, placing a hand on his thigh and praying he didn't get the wrong idea, "we'll get this sorted out." She patted him then returned her hand to her lap, entwining her fingers to stop herself showing him any more affection in the form of touch.

How would they get it sorted out, though? If Barry was experiencing the same thing they were, how could they get in contact with Rivald? Without Leyton being able to cross over into the Dreamworld, they were stuck here on their own, making all the decisions by themselves.

And there wouldn't be any decisions to make if Leyton hadn't taken that man back there. We could have had a nice long break while things went on in Dreamworld and when they were fixed, we'd return to work.

She nearly laughed at that. Work.

"Hey," Graham called hoarsely. "That wouldn't be the case."

What? Fuck, she'd forgotten Leyton had said Graham could still read minds. "What do you mean?" she asked, twisting to look at him.

He appeared uncomfortable, sprawled on the floor like that, his body rocking from side to side as Leyton swerved and took more corners a little too exuberantly.

"You'll get us noticed," she snapped at Leyton, giving him a spiteful glare. He might not care about being arrested, but she did. "Drive properly!"

She returned her attention to Graham.

"Those in the team I work for can all still function as normal. It's just your team that seems to be affected," Graham said. "There is a reason for that, and I'll explain it once we get to Barry's."

"Why can't you just tell us now?" she asked, eager to have her mind put at rest.

"I don't want to have to explain it twice," Graham said.

He set his jaw, and she knew she wouldn't be able to coax any more out of him.

Fucking hell.

She had not envisaged spending her evening like this.

"I heard that," Graham whispered.

"Good for you," Jessica said.

* * * *

With Jase propped up beside him, Dan felt all kinds of wonderful. He shouldn't, not when Jase had been through what he had, but to finally have him beside him like this again — *wanting* to lean on him and go to sleep — was something he hadn't thought to experience again.

Barry had gone into the kitchen to set more coffee on to brew and to think about what to make for dinner. Dan was glad of the privacy. He could stroke Jase's hair without feeling self-conscious and look down at his face, taking in the sight of him without someone else seeing his emotions, how being with Jase made him feel. He needed this time alone, to come to terms with how their separation had affected him, to think about whether he had any chance of being in Jase's new life. Could he only be there for him as a friend? Stand by if Jase went back to that Karrick guy, knowing Jase would be treated like shit again, Dan being there to pick up the pieces every time?

He admitted he wouldn't want to see Jase so upset, but if Jase chose to return to Karrick, Dan would be there on the sidelines for however long it took. Their time apart had shown him how much he loved the little blond—and being near him any way he could was better than not at all. *Suck on that, Dad.* Because for once in his life, admitting he loved another guy didn't carry the feelings of shame and disgust, didn't even echo with his father's derision as it had in the past. Jase needed him, and he could shut out the past to be what Jase needed.

Jase slept soundly, his breathing even. That meant he wasn't having one of those weird dreams where he always woke frightened and confused. Dan had seen that scenario many times, didn't fancy seeing it again either, but he would if he had to. Not accepting Jase for who he was had been one of their problems—his problems—in the past. He couldn't make the same mistake twice.

Barry popped his head around the door. "We have company."

"Fuck!" Dan's stomach rolled over, and he placed his free arm across Jase.

"Not that kind of company," Barry said. "I looked out the bedroom window while I was making a bed up for you in the spare room."

A bed. I'll be staying here?

"Oh. Right. Well, thank you." Dan's face grew hot.

"Well, you'll be good for Jase, I think," Barry said. "He could do with having you here, and there is no fucking way he is going back to his apartment now. Anyway, back to the company. It's Leyton, the strange guy I told you about. He'll come off as a whacko, but just ignore that. Although he doesn't do very nice things, he won't hurt you. Not when he knows who you are and that you're one of us." Barry shrugged. "Not one of us, but someone he can trust. You are, aren't you?"

Dan nodded. "Hell yeah. I'm here for Jase, and if that means keeping all this...odd shit to myself, then that's what I'll do, all right? I don't want him hurt. I'll do whatever to make sure he isn't, including shutting my mouth."

"Good. I'll go and let him in, then."

Barry disappeared, and Dan listened to the sound of the front door opening then Barry muttering, "What the fuck have we got here?"

Dan's stomach clenched. He didn't have a good feeling about this visitor. Maybe it was because of what Leyton did that freaked the shit out of him—but something told him otherwise. He knew that when Jase woke up, there would be a whole new bunch of crap to get through. Intuition flared, and he nodded absently, taking a deep breath to calm his fast-beating heart.

I can do this. I can deal with this kind of shit. For Jase.

Barry entered the living room followed by a pretty woman. Dan frowned, sure that Barry had told him

Leyton was a man. A guy was thrust through the doorway then, frazzled-looking, arms behind his back and a black sock hanging out of his mouth.

What the fuck?

Christ, this changed things a bit, didn't it? It was clear to him this man had been abducted and brought here. Why else would he have — *is that rope?* — around his wrists and a sock in his mouth?

Oh, God. Jase, stay asleep, man. Just stay a-fucking-sleep.

Another man came in, his face scarred, a frown so deep on his brow it appeared permanently carved there. The woman walked over to a chair and sat, smiling at Dan with an expression that said loud and clear that she wondered who the hell he was.

I'm thinking the same about you, love.

The scarred man shoved the bound guy forward then pressed a hand to his head so he folded to the floor. "You can sit there for now, Graham, until we determine whether you are one of us — whether you can be trusted."

Barry stared from Graham to the scarred man to the woman. "What the *fuck* is going on *now*?" he asked.

Chapter Eleven

Dan sat up straighter, nestling Jase more securely against him, and Barry sighed. *Perfect timing, Leyton, as usual.*

"You want to take Jase into the other room?" Barry asked Dan.

The kid shook his head, eyes wide, face pale, arms tight around Jase. "I'll stay. This is part of...whatever, right? I should know what's going on."

In for a penny. Barry just shook his head, resigned, and turned to Jessica, lifting an eyebrow.

"Hey, don't look at me," she said. "He came to me with this guy. What was I supposed to do?"

"Keep me out of it?" Barry suggested.

Leyton made a strange sound and Barry turned to him. "What?" he snarled at the Killer.

"Don't any of you get it? There is no keeping out of anything. Who's he?" Leyton pointed to Dan, uneasiness making him twitch.

Barry recognized the beginnings of panic in the back of Leyton's too-wide stare. "He's good. Never mind him. Just tell me what happened. Start at the beginning. I need to know everything."

Leyton swallowed then took a breath. He offered a short, sharp nod and told the story about grabbing Graham and not being sure why he had, and of picking up Jessica in hopes she would know what to do next.

Barry nodded. "Coming here was, I suppose, the best option at that point," he told her. "Leyton, did you drive past the park by any chance?"

Leyton nodded. "On the way to see Jessica. I had to stop on the bridge and secure the caravan door. Why?"

Barry glanced at Graham. "Because he's only got one shoe on." He fixed his gaze on Graham's face, studying the man who was too calm sitting trussed as he was in the middle of Barry's living room.

"You found my shoe then?"

Barry was so startled by the voice in his head he actually took a step back.

"Oh, fuck!" Dan swore and scrambled deeper into the couch, hauling his feet up under him in an attempt to get farther from the man on the floor.

Graham's eyes had gone pitch black. He stared up at Barry, but his face was slightly slack, as though he saw nothing and whatever he was doing required the utmost concentration.

"It does. This is difficult. Can you please remove the sock from my mouth?"

Barry frowned. "How are you doing that when none of us can?" he asked, reaching for the sock to yank it free.

Graham took a few seconds to work up to answering. "With great difficulty, actually. It gets harder every time."

"Why is that?" Barry crouched to peer into the man's now-pale eyes. "And how did your other shoe get dropped beside the creek off the bridge near the park?"

Graham sighed. "I have talented toes."

"What?"

The man shifted, bringing his bare foot around and wiggling his toes. "Freakishly agile. Who knew it would come in handy someday. I had just enough reach with my foot to get the caravan door open. I kicked my shoe, my wallet and my car keys out. Just thought maybe someone would find them and wonder."

Barry sighed. "I found them." He stood and glared at Leyton, who was smiling with a look of relief. "Don't get ahead of yourself there, big guy. I found his shoe and his keys. Not the wallet. I actually called the cops. I thought it was a lead on a new case. I wanted the authorities in it from the get-go—thought maybe if they brought one down themselves for once, they'd get off our backs for a while. They will scour every inch of that roadside, and they'll find his wallet. What then?" Barry jabbed a finger in Graham's direction. "He becomes a missing person with a name and a last known whereabouts instead of a mysterious shoe and set of keys on the side of the road."

"I am just glad I hadn't messed up and left the door unlatched," Leyton said. "I thought I was losing it. Slipping up, not checking I had the door closed properly. I'll have to secure a better lock on it. From the outside."

"You have to stop using it to transport your prey," Barry told him. "Do you know what will happen if the authorities ever get their hands on it? Not even your horned man will be able to save you then. Use your head, Leyton!"

"Don't you dare tell me how to do my job!" Leyton shouted, fists clenching, eyes blazing too darkly.

"Guys!" Jessica hopped up from her seat. "Guys. Stop it!"

Barry turned on her. "Do you have any idea how fucked we all are if he gets caught?"

Jessica's hands tightened into tiny fists and her face set in lines of anger. "This is not productive, Barry. Lay off him. He's doing the best he can. Just like the rest of us. He needs Rivald more than we do. Cut him some slack."

"Jessica—"

"Don't." She turned on Leyton. "Because he's right. You need to be extra careful, Leyton. You need Rivald the most, and without him you're the most vulnerable. Please. We all need you to be strong now."

Leyton nodded and visibly forced himself to relax. "Okay. You are right. I need to be more careful. It is hard."

She nodded. "I know it is. But you have to try. You know Rivald best. What he would want. We're counting on you."

Again, Leyton nodded. "You are right. Of course you are right."

"Good. Now." She turned to Graham. "About whatever it is that's blocking us. What do you know about it?"

"I don't know all of the details," Graham told her, instantly giving her his full attention.

Barry marveled at her calm, clear control of their volatile Killer, and her no-nonsense takeover of the impromptu interrogation. Wherever the victim of a few short months ago had gone, she was in control now, and he had to give Rivald credit for finding her. She was quickly becoming the glue that held them all together. Maybe she had started out as the bait for the scum Leyton hunted, but since then, she had clearly grown into her role as the sane, calm one, and it set Barry at ease. Just having her in the house left him a lot less jittery than he had been ever since Tag had left on his conference.

"Then tell us what you do know," Jessica said.

"There is going to be a Winnowing."

"A what?" she asked.

"Winnowing. It happens every so often when He feels the Dreaming is getting too high-profile, or someone is getting too dangerous." He shot a withering glare at Leyton. "Usually a Killer. One of yours went rogue recently, if I'm not mistaken?"

Barry shrugged, trying not to think about the mess he'd found in the basement of this very house when the team had stopped that rogue Killer a few months before. She had gone off her head and tortured and murdered innocents. The team had had no choice but to bring her down.

"Most of that was before my time," Barry said, glancing at Jessica and nodding.

She sank back into her chair and adopted her habitual pose, curled in on herself, silent and watching.

Barry returned his attention to Graham. "All I did was clean up the mess. I didn't know her or why she turned."

"Because she was insane," Leyton mumbled, shivering.

"Right," Barry agreed. "And we're not."

"*I'm* not," Leyton protested. But he did so quietly, his arms crossed over his chest.

Jessica glanced up at him, and Barry thought he actually saw pity on the girl's face.

"There is a barrier, of sorts," Graham went on, drawing their focus back to him, "between this world and the Dreaming world. I don't really know if the barrier is thinning, and that's why some of us are being affected like we are, or if the barrier is thinning because some of us are having difficulties. The Winnowing might be happening because of dangerous cases like your rogue, or she may have gone rogue because the veil thinned to allow Him better access to this world."

"The chicken or the egg," Leyton mused.

"One motherfucking chicken from hell, if you ask me," Barry replied.

Jessica snickered and leaned back in her chair, tucking her feet under her. "So," she said, "that maybe explains the issues we're having, but it doesn't tell us what to do about it."

"You could start with untying me," Graham suggested.

Barry didn't move. He didn't know this guy. He'd just been abducted and driven all over the city, his life threatened, and Dreamer or not, he would have to be some kind of pissed at the treatment he'd received so far.

"Look, we're all on the same side, right?" Graham squirmed, no doubt trying to ease some pressure on his arms. "I'm hardly going to call the cops on you. What would I tell them?"

No one spoke.

"This is happening to all of us," Graham continued. "Whatever is going on, we have no one to guide us. I can't reach Morland, and I don't dare try to contact Karrick."

Forgotten on the couch, Dan suddenly straightened, a snarl grinding from his mouth.

"You work with Karrick?" Barry's protective instincts put him between Jase and the bound man.

"To hear him tell it, I work *for* him. He's our Killer."

"Who else is on your team?" Barry asked.

"Me and Karrick and two other Dreamers. I haven't heard from either one of them in weeks. Not unusual at the best of times, but with everything going on, I would have expected them to check in. If they spoke to Karrick, he didn't mention it. But then, he hasn't exactly been himself lately, either. Last time I spoke to him, he was adamant he had found another Dreamer for us, and he was going to clean the kid up and get him under control."

"Like hell," Dan growled.

Next to him, Jase slept on, oblivious to the way Dan gathered him even closer.

"Calm down. Jason is not going anywhere." Barry crossed his arms over his chest and turned back to Graham, glaring at him. "No. Where."

Graham shrugged as much as his bonds allowed. "I don't want him. Karrick does. For whatever scheme he has going, and I know he's got something going on, because his thoughts have been closed to me for almost a month. Anything he tells me in person could be the truth. Or he could be lying through his teeth. I have no way of knowing." An emotion, dark and deeply angry, passed through Graham's eyes. "He's never closed me out before. Something is up with him, and I intend to find out what. I want to know what happened to the rest of my team, and for that"—he shrugged again—"I probably need your help."

"Lucky for you I'm a P.I., then." Barry crouched in front of him. "But I promise you, anything happens to one hair on the heads of anyone in this room, and I give you back to Leyton. Dreamer or no Dreamer, this is my family. You fuck with that, I will come for you."

Graham nodded. "Fair enough."

"All right." Barry stood. "Leyton, let him go. I have some calls to make. I'll see if I can get Ross to make the investigation into Graham's disappearance go away."

"Say hey to him for me," Jessica said.

"Call him yourself, Jess. Throw the poor man a bone."

She smiled but shook her head. "He doesn't really want me. This shit... It's all too much."

Barry glanced at Dan then back at her. "Tell that to Dan here. Or Tag. If Ross didn't want you, he wouldn't keep after you. Call him."

She smiled again but didn't say anything else as sadness crept into her eyes and she hugged herself.

One thing Barry had to give her—she hadn't lost her sense of compassion or her stubbornness. No matter how many times Barry's ex-police partner, Ross, used a poorly veiled excuse to see her, she continued to insist she felt nothing for the cop, that he didn't want to get involved with a Dreamer, even though he knew all about what they did, and even helped cover their tracks with the officials. Why she stubbornly refused to see he was up to his balls in 'this shit' was beyond Barry.

Chapter Twelve

Mist curled around Jase's legs. Cold dampness soaked through his jeans and he shivered.

"Who's there?"

No answer. Just the tightening grip of the cold as it seeped up his thighs. He took a few steps back, but the mist followed, winding up over his hips and caressing the bare skin of his stomach with sharp, sticky fingers.

"Stop it."

His voice had squeaked and he whimpered as the foggy fingers dug into his flesh. Warmth trickled down into the curling hair at his groin. He didn't know how or when he'd become naked. He scrambled back, but there was no escaping the clutching grasp of the mist.

"Leave me alone!"

The slow, almost gentle slicing continued at his abdomen and he screamed. The pain jolted him awake.

He stared into darkness, eyes wide and staring, but seeing nothing.

"Who's there?"

A skittering sound off somewhere behind him had him spinning. There was no light. No hint of shape or shadow. His bare feet scraped across rough planks.

"Please. I can't see."

He lifted a hand to find himself bound and the skittering getting closer. His ankles were tied, secured to something heavy or stationary. He couldn't move. The scratching came closer. Something dashed over his toes and he yelped. All surrounding sound stopped and he listened to his own harsh breathing in the dark.

"Hello?"

Nothing. Just the sounds of tiny claws again. Then something sharp nibbling at his toes. He thrashed, screamed, as that something clawed its way up his leg. Cold mist swirled up, clutched at his throat and he stumbled back, fell, landing hard on a grassy slope.

Mist spiraled around him, thrusting toward him, and he crawled on hands and knees away from it. It couldn't touch him. He mustn't let the mist touch him. It hurt too much. More than he liked. In ways that left him weak and afraid and he hated that touch.

His ankle ties fell off. Scampering away, he clambered to his feet then ran. It followed. One glance back was enough to know it was only biding its time. He would never outrun it. Never get away from what it wanted of him.

Ahead, he could hear traffic and instantly knew he was near the park. The road was only a few short yards away. He was close to safety. Close to the old place he'd shared with Dan. Close to home.

He stumbled then fell, closing his fingers over something damp and cool. He glanced down to see a square of leather under his palm. A wallet.

The fog cascaded in a shower of stinging, tiny blades, drawing blood as it shattered over him like a pane of broken glass.

His screams finally woke him for real...

Jase woke in a strange place. There was no squabbling from the couple next door coming through the thin walls of his new apartment. No sounds of the construction outside, nor did he wake to the eerie, unnerving silence of Karrick's bed. The familiar smell of Barry's too-strong coffee reached his nose.

"Wha—?"

"Shhh." A hand caressed his forehead, sweeping away the stray hair. "You're okay."

"Dan?" An unhinged memory surfaced. One of being face down, forced… He shuddered.

"I'm here, babe. Never going away again."

"Dan?" He couldn't quite believe it was real. Didn't dare believe it. He touched his stomach. No marks, no blood, no lovingly carved lines of red. Scrambling, he kicked the sheets away and inspected his toes. No teeth marks.

"What is it?" Dan watched him from the other side of the bed. "What did you dream?"

"Nothing." Jase sat up and crunched himself tight to the headboard, knees to his chest. "Nothing. Forget about it. What are you doing here?"

"Come back down here," Dan demanded, patting the mattress beside him.

Jase shook his head. "Why are you here?"

Dan bit his lip, making Jase long to reach out and touch the whitened skin and tell him to stop biting. He would worry it raw.

"I made a mistake, Jase. I screwed up. I'm so sorry."

"Sorry?"

"I should have held onto you."

"You're back?"

It had to be another dream. Jase shifted, scooting across the bed to get nearer the edge. This was not real any more than the razor blades or the rats or the mist. It was a trick to make him weak. Make him want what he couldn't have.

Dan shot a hand out and closed it around his wrist. "Don't."

"Let me go!"

The fingers tightened and Jase winced.

"I won't hurt you." Dan sat up, sliding after him and wrapping his arms then his legs and his whole body around Jase. "I won't hurt you again, Jase. I promise. I'm not leaving you again. Lie back down. Tell me what you dreamed. I'll help you."

The warmth was real. The tight embrace and the feel of Dan's hot breath on the side of his neck was real. The slick wetness of his tongue against Jase's skin, followed by the sharp bite of teeth was very, very real.

"Relax," Dan whispered. "I've got you now."

Another lick. Another bite. Just hard enough to cause a twinge of pain then it was gone and Jase's blood rushed in his ears. He tilted his head to one side and offered the spot again.

Dan's tongue trailed a slow, firm path over the exposure. His teeth grazed back along the skin and Jase tensed, anticipating the pain that never came.

"You like that," Dan whispered. Not a question.

Jase groaned, squirmed, but Dan had him in a full body hug. There was no escape.

Teeth closed over the shell of Jase's ear and he gulped past the sharp tingle of sensation that skittered over his skin and lit up his entire body. Dan's hands moved, gliding up his torso and stopping on his pecs. He played a light, tripping dance over Jase's nipples, teasing them up into hard nubs before taking them both in his fingers and twisting. Jase arched out, a moan falling from his lips.

"Yeah, you like that," Dan said. "All that pain."

He twisted again and Jase arched higher, groaning.

"Puts you in the here and now."

One last twist finally wrung a sharp cry from Jase and a long, uncontrolled whimper as he came back down to slump against his lover's chest.

"That's it."

Dan's touch turned gentle, and Jase pressed against him.

"You lie down now, Jase. I'm gonna take care of you." He slid from behind Jase and pushed on his shoulders. "Lie down. It's gonna be okay."

"This is real?" Jase lay back but didn't take his gaze off Dan, terrified that if he did, even for the time it took to blink, the mist would be back. It would have fooled him into thinking he was with the one person in the world he wanted, the one he trusted with everything, when really he was just trapped in another Dream that would only end in terror and death.

"I promise you, this is no dream," Dan assured him. "You feel this." He ran his hand down Jase's arm to his wrist and picked it up. "You feel me?"

Jase nodded, watching as Dan sucked one of his fingers into his mouth and swirled his tongue around.

"Good boy. Spread your legs."

"What are you going to do?"

Dan grinned. "You. Okay?"

In a flash, Jase recalled everything Karrick had done. "I—"

"Not like any other guy has ever done, babe. Not like any Dream, not like anything you've ever known before. You trust me?"

Jase searched his lover's face, his eyes, looking for the deception. The uncertainty. "Why?"

"Because I know what you need now. I know what I need. We can do this. Together. Always together. You want me in you or not?"

"I don't know," Jase replied truthfully. "I—"

Dan leaned down and covered his mouth, taking a kiss Jase found himself eager to return. The heat of Dan's body over his was overwhelming. The safety in the scent of him, in his touch, even the bright spots of pain he offered, was too much to resist. He wanted it. He wanted the assurance he wasn't alone. That he wasn't a freak. He wanted Dan.

But he was afraid. What about when he Dreamed? What about when Dan looked at him with fear and disgust in his eyes? It had happened before. It would happen again.

"I know what you're thinking," Dan said, straightening and taking both of Jase's hands in his.

"You do?"

Dan nodded. "You're thinking about what happens when you Dream and I freak out. What do you do after you trust me and my promises and I renege?"

Jase stared at him, waiting.

"I talked with Barry. It ain't gonna happen, babe. He told me all about him and Tag. How they split and got back together. How much he relies on Tag, and you can rely on me like that. I'm always gonna be here. I swear."

Jase just watched him, unsure if he could really believe his words.

"I swear." Dan kissed the backs of his knuckles on one hand. "I give you my solemn"—he kissed the other hand—"unwavering"—he raised Jase's hands and pressed them to the pillow above his head—"absolute word"—he leaned over Jase, gripping both his wrists in one hand and Jase's chin in the other—"on everything either one of us believes in, that I will not leave you, ever. I will always be here to keep you in the present. I won't let the mist drown you. I won't let the Dreams take you. I won't let the darkness keep you. You're mine, now, and mine you'll stay. You understand?"

"Why?" Jase pulled in a tight breath.

"Because I love you."

Jase frowned, but Dan went on without letting him respond.

"I want you. Dreams. Pain. Everything. I want you. I'll have you. If you'll have me."

"This isn't a Dream," Jase said at last, finally believing.

"This isn't a Dream."

Dan leaned down and kissed him until he saw stars and couldn't breathe. Until his chest hurt and his arms were numb and he wanted it to go on forever. When Dan finally pulled back, it was to look Jase in the eye, no smiles, no hint of anything other than direct, honest truth.

"You're my dream," Dan said. "The best kind, and I'm going to make the good ones come true for both of us."

"How?"

"First, by taking back what he tried to claim. I'll cover every bruise he left on you with one of my own, if I have to."

"You don't," Jase assured him. "Just let them heal." He shifted his legs apart as far as they would go under Dan's restrictive weight. "You can have me, though."

Dan nodded. "Good." He drew Jase's hands back down and arranged them, inner wrists together in front of him. "Don't move."

Jase watched him yank his belt free of the jeans on the floor and fish in the bedside table. A sly smile crossed Dan's face as he pulled forth lube.

"Nice." He caught Jase's eye. "That asshole use condoms?"

Jase nodded.

"There been anyone else?"

Jase shook his head.

"Me either. Gimme your hands."

Jase lifted his hands enough for Dan to wrap the belt around them.

"This isn't ideal but it's all I got at the moment. You tell me if it's too tight. I'm not out to maim you."

"It's okay."

"Good. Spread."

Jase did, lifting his knees and planting his heels, watching as Dan spread lube on two fingers and leaned close.

"Hard and fast," Dan promised, shoving the slicked fingers into Jase's body.

Jase closed his eyes, moaned, craving more of a stretch than two slim fingers offered. He opened his mouth to say as much when a sharp sting bloomed across his chest. He gasped.

"Open your eyes," Dan demanded.

Another sting, and Jase complied, gritting his teeth as the free end of the belt whistled and came down across his chest again. And again.

God, it hurt. It dug into him and boiled his blood. His cock stiffened and he threw his head back, wanting to howl out the demons and the darkness. Wanting to use each gratifying blow to release the terror of what he couldn't control and give the rest of it to Dan to manage for him. He wanted to be free.

The strap fell across his nipples and the added sting at last freed his voice in a ragged cry. Above him, Dan glowed and struck again.

"That's it," he encouraged. "Just let it go."

Jase lost track of the belt's blows, of Dan's words, of everything but the release of letting the pain be all that mattered. It hurt and it healed at the same time. It grew until the red heat of it was all he knew, then Dan's fingers left him and there was the stretch he craved, splitting him open as Dan fucked him.

The belting stopped when Dan raised Jase's hands above his head again and leaned down to kiss him as they fucked. The scratch of Dan's chest hair over Jase's tenderized skin was an added dimension of sensation and it sent him into spinning ecstasy he didn't want to come down from.

He didn't remember coming. Physical release was a small thing next to the emotional floodgates, and he spent as much time cradled in Dan's arms afterwards, shivering and bawling as he had high on the perfect mixture of pain and pleasure. Dan held him close, pressing a cool cloth to his burning skin and cooing silly words into his ear. Letting him cry like a baby was not something Dan had ever indulged before. It was more of an answer to Jase's fears than the lovemaking or the sadism had been.

He could be what he was in front of this man and not worry Dan would turn away from him.

Eventually, they made it out of bed, out of the shower and down to the kitchen. Barry was standing by the sink, coffee in hand, gazing out of the window. He turned when Jase entered the room.

"You are not a quiet pair, I'll give you that," Barry said. The bantering look vanished when he caught sight of Jase's chest through the open buttons on the too-big shirt he was wearing.

Self-conscious, Jase pulled the shirt closed. Dan was around in front of him in a heartbeat, gently doing up the buttons and shielding him from Barry's view.

"Don't, Dan. It's fine."

He tried to brush Dan's hands away, but he closed his fingers over Jase's and leaned close to kiss him.

"Mine," he whispered, and the possessiveness of it brought a smile to Jase's lips.

"Yours," he agreed.

"Good. We've established who belongs to whom." Barry fixed Jase with a look. "And that everyone is happy with the arrangement?"

Jase nodded. "Don't judge. We don't have to stay."

"You're welcome to," Barry reassured him "My only opinion on the matter is that it's safe, sane and —"

"Consensual," Jase said.

"Good." The P.I. turned back to the window. "Tag will be home soon. You'll have to deal with him. He's maybe not as open-minded as some."

"I can deal with him," Jase assured them both. "I can deal." This time, it was his turn to reach up for a kiss and Dan obliged him.

"Good." Barry swiveled to face them. "Because I think I know how to find out what Karrick is trying to do."

"How?"

"You have to go back to him."

Dan snarled and hauled Jase behind him. "Over my dead body!"

"Don't tempt fate around here, Daniel. It came too close to that once already. I'm not interested in taking another chance. But we have to get inside his head, and if Graham can't, then the only other person we know who even has a chance is Jason. It's the only way to figure out what's going on."

"What is he talking about? Who's Graham? Dan, what happened?" Jase asked. Insidious, the fear was back. Fear of losing what he'd just found in Dan.

Terror of being on his own again. "What does he mean it almost came to you dead? What does that mean?"

"Fill him in," Barry told Dan. "I have to meet Ross and explain about Graham. See if we can head things off before the police get any more involved. We've got to find that wallet."

Mist cascaded over Jase, shards of it burning into his skin, red-hot points of pain he couldn't bear. He couldn't scream. He had no voice left. Curling into a ball, he sobbed and prayed for it to be over. The cold square of leather pressed into his palm and against his chest like an anchor to what was real. His voice burst and howled.

"Jase!" Dan said.

Jase shook, hard, and felt hands gripping his arms.

"Jason, babe, look at me! Barry! Do something!"

Jase blinked into the brightness of the sunlit kitchen. Dan stared at him, deep brown eyes wide, face pale, terror and determination mixed in his expression.

"What just happened?" Dan demanded.

Barry stood behind him, features set in a grim frown.

"What was that?" Dan turned to the ex-cop. "What—"

"I don't know," Barry admitted. "It's never happened to me. I Dream when I'm asleep, not when I'm awake. If Rivald wants me when I'm awake these days, he calls my cell, just like anyone else. Well. At least he did before he dropped off my radar completely. Before that, I always knew when he was trying to get my attention." He made a wry face. "It was a dark and foggy night and all that."

Jase shivered and Dan drew him close.

"So what just happened?" Dan asked again.

"You said something about a lost wallet?" Jase asked, fighting to hold onto the ragged edges of the strange vision.

"Yeah, so?" Barry peered at him, concern edging his expression and sharpening his voice.

"I know where it is. I saw it last night."

"Dreams don't work that way," Barry began.

Jase pushed himself free of Dan's embrace and glared at his boss. "Mine *do*. I don't know why. I just know that mine are clear. They're telling me something, and today they're telling me there's a wallet in the grass off Peer Street, just outside the park on the far side of the bridge. You want it? That's where you'll find it."

"What else did your dreams tell you?" Dan demanded.

Jase shivered and wrapped both arms around himself. The movement folded the skin of his chest and pressed the crisp cotton of Dan's shirt against him, reminding him of the morning's activities. The reminder calmed him. "I can't really remember."

"Well that's helpful," Barry muttered.

"Hey." Dan draped his arm over Jase's shoulder and leaned on his lover. "Back off. He's doing his best."

"Yeah." Barry turned back to the view out of the kitchen window. "I know."

Barry fought to rein in his frustration and his temper. He had no business taking it out on these two. They were doing remarkably well, all things considered. He knew how he dealt when he didn't have Tag around to ground him. He picked up his whiskey-laced coffee and took a burning swallow.

He was still trying to find a way to kick Jase's memories into gear without traumatizing both young men, when his cell rang.

He glanced at the caller display, sighed and answered. "Hey, Ross. What's up?"

"Got some good and some not so good news. First, you lucked out. The park scene is being released. We didn't find anything. Not that we had enough time to really scour the place, but something bigger came up. We needed the personnel elsewhere."

"This the not so good?"

"Yeah. Dude, you need to see this."

"I got no badge, Ross. You know I can't show my face at a crime scene."

"Don't care. If this isn't to do with you and your scar-faced Killer freak, I don't know what is."

"Don't call him that." An unreasoning wave of protectiveness flushed through Barry. "Leyton can't help the way he is. Be nice."

"Um." Ross snorted. "Fine. Still. This shit's got me worried, Barry, and you need to get here before they take the body down."

"Jesus."

"Hurry." Ross gave him the address.

Not far enough from the sanctuary of Barry's little house for his comfort.

"Be there in five." Barry turned to the young men huddled at the breakfast bar. "I need you two to go over to the park and fetch that wallet. I have some business to take care of."

"You want us to come with you?" Jase asked.

"No. Bad enough I'm going to show my face at a murder scene. I want to keep you out of that shit if I can help it. Go find the wallet and come straight back here."

"Yeah." Dan tightened his fingers around Jase's. "No problem. We'll be careful."

"Good."

Chapter Thirteen

Karrick sat upright from resting on his sofa. He closed his eyes and cocked his head, waiting for the instinct that had made him move so quickly to reveal exactly what he'd sensed. Digging his fingers into the top of the sofa, he breathed steadily to unruffle his jittery nerves. Not that he was frightened—no, never that—but having been as relaxed as he had then ripped out of his calm state... It was a shock to the system.

He'd been on the way to Morland's cave when something had made him pause. A whisper of sound—feet walking on undergrowth? At first he'd thought someone had followed him into his trance, dogging his steps in order to see where he was going, and he'd stopped just as reality was changing into the Dreamworld landscape.

The shift backwards from one realm to the other had made him feel sick, disoriented, and he swallowed now, opening his eyes to glance around the room, wary that someone was in his living room in disguised form.

That was the problem with the fog and mist. Sometimes, if he wasn't fully alert, he didn't know it was there until it grew thick and swarmed around him.

"Anyone there?" He waited for a response, knowing if someone *was* there and they intended to do him harm, they weren't likely to announce themselves while he was on guard and ready.

As he suspected, no one answered, and he realized he had nothing to fear inside his home. Sudden clarity came, and he stared at the wall beside the living room door, seeing precisely what he needed to see, displayed as though on a projector screen.

"So he let you out of his sight," he murmured then stood, grabbing his coat on his way out of the front door. "You'll be in mine soon."

He got into his car and went as far over the speed limit as he could without drawing too much attention to himself. The journey to the park went smoothly, other vehicles on the road swiftly veering out of his way by his power of thought. The drivers would be unaware they'd even shifted across the road, continuing their travels after he'd driven past, the seconds it took for them to move wiped from their memories.

Fuck, I love being me.

A Killer didn't usually have the ability of a Tool Master, but somehow Karrick's aptitude for growth had increased. This was how he knew he was meant to be in Morland's shoes—how he was supposed to be the man in the cave giving orders, although he fancied when he took over he wouldn't operate from the Dreamworld. He liked this one far too much. The comforts, the ease of living. The many tight arses just waiting for him to breach them. Cave life and being away from the wonders of humankind wasn't to his liking.

He swerved down a track beside the park and stopped his car inside a huddle of trees, pleased that their abundant leaves draped low enough to hide it. Engine off, he shoved the keys in his pocket and took a moment to lean his head back on the seat and close his eyes. It didn't take long for a vision to form. There Jason was again, walking through the undergrowth just as the earlier whisper of sound had promised. Jason glanced from side to side, gaze on the ground.

What the hell are you looking for?

Karrick breathed deeply and absorbed Jason's surroundings, letting his location seep into his mind and body, where they settled as a compass to the young man's whereabouts. Karrick got out of the car, pressed his key fob to lock it, then headed forward into a thicker stand of trees. He walked for a short time until he came upon a grass-covered ledge that spanned quite a way to his left and right. He looked down a bush-speckled embankment to a small forest below and knew Jason was in there somewhere. The park spread out on the other side of the forest, and from here Karrick had a bird's-eye view. Several people were around—some walking dogs, children playing on the swings and slide, and others jogging.

Karrick thought of Jason again and focused on exactly where he was inside that forest. As though a beacon showed him the way, Karrick scanned the tops of the trees then stilled his gaze to the left where the forest butted the road he had traveled to get here.

"I'm coming, cherub," he whispered, a shiver of excitement skittering down his spine. He reveled in the way the shiver spread outwards, a million tiny fingertips skating over his skin, creeping around his sides until they reached his stomach and stopped their intimate fondling.

He rolled his shoulders, jogged down the embankment and reached the bottom in short time, entering the forest and letting the internal compass lead him. He weaved through trees and bushes, the daylight minimal due to the density of the leaves above, the way ahead murky with shadows that spoke of hidden menace — menace that didn't cause him any unrest. He was up for dealing with whatever presented itself, be it a rogue Dreamer or Jason himself. The only menace here was him.

A crackle of sound had him halting. Unsure if his feet touching the ground had made the noise or whether it was someone or some*thing* else, he waited for a moment. His breaths sounded loud, ragged, and he found it difficult to hear anything but them for several seconds.

"It's around here," Jason said. "I know it."

Karrick tilted his head. To have heard his voice so clearly meant Jason had to be close. The compass pushed Karrick forward. He trod quietly and slowly, narrowing his eyes to better see through the gloom.

There! Although a brief smudge of movement that quickly disappeared, Jason's blond head had popped up above a bush he was standing behind. Then it was gone.

What the hell are you doing?

Another head appeared, as well as shoulders, and the person raised his hand to scratch the back of his head. "Are you sure we're in the right place?"

Daniel. This is not how things are meant to be.

Karrick clenched his teeth. Anger threatened to spread through him, making him unreasonable — something he couldn't risk. He resisted darting forward to grab Daniel and throttle the damn life out of him, to feel the man's Adam's apple break beneath his pressing thumb, to see the light of life dim in his eyes. To hear Jason pleading for Daniel's life, Karrick telling him he needed no one but him, that Daniel wasn't the one Jason ought to be pining for. Daniel was going to prove a bind, getting in the way of Karrick's plans.

Something had to be done.

"Found it!" Jason said, standing upright.

The pair bent their heads to look down at whatever Jason held. They spoke quietly, and a slight snapping sound occurred, as though they had pulled something open. Karrick took a few steps forward to try to discern what they were looking at was but saw nothing. The men were standing too close, the tops of their arms pressed together, the gray-colored light making it impossible to see. Karrick stared, letting his vision blur, and tried to drag up an image of them in his mind's eye — an image from in front of them, but something was blocking his attempt. He frowned and tried again, pushing at the invisible force that seemed to stand between him, Jason and Daniel.

How was that happening when Rivald's Dreamers had lost their powers? Had something happened in the Dreamworld since he'd been there last?

Karrick shifted from foot to foot, moving something on the ground.

"Someone's here," Jason said, swiftly spinning.

Karrick ducked behind a wide tree trunk, pressing his back to it, splaying his hands on the rough, moss-covered bark.

"We should get back to Barry," Daniel said, his voice strong, not a pinch of fear tinting it.

So he's grown some balls, has he? Become the protector?

Karrick almost laughed.

I thought the little prick would have learned not to mess with me by now.

The sound of shifting footsteps pulled Karrick from the dangerous territory of getting lost in thoughts of killing Daniel. He waited until the noises were more muted before he twisted to peek around the tree. Jason and Daniel were walking briskly away from him, and despite the shadows, he was able to make out Daniel's arm draped across Jason's shoulders, the white of his hand standing out starkly, taunting him.

"He's mine, you little bastard," he whispered. "No one takes anything from me."

Rage began a slow burn inside him and, unable to stop it, he pursued, hands clenched into fists. He kept a good distance between them until the men in front reached the clearing where the park proper began. They stopped, remaining inside the treeline, looking out on the expanse of grass. Karrick wouldn't get a good chance like this again today. He drew a knife from his inside coat pocket then held it up as he ran, thankful that his feet made no sound on the soft, spongy ground. As he drew closer, a band of joggers came into view. It was now or never. Karrick raised the arm holding the knife and threw his weapon, watching it spin end over end through the air as though a spotlight illuminated its progress.

Jason shook his head. "Move!" he yelled, dragging Daniel to the right.

The knife found its home, but not the one Karrick had intended. Instead of the blade burying itself hilt deep in Daniel's back, it was instead embedded in a jogger's temple. The force of his throw had been harder than he'd thought if it had gone through bone like that. The runner went down with a scream, knees hitting the grass, then he folded, falling onto his side.

The side where the knife protruded.

Pandemonium broke out. The other joggers shrieked and moved to help their fallen friend. Daniel staggered beside Jason, still being wrenched away from the scene, and they hugged the treeline until they disappeared from Karrick's sight.

"Fuck!" Karrick breathed.

He had to go back the way he had come. Had to get home. Enter the Dreamstate. Morland was needed to remove Karrick's fingerprints from that damn knife.

Daniel's chest hurt from running so fast. "We should go back," he panted out. "Can't just…leave like that."

"We have to," Jase said, holding Daniel's wrist tighter. "We can't risk being associated with crimes. Ross can't sort everything all the time. Come on, this way."

Jase led him down a deserted narrow path, high bushes to either side, giving the impression they'd entered a maze. Jase let him go and as he ran, Daniel rubbed his wrist, the skin sore. He glanced back, able to make out the dark huddle of people surrounding the fallen jogger, their forms blurring into a single solid shape as they stood so close to one another. He whipped his head back around to find Jase way ahead and waiting at the end of the path, bending over, hands on his knees as he caught his breath. Daniel reached him and did the same, his lungs burning, his throat dry, his pulse hard and insistent at his temples.

Jesus, that poor fucking guy…

He glanced at Jase, who, by the looks of him, had just thought the same as he had.

"We can't go back, all right?" Jase said, standing upright and wiping sweat from his forehead. "That's the way things are, the way it has to be."

"I get it," Daniel said. "I do, but what if someone says they saw us running? What if *we're* suspects? That knife came from behind us, but it could look like one of *us* threw the fucking thing."

"It could, but it'll be okay. Barry will know what to do." Jase glanced behind Daniel. "We really ought to go."

Daniel didn't dare turn around to see what was going on back there. If someone was heading their way… "Shit, we need to get the fuck out of here, don't we?"

Jase nodded.

They ran along a path that surrounded the park until they reached a housing estate. There, they lost themselves in the labyrinth of streets, coming out on the other side where that estate bled into the one Barry lived on. Feeling safer now, Daniel slowed to walking, his face dripping sweat and his legs wobbly from being unaccustomed to the exercise.

"Wait!" he said, seeing Jase still running.

Jase stopped and as he turned around to face Daniel, he lifted his hands to grip at his hair. His eyes widened, and his lips skewed as though someone had hooked a finger inside the corner of his mouth and pulled.

"What the fuck?" Daniel lunged forward, holding Jase in his arms as he sagged against him. "Jason! What's happening? Shit!" He glanced around, seeing no one in the street they were in. "Fucking shit!"

Jase lowered his hands from his hair and pawed at Daniel's coat, gasping for breath. He rested his cheek against Daniel's chest, and all Daniel could do was hold him and stroke his back until whatever the hell had given Jase grief passed.

"You'll be all right," Daniel said. "Just breathe. Just concentrate on clearing your head." He was guessing Jase had experienced another vision, hoped he had because if Jase had endured some form of attack, he wasn't sure what the fuck to do.

"It was Karrick," Jase said, voice breathy. "Karrick threw the knife."

"Oh, shit..."

"And he did something else too. Earlier."

Daniel guided Jase along the street, supporting his weight. "I'm taking you back to Barry's. We shouldn't be out here with that nutter around." Daniel's stomach muscles contracted and he had to force himself not to buckle with fear. That man was a nightmare, someone he never wanted to see again.

"No, not Barry's," Jase said. "I have to go to where Barry is."

"Why? We'll be safe at his place until Barry gets back."

Jase straightened, and although he walked slowly, he appeared a hell of a lot better than he just had. "No. I saw something else, something Barry will want to know."

Chapter Fourteen

Barry had hurried out to his car and headed to the address Ross had given him. It was a loading warehouse on the pier, wide open to the harbor and hardly a secure area. He'd parked in an unobtrusive spot in a nearby alley and jogged the rest of the way to the outer edge of the commotion surrounding the warehouse. He'd waited damn near forty minutes for Ross to come and get him, and while he'd hung around, he'd entertained thoughts of Tag. How he missed him. How, if Tag were here, Barry wouldn't feel so off-kilter. Tag would have suggestions, offer ways to deal with this crap as it happened. As it was, Tag tried to help when he rang Barry at night, but hearing things after the event wasn't the same as Tag being by Barry's side. If Barry had known how long Ross was going to be, he'd have called Tag, even if it was just to hear his voice.

Ross came toward him now, apologies written all over his face.

"So?" Barry asked once he was within earshot.

"Sorry about that. I had to wait for a few officers to leave."

"The ones who wouldn't like me being here, I take it."

"Yep. Come have a look. I've cleared out all non-essentials. The rookie who's left doesn't know you, and the coroner isn't going to mind you being here."

"Efficient."

"This is important. Come on."

They entered the echoing space and Barry stared at a body, slumping from rope bonds holding the slight form to a wooden pillar in the middle of the open space.

"Oh, Jesus," Barry whispered.

Blood had congealed across the young man's stomach, around his feet and fingers. Blond hair hid his face, but Barry felt the aura of terror still lingering in the fading echoes of his screams and pleas.

"Hard to tell, really, with all the animal damage," Ross said, obviously fighting to keep his voice level and professional, "but it looks like there was something carved into his flesh over his stomach. We won't know if he was brought here for the rats before or after he died until the coroner is through —"

"Before," Barry whispered. He couldn't explain how he knew. He just knew. Foggy whispers of pain and fear still lingered in the corners of this place, and the Dreamer in him could feel them.

"Well, when Sally's done with her report, I'll let you know what she finds. If there was something specific carved into him, we'll probably never know what it was."

"Hurt me."

Both men turned to find Jase standing at the entrance. All color had leached from his face. His eyes were wide and staring, and every ounce of the horror Barry felt hovering in the dark places around him was reflected in the young man's face.

"I told you—" Barry began.

"He carved 'Hurt Me' into his stomach," Jase said. "And Barry's right. He was alive when he was left here."

"Who did?" Ross asked, approaching Jase. "Who did this?"

Jason ripped his gaze from the dead youth to look at Ross. "He looks—looked—just like me."

"Who did this, Jason?" Ross asked again. "Do you know? Because if you do, you need to tell us."

"There's only one way to stop him," Jason said, turning his attention to Barry. "You were right. I have to go back."

Barry stared at Jason, wondering if that was such a good idea now. If Karrick had killed this man here with Jason in mind as he'd selected him, Jason would be in danger if he returned to the Killer's house. "I don't know now. I mean..." He glanced back at the body, lifting one hand then dropping it to his side again. "He might have been practicing, picking someone who looked like you to see how it felt to kill him—kill you." He faced Jason again. "Do you understand what I'm saying?"

Jason nodded.

Barry looked at Ross. "It's Karrick."

Ross paled. "Oh fuck."

"Best you leave it to us," Barry said.

Ross nodded then scrubbed his hand through his hair. "Right." He paused. "Right."

Daniel appeared by Jason's side. "Hey, you didn't wait. I called out to you, Jase. Didn't you hear me?" He caught sight of the body. "What's going—? Oh, fuck me. That's...that is just fucking wrong!" He folded over, his body convulsing with heaves.

"Get him out of here," Ross said, jerking a thumb at Daniel. "Last thing I need is his puke contaminating the scene. I can't explain *that* away."

Barry nodded. "I'll be back in a bit, Ross." He stepped forward, gripping Daniel's elbow and leading him toward his car. He glanced over his shoulder. "Jason!"

The young man followed, reaching Barry's side and matching his pace. "Karrick's crazy, Barry, bloody crazy."

"That's the understatement of the damn year." Barry shook his head. "I'm taking you two home, then I'll come back here. You do *not* leave the house until I return, understand?"

"Yes," Jase said, "but there's something I have to tell you."

"Aww, fuck," Barry said. "What now?"

"Let's get Dan in the car first."

Jase held a heaving Dan while Barry opened the rear door and helped Dan inside. His cop's mind was going a mile a minute as he tried to figure out what the hell could have happened, what could have gone wrong with the simple act of picking up a wallet. He wished he'd sent Graham with them to collect it. They'd have been safer that way. But who was to say anything had happened to them? He might just be expecting the worst. Then again, that wasn't surprising, was it? Things hadn't been normal for a long time, and the worst usually did happen.

After making sure Daniel sat with his head wedged between his knees and a carrier bag was beside him in case he was sick, he closed the door, leaned against it and stared at Jase. "Give it to me."

"We got the wallet." Jase pulled it out of his coat pocket. "And he is who he says he is. Well, the credentials in his wallet say his name is Graham. Doesn't mean that's who he really is, does it? He could have just had these made to make us think he's Graham Green."

Barry nodded, taking the wallet and popping it open. "Wouldn't be the first time someone's done it. What else?"

Jase craned his neck to try to see Daniel. "Is he all right?"

"He will be. It's not every day you see a dead body, is it?"

"Or two," Jase said.

"What?" Barry let out a rush of breath, his heart rate kicking up a notch. "What the hell went on?" Anger at whoever was directing the latest events burbled inside him, and he had a hard time fighting the urge to swivel round and slam the side of his fist on the top of his car. To prevent Jase babbling in a rush, he said, "Start from the beginning."

"We went there, straight to the spot where it was, only I couldn't see it at first. And we were followed." Jase put his head down and scuffed at loose stones on the ground. He rammed his hands into his jeans pockets, biting his bottom lip.

"Shit. Who by?" *Like I don't know...*

"Karrick, but we didn't know until... Shit, it was nasty." Jase shook his head as though trying to erase thoughts from it.

"Take a deep breath then go on." Barry clenched his hands into fists and pursed his lips. Karrick needed eliminating. He never thought he'd wish death on a person—his oath as a police officer and his morals had prevented him from wanting such a thing in the past—but when it concerned Karrick... Christ, with him out of the picture, he had a strong suspicion none of this crap would be happening.

Jase was taking his time preparing himself for what he had to say, and Barry's mind went to Leyton. Could their Killer take Karrick out? Leyton was a vicious bastard when he needed to be, but Karrick seemed cannier, more able to outwit, out maneuver and goddamn out everything Leyton might throw at him. Leyton had a soft side, and despite being a man who killed because that's what he felt he'd been born to do, he wasn't totally psycho- or sociopathic. He had feelings. He felt compassion, and he had a strong need to be accepted and loved. Barry doubted Karrick had the ability to feel or to give a shit about anything except what he wanted. Sending Leyton out there to kill Karrick might be the end of their Killer. Odd as it sounded, Barry had grown fond of the crazy shit and wouldn't want him harmed.

But what choice do we have with Rivald keeping silent — or being kept silent?

Not knowing what was going on was doing a number on Barry, and as he pulled his mind away from things he perhaps shouldn't have been thinking or wishing for, he almost snapped at Jase to get a move on and tell him what had happened. That wouldn't do any good, though. Jase was messed up enough as it was, and Barry pressuring him might make Jase take a giant step backwards, closing himself off and enduring his Dreams and visions without sharing the burden.

"I thought I heard someone in the forest with us, so we headed for the clearing," Jase said, his voice shaking. "And there were people about when we got there, so I felt all right, you know? Then...shit, then these joggers came along, and I got the strong sense whoever had been in the forest was right behind us, like he was breathing down my neck. So I told Dan to move, and... God, one of the joggers...a knife went into his head—into his head, Barry! And he went down and he landed on the knife and I kept thinking that would have made it go in deeper and we were running and I felt bad and—"

"Stop!" Barry said. "Take your time."

Jase closed his eyes and inhaled through his nose. When he opened his eyes again, he said, "I knew it was Karrick. I don't know how. Maybe I smelled him or something, but it was him."

"What happened then? How did you know where to find me?"

Jason shook his head as if clearing it of the images inside. "We were on our way back home and I got one of those visions again. I saw Karrick killing that guy in there." He jabbed his thumb over his shoulder. "And what you said about him doing a test...seeing how it would feel if...it was me. I knew that too. The Dreams were bad, but seeing stuff when I'm awake? It's freaky. Scares the crap out of me. I get no warning they're coming."

Barry lifted a hand and placed it on Jase's shoulder, gave it a little squeeze. "It'll be all right." He didn't know how it would be, but he'd have a damn good go at trying to make sure it was.

* * * *

Jessica stared across the living room at Graham. When everyone had left earlier, Leyton going into Barry's office to try to get into the Dreamstate and reach Rivald, she'd untied Graham, hoping he

150

wouldn't turn nasty once he was free. He hadn't. She'd made them tea, him following her into the kitchen while she made it, and he'd acted normal, as though he was there because he wanted to be.

And maybe he was.

"Karrick is bad news," Graham said, staring down at the carpet from his perch on the armchair. "But you've already gathered that, right?"

Jessica sighed. "Yes, and so are many other people I've come into contact with lately, except the ones in our Dreamer family." She paused to smile. "Although I found them odd to begin with, especially Leyton."

"That was a nasty business," Graham said. "What you went through with him, I mean."

Graham must have been inside her head, probing to find that information. "Yeah, but he'd been misled." She shrugged. "He took me because he wanted to save me from another murderer and he was convinced I was someone else. He'd been promised the love of his life and he thought it was me."

"Still thinks it's you," Graham said quietly, "if the way he looks at you is anything to go by."

Jessica glanced at the doorway. "Shh. He might hear you."

"He won't. The office door is shut." Graham sighed. "I'm surprised he left you in here alone with me."

"He knows deep down you're not bad. He's been confused lately, that's all. What with everything going haywire... Shit, *I've* been confused lately, although I'll admit I wasn't sorry when Rivald didn't contact me. I just assumed things had quieted down, you know? That the city had a break from the mad people who enjoy killing." She studied him, seeing goodness in his eyes that he was a proper Dreamer, one who just wanted to put right the wrongs. "Why the fuck did this have to happen to me? You ever wondered that about yourself? Are we chosen from birth? Is that it? Are we born with it and have to wait until whatever we have inside us grows or something?"

"I'm not sure, but I know exactly what you're going through. I didn't become a Dreamer until my thirties. It shocked the shit out of me when I had my first Dream."

"But I'm not the same as you," she said, twirling her cup around then taking a sip. "I'm used as bait, and I find it really hard to reach the Dreamstate. Usually Rivald comes to me because it's easier that way, although his sudden appearances... I'll never get used to those. Or the way he can direct my movements and make me say and do things."

Graham chuckled. "I think they enjoy playing sometimes, Rivald and Morland. Maybe they get bored in the caves."

"Maybe." She smiled. Sighed. "I never thought I'd hear myself saying this, but I wish Rivald would appear now. Arrive in his creepy-as-fuck misty way and let us in on what's happening. And even though he's some weird horned...thing, I'm worried he's been hurt, that someone's got to him."

"Karrick will be behind whatever's happened," Graham said. "He started acting strange a while back and I knew things weren't right."

Jessica opened her mouth to say something but the sound of the front door opening then closing stopped her. She twisted in her seat to look at the doorway. Barry came in, Jase and a sick-looking Daniel trailing behind him.

"Karrick's been doing what he does best," Barry said, remaining near the door while Daniel and Jase sat on the sofa by Graham.

Graham sighed. "Who has he killed?"

"Some young kid and a jogger. Neither kills were for the good." Barry grimaced. "I have to go back to the kid's crime scene. Need to see if Ross can sort things out where witnesses are concerned with the jogger. Jase and Daniel saw it…"

Jessica shivered and shifted her gaze from Barry to the two younger men. Her first concern was for Jase, who struck her as the weaker of the two, the one who needed cosseting. What she saw was a different story. Daniel appeared shaken to his bones, and Jase was the one comforting him.

"Look after everyone," Barry said.

Jessica nodded at him.

Barry frowned. "Where's Leyton?"

"In your office," she said. "Trying to reach Rivald."

"Fucking good luck to him, then," Barry said, moving to leave the room. "In fact, fucking good luck to all of us, because this shit's only just getting started."

Chapter Fifteen

At first, Leyton attempted to get comfortable seated at Barry's desk, but the untidy stacks of papers and photos and pens strewn over the surface defied his ability to shut them out. He found himself alternately lining the papers up in neat rows, or obsessively smoothing his fingertips over the button placard of his shirt in an attempt to keep his hands off Barry's things.

How the man got any work done at all in the midst of the chaos was beyond Leyton.

He moved to the couch, laying out on his back and folding his hands over his chest. Four or five times he found he had to still his fingers from sliding down the front of his shirt, checking every button was secure and straight, the holes lined up neatly. The unease of Barry's messy space took too long to dissipate. He couldn't focus on his own breathing, let alone find the still and quiet mind space needed to contact Rivald. Besides, the cushions of the couch were too soft. It felt like they were going to envelope him in their hot, sticky leather clutches.

Finally, he settled on his back on the floor. More used to the thin mattress of his van's bed, the floor at least offered some sense of support and protection.

Closing his eyes and concentrating hard on drawing in one breath at a time and letting each out again in a long sigh, he managed at last to find the calm center of himself where even Mother's voice could not reach.

He drew a mental picture of the entrance path to Rivald's cave, well aware he was constructing something in his head he did not feel in his heart the way he should. He just hoped this would at least offer solace if it didn't net him the result of actually contacting his mentor.

There had been a time when he'd hated Rivald. After he'd learned that Jessica was not his chosen life partner, he'd wanted very badly to destroy the horned creature. To make him pay for the pain he'd caused. Leyton wanted to blame him for the loss. But as the months passed and his team had come together in destroying the evil of the city, a subtle shift had occurred.

Maybe Jessica wasn't the love of his life. Maybe she wasn't destined to love him back. It didn't change how he felt about her. It didn't have to mean the purity of his feelings had to be sullied because she didn't feel the same. Besides, he'd needed so badly not to be alone. He'd needed it so desperately he'd allowed Mother to plague him long after her death, just so he didn't have to face the endless days with nothing and no one. He'd needed someone and he had allowed himself the illusion of believing he himself was loveable to someone like Jessica.

He didn't need that illusion anymore. He didn't need to be loved. Being needed was enough. And she needed him. They all did. They could not do what they did without him, and if they could not bring the evil to justice, the dreams would drive them all mad. So they needed him. If he could not be loved, it was enough to be needed.

"Philosophy, Leyton? So New Age of you."

"Rivald!"

"You sound surprised."

"I am. Where have you been? Why have you been so hard to reach? What is going on?"

"Slow down. This is difficult enough. I need you to get deeper into the Dreamstate, Leyton. Focus. I need you..."

The faint voice in Leyton's head faded into the distance. He fought panic at the idea Rivald was not strong enough to maintain so simple a contact, and once more envisioned the entrance to the Tool Master's cave.

He built his image, stone by stone, recalling each hillock of crumbling rock, every carved symbol on the walls. He knew the path like he knew his own van. He knew the dips in the rocky trail, the way the pool lapped at the stony edge of its shallow bowl, exactly how it ebbed and flowed with the imagined beat of Rivald's heart, and the way the tumbling wall of rocks at the far edge of the water cascaded in a lumpy pile into the darkness of the underground pond.

Carefully, slowly, he made his way along the path, reconstructing every inch of it from memory, and as he approached Rivald's throne, he could begin to feel the heat of his master's presence, see the shadows dancing on the wall behind the horned man and feel the pinch and stab of gravel under his stockinged feet. The stench of sulfur and char rose to greet him and he at last began to relax.

The images took on substance as he crossed the cavern floor to kneel at his master's feet.

"Very good, Leyton," Rival encouraged. "You are getting stronger again. I am pleased." The weight of Rivald's three-fingered hand rested on the top of Leyton's head and he let out a sigh.

"Again?" Leyton asked softly.

"You lost focus for some time. But here you are, back with me again. This pleases me, Leyton."

Leyton looked up into the dark shadows of Rivald's eyes. Nothing ever showed there but blackness. The face of the creature never changed. Whatever calm Leyton felt in the horned man's presence was projected somehow outside of obvious body language.

"Things grow precarious, Leyton. I need you to be up to the challenges that are in store for you."

"What challenges, Master?" How long had it been since he had uttered that title and meant it so fervently as he did in that moment? Too long, he realized.

Rivald moved his hand, sliding it down to cup Leyton's chin and lift his face. "In the days to come, you may find yourself asked to perform tasks that you do not fully understand. You will find your urges are harder to control, and your appetites...fiercer. It will be difficult, but at times, you will be forced to rely on people you may not fully trust, and to do so without completely understanding all my reasons for requiring it. Your loyalty must remain without question, Leyton, or everything we have built will fall."

"Does this have to do with the Winnowing?"

"And who told you about that?"

"A man named Graham. He's a Dreamer, but he doesn't work for you." Sudden uncertainty assailed Leyton. "Does he? Are there others you speak to? Others I do not know about? That you have not told me about?"

"There are other Teams, Leyton. Some with Killers more cunning and more vicious that you will ever be. There are Tool Masters with fewer scruples and no morals. I chose you because you have great potential to be something more than a simple killing tool. You have potential to be something the Dreaming world has never seen. But you cannot achieve this alone. Remember that."

"But who will help me?"

This news excited Leyton, vindicated him. He had always known he was destined for something big. Rivald had all but confirmed that he was going to be important.

"Some answers I cannot give you. Some paths you will have to find on your own, and you will have to lead others down them. And I cannot tell you what you will find at the end. Often, the destination is defined by the route you take to get there. The decisions you make along the way. I cannot make those decisions for you."

"But you can advise me. You've always advised me. You've always told me what to do. How—"

"Those days are ending, Leyton."

Leyton remained very still, on the verge of being thrown from the Dreamstate by his distress. "I don't understand. What have I done? Why are you doing this?" It sounded very much like Rivald was preparing to let Leyton go. To leave him to his own devices.

"Eventually, every person must leave their childhood behind. I have watched you grow, Leyton, and it saddens me to know that our time together grows short. But there will be a void soon. It will need to be filled, and there are few with the strength, the ruthlessness balanced by the compassion necessary to fill it. We have all chosen our candidates. Once the Choosing is done, we may no longer interfere with the process. I have faith in you. You know your Team. You know what each of them needs to fulfill their roles. Make sure they have it, and trust them. I hand-picked them for you. Use them to their best advantages, and do what I know you can do."

"But what about you?"

"Do not worry about me. From this time forward, my role will be strictly enforced. You will be shown your target. How you deal with that target will be in your hands. I will not be able to lead you as I have done in the past. You will have to trust your instincts."

"They have been off lately," Leyton said, worried that he was not up to this new task. "I picked up Graham. He was one of us. I do not know where that impulse came from."

"Trust your instincts, Leyton."

"It was an impulse." Leyton sat back on his heels. The movement freed him of Rivald's touch and he stared inward, focused on the memory of meeting Graham in the parking lot. "I had been driving. Feeling…at loose ends. I was not paying attention to where I was going. I was just driving, hoping you would guide me to where I needed to be. It had been weeks since the last kill. Almost, no, definitely a month. A long time. I thought I should be feeling something about the next target, even if it was too soon for another kill. I should have been feeling *something*. Maybe I wanted to feel the pull, so I imagined it?"

He looked up, but Rivald's face was as stoic as ever.

Leyton found his fingers running down the front of his shirt, his mind silently counting his buttons. He placed both hands in his lap and clasped them there.

"No. I did not make it up. Yes, I was starting to feel restless. Starting to feel the burn deep inside, but I could control it. It was not getting the better of me. That impulse came from somewhere." He frowned. "It came from somewhere, but not you and not me."

"How do you know?"

"It was cold."

"Cold?"

Leyton nodded. "I feel this" — he waved a hand up and down in front of his chest — "warmth when you lead me to my next target. I don't know how to explain. A *rightness*. I never question it. Never."

"But you did this time?"

Again, Leyton nodded. "I did, but I didn't. I thought it was wrong, the feeling. The feel of the target, the" — he waved both arms this time, trying to convey with his hands what he couldn't find the words to explain — "the energy was all off. Too sharp and frigid and demanding. Too...*controlling*."

"Then why did you ignore that instinct? Why did you grab Graham?"

"Because when I decided to turn the van around, not go to the appointed place, but to leave him alone, I felt a wave of...revulsion. A sickening sensation, like something terrible would happen if I didn't nab him. I didn't know why I had to, but I knew that if I left him there, it would be terrible." He lifted his gaze again and smiled at Rivald. "And it turned out all right. It turned out we needed to meet him, so I was right."

"There. You see?" Rivald stood and held out a hand to Leyton. "I have chosen well. You will prevail, Leyton. Just as long as you heed your instincts. And trust your Team."

"They do not like me."

"You would be surprised how they really feel about you. Besides, what choice do you have?"

Leyton sighed. "None, I suppose. It would be easier if I knew you were watching over me."

"I did not say I would not be watching, Leyton. I said I could not interfere. I will be watching. Closely. If you fail, it falls to me to make sure your failure is dealt with. You are my creation, after all."

"What does that mean?" Leyton asked, fear gripping him with cruel fingers.

"It means what it means. Do not fail, my child. Do not fail."

Chapter Sixteen

"Is he ever coming out of there?" Jessica asked no one in particular.

Barry shook his head. "Be patient. He's probably the only one of us with the strength or experience to actually reach Rivald. We have to just wait and hope he manages it."

Barry wanted to have as much faith as he made it sound like he had, but every single attempt to reach their Tool Master lately had failed. He could not even read Jessica from across the room. His Dreams had been so vague as to be useless, if no less terrifying than they ever were. It kept him awake nights, knowing what waited and knowing he would be able to use none of it.

What was the point of Dreaming if all the Dreams did was scare the shit out of him and make him wish Tag were not on the other side of the continent?

On the far side of the room from where Barry slouched in the armchair, Dan was sitting on the sofa looking pale and disheveled. Jase sprawled over the cushions, feet dangling from the arm, sound asleep in

Dan's lap. He lay peaceful, and as the minutes ticked past, the haunted, terrified look slowly seeped from Dan's features. He stroked Jase's hair and laced their fingers when the blond stirred and muttered, and immediately, Jase calmed without even waking. Another notch of fear visibly eased from Dan as he settled deeper into the couch. The display made Barry think of Tag again, of how he calmed with Tag's touch.

"I gotta make a phone call," Barry said, abruptly standing, hustling to his bedroom then shutting the door.

He dug his cell form his pocket and hit speed dial, flinging himself onto the bed.

"Hey," Tag's rough, deep voice crooned over the connection.

Barry flopped back on his pillow. "Hey."

"What's wrong?"

Trust Tag not to need more than one syllable to know there was something up.

"Long story. I'm sure Ross will fill you in on the details."

"Don't want those details. I want yours. What's wrong?" he asked again.

Barry closed his eyes, pinched the bridge of his nose and bit his lip. He couldn't... If he opened his mouth, the plea would come out, and Tag had a job to do. Responsibilities. A life in the real world.

"Barry..."

"Come home."

Shit.

He had meant to keep that in. He could not ask Tag to drop everything and rush to his side just because he'd had a few bad Dreams.

"Plane landed ten minutes ago. I'm getting a cab." And to suit action to words, Barry heard him call faintly to a taxi, then the phone was back close enough to Tag's mouth that Barry could hear him breathing a little bit hard as he slammed the car door.

"How did you know?" Barry asked, dumbfounded that Tag could possibly be as close as the airport, less than a fifteen-minute car ride away.

"Babe, I can feel your heartbeat from here. I feel it every time fear twists in your gut, and I know when you don't sleep. I can practically taste your awful coffee and cheap whiskey. I'm coming home. Hang tight."

The phone went dead and Barry lay there, in shock. How was any of that possible?

Simple. He had dreamed it. He had imagined the entire conversation. Tag was at his conference eating bland hotel food and sleeping in a lumpy bed at night and listening to boring lectures on the latest crime scene analysis procedures.

Without rising from where he lay, Barry twisted so he could see the clock. Nearly dinner time, and he had a house full of people. The least he could do was order pizza or something. Normally, he'd get Jase to cook, but the kid was wiped out. He wasn't about to wake him from a sound sleep for anything.

Then, as if he was sitting in the other room next to the front door, he heard a key in the lock, and bits of jittering restlessness in his chest slipped into place. Calm filled him. He sat up.

"Tag."

Rushing to the other room, he flung the door open, reaching for the man on the threshold.

"No!" A body hurtled at them, hands flinging Barry aside, and the next thing Barry knew, Leyton was plunging a kitchen knife deep into Tag's chest.

Blood spurted everywhere. Tag's face went pale, then slack. Light drained from his eyes and he slid down the door frame, landing on his back on the threshold. Barry's body gave up on him, and he fell heavily, numbly, to the floor. Inside his head he was screaming, his eyes wide as he took in the redness — so much redness.

"What did you do?" he whispered, crawling to Tag to grip a hand that didn't grip back. "Leyton!" With a sudden burst of energy and anger, he shot to his feet, grabbed the scarred man and threw him to the floor, wrapping both hands around the Killer's neck. "What the fuck did you do?"

He shook and shook while Leyton scrabbled at his fingers and kicked at the floor trying to loosen his hold or dislodge him. Other hands pried at him, trying to separate him from his goal of wringing the life from the murderer.

"Barry!" Someone grabbed his hair and hauled on him, but it didn't matter if they tore every strand from his head. He was going to kill the fucked-up bastard for this. Kill him and fucking rip his goddamn guts out and wear them like a trophy.

A heavy blow landed on the side of his head. He felt himself falling, torn away from Leyton, and he fought with every ounce of fury and hate in him to get back at the man.

"What in bloody blazes is going on!"

The voice boomed through the room, stilled everyone and silenced every sound but Barry's own harsh breathing.

"Tag?" He blinked up from where he lay, sprawled under Graham's weight. "What...?"

He looked to the doorway. There was no body. He glanced to where Jessica was kneeling next to Leyton's still form.

"Oh, God." He tried to wipe sweat and hair from his eyes only to find Jase holding his arm down and Dan blinking at them all in horror. "What did...? Oh, God."

Relaxing under Graham's and Jase's restraint, Barry felt the world rush back in on top of him. "Let me up."

Jason released him immediately. Graham hesitated.

"I'm fine! Let me the hell up!" Barry snapped.

"It's okay," Jason assured Graham. "Let him go."

Barry crawled over to Leyton's side and tentatively touched his still face. "Is he...?"

"No," Jessica said, her voice tight and angry. "What happened? Why did you do that?" She glared up at him, fury in her face. "Why?"

"I thought..." Barry pointed to the door, to Tag, still standing there, suitcase abandoned on the porch behind him. "I thought. He..." He pointed back to Leyton, brow folding under his confusion.

"You had a vision," Jase said.

"I don't *have* visions!" Barry snarled. "I don't! Leyton..." He shook the man by the shoulder and got only a low moan in response. "I don't know what happened. I swear. I thought he'd killed Tag. I thought..." He looked up again, unsure if there really was person in the doorway or if this was just another horrible dream.

"I'm not dead," Tag said. "Whatever you saw, it wasn't real, babe. Get up."

Tag held out a hand, but Barry backed away.

"You're not real."

"Yes, I am. We just talked on the phone. I was getting into the cab. I told you I was here. Now get. Up."

Slowly, Barry climbed to his feet, still not willing to reach out to his lover in case that, too, proved to be a hallucination. He couldn't stand it if he reached for the hand and found only empty space, or worse, an actual body, and the first images had been the real ones.

Tag's eyes narrowed. "Go into the bedroom, Barry. Wait for me there."

"But..." What if he was real? How could he just walk into the other room and turn his back, let Tag out of his sight? What if something happened?

"Go." Tag touched his arm, and the warmth of fingers on his bare skin was oh so real and tangible.

"Tag..."

"Go."

Barry nodded and stumbled away. He heard more orders being dished out. He heard Dan say something about first aid, and a few minutes later, Leyton's hoarse voice asking why he'd been attacked. Then the door swung shut and Barry was alone.

* * * *

"And you thought I was the volatile one," Leyton croaked, glaring at Jessica as though she could have done something to stop Barry.

"I didn't know he was going to lose it, did I?" she asked. "No one knew. He was holding it together pretty well, I thought." She crossed her arms in front of herself and slumped into her chair. "Welcome home, Tag. You're early."

"Yeah." Tag threw his satchel on the floor next to the hall doorway and turned to glare at them all. "And a good fucking thing too. What the hell is going on? I could tell from across the country Barry was losing it, and you all sit here like you're surprised? Are you all stupid?" He turned to the strangers in his living room. "And who the hell are you two?"

Jase piped up, taking the hand of the small, dark-haired man at his side. "This is Daniel. You've heard me talk about him."

"He dumped you." Tag's jaw set. He would heave to the curb anyone who disrespected this Team.

"He didn't understand," Jase replied, defending his man. "He does now." He pulled Dan away from the group and they huddled onto the couch, both of them sullen and silent.

"And you?" Tag asked, turning to the older man.

"Graham Green." He held out a hand. "Fellow Dreamer."

"Fuck." Tag ignored the hand, instead rasping his own across the back of his neck. "Perfect. Another one. Anyone want to tell me why the hell you are all trying to kill one another?"

They began speaking over each other in an attempt to explain the inability to communicate, the lack of direction and the danger to Jase from another Killer. Before Tag could shout them down and demand some sort of order, Leyton, of all people, quieted everyone with a sharp slap of his hand on the wall.

"Enough!" he growled, clearly having difficulty speaking. "Jessica. Explain."

She shot Leyton a startled glance but obliged, telling Tag about their communications issues then handing the tale to Graham to explain his presence. Jase quickly filled him in on the murders.

Finally, Tag turned back to Leyton. "So none of that explains why Barry tried to strangle you."

Leyton shook his head. "Only he knows what he saw."

"If I had to guess," Graham spoke up, "I would put forth that Barry was half asleep when he came out here. Maybe half in the Dreamworld." He shifted his feet, straightened his hopelessly loose tie, and sighed. "I think perhaps Karrick managed to get at him. He has a knack for manipulating other Dreamers. Not like a master can do, but disturbing just the same. He's always been able to get into our heads more easily than the rest of us can to others, and he can make Maggie—she's one of our Dreamers—see things that aren't there. If he's getting stronger—and I think maybe he is—there's a chance we're all vulnerable to him when we enter the Dreamstate. And even out of it."

"Perfect," Tag said again.

"And if Barry was thinking about Tag when he entered the Dreamstate, it would have been easy enough for Karrick to make him think he saw Leyton hurt him," Jase added. "I can't think of anything else that would make Barry attack him like that."

"It's classic Karrick," Graham agreed. "Turn us against each other."

"Us?" Jessica asked, lifting one nicely plucked eyebrow.

Graham shrugged. "Someone nudged Leyton to pick me up, tried to manipulate him into killing me." He looked over at the Killer. "Thankfully, you have better instincts than that or I would be dead. I know I should be loyal to Karrick, but he's been the go-between for me and the rest of my Team for months now, and I have heard nothing from them or about them. What if he's managed to get at them? I don't trust him. Where else am I going to go?"

"Fine," Tag decided, trusting his cop instincts about the man. "You stay. You all stay until we have more information. Safest place. But keep out of my way. And Jason..." He turned to the younger man. "You know the drill. Every last drop. I want every ounce of booze in this house down the drain, now." The last thing he needed was Barry going back on the bottle.

Jason nodded and got up from the couch, Dan and Jessica following.

Tag spun without another word and went to the bedroom.

Barry was pacing the floor between the bed and the window when Tag entered.

"Hey."

His lover jumped at the sound of Tag's voice, hesitated, then crossed the room and took Tag's face in both his hands, leaning into a kiss that burned through the weeks apart and got Tag's blood boiling. Just when Tag figured there was going to be no talking until there had been fucking, Barry broke away and began pacing again.

"I didn't mean to hurt him," Barry said.

"I think he knows that."

"I saw it, Tag, I swear I did. He put a knife through your heart. Why would he do that?"

"He didn't, Barry. It was a Dream."

"A waking Dream? Tag, I don't have those. You know I don't have those." He shuddered, and Tag could just imagine Barry's horror at the thought that waking or sleeping, he would never be sure what was real anymore.

"I don't know what it was, Barry, or why, but" —he grabbed both of Barry's shoulders on the next pass and turned his lover to face him— "but right now, you have to calm down. You hear me? You have to calm the fuck down."

Barry stopped, his gaze settling on Tag's face. "I almost killed him. I could have. Why? He should be faster than that. Faster than me. How did that happen?"

"He didn't expect it, did he? He trusts you."

"Trusted. How can he now?"

"Don't worry about that right now. Right now, you have to get yourself under control. If you don't, this will keep happening. How much have you been drinking?"

Barry grimaced and his gaze shifted away. "Too much."

"Well, no more, I'm back. Let's get you cleaned up."

Barry nodded and allowed Tag to lead him to the bathroom.

Tag watched as Barry stripped his clothes off then dropped them into a heap on the floor. He was thinner than he had been two weeks ago. The drink did that to him. Jase would have to stay for a while and hopefully get a few decent meals into them. He could use some good home cooking himself, and besides, he was mostly sure he was over the pangs of jealousy the younger man's presence had a tendency to cause.

"Into the shower with you," Tag said as he turned from adjusting the temperature. "Come on."

Barry obeyed, mild and less frenetic now, although his gaze still darted about the room, fixing on every plume of steam, and his fingers twitched.

Tag followed him into the shower and proceeded immediately with touch therapy he knew from experience would bring Barry down from the Dreaming frenzy of fear.

"You're okay, now," Tag promised. "Safe. I've got you, and no one is going to hurt either one of us."

"Don't make empty promises," Barry said, splaying both hands on the wall while he arched his back into Tag's touch. "Just don't."

"Fine. Then we'll be careful." Tag leaned and kissed the tense spot between Barry's shoulder blades, began to knead the muscles, and moved closer so their bodies made contact. "We'll stick together. No more conferences for me."

Barry nodded, sighed, and tipped his head back so it rested on Tag's shoulder. "Want you in me," he whispered, his voice thin with need and desperation. "Please."

Tag moved his kisses to Barry's shoulder and canted his hips so Barry could feel his growing hard-on. "Want that too," he assured his lover. "Missed you so much."

"Promise this is real," Barry said, uncharacteristically voicing his fear.

Tag nudged at his arse with his cock. "Very real. Nothing more real than me fucking you into the wall, lover." He put pressure on Barry's shoulder to indicate he should bend then grabbed the lube from the shelf.

"And then into the mattress, the floor, wherever, whenever. I hope your house guests don't mind. They'll get an earful."

Barry groaned as Tag stretched him swiftly with his fingers. "Do it now," he pleaded. "Fuck, Tag, just do it."

Tag didn't see any point waiting. He pushed his way into Barry's tight entrance, listened with satisfaction to the hiss of breath he'd come to recognize as Barry's unconscious signal that the burn was just right, and he began to thrust.

He didn't even give Barry the chance to find a counter rhythm. He just fucked to make up for two weeks apart. For Barry's loneliness, and for his own, and to undo the tangle of nerves and fear that had bound his man up in knots while he'd been gone.

Barry came first, with a loud cry and buckling knees. Tag pulled out, still hard and aching, and Barry whimpered.

"You didn't—"

"I told you," Tag said, pinning Barry to the wall and rubbing his cock along the crack of his arse. "I'm going to fuck you six ways to Sunday. You'll have to eat breakfast standing up. We've got all night."

Barry sighed and bent his neck to give Tag access to his neck and the tender skin that would be marked with bruises before the night was done.

"Welcome home," Barry whispered.

"Good to be home."

Neither of them spoke more about what the next day would bring. For now, there was just the lovemaking and the release they both needed.

Chapter Seventeen

Karrick stood in the Dreamworld opposite Morland, who sat on his throne, as usual, like he was God's gift. About to think uncharitable thoughts, Karrick stopped himself. He didn't need Morland reading his mind and finding out what he really felt about him—what he was really up to.

"The fingerprints are gone from the knife," Morland said airily, waving his hand in the way of England's royals. "But I must say it was unusual for you to make such a mistake. Did you allow your anger to get the better of you?"

Karrick was fucked if he'd admit such a thing. "No, fate had other ideas, that's all. The joggers seemed to speed up as I threw the knife, and Jason must be becoming more than he was, because he sensed I was there. The knife had been perfectly aimed at Daniel's back. If Jason hadn't dragged him away..." Karrick paused. He sounded as though he was over-explaining himself, that he needed Morland to believe him and he hated that. But maybe that wasn't such a bad thing. If Morland thought Karrick was still the same Karrick he'd been before, things would work out better.

"I saw it all," Morland said, sneering. "I felt your anger overruling your common sense. If *you* did not feel your ire, then perhaps it is not a good idea for you to be our Killer at this present time. Losing your focus is not an option now. I need you to get ready for the next phase. Rivald's team needs extinguishing."

Karrick battled the urge to roll his eyes. Like he hadn't known that. "Why do you think I made Leyton kill that Tag person just before I crossed over to here?"

Morland laughed, a nasty cackle that set Karrick's nerves on edge.

"You did not succeed. Leyton did not kill Tag. You only managed to make Barry *think* he had. You made Barry see it happen, yet it did not. Tag is still up and about—up being the main word here." He laughed again, for far too long. "He is currently fucking Barry, you know, and it makes for pleasurable viewing. Why, you really ought to take a peek."

Karrick grimaced. "No, thank you. I'd rather not sully my psyche with those types of images."

"Ha! You make it sound as if you are against that kind of union, that seeing such a coupling would be against your beliefs, but I know the way you are, who you are, so therefore it must be the thought of *who is* fucking that makes you disinclined to watch them." Morland closed his eyes and smiled. "They are having a *very* good time."

Karrick shuddered, staring at Morland in horror as the man-beast's cock, uncovered by garments, sprang up, hard and bobbing. Karrick turned away, wiping his disgust from his mind.

Fuck, how did my plan not work? How did Leyton not do as I intended? Is he getting stronger too? And how the fuck had he not realized it was Barry's mind he was manipulating and not Leyton's? What the hell was wrong with him? Between the blackout with Jason and this, he feared he had more to worry about than just losing his temper.

"Leyton was oblivious to what you wanted," Morland said.

Karrick cursed himself for thinking, for leaving his mind open for his master to probe. He looked at Morland, who was palming his long, thick cock, eyes open, gaze directed at Karrick. Maintaining eye contact and trying to block the hand movement going on in his peripheral, Karrick decided to take the route he hadn't wanted to take.

"What did I do wrong, Master? Please, tell me, so I don't repeat the mistake." It pained him to have said that, to hear the pleading note in his voice, but if Morland thought he was better than Karrick, it would be to Karrick's advantage. His master would be so puffed up at being more knowledgeable that he might not look too closely at what Karrick planned to do. He raised a screen in his mind so he could think the one delicious thought that kept him going—*I am going to rip you from your throne and take your place. Soon, so very soon.*

"You had too many people on your mind," Morland said. "You did not concentrate just on Leyton and getting him to stab Tag. You were thinking of Barry too, and, of course, you had your little man on your mind, albeit at the back. Jason is important, as you know, but he must only be eradicated if it appears he will not bend to your way of thinking. If he will not come over to our side. At present it appears he will not, but that is because he is surrounded by those who care for him. If they were all gone, he would only have you to turn to for comfort. Am I making my request clear? Do you need more clarification?"

"Everyone must go but Jason." Karrick paused, as though thinking hard, except he knew exactly what he wanted to say. "What do I do if Jason doesn't turn to me?"

"You must make him. None of your tactics have worked in the past with him. Yes, he enjoys pain when you have sex, but you have not quite got it right, have you? Your form of pain makes him feel abused. The kind he wants takes other pain away, the pain in his mind. You must learn the difference and then he will be yours. Ours." Morland gave his now-hard cock an extra forceful tug. "Ah, yes, he will be a good addition to our Team when I become sole Tool Master of these parts." He giggled, high-pitched and strange-sounding. "I wonder whether Rivald's ears are burning…"

Morland jerked his hips up, thrusting his cock through the semi-circle his hand had created. Karrick lowered his gaze, unable to stand watching the man come. He shut the sounds of Morland out — the grunts, the moans, the *ah-ah-ah* — and waited until his master had finished.

"I am disappointed you did not wish to watch me," Morland said. "It makes me think of what I said earlier. That who you are watching makes a difference. I rather thought a man masturbating was your thing."

Karrick chose not to respond. How could he, when his answer would have been yes, it *was* his thing, but he had to find the man attractive in order to get off. Seeing a man-beast jerking off did nothing for him.

Morland cleared his throat, obviously needing an answer.

"I thought it best you had privacy, me respecting your need for release even though I am here. I understand how it is to be unable to wait."

"That is very thoughtful of you. Now," Morland said, his flaccid cock hanging over his scrotum, "it is time you went back and did your job. I shall be busy but it does not mean I cannot look in on you from time to time. I am trusting you to do this the way it needs to be done."

Karrick nodded then left the throne room, jogging through the fusty cave and coming out onto the barren landscape. He sucked in a lungful of air and shook the images of Morland from his mind. Glancing across the way, he stared at Rivald's cave and tamped down the need to go in there and kill the fucker. With him gone, Karrick's only remaining tasks would be to murder Rivald's Team, which appeared to include Graham now, and take care of Morland.

But he couldn't. With the Winnowing and the rules here, if he went against the standard practice, he risked not getting what he wanted – Morland's job. No, he had to play it by the book, much as it pissed him off, but he'd have a damn good time while doing it. He wondered who to pick off first. Tag was a good bet, which was why he'd chosen him in the first place, but they would all be on guard now, waiting for something to happen to Tag. Jessica was the weakest link, perhaps he should go for her. Then he thought of Graham.

I should have got rid of you ages ago. I knew you'd be trouble when you started asking questions, started getting too big for your stinking boots.

Karrick turned away from Rivald's cave and walked toward the darkness ahead, waiting for the pull of the real world to start its pleasing tug. As he floated into it, his body drifting through the ether, he nodded to himself, coming to a decision.

Graham? Get ready. I'm coming for you.

* * * *

Maggie Reynolds sat at her kitchen table and gazed out of the window at her back garden, which was shrouded in darkness at the far edges but lit by a set of spotlights she'd had mounted on the wall outside next to the window. She'd been able to tend to her garden more often of late, spending most days weeding and pruning, even planting new shrubs and sprinkling grass seed on the lawn where patches of earth had started showing through. She didn't understand how that had happened when she didn't even walk on her grass, preferring to sit in the sunshine on her raised deck.

She touched a tress of her short auburn hair at her temple, a style ideal for her line of work. She couldn't be doing with having to tie it back if she was in a rush. The bedhead look suited her oval face and suited her needs. One jam of her hand through it and she was good to go. Thankfully she wasn't the sort who had to plaster makeup on before she left the house either. God, the times she'd had to leap out of bed, dress and leave, not even going into the bathroom for a quick wash. Still, her job thrilled her, was unpredictable, and even though she'd resisted being a Dreamer at first, she wouldn't change a thing now.

With no family or that many friends, she'd soon found a family in her Team, and the friends she'd had in her previous life had drifted away when she'd had to constantly tell them she couldn't make it to this meal or that party. Her only non-Dreamer friends now lived in another city miles away. She'd grown accustomed to the solitary life and getting to know herself — getting to like who she was and enjoy her own company. But lately she hadn't seen much of anyone except people in the supermarket, or the guy in the corner shop when she went to buy her newspaper and daily packet of cigarettes, or people walking past the front of her house on their way to God knew where.

Her Tool Master, Karrick, hadn't contacted her for the longest time, and it had begun to bug her. She'd been a Tool for twelve years, a Dreamer used to working at least every other day, and now boredom at having time off was setting in. She'd tried to contact Karrick via thought but had been met with nothing but empty space. It had worried her — frightened her, if she were honest — as the other Team members had been unreachable too. No one had visited either, and that was damn odd. Graham liked to sprawl on her sofa and watch TV every so often, and it was unlike him not to touch base with her at least once a week.

She knew nothing had happened to Karrick, though, because she'd seen him the other day when she'd driven past his place when her worries had gotten the better of her. Even though he'd seemed fine as he'd walked to his car, the sense that something was wrong plagued her. Perhaps there was a lull in business, or maybe she wasn't needed for whatever jobs were going on at the moment. Her role as Mind Sweeper wasn't always necessary. Sometimes things went down when members of the public weren't around. No one needed to forget what they'd seen then, no one needed to lose minutes or hours of their lives — her talent leaving them oblivious to having really witnessed a horrific murder or members of her Team doing things that were against the law.

Another thought came then, one that made her uncomfortable. What if she wasn't needed *at all*? What if a younger Mind Sweeper had joined the fold and Karrick hadn't had the balls to tell her? She dragged her laptop across the table then switched it on, accessing her bank online. Her wages had been deposited yesterday, as usual. Nothing untoward there.

Frowning, she stood and went over to her back door, pressing her palm to the glass. Her breath fogged the pane, so she leaned back a little in order to look at her pretty flower borders, her fountain that sprayed delicate squirts of water up into the air.

At the dark figure in the shadows at the bottom of her garden.

She jumped back, heart pattering way too fast, then walked in reverse, reaching behind her to feel for the wall where the light switch was. She flicked it and the room went into darkness, making it easier for her to see outside and harder for whoever was out there to see in. Normally she wouldn't feel afraid. Normally the sight of someone on her property wouldn't make her feel sick. Normally she'd have yanked the door open and strutted out there, knowing Karrick would hear her mind communication to him that she needed help.

But things weren't normal these days.

She ducked so she was hidden by the lower wooden portion of the door and, feeling foolish, scrabbled toward it on her hands and knees. She reached up and twisted the key, feeling infinitely better when the lock met with the keeper. Now, if that person outside wanted in, he or she would have to make a damn load of noise doing it. Breaking glass or a foot kicking the frame would attract her neighbor's attention.

She turned and made her way to her table, a speck of hard dirt digging into her knee. After dislodging it, she lifted her arm and patted the table top, relieved when she touched her phone with her fingertips. If Karrick wasn't available by thought, she'd call him, tell him to come over, providing she didn't get dead air like she'd had before. Even if the figure in her garden had gone by the time Karrick arrived, it wouldn't matter. She could ask him what the hell was going on. He could find out who it was and sort them out.

Sitting with her back against one of the table legs, she dialed and waited. The ringing was loud in her ear, but she also picked up a faint ring elsewhere. She cocked her head, straining to work out where it was coming from. It sounded as though it was outside.

"Yes?" Karrick answered.

"It's Maggie. I need you. Someone's in my garden."

"Stand up."

Automatically, she did as he'd ordered and glanced at the door. The figure stood on the other side of the glass, and for an instant she almost screamed, seeing only a man instead of who really stood there.

"You!" she said, laughing, her nerves unwinding and the rush of adrenaline abating. "What the hell are you doing out there?" She rose to unlock the door, closing her phone. "You scared the shit out of me!"

"Sorry," he said, smiling. "I needed to make sure you were alone."

Maggie stepped back and Karrick entered, flopping down casually into a chair at her table. She closed the door, switched the light back on then joined him.

"Of course I'm alone. When do I ever entertain anyone?" She laughed again, sad inside that there was no one special in her life. No one she could trust enough to have an intimate relationship with, no one who would understand what she did and why she might need to scoot out at odd hours of the night with no explanation as to where she was going. And constantly Mind Sweeping a partner wasn't exactly something she relished doing. No, better to remain alone.

"Oh, I don't know," Karrick said. "Graham sometimes pops over."

"He does," she said, getting up and going to the fridge to pull out two small bottles of Coke. "But I haven't seen or heard from him in ages." She handed him a drink then sat opposite. "I haven't heard from *any* of our Team, including you!" She smiled to make sure he knew she wasn't angry, even though she had been at one point.

"Sorry about that." He unscrewed his bottle lid, looking far from sorry. "Things are going on, things that meant we've not had to concentrate on working lately."

"Oh, right. Do I need to know?"

"Ah," he said, "just that Winnowing crap I told you about a while back."

"Are we safe?" she asked, opening her drink. "I mean, we're likely to win, right?"

Karrick laughed. "Of course we are. Nothing to worry about there. It means we have work to do now, though, and I need your help. But only you can do it. I don't trust the others."

She frowned, suddenly chilled at the way his tone of voice had changed. It had grown harder. Cold. Mean.

"What?" she said. "But our Team is solid. There's no way anyone would go over to the other Team."

"They already have." He took a long pull of his soda and eyed her down the length of the bottle.

"You're kidding me, right? Who the fuck has defected? Who would do that to us?" Anger and bewilderment fought for prominence inside her and she swallowed down a shot of bile.

"There's something I have to tell you and it might be difficult to take in." Karrick twisted his bottle on the table top, studying it instead of looking at her. "The person who has joined the other team...he's gone mad, thinks I'm someone to fear, that I'm not the best Killer for our Team. I think he wanted to take my place, and when I told him Morland didn't want that, he went to Rivald's Team and gave them some trumped-up bullshit about me being out there to get them." He laughed gently and looked up at her. "Like I would *do* that, Maggie. How could I when I respect the Winnowing, respect the way things are? I wouldn't fuck about with the rules, you know that."

She had no reason to doubt him. He'd always been fair to her, an excellent Killer and leader, and she respected him. It had only been recently she'd begun to wonder if he didn't afford her the same respect, that it wasn't a two-way thing, what with him failing to contact her, to at least let her know why things had gone quiet.

"I couldn't contact you, Maggie, for reasons I'm not allowed to disclose. Please understand it hurt me to do that. If I could have let you in on what's been going on I would have, but if I had, it would have meant me going against Morland, against Him, and I just couldn't do it."

"I understand." She reached out and covered his hand with hers, giving it a little squeeze. After taking a deep breath, she asked, "So who defected? Who do I need to Mind Sweep?"

Chapter Eighteen

Maggie stood outside some guy named Barry's house. She zipped up her black slim-fit coat and put her hands into her jeans pockets, then leaned on the house wall beside the front door. Karrick drove away, and she watched until his tail lights disappeared as he turned the corner to park in the next street like he'd said he would. Light spilled from the living room window of the house, the curtains undrawn, affording her the perfect view inside. She wondered why those gathered hadn't detected her presence. One of them ought to be able to sense when something was wrong, when someone was hanging around. Granted, she hadn't had any inkling that Karrick had been in her garden until she'd spotted him, but with the other Team all gathered in the same place, surely *one* of them had the ability to sense trouble?

She'd been given her instructions by Karrick and, even though she'd disbelieved him at first, she'd accepted that Graham was the one who had gone against their Team. And she agreed with Karrick—it *did* make sense now why only Graham visited Team members at least once a week and no one else had. He'd been spying on them all, seeing if he could feel them out and get them on his side. Seeing if any of them were likely to believe his lies about Karrick. Well, Maggie wasn't about to be used like that. She wasn't about to go against their Killer, not when Morland was more than happy to have him in that role. Morland knew more than any of them, so if he trusted Karrick, then who was she not to?

Glad of the night hiding her presence, she moved to stand behind a bush on the other side of the garden and stared through the window into this Barry's living room. A few people were inside, sitting on a sofa and a couple of armchairs, drinking tea or coffee and laughing. That hurt, seeing them like that. It brought it home that her Team were loners, with no get-togethers, no fun evenings when they didn't have to work. She felt a twinge of sadness that only her Team would make it through the Winnowing — sadness for this Team, who plainly loved one another — but it went away quickly. It was survival of the fittest in this game, and she didn't intend on being a member of the losing side.

Then she spied Graham, sitting slouched against the wall by the internal door — one of them, a part of them. Anger boiled inside her. Who the hell did he think he was? How could he *do* that to her Team? To Karrick, who had always been so kind and just? These people had clearly believed his tales. They interacted as if he'd always been one of them. Oh, she knew some people were fine actors, but to have been *so* duped, *so* taken in… Well, it pissed her the fuck off.

She began a slight mind probe, watching Graham for signs that he knew she was inside his head, albeit on the fringes. He appeared unaware, and she wondered if his acting skills were being used now. She had no way of knowing unless she pushed further. Karrick had told her he would enter Graham's mind from inside his car to keep an eye on things then come to collect her and Graham when she'd completed her mission. After that, she had no idea what was in store for Graham and she didn't much care. He'd put them all in danger, had thought only of himself, and if it meant he had to be punished for it, then so be it. She'd accepted long ago that some people had to be killed, had gotten over feeling guilty, thinking about their families and the gaping hole Karrick's handiwork had left behind. Karrick killed killers, just as that man in there did, the scarred one who kept twitching and fiddling with his shirt buttons. Karrick had described him to her, described everyone so she'd know who was who, who did what, and who was more likely to do her harm if she was discovered. It seemed the only one she had to fear was Leyton. The young guy, Jason, he might pick up on her being there eventually, and maybe the one called Barry, but he and his boyfriend weren't in the living room.

She glanced to the upper floors, making sure the latter two weren't watching her from above. The curtains were shut tight in both rooms, so she relaxed and continued her entry into Graham's mind. She stared at him then made her gaze less concentrated — everyone seemed to know when they were being stared at, didn't they, no extra-sensory perception needed there. She didn't want him glancing across the room and spotting her shape behind the bush.

Graham was laughing at something the young woman — Jessica, was it? — had said, so Maggie dove in quickly while he was occupied with thoughts of whatever she'd been talking about. He didn't know

Maggie was there, she was certain of it, so she roamed, going into the crevices, the places where he kept his innermost secrets.

What she discovered shocked her, but not as much as it would have if Karrick hadn't explained what she'd find. He'd warned her she would see the lies as truths, that Karrick *was* a bad man, that he *did* want to take over Morland's job—and that was because Graham truly believed it.

My God, Graham, how on earth can you entertain this shit?

Graham sat upright, his laughter gone, a serious expression smothering the previous one of merriment. Shit. He'd heard her thought. He shook his head and frowned, staring at Jessica as though he thought she'd mind-spoken to him. It was obvious she hadn't, as she was talking animatedly to Leyton, who'd stopped twitching and stared at her with adoration in his gaze.

The poor man's in love with her and she doesn't love him back.

That was so painfully obvious it made a twist of sorrow writhe in Maggie's gut. She'd been in Leyton's shoes once or twice and it hadn't been pleasant. Maggie returned her attention to Graham, who had gotten up while her focus had been elsewhere. He said something to Jessica, and she nodded in a 'go ahead' way. Graham left the room, and Maggie looked through his eyes and saw him heading for the front door. She ducked behind the bush and waited.

The door opened, and Graham stood on the threshold. He stepped outside and glanced about, his frown still in place, his arms bowed at his sides, hands clenched as though he was readying himself for an attack. Leyton came out behind him—she picked up Graham's knowledge that the scarred man didn't trust him out here by himself—and both men scanned the area.

"There's no one here," Leyton said.

"Maybe we're meant to think that," said Graham. "Maybe Karrick's done a number in our heads like he did with Barry. Maybe we're not seeing what's really there."

What's he going on about?

Leyton nodded. "We will never know until it is too late. Until whatever Karrick wants us to see or do is seen or done. I dislike this. Not knowing whether something is real or not is unsettling."

"Tell me about it." Graham peered at the hedge Maggie was behind. "Someone's over there." He pointed to her hiding place.

Quickly, Maggie erased that thought from his mind then zipped into Leyton's head to do the same. Then she returned to Graham.

"I'd like a moment to myself if you don't mind, Leyton," Graham said.

"I cannot allow that."

Fuck!

"I promise you," Graham said, "there's no way I'll return to my Team. *This* is my Team now."

Leyton gave him a sideways glance, seemed to weigh something up then nodded. "All right, I'll trust you, but if you run, if you go back to them, I'll hunt you down and find you. My burn will see to that."

Burn?

Leyton went inside, closing the door, and Graham began to stroll around the garden. Maggie held her breath as he strode past the bush, and when he was out of sight of the living room window and anyone inside who had a mind to look out, she blanked his mind. He aimlessly wandered onto the driveway then ambled down the street, looking as though he had no clue where he was or what he was doing here.

That was the idea.

She clambered out of the bush then followed him, watched as he turned the corner. Reaching it herself, she was pleased to note Graham headed straight for Karrick's car. She searched Graham's head, seeking Karrick to see if he'd entered his mind too, but there was nothing there, just a blank void. Graham shuffled past the car, and Maggie expected Karrick to get out and grab him.

He didn't.

She stopped walking and leaned against a tree trunk, easing out of Graham's mind so he wasn't too disoriented once she had fully removed herself. Before she left completely, she planted the idea that Graham had come out for a stroll and it was perfectly natural that he was in this street at such a late hour.

* * * *

Karrick waited for Maggie to walk past his car before he got out. On the pavement, Graham blinked rapidly, frowning and looking around. He shook his head then appeared all right again, giving a slight shrug before following Maggie down the street. Karrick lunged, gripping Graham around the neck from behind and pressing the side of his forearm into Graham's throat. The man struggled for a few seconds, going limp soon after.

Karrick spotted a man on the other side of the street, staring his way.

"Maggie, wait. I have a witness."

At the end of the street Maggie turned and began retracing her steps. As she drew closer, he jerked his head at their peeper and, once she'd spied him, Karrick hauled Graham to his car then bundled him into the trunk.

He opened the driver's door and stared at Maggie. "Once I've driven off, sort that nosy bastard then go home. I'll be in contact. I'll need your help again. I'll explain more soon."

Maggie nodded. Karrick drove away, glancing in his rear-view mirror to see the man jolt then scratch his head. Karrick let out a roar of laughter. The poor fucker was probably wondering why he'd even come outside. Swerving left, Karrick made for the park, finding amusement in the fact that he was going to dump Graham where Jason had found his wallet. He parked where he had before and dragged his lifeless body through the forest, keeping alert in case the police were still around due to the jogger incident. He dropped Graham on the ground then kicked the shit out of him, gaining pleasure from it even though the dead man couldn't feel a thing. Karrick's only remorse was that he hadn't been able to torture Graham before his death—that the man had been given a relatively painless passing—something he hadn't deserved.

After going back the way he had come, Karrick got into his car and sat for a moment, eyes closed. He tried to get a thought message to Morland, to ask him to remove any traces of Karrick or his car fibers from Graham. A miniscule stray carpet strand would be all that was needed to get the cops on his tail. Still, now he had Maggie back in the game, he didn't have to worry about that. Any officer who chose to visit Karrick—should Morland not get his message—would find their minds wiped of anything to do with him. And if he had to, Karrick would send Maggie into the mind of a cop in the police station and have them destroy any indication of evidence from papers and storage.

I told you, Graham, that I was coming for you. Now, who's next?

Chapter Nineteen

The glass in Jase's hands slipped from his fingers then shattered, spraying his bare feet with the shards. The feel of it brought back the terrible dream of the death of the boy who looked like him and he shuddered, but then that memory drifted away on the fog that almost always seemed to inhabit his mind these days.

He flared his nostrils, smelling blood, but no. That was wrong. There was no blood in this vision. Just encroaching darkness and burning lungs...

"Jase!"

Dan's voice drifted through the fog, far off but demanding. Fingers dug into his biceps and he winced, blinked, and Barry and Tag's kitchen coalesced around him. He gasped, drawing breath into his lungs and fighting back the black spots.

"What happened?" Dan asked.

Jase fixed on him, on the cool tenor of his voice, and swallowed.

"He's gone," he whispered.

"Who?"

Dan frowned, but there was no fear in his eyes, and for some reason, that caught Jase's attention, focused him, and the vision settled more firmly in his mind.

"Jase, who's gone?"

"Graham," he said.

"He went for a walk," Leyton said from the doorway. "Said he'd be right back."

Jason shook his head. "He's gone."

"What do you mean?" The scarred man straightened from where he had been leaning on the door frame, his expression turning dangerous. "If he ran—"

"No. Not gone like left. Gone, like…gone."

* * * *

A low groan brought Graham to full consciousness. It was a moment before he realized the sound had come from his own throat. He shifted. Pains, some dull and some sharp and grinding, registered from a dozen places on his body.

"You should really refrain from moving just yet," a voice said in his head.

It was enough to freeze Graham in place. "Morland?"

His voice seemed to fall into the misty air around him then disappear.

"Be still. Silent. Let me get my bearings."

"Who are you?" He knew the distinctive feel of each one of his Team members, and this voice didn't feel like any he knew. Of course, at the moment, his head felt like someone had tried to stuff it to bursting full of cotton, so perhaps the problem wasn't the voice but his perception.

"All right. Better. Still. Try to remain calm."

"Calm." In fact, the vibration of fear had already begun deep in Graham's chest, and if he didn't get it under control, it would bloom to full-grown panic, complete with shortness of breath and vertigo.

"*Yes.*" The voice began to sound slightly irritated. "*Calm. And be thankful. That actually went rather better than I anticipated.*"

"Better?" Graham's voice rose to a croaked rasp. Every part of him hurt and this disembodied voice thought it hadn't gone so bad? "If whatever happened had gone any worse, I'd be dead."

The voice remained conspicuously silent. Not exactly reassuring, given that he hurt in places he wasn't aware even existed before now. He tried to sit up, but pain radiated through his torso and ground up his spine.

"*You should try to remain still while I assess the damage.*"

"Let's just go with extensive and skip to the next bit."

He received the mental equivalent of raised eyebrows and a growl, which interested him. Whoever this jerk was, he was a damn sight more expressive than Morland.

"The next bit. You know," Graham muttered, trying to ease into something resembling a more comfortable position. "The part where you tell me who the hell you are and what the fuck you are doing in my head."

"*Oh that.*"

The following mental chuckle had Graham grinding his teeth.

"And maybe where in God's creation I am."

"*That last one is a tricky one. Can you walk?*"

"Can we discuss standing first?"

He sensed a sardonic smile and grunted as his side shot through with fire when he moved his arm.

"I am sorry about your ribs. It could not be helped."

"I'm sure." Graham eased back to the ground with a whimper. "Where am I?" He'd let go of who he was conversing with. It wasn't Morland. It wasn't anyone from his old Team, and he felt sure he would know if it was one of Leyton's people. That left only his new Tool Master — if Rivald was indeed that.

"It's hard to breathe," he said after a few moments of silence.

"I can sense that."

"And I can't see bloody anything."

"I am aware."

A frightening thought occurred to Graham. "Am I dying?"

More silence.

"Can I at least know your name?" he asked, fighting to keep the panic in check.

"My Team call me Rivald. Please try to stay calm. There is only so much I can do, but what I can do will be infinitely less effective if I have to fight a panic attack to achieve it."

"Rivald." Graham latched onto the name, a solid handhold in the fog. "What are you trying to do?"

"Stabilize you as much as I can. There is only so long your body can remain where it is. I would rather have you safely disposed of before dawn."

"Disposed of?" If this creep was trying to calm him, it wasn't working. It was only making things worse to say things like 'disposed of'. Fog thickened around Graham. He couldn't see it, but he could feel it condensing on his skin, crawling over him, exploring his damaged body. Creeping him out.

"What's going on?" His body was going numb. The only connection he had to the world outside his own head slowly diminished until he could barely feel any of the aches and pains of his flesh. That was far less comforting than he might have expected.

"Concentrate on getting to your feet. Follow me."

"What?

"Do it."

The fog coalesced into a vague form, crouching over him. He could sense it there, see it in his mind, though he knew it wasn't something he was seeing with his eyes.

"Get up."

Graham concentrated, thought about hefting his unresponsive body to sitting then standing. It moved sluggishly, as though his thoughts controlled it, but did not inhabit it. When he tried to look at himself, it was all wrong. He could see the whole of himself from a wrong angle.

"Fuck!" Panic assailed him and he was abruptly thrust back into a world of burning pain and dark. His lungs spasmed, his head spun. He couldn't breathe or think past the ringing in his ears.

"If you insist on this foolishness, I will have no choice but to leave you here."

"I'm dying." Graham's thoughts spiraled into the same dark void as his vision. His body's aches grew distant again, but not in the same muffled way as before. Just absent. This was a sense of separation he could not breach.

"You fool! I see I will have to do this the hard way. I had hoped for your cooperation."

The world truly went black. Graham lost all sense of place and self. He was tangled in a web of shadows and pain and sticky, invisible threads of *what if.*

I'm dead. The thought sent him careening into panic. The web clung to him, held him, stopped him moving forward into the unknown darkness or going back to the pain of his body.

"*Is that what you want?*" The voice came, low and sinister in his head.

"Am I dead? Is this death?"

"*One would think that was a much more straightforward question to answer than it actually is.*"

"What does that mean?"

"*It means death is not an either or. It never has been. It's more of a continuum, and with the veil as thin and flexible as it is, even the very extremes of that scale are not what they once were.*"

"What?"

Graham turned to the vague sense of *something* at his side. He saw a man, taller than himself, and broader in his shoulders, with thighs like the trunks of young trees, but still not nearly as massive as his recollection of Morland.

"You have horns."

"And you have anxiety issues. Foolish of your master not to cure that."

"Can I help it if I find dying unnerving?"

"Is it?" Rivald's form shifted. He walked a few steps, trailing a swathe of that dark fog in his wake. He stopped and looked back. "Funny. I don't remember it being that way."

"Well it is!" Graham fought another wave of nausea and the tightening in his chest.

"Interesting."

"So." Graham took a few steps after his new master. "Am I...?"

"You are." Rivald tilted his head to one side. "Behind the veil, I suppose would be an adequate way to explain." His ghostly image solidified into a very real-looking man, complete with hooves and horns.

He motioned to a lumpy mass sprawled on the ground at his feet. "A rather elegant solution to death by exposure, though inelegantly executed, thanks to your inability to control yourself."

Graham stared down at his own battered body. "How?" He looked around himself, seeing that he was inside some kind of cave, near the entrance to a large cavern with a dark pool behind him and a stone throne of some sort beside that. The body lay at the head of a rocky path that he assumed led out of the cave. "Where?"

A look of resignation passed over Rivald's face. "The Winnowing. I am afraid there is no stopping it now. Your Team has splintered. Your Killer is on the verge of going rogue, and mine is only very slowly coming into his true power. There is every chance this culling will remove both Teams—or at least substantial parts of them—from the landscape. There will not be enough Dreamers for two masters. I had hoped to avoid this. I have no argument with your Morland. It seems he feels differently about me."

"Wait a minute. You're talking about Karrick? He's gone rogue?" He turned back to his own limp form on the ground. His heart sank. "He did that?"

"Not alone. There are broken paths in your thoughts. Things obscured. You have a Wiper on your Team."

"Of course." Graham forced his attention back to Rivald and the conversation, trying to control the downward spin of his thoughts. "Maggie. Doesn't every Team have one?"

"No. Dreamers like Maggie are rare and precious."

"Your Team doesn't have one?"

"No. The only Dreamer more valuable than a Wiper is a Visioner, and they are literally one in a million. He, Himself, cannot predict when one will appear."

"But one has." Graham didn't know how he knew he was right.

"Perhaps. It can be very difficult to tell sometimes. Most Visioners go quite mad before they come into their talent. Without the right support..." Rivald shrugged one big shoulder.

"Jase?"

No answer.

Graham pressed on. "What causes a Winnowing?"

"Imbalance. Too many Dreamers, or not enough who can access their Dreams and understand them for what they are."

"Or perhaps two rare and powerful Dreamers in close proximity. Or two unstable Killers?" Graham ventured.

"Sometimes it isn't about the Dreamers at all. Sometimes it is about the sheer number of people with too much blood lust, killing each other for sport. Imbalance thins the veil. That affects everyone, Dreamers and non-Dreamers alike. It creates chaos." Rivald stalked to his chair and sat. "Chaos can get...messy."

Graham spared one last glance for his inert body then moved closer to Rivald. Strangely enough, the odd creature's nearness was comforting in this fog-laden realm. "You don't like messy, do you?" he asked.

"I prefer order."

"As Leyton does. He's the same. I've noticed he likes things the way he likes them and gets...cranky when things get out of hand."

"He is very cranky at your disappearance," Rivald agreed. "I am afraid he will not understand why you walked off after telling him you would not go far."

"I didn't." Graham frowned. "I don't remember."

"Of course you don't, because your friend Maggie has fiddled with your thoughts, and his. That will push him beyond merely cranky, I think."

"Maggie? No. She wouldn't."

"But she has. She must have. I can see into your thoughts and some are missing. Or re-arranged. Who else could do such a thing?"

"That would mean she helped Karrick." Graham shook his head. "I can't see her doing anything like agreeing to help him murder me. She wouldn't."

"She has."

"Then he's told her some lie. Manipulated her in some way to make her think he had a good reason." Graham started back toward his body, determined to get to his Team mate and rescue her from Karrick.

"I wouldn't," Rivald warned. "Re-entering your body at this juncture could very well give Karrick the result he hoped for."

Graham stopped, staring at his own battered frame. "I have to go back. Tell her the truth."

"Would she believe you?"

"Over him? Yes." But would she? Graham wasn't sure. He wouldn't have thought she would agree to help Karrick kill a friend, but what if Rivald was right? There had to be some reason Graham couldn't recall the last few hours. Everything up to and including the feeling of acceptance sitting in Barry's living room chatting with Jessica and even Leyton was perfectly clear. So why couldn't he remember leaving? Or meeting Karrick?

"We must entertain all possibilities," Rivald said, "including the one you propose—that he lied to her, manipulated her in some way. Perhaps she was unaware of his true intentions. The difficulty with being a Mind Wiper is the inability to tell truth from the fictions sometimes. They are rather easy to lie to. It is a balance to their gift. If they always knew and understood everyone's thoughts, imagine the power they would wield. Maggie is vulnerable, Graham, and perhaps the very safest place for her right now is close to Karrick's side, with him believing she is allied with him. As long as he sees a way to use her, he will keep her safe."

"He could destroy her. Make her do something that will get her arrested or killed."

"He could." Rivald stood and approached the pool, gazing into the black depths. "But if he sees she is not with him, that she doubts him, he will have no use for her, and he will certainly kill her. She already knows too much. She knows about you. He cannot risk her telling anyone he had anything to do with your disappearance."

The man was right. Graham had never felt so helpless.

"Fine. But as soon as we can, I need to tell her the truth." Graham didn't like the idea of Maggie believing he was the bad guy. He turned to face the Tool Master and the pool. His attention caught at the way the waters shimmered and colors seemed to rise from the water.

"Pay attention," Rivald told him. "Projecting my thoughts like this is difficult, but I believe you need to see what I see."

Graham stared into the water. On the surface, an image of Barry's living room began to take shape.

Leyton was there, standing in the doorway to the kitchen. Jessica, Barry and Tag stood in a semicircle around Dan and Jason. Jason was pale as a ghost and clearly shaking. His lips moved, but Graham heard nothing for a moment.

"Focus," Rivald said, and a moment later, faint but distinct voices came to him.

"Gone," Jason was saying. "I can't even feel him. Something's happened."

"What?" Leyton was tense. His voice cracked and his hands clenched and unclenched. One hand kept rising halfway then falling again, and Graham actually felt him struggling against the desire to play with his buttons, to line them up properly.

"Let him concentrate!" Dan snapped as he put an arm around Jason. "Come here, babe. Sit down." He led his lover to a chair and they both sat, Dan on the arm and Jason perched on the edge of the seat, holding his head.

"This is crazy," Barry muttered. "What is Jase trying to do anyway?"

"See what happened," Jason said without looking up. "Please, just be quiet."

"You can't make the Dreams come," Barry insisted. "It doesn't work like that!"

"Shut up!" Jason winced at his own raised voice and pressed his fingertips to his temples. "I can get so close. I can see him. A shadow behind him." He shivered. "It's Karrick. I know it is. Karrick has done something."

"Done what?" Jessica asked softly.

Jason sighed and lifted his head. "I don't know. I can't see anything else, but..." He shook his head and leaned into Dan's arms. "Karrick's a Killer, isn't he? Don't think it takes much imagination."

"He killed his own Team member?"

Everyone looked horrified, and a few of them glanced at Leyton.

This time, Leyton gave in to the impulse and his fingers played restlessly, quickly over his buttons. He looked to Jessica first and she managed a smile.

"So what do we do now?" she asked. "Oh, you poor idiot, Graham. He should have stayed where it was safe. With us."

"But..." Graham stepped back from the pool. "I'm not..." He turned to Rivald. "Am I? You said..."

Rivald shook himself and the visions quickly dissipated. "The veil is thin enough that I managed to manipulate it. Your body is, technically, where Karrick left it. You are here. I managed to stretch a ragged edge of the veil over your physical form, so to speak, and it should be enough to keep it in stasis and free from detection, at least for a while. Hopefully long enough to resolve this."

"You can get through to them. Just tell them. Tell them where I am. That I'm not dead!"

Rivald shook his head. "I cannot."

"You have to!"

"I made my vow not to intervene in such matters. Whatever happens now, it is up to them. Up to Leyton to lead his Team down the right path."

"You think Morland is going to take that same vow?"

"He must."

"Even if he does, I know him. He won't keep it."

"I fear you may be right about that. Nevertheless, I have faith in Leyton. In the Team. I will not break my vow. Nothing the Team does, win or lose, will mean anything if I do. If you want to become one of my Team, you must have faith as well."

"Don't have much choice, do I?"

Rivald lifted his head, great horns rising like some kind of twisted halo. "There is always choice. Mine was to help you. For that I may face punishment of my own, but it was my choice. You may choose to accept that help or reject it. No one is stopping you going back to your body and fighting your own battle."

"I could go back?"

"I cannot guarantee you will survive, but of course you can go back."

"You can't guarantee I'll survive either way, can you?" Graham guessed.

Rivald's gaze bored into him. "No."

"Then why should I do this your way?"

"Because you deserve better than Karrick. Better than Morland. Live or die in the end, you deserve to know you are valued."

Graham snapped his mouth shut. He couldn't remember anyone on his Team saying anything like that to him. Except maybe Maggie. In fact, he couldn't remember anyone in his life treating him like he had any real value. "You." He swallowed. "You believe that? About me?"

Rivald bowed his head slightly. "I believe that about all my children."

Children? Graham took a step back. *He can't mean that. Not literally, surely.*

Rivald's eyes glowed briefly as their gazes met, then the huge creature was turning away, heading back to his throne and taking his seat. When Graham got another look at his face, his eyes were once again dark and his attention *elsewhere.*

"This is fucked up," he whispered, glancing between Rivald, his own body, and the pool. "What the hell do I do now?"

Chapter Twenty

"What if Karrick has killed him?" Jase asked.

Dan sat opposite him on the bed in the guest room, haunted and worried. "What if he has? I'd feel bad for the guy, but he isn't one of us, is he? If he can't trust his own..." He shuddered. He hated saying the word. Hated calling Karrick—or Leyton, for that matter—what they really were. It was too freaky. "What are we supposed to do about it, Jase?"

"Help him. I mean what if...what if he isn't dead? What if he's just in trouble and we're all sat here like idiots assuming the worst, and he needs us? What if, right now, he's just trapped somewhere? Waiting for us to help him and we just...don't? I sense this but I don't know what to do about it."

"God, Jase." Dan shuffled closer on the bed and took Jase's hand. "You can't keep doing this, okay? It's one thing to try and interpret the Dreams. Even try to anticipate them, see deeper into them, or whatever it is you do, but you can't take on every single victim like they're your last family member on Earth. You'll never save them all, and you'll make yourself crazy trying."

"Especially when I fail, you mean?" Jase asked, yanking his hand away.

Dan clenched his jaw around a growl of frustration as he watched Jase rise and start to pace. "Yes," he said at last. "Especially when you fail. Do you really think that won't happen? At least some of the time?"

Jase stopped, turned and strode back to Dan, his fists clenched. "I thought you said you were going to try. That you were on my side." He turned again, and the pain in his eyes was worse than a physical blow. "You promised you would try."

"I am on your side. I am, Jase, I swear, but one of us has to be realistic here. You have an incredible gift. I don't understand it. I don't like the way it tortures you, but I get that you need to try and use it. I only want to make sure we both understand what the reality is. People die. And it's horrible. More horrible because of how you feel the way it happens. At some point, we have to accept that no matter how hard we try, we won't be able to save them all."

"I wish—" Jase heaved in a deep breath. "That sucks."

Letting go a sigh of relief, Dan got up and went to him, standing behind him and placing a hand on each of his biceps. "I know. And I'm sorry."

"It's not your fault."

Jase shuddered slightly and sank back until Dan was holding most of his weight. The trust inherent in the way his lover closed his eyes and put all of himself into Dan's hands like that left his heart jittering.

"And it's not yours, either," Dan said. "The sooner you realize that, the better."

"There is something I can do."

The hesitant edge to Jase's voice put Dan on alert. He tightened his fingers around Jase's arms.

"Karrick—"

"No."

"Just listen—"

"No." Dan fought to keep himself from gripping so hard he left bruises.

"Dan, please—"

"No!" Dan spun him round, gripping him again so he could look into Jase's face. "Don't even ask, because I won't let you."

"You don't own me," Jase said, more calmly than Dan would have expected.

Dan drew in a sharp breath. "Who says?"

"I do." Jason twisted to get free, but Dan only held on tighter.

"I just got you back!" Dan wanted to haul Jason against him, hold on hard—so hard they became one and Jase could never be out of his sight again.

"Would you listen to me?" Jase yanked free, his arms red with finger marks where Dan had held him too harshly. "You swore to listen to me, to help me."

"To protect you!"

"And what about you? And everyone out there?" Jase flung a hand toward the door. "Who protects all of you?"

Dan shrank back from Jase's frantic shouting. How had they gotten to this ugly place again so fast?

"I...can see it!" Jase gestured to his head, hands shaking with his vehemence. "I know, and don't ask me to explain how I know, because I can't, but I *know*. It's me. He's fixated on *me*. He will do anything and everything to get me. I know I'm special, one of a kind that any Team would be pleased to have—and to make sure his Team gets me, for him that probably starts with getting rid of you."

Dan opened his mouth, shook his head, but Jase clamped a hand over Dan's lips.

"*Listen to me!*" Jase said. "I just got *you* back. I am not going to lose you like that. I am not going to walk into some godforsaken warehouse and see *you* tied to post and eaten by rats!"

Dan shook himself free. "It won't come to that."

But Jase was shaking his head, hugging himself and backing against the wall. "You don't know."

"Neither do you."

Dan watched his lover shrivel in on himself, sink to the floor. He crouched in front of Jase and tried to look into his eyes, but his lover kept his head down, his fingers jammed into his hair.

"Jason, look at me. You have no way of knowing—"

"I saw it." A low moan of misery grated from him. "Dan, I saw it. Just like that poor kid, but it was you. I saw what he did. What he wants. Everyone. He'll hurt you all until I have nothing left."

He lifted his head, and the utter terror in his eyes knocked Dan to his arse on the floor.

Jase grimaced. "If I go to him willingly, he'll have no reason to touch you. It won't be worth the risk if he has what he wants."

"He almost killed you. What he did—"

"If I knew you were safe, I could handle it."

Dan just shook his head, lost. "How do you expect me to agree to this?"

Jase's eyes watered. He didn't even try to blink away the tears. "I don't. How can you?"

"So what the hell do we do?"

Jase crawled forward into Dan's ready embrace. "What we have to. It isn't just about you and me, Dan. He'll take them all, and it's horrible what he'll do."

"How do you know? Maybe—"

"I can't explain. It's a feeling. Different from when I dream a dream of might-be. Even different from when I dream of already-is. Like with the kid. I knew that already was. That I couldn't help him. It's like...it's like if I don't change the path I'm on, everything I saw will happen, and I will be alone, and Karrick'll be all that's left. Where will I go? What will I do without Dreamers other than him?" He lifted his head. "Without you, right? I have to change the path."

"No one else will let you do this either, Jason."

"Then you have to help me. You have to get me out of here when they're all asleep."

"Really?" Dan pulled back to glare at him. "You really expect me to—"

"Yes." Jase touched his face, snuggled closer. "Please, Dan, help me do this. It's the only way."

Dan pulled him firm and hard against him. "This is insane," he said through clenched teeth.

"Please."

"You want me to agree to another man—" He tightened his arms, probably squeezing the breath out of Jase. "How am I supposed to do that?"

Jase pushed and shoved until Dan had to relinquish his grip. "I got you something. Before." He swallowed and ducked his head. "Before we split. Just wait." He went to the closet then hauled out a wooden box about the size of a tool chest, clasped and hinged in brass.

"What the hell is that?"

"Just open it." Jase shoved it in front of him and sat on the bed.

Intrigued, Dan unlatched the box to open the lid. Inside nestled what appeared to be a fondue pot and an assortment of candles, along with a lighter and fluid and a bottle of oil. A smile spread over his face. "Is this what I think it is?"

Jase's half grin met his and he nodded. "A candle pot." He went back to the closet to take out a sheet of thick plastic and a painter's drop cloth.

"Jase." Dan studied the paraphernalia.

"See, I figure when I get back, you'll have this. You can use hot wax all over my body. You can use it to pull everything he does out of my skin. I'll be like new. Just yours. No one but you will ever come near me again."

Dan closed his eyes, unable to meet Jase's eyes. "Jase."

"Please, Dan, you have to understand. I know in my gut this is what has to happen. I know it like I know my own name. Because nothing can happen to you. Whoever else is out there that can hurt me, they will never be you. It isn't the pain I need, it's you. It's the way you touch me, the way you look at me. It's just you. If I don't have you, I have nothing. I won't be able to control what's in my head. I will go crazy. Without you, nothing will stop that. I *need* you, and this is the only way to keep you alive. You have to trust me."

"Go take a shower," Dan said gruffly, shutting the box and sitting back to stare at the closed lid.

"Dan—"

"Just go."

Chapter Twenty-One

Leyton cursed himself. Rivald had told him to go with his instincts, and he hadn't. When he'd first set eyes on Graham. he'd known something was off— otherwise, why would he have grabbed him? Then he'd taken him to Barry's, and everyone had seemed to overrule him. Graham was good. Graham was on their side. Well, now look. Graham had said he was going for a walk and he hadn't come back. Leyton had believed everyone and now a rogue Tool was walking around, possibly off with Karrick, ready to take them all down.

But the lad, Jason, had said that wasn't the case. Could Leyton trust his word? Oh, he knew full well how Dreaming worked, how information was passed along, but Jason appeared to be different. He could see things in the now, without resting with his eyes closed in order to seek information. Was that even possible? Visions outside of Dreaming? There had to be more going on than Rivald had told him, but then...why hadn't Rivald told him everything? Why would he keep things from Leyton?

I don't understand!

He left the living room, fuming that Jason and Daniel had just gone off upstairs, leaving Barry, Tag, himself and Jessica to try to work out what the devil was going on. Jason was being treated like a child, cosseted and pandered to, and Leyton didn't think that was the best course of action. The lad needed to nurture his courage, learn to face things head-on instead of allowing everyone to shield him from having to deal with the horrors. Leyton had had to grow up fast, to understand that he had a job to do. The fact that Jason was a sensitive chap probably had something to do with it. Leyton enjoyed killing, always had, so he supposed he ought to cut Jason some slack.

Not everyone's made the same.

But there was one thing he knew for certain. Without Rivald's contact, they were all lost. Without Dreams showing them the way, it was down to them to work out what needed to be done. Rivald had said as much, and him basically telling Leyton it was up to him to fix things…

How can I fix what I don't know is broken?

As he strode along the hallway, he ticked things off in his mind. Barry's Dreams had stopped, yet he'd had a weird vision, much the same as Jason had. Was Barry evolving into someone who could see things in the now without stepping into Dreamstate? Were he and Jason the same in that respect? Were there other types of Dreamers they had yet to learn about?

In Barry's office, Leyton sat at the desk and closed his eyes. He was confused. Everything was changing. Why couldn't it stay as it had been before? He Dreamed and found out who he needed to kill. Jessica met up with the killer to lure them to a place where

Leyton could murder them. Barry, Tag and Rivald cleaned up the mess. Now... God, now they had Jason and Barry seeing things as daydreams, Karrick interfering, creating live scenarios and supposedly taking Graham away, Rivald unable or unwilling to help them...

For the first time in a long while, Leyton wanted to cry. He knew deep inside he had to fix this, to ensure every one of their Team came out unscathed after whatever the hell was going to happen, happened. But how close was the major change? It could be months that they wandered around like this, useless, their lives without meaning. *His* life without meaning. If he couldn't kill, if he received no instructions on *who* to kill... He would go insane. He might even kill someone by accident, just because the burn had started and he couldn't control his actions.

He needed to speak to Rivald again. Yes, he'd been told to go it alone, that Rivald couldn't intervene in what was happening, but this latest turn of events made Leyton want to go out there and kill this Karrick. But what if the other Killer hadn't done anything to Graham as Jason had said? What if Karrick was at home, minding his own business? Leyton couldn't just turn up there and eradicate the man. What if Graham had decided to go it alone too?

He concentrated on reaching the Dreamstate, catching a glimpse of the rocky terrain and Rivald's cave in the far distance, but the visual was smoky, indistinct. He pushed harder, channeling all his energy into crossing over, but although he could see the shadowed shapes of the place, it wasn't enough.

"Help me, Rivald," he murmured, stretching his powers to the limit.

His head throbbed, and a sharp pain streaked across his forehead. He bit back a shout and pressed forward, but it was as though an invisible force prevented him from stepping farther. The gauzy landscape taunted him, frustrated him beyond measure, but something inside told him not to give up.

"Trust your instincts, that's what you said," he whispered.

With a hard mental shove, he popped through the mist and found himself on the outer edges of Dreamstate. Rivald's cave was there, as was Morland's, but it was the black pool he had come to visit. How he knew he wasn't sure, but he sought it out and stood beside it, staring into the melted-tar-like substance. If Rivald couldn't tell him anything, maybe the pool could.

He stared at it, waiting for a voice to come out of the darkness. He wasn't sure what to expect, just had the sense this was where he needed to be. He cleared his mind until only his *self* remained.

The pool rippled, concentric circles, as though someone had dropped a stone into the center from a great height. Each curve of every ripple grew lighter, like a crafty sun hid somewhere, only allowing one ray to glance across the liquid to highlight the swells. The faces of his Team appeared in the lightened areas, one per ripple, and as they reached the edge of the pool, they appeared again in the inner circles, a never ending journey across the surface. What did that mean? Leyton wanted to understand the message—for there *was* a message here—but failed to make any sense of it.

The circle in the center widened, and shapes, shadows and colors appeared there. Rivald's image became clear, him sitting on his throne with Morland dead at his feet. The dawning of realization began in Leyton's mind, and he knew that Rivald would win whatever fight they were going through. Rivald would lead whoever was left in both Teams, merging them into one. But how could this be? How could Karrick be thwarted? Leyton could try to kill him, but what if the other Killer was more experienced? If Graham had been taken, Karrick was certainly more wily than Leyton.

That needed to be remedied. Leyton himself needed to embrace change, to draw it to him in order for him to help Rivald in this battle. No more 'just Dreaming'. No, he had to take matters into his own hands and deal with Karrick. He pulled back from the pool, withdrawing into the real world, and opened his eyes. He'd go to the others and explain what he'd seen. They would help him. Doing this alone wasn't something he felt he could manage, and keeping them in the dark didn't sit well with him at all.

Besides, for the first time in what seemed like forever, he was frightened.

* * * *

Karrick rested on his sofa, agitated. Something was bothering him. He'd killed Graham, he had no doubt about it—he'd felt for a pulse when he'd dumped him at the park in the forest and it wasn't there. No, it was something else.

"What the hell is it? Think! Think back!"

He closed his eyes and went backwards in his head. He'd put Graham in his car. Had taken him to the forest. Checked he was dead then left him there. Had someone seen him, was that it? Morland had assured him the fingerprints and fibers were gone, so that wasn't something he needed to contemplate. Maybe, if it hit the news that a body had been discovered and someone had witnessed him as the one who had put it there, Maggie could do her thing. Mind Sweep the witness until there was nothing left in their heads to recall about Graham or Karrick.

He nodded, satisfied he'd covered all angles but annoyed he'd had to go over it all again like this. He was usually so on top of everything. One step ahead.

Yet still a voice nagged inside his head, the tendrils of *something* floating, causing him unrest. He could visit Morland again, but that would mean admitting he'd fucked up, that he needed help. The fact that he'd killed Graham, one of his own Team—what message had that sent to Morland? That Karrick was ruthless, even when it came to their Team, their family? Why hadn't Morland seemed bothered that Graham was dead? Why hadn't Karrick been severely reprimanded?

Karrick would have to deal with these issues by himself, leaving Morland out of the loop. He didn't want to know *what* Morland truly thought. Much as he hated to admit it, and despite Karrick planning to usurp Morland, the man-beast had been his master for a long time, and oddly, Morland's disappointment in him wasn't something he felt he could deal with at the moment.

And that's insane! I don't usually have a conscience. This isn't right. These feelings. Emotions. Everything is wrong. Off.

He tried to clear his mind so only what was bugging him remained, but if he didn't know what *it* was, how could he make it show itself? His logic wasn't working properly, but at this point he was willing to try anything in order to discover the problem. He had to regain control.

What if Maggie did something to me?

He sat upright, swinging his legs to the floor then pushing himself to his feet. He paced, one hand to his mouth, clenching the other into a fist.

He'd have to go back out. There was nothing for it but to return to the forest, if only to put his mind at rest that Graham was definitely dead.

* * * *

Karrick stood in the spot where he'd left Graham and glanced around. The body wasn't there.

"Fuck. Fuck!"

He ran things through his mind once again—yes, this was definitely the spot. So where the hell was he? Had he been found already? Or was he still alive and had crawled off somewhere? And why had Karrick been so stupid as to return to the scene? The cops watched for this kind of thing, for killers to revisit.

What the fuck am I playing at? Why aren't I thinking like I usually do?

Had Graham's pulse just stopped for a short while?

"No, you were dead..."

He clenched his teeth and did a quick jog of the surrounding area, checking for disturbed undergrowth where Graham could have dragged himself along. *That* was the only reason Graham wasn't here, of course it was. If his body had been found by the authorities, everything would be mayhem. The body would still be in place, and officers, forensics, and possibly the press would be milling around.

"Shit!"

Other thoughts came to him then.

What if Maggie defected? What if she's told the other Team what I've done? She could have got inside my head to

219

know my plans. She could have... Maggie, Maggie, Maggie, you silly, silly, girl...

* * * *

Maggie was exhausted. Mind Wiping always did that to her, although not as hard as it had done at first. Now she was able to control the tiredness a little better, but having been restless all day out of boredom then doing the job for Karrick, her body and mind were ready for sleep now. She showered, standing under the spray with her head down, just letting the water ease the aches from her muscles. She thought about tonight and how Graham had turned on them like he had. How could he have done such a thing? Thank God she was still in Karrick's favor. There was no way she'd cross him. He was their Killer, and no amount of coaxing would make her go over to the other side.

She shut the shower off then stepped from the tub, drying gently, her arms heavy. She couldn't be bothered to rush, yet at the same time all she wanted was her bed.

A loud knock on the front door startled her and she frowned, wondering who the hell would be calling on her at this time of night. Maybe Karrick had called a meeting and one of the other Tools from their Team had come to pick her up. No, that was silly. They'd have phoned, surely...

Not if it was so important they couldn't risk a phone line.

Quickly, she dropped the towel and scrabbled into her dressing gown, walking from the bathroom and through to the living room, tying it along the way. In the hallway she went to the front door and peered through the peep hole. She staggered back a little, shocked at who stood on the other side. It was that young man from the other Team house. Jason, was it? What the fuck was he doing here? And how did he know where she lived? How did he know who she *was*?

She moved in front of the door again and pushed to enter his mind but found nothing but blankness. Ah, so he had the ability to shield himself, did he? She'd see about that!

"What do you want?" she asked, making her voice low and angry-sounding.

"Uh, hi. You don't know me, but um... Listen, this is going to sound crazy, but I had... Fuck it!" He took a deep breath and stared at the door. "I had a vision, okay? Just before I left home to go and see—well, it doesn't matter who—I had a vision and you were in it."

She laughed. "So what? Like, people think of others all the time. They say everyone who's been in our dreams we've seen before, even if we'd swear they were strangers. We'd have seen them in the supermarket or whatever, just a glance but our minds store the image. See what I'm saying?" Did she sound convincing, or was she making it clear she knew exactly what he'd meant? She wasn't sure so decided to press on as though she was New Age and was well down with this kind of thing. "But wow, that doesn't explain how you knew where I lived. Was that in the vision too?"

He's going to know you're ripping the piss out of him...

"Yes, it was," he said.

She tried a mind probe again and failed. *Shit...*

"Look," he said, stepping back from the door a bit. "Even if this sounds mad, you need to watch yourself with Karrick. He isn't as he seems, yeah?"

Oh, so that's their tactic, is it?

"Who the hell is Karrick? Are you some freaking nutjob or what?" She clamped her mouth shut to stop herself defending him, giving herself away.

The man shrugged. Turned to his left and said, "She's not listening. What do I do, Dan?"

"I don't know. Shit, I just don't know," Dan said.

"Look," Maggie snapped. "Go away. I don't know who the hell you are or what your game is, but you need to leave me alone before I call the police!"

Go away. Just...just go away!

Jason stared at her door one last time then disappeared. With a sigh of relief, she went into her living room in order to look for her phone. She needed to call Karrick, alert him that the other Team were poking their noses into places they shouldn't be. Casting bad light on him. She couldn't find it so scoured the flat, the creeping thought worrying her that she'd dropped it in the bushes outside that Barry man's house.

Oh, God...

Someone knocked.

"Oh, for fuck's... If it's that bloody man again..."

She went back to her front door. Peered through the peephole once more.

Karrick stood on the other side.

Chapter Twenty-Two

"Look, we tried, all right?" Dan hurried faster down the sidewalk away from the woman's house.

"But what if she doesn't believe us?"

"Jase, I swear. You care too much. How the hell do you expect to chase down every single vision? Warn every single person you dream of that the next time they open their front door or get on a bus or go to a bar will be the time they get slaughtered?" He sounded so angry. So frustrated.

Jase followed miserably in his wake. "So what?" he said after a while, shoving his hands deep into his pockets and scuffing along in Dan's footsteps. "Am I supposed to just not try?"

Dan stopped and whirled on him. "You can't—"

"I swear, Dan, if you tell me one more time I can't save everyone—"

A scream from the dark behind them shattered the night then cut off abruptly and was followed by a slamming door and a squeal of tires. They both froze, staring back the way they had come.

"Oh, God—" Jase pivoted to go back, but Dan's hand closed around his arm.

"No!" Dan hauled him backwards. "No, Jase. You did everything you could. Come on!"

"But—"

"No!" Dan pulled harder, nearly yanking Jase off his feet.

He knew Dan was right. The woman was dead or gone, taken by that maniac to whatever fate he had in store for her. Giving in to Dan's frantic tugging, Jase finally moved away from the house and into the night.

They reached a safe distance of a few blocks, got on a bus and rode it across town. Slumping in the back, out of breath and shaking, they huddled close and silent.

"Now what?" Jase asked, as they finally found their equilibrium again.

Dan just shrugged, lips a tight line, dark eyes shielded and fixed on the grubby rubber flooring.

"You have to go back to Barry's," Jase told him.

Dan shook his head stubbornly. "Not without you."

"Dan, please. I have to know you're safe."

"And what about what I need?" he asked. "What about me needing to know that crazy bastard isn't carving you to ribbons?"

"He won't."

"You don't know that. You said yourself, he was out of control that time. He's unstable. Hell, even Leyton doesn't just lose it and try to off people and not remember doing it."

"Dan, we already had this out. I'm going back to Karrick. I have to. It's the only way to keep him under surveillance. Maybe to stop him doing whatever he's going to do."

"You don't know he's planning anything."

"Yes, I do. It's big, and it will hurt all of us if we don't stop him. And you have to go back to Barry and tell him where I am. I'll try and find out if he killed that woman. I'll try and get in touch if I can. Maybe I'll be able to reach Leyton. But if I can't, you have to tell them where I am."

"I hate this."

Jase nodded. "I know, babe. I do too. I swear I'll make it up to you. You'll have every part of me when I get back. You can do anything you think you need to do to me to get him off my skin, out of my head — make me forget he ever touched me. I promise."

Dan stared fiercely into middle space for a few seconds before yanking the bell and grabbing Jase's hand. "Come on," he ordered, pulling him up off his seat and down the aisle. "Get off." He practically shoved Jase out of the door and onto the sidewalk.

"Where are we going?" Jase asked.

The bus had just passed over the bridge, and Jase fetched up against the end post of the railing, forced to stillness under Dan's restraining palm and his dark glare. He groaned as Dan pinned him there, knee tight to his crotch, other hand in his hair, breath hot on his neck.

"Do you remember our contract?" Dan asked quietly.

Jase swallowed hard and nodded. "Yes," he barely managed to whisper.

Dan hadn't invoked that contract in months.

"I can fuck you — anytime, anywhere. You remember that?"

Jase nodded again. "Yes."

"Right here on the side of the road if I want." He licked up Jase's ear, breathed on his neck, and bit, hard.

Jase whimpered. "Yes."

"When you go to him and knock on his door, you're going to smell like me. You'll feel me. Inside you. Outside. My bruises, my spunk. Me all over you."

Jase sucked in a breath as Dan's knee pressed up, crushing him, hurting him and making him hard.

"Remind him he failed. Whatever he thought he was going to do to me with that freaky-arse stare of his, he failed. You're still mine. You always will be."

"Always," Jase whispered.

Dan's hand tightened in his hair and he lifted his weight off Jase.

"Shoes off," he commanded.

Jase scuffled to toe off his sneakers.

"Socks," Dan instructed, once he'd succeeded.

It was harder to get his socks off with Dan's grip on him and his proximity, but he finally managed.

"Good boy. Now pick them up." He released Jase long enough to allow him to gather the discarded items and tuck them under one arm.

The instant Jase straightened, Dan gripped him again and pulled him away from the railing. Jase had to obey or have his hair ripped out. Dan guided him ahead, down the embankment toward the grassy verge beside the river. His bare feet in the gravel and dust along the road, in the cold dew covering the grass hurt after only a dozen steps. At the base of the bridge, Dan's curt instructions to drop his pants and lift his shirt made him tremble.

"Here?" he asked, striving to make his voice strong.

"Now," Dan confirmed.

Jase swallowed repeatedly, dropped his shoes and socks then undid his jeans. Traffic streamed past above. Probably no one could see them down here. Not from a speeding car, but if the light changed or a train went by on the next block and traffic backed up, they very well could have an audience.

Obedient, Jase pushed his pants to his knees, slung his T-shirt behind his neck to leave himself bare, throat to thighs, and placed both palms flat against the cold concrete of the bridge. He listened, silent, as Dan spat into one hand. The night noises weren't enough to mask the sound of skin brushing skin when Dan palmed himself.

"Spread," Dan commanded.

Jase did, shuffling his aching feet apart in the freezing grass. His jeans stopped him getting very wide, which forced him to bend forward to allow Dan the access he was going to require.

Penetration with spit and nothing else hurt like hell. Dan held him still, both hands gripping his hips now, fingers digging into flesh over bone. Jase sucked in breath after breath, clenching his hands, knuckles rubbing on rough cement. It took more than a few long, hard strokes for his passage to accept Dan's girth. His lover was right. He was going to feel this for some time after. When his body finally conformed to Dan's will and the fucking picked up pace, he was sweating with the exertion of holding still.

Releasing one hip, Dan snaked his fingers back through Jase's hair and pulled, relentless, until Jase's neck was kinked, his throat exposed, his muscles at the limit of what could be forced. It took all Jase's strength to keep himself from being fucked right into the stone. He locked his elbows and pushed back into Dan's thrusting.

His shoulders began to ache. His arms trembled. His knuckles and his scalp stung. His cock responded, bobbing between his legs as his balls drew up. As if reading his mind, sensing his imminent explosion,

Dan reached around and gripped his cock, not to pleasure it, but to squeeze it tight and prevent him coming at all.

Jase sobbed, struggling to drive into those unforgiving fingers, but Dan refused him release while he took his own, letting go of his orgasm and his spunk into Jason's body. Jason could feel him throb inside his arse and he strained for his own release. Still, Dan denied him, pressing him up against the bridge, forcing his arms to give, leaning on him and breathing hot on the back of Jase's neck.

"You take this" — he squeezed Jase's cock more painfully — "to that animal, and when he touches you and you come in his bed, you remember it's me allowing it. This" — he squeezed again — "is mine. You mark his bed with it, and think of me when he touches you. You understand me?"

A ragged cry tore from Jase's throat and he nodded. "I understand."

"Your heart and your soul, your Dreams, your body belong to me. No matter what he does. Never forget that."

"I won't forget," Jase whispered.

Dan's fingers in his hair made his scalp scream in protest. The muscles of his neck twisted into knots that would take days to work out. The rough surface of the bridge dug at his chest, scraping over skin and leaving scratches beyond burn, not quite deep enough to draw blood. Marks that would sting every time he sweated or showered, every time anyone touched him there. The bruises on his hips would smart when he walked, when he sat. At every touch, he'd remember Dan's hold on him. His arse stung and burned as Dan's cum leaked out and down his thighs. It would dry and pull at the short hairs there, every step toward Karrick reminding him where it had come from. His arse twitched around Dan's cock. His frozen feet burned on the uneven ground.

Dan had marked him, head to toe with sensation that wouldn't fade quickly.

Closing his eyes and releasing all his tension into a deep sigh, Jase wilted between hard concrete and hard muscle.

"Beautiful." Dan kissed his shoulder. "Perfect."

For a few minutes, they remained so. When Dan's erection was completely gone and Jase's pulsed with every beat of his heart, Dan took a step back.

"Dress now, Jase," he said softly, trailing his fingers through the sweat along Jase's spine.

Jase nodded and wiped his cheeks. It would only upset Dan to see tears on his face now. He stuffed his hard-on into his pants and found his damp socks. He got them and his shoes back on, cramming sore, achingly cold feet into sneakers then turning.

Dan took his face in both hands and kissed him soundly. "You meet me here. Two evenings from now, or we're coming to get you. Understand?"

Jase nodded again.

"Good." He released him and stepped back. "Go."

Jase turned abruptly and fled.

He didn't look back. He couldn't. If he saw Dan standing there watching him, he'd change his mind. That couldn't happen. This had to be done. He knew it did. There was something he needed to know and he had to be close to Karrick to figure it out.

The bridge wasn't that far from Karrick's house. It took him less than a quarter of an hour to reach the big brick dwelling and he didn't think before striding up to the door and ringing the bell. He couldn't afford to think and risk hesitating.

Karrick had to believe he wanted this with his whole being.

He had no illusion how it would go. Listening to Karrick's footsteps stomping down the stairs toward the door, he knew as soon as the bigger man caught sight of him, smelled him, he'd know.

He'd claim Jase immediately, brutally, rub his own scent over Jase's skin to eradicate Dan's. Jase braced himself as the door swung open.

"Right on time." Karrick sneered down at Jase and held up a length of rough rope. "I've been meaning to redecorate. I have just the place for a new ornament." He stepped aside and motioned Jase onto the welcome mat. "Do come in."

* * * *

Dan watched his lover flee. Every fiber of him longed to call him back, hold him, tie him down if need be, to keep Jase with him. But one small, distant, alien whisper in the back of his mind warned him not to.

Jase was the key to Karrick.

What made his pretty little twink strong and resilient was the thing that made Karrick weak. Jase craved pain and the headspace where he could escape his Dreams. Karrick would give it to him, Dan knew. Possibly more than Jase could handle. But something in the Killer had stopped him destroying Jase, and that restraint went against Karrick's nature. That moment when he made the decision not to kill, he was at his most vulnerable. That's when they would be able to stop him.

For some reason, Jase was the one toy Karrick had not been able to bring himself to break. Dan had to believe that fact wouldn't change.

Steeling himself for the anger he would face, he hurried back up to the road, pulled out his cell then called a cab to take him to Barry.

Chapter Twenty-Three

"You *what?*" Barry was livid. His face took on a frightening shade of red. "We got him back! Not so you could — Jesus *fuck*, you bastard! How could you let him — ?"

"Barry." Tag laid a hand on Barry's arm.

Dan eyed Barry's tight fist and Tag's firm hold on him.

"Don't you fucking tell me to calm down," Barry warned, glaring at Tag.

Tag lifted both eyebrows. "Smashing Dan's face in is not going to help."

"It'll make me feel a fuck lot better."

Tag actually grinned, but didn't, Dan noted, loosen his grip.

"Me too," Tag said. "Unfortunately, we need him conscious, so please, lover, retrain yourself, at least for now."

Barry growled and finally loosened his fingers. "Fine." He shook Tag off then stalked to the kitchen sink to stare out of the window. "Tell us everything," he demanded, meeting Dan's gaze in the reflectior.. "Every fucking detail."

Dan pursed his lips but nodded and proceeded to explain where he and Jase had gone and why.

"You're a fucking idiot," Barry snarled. "Leaving him marked up like that. You have to know it's going to trigger Karrick to do the same. You have any idea what he'll do to him to get you off—"

"Barry!" It was Jessica who interrupted him this time. "Don't make it worse." She laid a hand on Dan's arm, sympathy smoldering in her eyes.

Forcing the sick knot in his gut to stillness, Dan nodded. "I know," he managed through clenched teeth, carefully shifting away from her touch. "Jase is tough—and he made me agree to this. And as long as Karrick's distracted with him, he's not out doing whatever the fuck he's planning. It buys us time."

"To do *what?*" Barry asked. "We have no contac: with Rivald. None of us know what the fuck is going on, and you've bargained away our only hope of figuring it out."

Dan shook his head. Jase had wanted it this way. Dan hadn't liked it either—could understand Barry's anger—but Jase would have gone ahead with his plans anyway, regardless of what any of them said. Dan wanted to say that, to tell them that he knew Jase better than any of them, but with emotions so high, he had a feeling his explanation would fall on deaf ears. Instead, he said, "Maybe not."

"How the hell do you figure that?"

Dan offered a grim smile. "I was thinking on the way back. Why would Graham run?"

No one spoke.

"Answer—he *wouldn't* run. So something has happened to him. And something has happened to their other Dreamer, the woman. She didn't listen to us, and..." He shuddered. He explained they had heard her scream. They'd heard it and hadn't gone back to help. "Karrick is alone now, he's not interested in working with his Team," he said, shaking the memory off. "And what is the worst thing for any of you to ever be?"

Barry shot Tag a naked look and nodded. "Alone," he admitted.

"Been alone all my life and done just fine," Leyton muttered.

"But you're not now," Dan pointed out.

Leyton glanced between Tag and Barry, then to Jessica and shrugged. "I don't have what they do."

"You're not built the same way, Leyton. You don't need what Barry and Jase do, because you're different. And you have Jessica," Dan said.

"Now wait one minute." Jessica raised both hands in front of herself and backed a step away from them all.

"Just listen," Dan said. "I've been thinking about this since Jase left me, wondering how he was dealing. He needs an anchor. He needs something to hold on to, to keep the Dreams in perspective, and I admit I haven't always been that good at it. But when we were doing okay, *he* was doing okay." Heat flushed up into Dan's face, but he didn't slow down. "When he needed a beating, I gave it to him. It's his touchstone." He looked at Barry. "You guys, you do whatever you do, and it works to keep you grounded, knowing Tag's there to give you whatever he gives you to make the Dreams bearable. Leyton always had his hope of a real life."

"I didn't get it," Leyton pointed out. His fingers flashed over his buttons, and he twisted each one so the holes lined up down his front.

"Didn't you?" Dan spread his arms out to indicate them all. "Jessica didn't leave, did she? Maybe what you thought you wanted wasn't actually what she's here to give you. I mean, bait?" He glanced at the woman with an apologetic shrug. "Face it. You just aren't every serial killer's type. You can't lure them all."

She frowned but didn't argue the point. "I'm a Dreamer too, though," she said. "I don't have an anchor."

"You don't Dream the way they do. Rivald comes to you. He tells you what you need to do. He puts you in the place Leyton needs you to be. You're Leyton's touchstone. There is nothing Barry and Jase won't do to protect me and Tag." Dan shifted his gaze to Leyton. "And nothing you won't do to protect her."

There was confirmation in Leyton's eyes, even though he didn't say anything out loud.

"So." Jessica glanced around the room. "We all just need someone for this to work, whether it's romantic or not? And the bait thing is just for show? I don't understand."

"Sadly, I don't think so," Dan replied. "If you weren't in real danger, you wouldn't be any use to Leyton. You'd just be a disturbance. You'd be the thing he wants that he can't have, and that would be a deadly distraction when he can least afford it."

"He still can't have—"

"I can protect you," Leyton growled, stepping toward her and forcing her back one more pace. "And I will."

"How, when we don't even know what's happening?" she asked.

"I—" Leyton glanced between them, skittered his fingers along his buttons and took a breath. "I managed to see into Rivald's pool," he confessed. "I don't really know what I saw, exactly. Only that Rivald will come out on top. He'll lead whoever is left."

"How do you know?" Barry asked.

Leyton shrugged. "I saw it. I *felt* it." He touched fingers to his scars and scowled. "He saved my life. My sanity. I'm going to give him a Team worthy of that." He wagged his head back and forth slowly, his brown eyes locking with each of theirs for scant seconds.

It was enough to send a shiver through Dan and leave him chilled to his core.

"Karrick is not worthy of Rivald," Leyton went on. "He'll have to die. If there is any of his Team left..." He shrugged. "We'll see."

"Seems he's already started taking care of his own people for us," Tag pointed out.

Dan thought he heard a slight tremor in the cop's voice, but it was hard to tell. He didn't imagine the way Tag's hand closed around Barry's arm or the stumbling step back Barry took when Tag pulled him farther from Leyton's cold glare, though.

"Jase said Graham was 'gone'," Dan cut in. "He didn't say dead. He said gone. So we have to get him back."

"How?" Tag seemed almost grateful for the distraction Dan had offered, and he broke eye contact with Leyton. There was no mistaking the shudder as he did so.

"Find his touchstone."

"And how do we do that?" Barry asked.

"Start at his place, probably. Find the person Graham will do anything to protect and..." He shrugged. "Yeah. I don't know what comes after that, but it's an idea, at least."

"Feels like grasping at straws," Tag muttered.

But Barry was already striding from the room toward his office. "It's an idea," he said over his shoulder. "If we all need a touchstone, an anchor to get strength, to help us do our jobs… I'll call Ross and get Graham's address."

* * * *

In Graham's apartment, Jessica stared at the three-drawer filing cabinet she was crouching in front of. The bottom drawer was open, and inside were folders filled with papers. She was amazed at his orderliness — in fact, the whole place was tidy in the extreme, as though he had OCD. A place for everything and everything in its place. It shouldn't take them all long to find what they needed — *if* he had an anchor.

Yes, she could understand Dan's thinking. Her anchor was her mother. Jessica had made sure to keep away from her as much as possible in order to keep her safe. She'd do anything — *anything* — to make sure her mother came to no harm.

It made total sense, even though her tie to Leyton wasn't exactly something she'd have chosen. The others loved their anchors, and that was what she was having a hard time trying to deal with. The thought of Leyton loving her like *that*… It made her go cold. But if it was just a tie, she could deal with it. The thing was, could Leyton see it that way? He'd convinced himself in the past that she was the one for him, a potential lover he could spend the rest of his life with. How difficult would it be for him to accept that their bond wasn't the same kind as the others?

He'll just have to learn to get over it. No way is he my kind of man. Not like that. Never like that.

She pulled a file open between fingers and thumb and with her other hand flicked through each piece of paper. They were just bills — electricity, gas, telephone. Quickly going through the remaining files and coming up with the same type of thing, she moved to the drawer above. Finding similar there, she pulled open the top drawer and steeled herself for the disappointment that she wouldn't be finding anything of significance.

She was right. Nothing of importance was in the filing cabinet, so she moved to his desk. He probably kept his more personal things in there. With only two drawers, one either side of the space where his chair sat, she sighed, thankful she wouldn't have to sift through too much. The left one held nothing but pens, pencils, a few paper clips and the usual assortment of office paraphernalia, so she shifted to the one on the right.

It was locked.

"Fuck it."

She felt beneath it for some kind of catch but didn't find one. Why did everything seem to be so hard lately? What force was in play that appeared to be preventing them all from moving forward? At a guess she'd say Morland had cast some mumbo-jumbo spell crap, altering the way things would normally work so it slowed them down, stopped them from being the Team to win this...this whatever the hell it was. Winnowing.

She huffed out a laugh, more from nerves than anything else, and poked around in a pen holder on the desk in the hope she'd find a key. Of course, there wasn't one, and she kicked the desk leg in frustration. A dull sound had her going down on her knees to find a small silver key sitting on the floor. She cursed herself—she'd bloody felt under that desk and had come up with nothing, yet the key had been there all along.

Grabbing it, she then slid it into the keyhole, her hand shaking, her nerves pinging. She had the sense that she'd find what they were looking for, and excitement breezed through her, making her reel backwards a bit so that she dropped the key.

"Calm the hell down," she muttered then took a deep breath. "Just calm the hell down."

Key in the lock once more, she managed to turn it and slide the drawer open. A large bill-sized envelope sat inside, cream, expensive paper, stuffed with what looked like letters. Handwritten letters. She took it out and sat in the chair, then removed the letters and placed them in a stack on the green desk blotter. Scanning the top one for a date—two years ago—she flicked back to the bottom of the pile. Five years ago. So he'd been corresponding with someone via snail mail—virtually unheard of these days, at least in her experience—for three years, then the letters stopped. Maybe they'd switched over to email for the last two years up to the present day, finally getting with the program and into current times.

She'd start with these for now. Turning the pile over, she began from the start, quickly realizing these were very private love letters. She felt guilty reading them, as though she were snooping in his diary, something that didn't sit well with her at all. Still, what else could she do? They had to find Graham's anchor, and it seemed to her that she had. If Graham had loved this woman, didn't it make sense that she would be the one thing he'd do everything in his power to protect?

Unless they split and aren't together anymore.

She thought of Dan then. He and Jase had parted ways, yet Dan had still been tied to him, still hadn't been able to keep away. The same with Barry and Tag. Was that what true love was like?

She grimaced.

I'll never know now, will I? It's not like I can have someone in my life, what with the way things are, the way things have to be. No one would understand the shit I have to do, and I wouldn't blame them either. Unless I count Ross, but he's not really interested in me like that. He just wants to be friends.

Uncomfortable with reading the depth of longing in the letters—from what she could make out, Graham and the woman, Sue, had spent the majority of their relationship long distance—she scanned them all until she reached the most recent.

Graham,

I don't understand. Your phone call was so odd, as though you weren't you anymore. What's going on? The last I knew I was coming to visit, like I always do at the end of the month, then you rang and said we were over. What? Like I'm meant to just accept that with no explanation other than you saying you don't love me anymore? When the hell did that happen? I mean, look at the date of your last letter and what you said in it. That you wanted to marry me, have kids, that you'd be moving up my way and we'd be able to have a proper relationship.

What happened between then and now? How can you just stop loving someone inside a matter of days?

I thought you were The One. You even said you were, convinced me you were this wonderful man who was so in love with me, nothing could keep us apart. Were you playing some kind of game? Is that it? Were you laughing your arse off for three whole years, reeling me in, intending to drop me all along?

No, I don't believe that. Call me naive, call me a stupid woman for believing you all this time, but I don't believe that and never will. We had something – still have it, I'm sure of that – and whatever's happened to make you call this off...

What has happened? Something has, I know it. I don't buy the bullshit you gave me. Please ring me so we can work this out. And if you really don't love me, then I want to hear you say it again. I want to listen to how you say it. See your face when you say it. Then I'll know for sure. Leaving it like this, well, it isn't right, is it? Not after what we had.

Please, call me again, or at the very least, write. You owe me that much.

I love you, always will.

Sue

Chapter Twenty-Four

Leyton sensed Jessica coming into the living room so turned from ferreting in a drawer of the TV cabinet to see her standing in the doorway.

"I think I've found his anchor," she said.

Leyton straightened then moved to her side. He glanced at a bunch of letters in her hand and frowned at having caught what a couple of the lines said. Graham had a lover, someone he cared deeply for, something Leyton had wished for yet had been denied. He glanced up at Jessica, who stared down at the words, and he wondered what was going through her mind. She looked tense, stiff, as though she worried that the love in those letters would give him ideas again.

"I'm well past that," he lied to reassure her. "You don't have to worry that I don't know where we stand. I can't say it was easy having to accept that you weren't the woman promised to me, that some crazy bitch who'd defected from the Team was instead, but I'll never press you for more. I hope you believe that."

That last bit was true. He wouldn't force her to love him or expect her to, but no one could make him not love her. He'd keep that secret to himself, love her to his dying day, make sure she was as safe as he could make her.

"I know," she said, looking up at him and giving a tentative smile.

That gaze of hers almost broke him. He had the urge to gather her in his arms and try the physical aspects of love on for size, but that would horrify her. And who could love a man like him anyway? Face full of scars, teeth that belonged to the people he'd killed He'd be alone forever, he knew that, and thank God he had the Team to focus on. If he didn't have them and this mess to deal with, he'd go insane with wanting Jessica, tormenting himself with ideas that they could be together when it was so clear they couldn't. How did you make someone love you?

You don't. And no one's loved me my whole life, so I should be used to that by now. Whatever. It doesn't matter.

"We need to show Barry," he said, the change of subject the only way he could stop himself wishing and hoping. "He's in the bedroom with Tag and Daniel."

She turned. He followed her along a short hallway and into a bedroom. Dan was on the floor searching under a single bed. Barry was checking the pockets of clothes in the wardrobe, and Tag was in front of a chest of drawers, reaching into the back of one as though looking for a secret panel.

"Jessica may have found what we need," Leyton said, proud of her, proud that she'd been the one to find those letters.

Barry let go of a suit jacket and strode toward them, hand out. "Let me see?"

Jessica gave them to him then crossed her arms over her stomach, tucking her hands beneath her arms. Barry quickly read a few, passing them in order to Tag, who had stepped to Barry's side. Daniel got out from under the bed and read over Tag's shoulder.

"So they stopped writing to each other two years ago," Barry said, frowning. "This last letter from her... I'm speculating, but with the sudden change of heart—what do you reckon to it being because Graham joined his Team then? What if he had to cut her off because he knew if they remained a couple, she'd either be in danger or would find out what he was doing?"

"I know how that feels," Jessica said. She shrugged. "What with my mother, me not seeing her as much... You feel you have to cut them off to protect them."

Barry nodded. "Makes sense. Won't know if that's the case until we ask Graham, but I'm willing to bet we're right."

"But," Leyton said, looking at Daniel, "if your anchor theory is right, if Graham has cut this Sue out of his life, he isn't using her as an anchor, is he? What I mean by that is, if she isn't close, isn't there to help him get grounded, she isn't really an anchor."

"Yes, she is," Jessica said.

Leyton turned to look at her. "How so?"

"My mother is my anchor. It doesn't matter that I don't go to her so she can ground me or help me to make sense of this shit." She smiled apologetically. "Just knowing I love her, that she'd be there for me if I *did* go to her and tell her everything, asked for help or whatever... It's enough." Her eyes glistened. "From reading those letters, I'd say Sue still loves him. Said she always would. Graham knows this, and so long as he can go to her if he absolutely had to, it'll probably be enough for him too."

Leyton couldn't imagine not seeing Jessica often, just using the memory of her to get him through, but perhaps she and Graham worked differently. Then again, just the promise of having a woman in his life for all time had kept Leyton going, so maybe he *could* go without seeing Jessica after all. He shuddered at the thought.

I don't ever want to be without her.

"So, what's next?" Daniel asked.

"Maybe speak to this Sue?" Tag suggested. "I can get Ross to run her name and address through the database, see if she's still living in the same place."

If she's anything like I would be, I'd never move house. I'd stay exactly where I was so that Graham would know where to find me.

Leyton shook his head, trying to rid it of thoughts like that. They wouldn't do him any good. Things were as they were, and the faster he accepted that, the better. They had a job to do, and they needed to do it fast.

Before the Winnowing was upon them.

* * * *

"You really are quite a beauty," Karrick said, prowling around Jase, who was naked on his knees in the living room, head bowed, submissive and ready to take what Karrick had in mind to give him. And if he wasn't ready? Tough shit.

How dare he come in here stinking of that other man?

Karrick calmed himself with thoughts that Jase had needed to be with that Daniel person in order to realize Karrick was the man for him. Yes, that was it. It was a small sacrifice that Karrick would be taking sloppy seconds, but needs must. A slew of satisfaction went through him as he imagined coming inside Jase's arse, his cum coating Daniel's—overpowering it, taking its place. That Daniel's mess would still be there was neither here nor there. The fact that Karrick's would be the only spunk Jase would be getting from here on out was enough to make him feel better. This was the way to go, to fuck Jase seven ways to Sunday and leave him in no uncertain terms that Karrick was the man he needed to purge the confusion that those Dreams of his gave him.

"I didn't think it would be long before you came back," Karrick said. "Back to where you belong. And you know you belong here now, don't you?"

Jase nodded, keeping his gaze fixed on a wall.

"Yes, you do." Karrick nodded. "We're destined to be together, you and me. You just needed to find that out for yourself. Needed to test the waters, so to speak. I suspect you found those waters weren't to your liking, hmm? That mine are purer, the taste cleaner, the nectar you need to survive."

Jase winced—he *had* winced, hadn't he?

"What's the matter?" Karrick snapped, annoyed that Jase might have pulled that face because of his words. "You may speak. Tell me."

"I'm sore," Jase said. "From *him*."

Oh, the way Jase had spat that word, it filled Karrick with a sense of power.

"Is his soreness not to your liking?" Karrick asked.

"No. I need yours." Jase winced again.

"I know you do. And I'm going to give it to you in a way you've never had it before."

Karrick smiled then strode over to a cabinet beside the door. He opened it to draw out a whip. Turned it over in his hands and soaked in the feel of it, relishing the power that surged through his body at the prospect of using it on Jase. The young man had undoubtedly enjoyed a whip in the past, but Karrick didn't intend on wielding it in the usual manner. No, he had other uses for it at the moment.

"This," he said, closing the cabinet door then striding back to Jase, standing in front of him with his legs a foot apart, "will always remind you of me. What I'm about to do will leave you in no doubt that I am the man you need, always." He sucked in a long breath, closing his eyes on the exhale.

"Yes," Jase said. "Only you. I only need you."

"That's right." Karrick opened his eyes and glared down at Jase. "So get up. That's it, up on your feet. Now go and stand behind that chair there. Yes, that's the one. Hold the top and bend at the waist so I have unhindered access."

He went to stand behind Jase. Admired the swell of his perfect arse, the pucker that had so obviously been used recently. Before he shot his load up there, he'd be pushing something other than his dick into that tight, greedy little place. He turned the whip around so he held it just below the handle. Placed the tip of that handle to Jase's hole.

And rammed it inside.

* * * *

Graham's feet ached. He'd been walking for what seemed like miles. The ride he'd bagged from a passing motorist had been a godsend, but the man had only been able to take him to the outskirts of this town. Although Graham had been here countless times before, he'd driven and only knew how to reach his destination by car. The housing estate he was on was alien, a spread of homes and front gardens he'd never seen previously. He had to work out how to reach the estate on the other side, where salvation and possible danger lay. Shoving thoughts of the danger from his mind, he pushed on, head down, hands in jacket pockets.

His interaction with Rivald filled his mind. Going against that man's wishes had been a tough decision to make. Rivald had advised that Graham remain in the veil, in Dreamstate, but shit, he hadn't been able to do it. Yes, he'd seen the sense in it, but for the past two years he'd been a Dreamer, part of the Team, and dropping the ball now hadn't been an option. How could he let others do their thing when everyone had become so splintered? Morland's Team was effectively a fuck-up, and Rivald's appeared to be on the ball and determined to see the Winnowing through—and win. He knew what side he was on—Rivald's, most definitely—but to get his mind back to where it needed to be, as sharp as he had to have it, and to restore his strength and equilibrium so that he could be of good use to Barry and everyone else, he'd chosen to go back inside his body.

That had been an experience and a half. So weird, sliding back inside something he'd spent his whole life in, yet feeling alien when he'd settled in. He'd been cold, but not the kind of cold one usually felt when the winter air wrapped itself around you. No, he'd been freezing, clammy and damp. And so very dead. It had taken around five minutes for him to get his body to accept he was back—five minutes that had passed like hours, with Graham thinking that at any moment Karrick would return for him. When he'd finally managed to get his body to accept him, to get his heart to beat and his lungs to fill like bellows, he'd staggered to his feet and felt more ill than he'd ever been in his life.

Now, it was like he'd just gotten over the flu, the remnants of it lingering in the background, reminding him that he'd really been quite sick. He had a mild headache, clearing now that he wasn't inside the car, and his limbs ached. Other than that, he was good to go, and the final energy he needed to make him one hundred percent lived a matter of minutes away. Half an hour, perhaps.

Sue. His Sue.

What if she's found someone else? What if he opens the door? What if she doesn't even live there anymore?

For the first time since he'd re-entered his body, Graham had doubts.

"Shit."

He walked on, tremors of worry skittering through him. He mulled over his reservations. He was so close to seeing her, to having his energy restored fully. And if she *was* with someone else? Just a glimpse of her should do it. A word or two, maybe. Something, anything that would remind him how much he loved her. He could cling to that, fill himself with it, then return to Rivald's Team and be of some use.

He reached her estate faster than he thought he would and made his way down her winding street. Her house sat in the middle of a terrace of three, and just the sight of it brought tears to his eyes and renewed hope. That and a knot of terror that he was drawing her into this shit, that if Karrick knew what he was doing, he'd come to find Sue and kill her.

"Fuck, what the hell am I doing?"

He walked up her path, noting the curtains were the same ones she'd had when he'd last been here. Cream, black flowers. But that didn't mean anything. Lots of people moved out and left some of their things behind for the next tenants. Perhaps it was for the best, that she wasn't here. Already he felt better, stronger, more himself. If just being at her house could do that, staying outside and staring at it might well give him all the power he needed.

Still, despite the fear that he was dragging her into danger — no one knew about her, and so long as Karrick didn't visit the Dreamstate any time soon or get inside his head, no one ever would — he knocked on her door.

His stomach muscles contracted, and his heart rate picked up speed. Should he turn away, get the fuck out of here, leave her to the life he'd ensured she now led? Lonely, she'd said that on the phone when he'd given her a call to tell her once again that he didn't love her. And he'd believed her too. She'd sounded so...so damn broken. But it had been for the best, yet here he was, undoing all the good he'd done back then. Putting her in the line of fire.

He stared at the glass panels in the door, telling himself that she'd be all right, that he'd see her then go again, urge her to maybe go and stay with her sister up north if he had to. A shadow approached, turned into a solid figure, one he'd recognize anywhere. The door was pulled wide, and he stood staring at the one woman who had captured his heart and ruined him for anyone else.

"Graham?" she said, squinting.

God, she was beautiful.

"Sue," he said, falling forward, reaching blindly for her. "I need you. Just for a minute, I need you."

Chapter Twenty-Five

Jase lay on his side in the living room, the floor hard on his bones. He was bruised, battered, and — as far as Karrick was concerned — thoroughly, sexually sated. Jase had told him he was, that Karrick had given him the best beating and fuck ever, but he'd lied through his teeth for the good of the Team. He'd shut everything out as much as he could as it had happened — mainly that it was Karrick doing what he'd done — and pretended that the whip handle had been Dan's cock, that the hands slapping at him, the fists punching had been Dan's too.

No amount of kidding himself had worked, though.

He dozed, safe in the knowledge that Karrick had gone to bed for a nap, that he'd be left undisturbed with his thoughts for at least an hour or two. He wasn't sure how long he'd been lightly sleeping when he'd seen a vision. A snippet at first, of Graham walking down a street then knocking on a door. Relief had poured through him that Graham was okay, but tension had filled his muscles so he was rigid and stiff. What was Graham doing? And where was he?

Jase would have got up, walked around to think more clearly, but before Karrick had gone for his nap, he'd drawn Jase's feet up and back then tethered his ankles and wrists together with chains. If he needed a piss, he'd have to do it where he was. If he needed to think, he'd just have to do it here.

In the vision, a woman opened the door, and Graham said something, falling forward into her arms. Jase concentrated to try to find out who she was, a snippet of information floating, something he could chase to give him enlightenment. There was nothing, but then he shouldn't have expected it to be easy. Their tasks were hard, and having to work out what the fuck was going on had become the norm.

Jase was able to follow Graham into the house and sit beside him on the sofa. Information shifted through his mind, informing him her name was Sue. She sat on the other side, and Graham held her as though it was the first time he'd done that in ages and the last time he ever would. Graham's emotions seemed to seep out of him and into Jase, and he felt utter sorrow at something Graham had done, yet relief that he was here now, with her.

Who was she, his sister or what?

A sound startled Jase out of his daydream and back into Karrick's living room. He opened his eyes. Karrick was hopping along getting his trousers on, then plonked himself on the sofa to pull on his boots. Who'd lit a fire under his arse?

"That bastard. He didn't die," Karrick said. "He didn't fucking die!"

Oh, God. He knows. He's seen Graham too.

"Who?" Jase asked quietly, acting puzzled as he dug one elbow against the floor and propped himself up. His muscles screamed at him to lie back down, but he felt at a disadvantage while lower and couldn't see Karrick as clearly as he'd like.

"None of your concern," Karrick said. "I need to go out. In the car. Somewhere up north a bit. I'll be back before you know it."

"What? Are you leaving me here like this?" The thought of being helpless, unable to do anything but stay in one place, had Jase's guts churning.

"Why not? It's not as though you have anywhere to be, is it?" Karrick eyed him shrewdly.

Jase shook his head, as if he were in complete compliance. "Of course not."

"So shut up then. I'd have left you there for hours anyway, as a lesson for your disobedience in going back to that Daniel person, so it makes no difference my leaving you here now."

Karrick rose then walked over to Jase. He hunkered down and held Jase's chin between finger and thumb. He pinched—hard. "You just stay here and have a think on our future. Think on your past and the mistakes you've made, too, and tell yourself that you won't ever make those mistakes again. Use this time as a way to reflect, to renew your life vows, and remember, I can log in any time and see what you're doing."

"I will," Jase said. "Think, I mean. I'll be doing a lot of thinking."

"Just make sure you do, cherub."

Karrick got up and left, the sound of the door being locked from the outside an anvil in Jase's belly. He closed his eyes and, while he thought Karrick's mind would be full of what he had to do next, Jase reached out to try to make contact with someone from his Team. He didn't hold out much hope, what with their connections being spotty at best, but he had to give it a go.

He had to warn them that Graham had gone to visit some woman called Sue, and that Karrick was hot on his tail, murder in his eyes.

* * * *

Karrick was pissed off beyond description. He'd only intended to nip into the Dreamstate to make sure Jase was being truthful with him. As far as he'd seen he was, so he'd prepared himself to return to the land of the living and maybe fuck Jase's arse some more. Something had stopped him, a presence, a scent he'd smelled before—one he shouldn't ever have smelled again.

Graham.

He'd spun to look behind him and, seeing no one, frowned in confusion. Perhaps Graham's essence had returned to the caves here after his death and that was what had got Karrick out of sorts and suspicious.

He'd walked over to the pool, just to make sure, and what he'd seen there had struck him like a solid punch to his stomach. Graham's image wavered on the water's surface, him in a car with some man Karrick had never seen before. They were discussing their destination, chatting as though they didn't know one another and were just being pleasant. Was this a snippet of Graham's past?

The rest of the image appeared—the dashboard, the road ahead—and on that dashboard was a newspaper. Folded, it was, with the title of it splashed in red across the top. And below that had been a date.

Today's date.

Karrick's mind had seemed to implode at that moment. Seeing red was an understatement. Everything he had been working toward whipped around him, in the pool, inside him, and he had the sense that it would all come crashing down around him because of that fucking man. Graham had a lot to answer for, and before he could wreak havoc, Karrick intended to reach him before he could.

He'd withdrawn from the Dreamstate, irate, the mess in his mind coalescing into one big mass of hate. And now he was in his car, belting it along the roads. eager to reach this place up north and find the man who had the potential to wreck everything. Graham was working for Rivald's Team now, he was sure of it, and whoever Graham had gone to visit may well help to snuff Morland's Team out. *His* Team.

"I will not have that," Karrick said to the empty road ahead. "I will not be thwarted."

He drove, a madman intent on doing battle, and it wasn't long before he came to some rough housing estate that had him turning up his nose. Who the hell would want to live here? Who would *choose* to live here? It wasn't his idea of a nice place to live, but then Karrick had expensive tastes, so anything below the standard of estate where *he* lived would appear nasty. It reminded him of where that Barry lived and brought on another fresh wave of anger.

Those people in Rivald's Team—they had to go. Really, they had to be dealt with so every single one of them ceased to exist. And whoever Graham was visiting with, well, they could be dealt with as well.

* * * *

"What?" Sue said, widening her eyes and shifting away from Graham on the sofa.

Her moving like that made him feel alone, crazy, her one word telling him what he'd suspected all along. That what he'd told her was too fantastical for any regular person to believe. He'd been right in the past to have just shoved her away by making out he didn't love her. But now he'd blurted the whole story out to make her understand the importance that she get to safety, he couldn't take it back. Couldn't unsay what had been said.

"I know it sounds mad," he said, reaching out for her only to have her recoil even more. "But it's true, I swear it. Everything I told you is true."

"Are you on drugs, is that it?" she asked, rising to go and stand on the other side of the room.

She had chosen to lean on the doorjamb, and the reason wasn't lost on him. It would be easier for her to escape, to get the fuck out of here, away from him. That he'd come across as insane was something he'd expected, but that she actually thought he was... Jesus Christ, it stung. Fucking stung.

"No," he said. "Not drugs, but I wish to God I *was* on them. Wish that was the explanation for all this. Hallucinations and whatever else comes with being high. But I'm not making this up—who the hell *could* come up with shit like this?—and what I've told you is the truth. We're wasting time. Karrick will come soon. He'll find you, know you're lying if you say I'm not here once I've gone." He folded his lips in on themselves and shook his head. "And he *will* kill you."

She widened her eyes again, but Graham got the sense it was more from her disbelieving him than anything else. She looked incredulous then changed her expression, which reflected that she was trying to work out how to help him — who to turn to for help.

"Sue," Graham said, going to rise then thinking better of it. If he stayed where he was she might not run. "If this were all a dream, a stupid thing I'd thought up, then what do you think my reasons are for telling you? I mean, come on. I told you I didn't love you to keep you safe, and I *know* you'd have me back if I admitted I'd made a mistake — so why would I feel the need to come out with this crap?"

"I don't know. Drugs do strange things to people."

She narrowed her eyes as if trying to see right into his soul. If she had that ability, she'd see many of the things he'd done, things he wasn't proud of. She'd also see the truth.

A swathe of light swept across the living room through the window, and Graham's stomach muscles bunched. He shifted his mind to semi-Dreamstate to try to see if whoever was driving that car was a danger to them, but there was a block there. Probably because all his emotions were wrapped up in Sue.

He returned to the here and now, conscious that his eyes going black might freak her the hell out.

She moved to the window then pulled the curtain across, leaning forward to peer outside. "Do you know anyone with a red Porsche?"

Oh, God. Oh, Jesus...

Graham bolted out of his seat. He strode to the window and nudged Sue aside, taking her place. Karrick stood at the end of the path, looking left then right. A knot of fear unraveled in Graham's gut, and for a moment he was unable to take action. He couldn't move, as if Karrick had immobilized him.

"It's him," he whispered. "Karrick."

Graham wanted to turn to look at Sue, to see if she believed him now, but he couldn't risk it. He had to keep his attention on the man outside.

"Then if he's as bad as you said he is, we have to leave," Sue said, her tone implying she was humoring him.

"This is *not* a fucking joke, Sue." He took a chance and looked away from the window to stare at her. If he could make her see how serious this was with his gaze... "Where does your back garden lead to? A path? The street behind? What?" His heart hammered, and fright was threatening to take up residence inside him.

She stared back at him, finally, *finally* showing him an expression that spoke of her possibly believing him—or that Karrick was a threat at least. "An alleyway, then at the end there's an entrance to the street behind."

"You need to use it. Now." He glared at her. "Now!"

"But I don't have any things. I need to pack!"

"What haven't you understood from what I've told you? He'll kill you. Isn't that reason enough to go without a suitcase full of clothes? Christ, just do it. Go!"

"Not without you," she said, fear in her eyes.

She rubbed her hands together, winding, winding, winding her fingers until he couldn't stand it anymore. He looked back out of the window, wishing she'd just do as he'd asked. Karrick was still standing at the end of the path. What the fuck was he doing? Trying to see inside before he knocked?

Graham erected a mindshield, hoping Karrick only thought Sue was in the house. If the man didn't think Graham was here—or that he'd even been here— perhaps he'd go away.

You don't believe that. You know he'll have come here to eradicate all threats. And for him to be here – he knows about me being alive. He fucking well knows.

Graham let the curtain fall back into place and a sudden sense of dread in doing so gripped hold of him. While he had been able to see Karrick he'd felt in control, but now, with just a curtain keeping him from seeing him...

"We need to leave," he said to Sue, walking toward her. He took her elbow and steered her out of the room, down the hallway, then into the kitchen. "We have to get out right away."

She tried to get her arm free but he gripped harder.

"No," he said. "Even if you still think I'm high, bear with me. Just...please, please do as I ask."

Worry must have shown on his face. She stopped tugging and let him lead her to the back door. She unlocked it then swung it wide. Graham stood in front of her and scanned the garden. Nothing was out there but a rotary washing line, all skeletal arms held up in what he fancied was exasperation – exactly what he was feeling along with a glut of terror and determination to get her to safety.

"Do you have a car?" he asked quietly.

"Yes. In a garage I rent."

"And where is that?"

"In the street behind. Next to the entryway down the alley."

"Your keys. Where are they?"

"What, my house keys?"

He loved her, but God, he wanted to shout a bit of sense into her right then. "Your *car* keys."

She reached out to a small wooden box situated on the wall beside the door. She opened it, revealing several sets of keys. Taking a bunch, which he presumed also had her house keys on it, she handed them to Graham.

"Right," he said, shoving them into his pocket. "It's time to go."

"Go where?" she asked, then bit her bottom lip.

"I don't know, but for the moment, anywhere other than here."

Chapter Twenty-Six

Barry was hacked off. They'd returned to his house after finding Graham's letters and now, after two hours had passed, they were still no closer to finding this Sue woman. There had been no address on her correspondence. The block to the Dreamstate seemed to be in place again. Leyton had gone into Barry's office to try to get information from Rivald on the woman but had come back out after an hour, exhausted and frustrated. Jessica was in there now. Fledgling as she was, she'd wanted to give it a go. At this point, they had to do whatever they could to get in contact with Rivald.

"So," Barry said, casting his gaze around the room at each of them in turn. "What the fuck do we do now? Graham's and Sue's whereabouts are unknown. Jase is at Karrick's and unreachable—you'd think because Jase is coming into his own he'd be able to get a message to one of us but he clearly can't. And Karrick? If he isn't with Jase, where the fuck he is, we don't know. But what if Karrick's been able to access the Dreamstate and knows everything that's going on?"

He sighed heavily. "I'm not happy about Jase being where he is. Yes, I know it's for a reason, but he isn't strong enough to do this, not strong enough against someone like Karrick. Fucking stupid to have gone there."

"Then maybe we ought to go and get him," Tag suggested.

Barry grimaced. "Yes, maybe we should. His silence isn't good. It's worrying me. I expect it's worrying you, too, Dan."

Daniel was sitting on the sofa, head back, eyes closed. "I didn't want him to go, didn't want him to do this, but…" He swallowed, shook his head. "He insisted he knew what he was doing. That he was the one to fix this mess." He opened his eyes and stared at Barry, his glassy gaze full of remorse.

Barry pursed his lips. Glanced at Tag then Leyton. "We all think we can fix this, yet to be honest, none of us have a bloody clue—not really. This is still so new to us. Well, not to you, Leyton."

Leyton paced in front of the window, his face scrunched up in what appeared to be pain. It didn't look pretty, what with his scars. Barry wondered about how Leyton felt to be so impotent. The man had always had access to Dreamstate, had always had his finger on the pulse. To be denied entry and not know what was going on must be playing havoc with him. Leyton never liked not being in control.

"I keep getting wisps of information," Leyton said. "But it isn't anything that makes sense. It's more like feelings, and I can't trust them because maybe it's just what I want to feel—or someone is making me feel them."

Barry bunched his fists. "Why didn't you say anything?" He had the urge to go over and shake

Leyton, slap him from here to kingdom come for being such a dick.

"Because of what I just said." Leyton stopped pacing and turned to face them all. "What if it's just hope on my part or planted information?"

"I don't give a shit *what* it is," Barry said. "Any information is better than this bloody silence we've endured so far. Tell us—whatever it is, fucking *tell* us!"

Jesus Christ, if I end up smacking him one, so help me God…

Leyton seemed to take forever to inhale then exhale Barry kept himself in check. Getting angry with anyone wasn't going to solve their dilemma. Tag reached out to take Barry's hand.

That's better. So much better…

"Karrick isn't at his place. Jase is there alone." Leyton frowned. "But the information came as me just knowing, as if I'd been told and it was a truth I knew. It wasn't an image, like it would usually be. Just…do you see what I've been trying to say? What if it *is* just a hope inside me?"

"And what if it isn't?" Barry snapped. "There's only one reason Karrick would leave Jase alone. Fucking hell!"

"Shall I go over there?" Leyton asked.

Barry turned to Tag for advice.

Tag nodded. "If Karrick isn't there, talk to Jase, see how things are. If Jase isn't in danger and feels he should stay, let him."

"What?" Barry said, widening his eyes and staring at Tag as though his man had lost his damn mind.

"Jase is the key, we've discovered that." Tag scrubbed at his chin. "There has to be a reason Jase is that key. If he's gone to Karrick's knowing, feeling it's the right thing to do, should we stop that? What if us interfering isn't in the plan—whatever that plan is, being as I still can't get my bloody head around it. What if we do more harm than good by removing him? We don't have much time, remember. The Winnowing..."

Dread pooled in Barry's gut, and he fought back a gag. This life he now led—one they all led—had been forced upon them, was something none of them—apart from maybe Leyton—wanted. A sense of unfairness drew sharp claws down his stomach lining, and he wanted to be sick.

Before he could answer, Jessica appeared in the doorway. Barry's heart leaped at the sight of her.

Please, let her have managed to get through...

"Did you...?" he began.

She shook her head, but it didn't seem to be in the negative, more to clear whatever floated around inside. Was Barry experiencing what Leyton had described? Feeling only hope, not truth?

"I didn't manage to get right into Dreamstate," she said. "But I did get there." She flopped onto the sofa beside Daniel.

"How far in?" Leyton asked.

"Literally one step. There were caves and the pool in the far distance. It was all dark behind me, beside me, and murky ahead. But I got there." She sighed, the air coming out of her in a juddering wave.

"Did you see anything?" Barry asked. "Get told anything?"

"Not full sentences, but enough for me to patch things together. It was windy there—I felt that was highly unusual—and the words or whatever the hell it was came to me on the breeze. Sort of shifted at me on the wind." She rested her head back and closed her eyes.

What, did she think she could go to sleep now? Barry resisted shouting at her.

Calming himself, he asked, "So, the information?"

"Oh," she said, sitting more upright and opening her eyes. "Karrick isn't with Jase. Jase is alone at his place. Those two things seem fairly certain. And Graham...I *think* he's found Sue. Can't be one hundred percent on that, though. But they're not safe."

Barry wanted to rage, to storm about the room, punching walls and getting his frustration out of him. *None* of them were safe until Karrick had been dealt with, but to know, to feel it in his bones, that Karrick had gone after Graham and Sue... Hopeless, it was all so fucking hopeless.

"I'm going to try to get to the Dreamstate," he announced.

Tag opened his mouth, but Barry held up a finger to stop him before he started to protest.

"I can try. Everyone else has," Barry said. "And if you're worried, Tag, then come with me. In the meantime, Leyton, go over to Karrick's place. If Karrick is there and you can take him out in your usual manner without coming to any harm yourself, do it."

Leyton nodded. "Oh, I will indeed."

He left the room at a run. The front door slammed, then Barry listened to the rumble of the Killer's VW van as he gunned it to life.

"What do we do?" Daniel asked.

"Sit tight," Barry said. "Hope Jase texts you. Sit with Jessica, because it looks to me as though she's falling asleep. She might be entering the Dreamstate again.

Watch over her. Any irregular breathing where you think it's bordering on dangerous, wake her."

Barry looked at Tag.

"And I'll be coming with you," Tag said.

Leaving the room, Barry went into his office, Tag close behind. Barry sat in his desk chair and stared at the ceiling. He was tired, God knew he was tired, but he wasn't relaxed enough to enable him to do what had to be done. Or to try. He closed his eyes, heard Tag take the seat in the opposite corner, and concentrated on clearing his mind. It was a difficult task with everything swirling around inside, but slowly, problem by problem, it all began to fade. One thought refused to be budged.

"What I can't stop worrying about," he said, "is the Winnowing. What it'll mean for mankind. Whether we'll even get through this."

"We will," Tag said. "You have to believe that. Otherwise, what's the point in us all being together like this? What's the point in any of it? We've all been chosen, dealt hands we didn't want, but we have to play them. If we don't..."

Barry shoved at the remaining issue in his head. It shifted a bit but still remained stubborn, clinging to his brain cells as though taunting him. "I don't think I'm going to manage this. Can't relax enough."

He heard Tag getting up. Felt the touch of Tag's hand on his knee.

"I'll deal with that," Tag said, easing Barry's legs open then going for his zipper.

"We don't...we shouldn't..." Barry gave up protesting.

"It's for the good," Tag said.

The blow job did what Barry had failed to do. It calmed his racing mind, increased his fluctuating heartbeat, and erased, for the moment of ejaculation, every thought he'd been thinking. As he came down from his high, Barry slumped in the chair, his whole body limp. He was aware of his deflated cock resting on his upper thigh. Of Tag stroking his hair back from his forehead. Of their ragged breathing.

"That's it," Tag said. "Keep your eyes closed and just *be*. No thinking. Just rest."

Barry floated through his mind, seeing nothing but blackness. He pushed away a pinch of frustration and did as Tag had asked.

Just be. Just sit here and forget it all for a little while. I'm so tired. So fucking tired.

The familiar fingers of sleep caressed him, clutching him gently, sweeping him along toward a blacker, more infinite area in his mind. He floated to it, glad of its pitch embrace, of how more stress was swiped away the closer to the blacker void he got. A breeze shunted over his face—it must have been Tag breathing—and he welcomed the coolness as it dried his sweaty face. He could have been on a beach with his eyes closed. He could have been anywhere at all other than his office. What he recognized was that finally he'd let go of all his frustration and felt able to allow the pressures to slide out of him, to drip away into a sea of confusion below, leaving him at peace for the first time is ages.

And there, in the distance, was the outline of a cave. Indistinct, but there all the same. A sense of euphoria stole over him, and he waited, not wanting to move in case he broke whatever tenuous tether held him here.

It didn't matter how weak the visual ahead of him was. He was in. Jesus Christ, he was in.

Chapter Twenty-Seven

Graham felt a bastard for what he was about to do, but he had no choice. They'd made it to Sue's car without incident, getting away with no one following them. He knew it wouldn't be long before Karrick picked up their trail, but for now, as they sat with the car idling down a remote track in the countryside, he had other things to worry about.

"Listen," he said, turning to look at Sue.

She had her elbow propped on the passenger-side door, her arm flat against the window. "I've done so much listening on this journey. I don't think I want to hear anymore. Why did you come to see me if you knew it would put me in danger? Why?"

"Because...because I needed you. Needed the strength you give me. You're my anchor."

"Is that what you call an ex-girlfriend these days? An anchor?" She rolled her eyes.

"It's more than that. You're the one who gives me the strength I need to be who I am. To do what I have to do. I told you what happened to me. All my strength had almost been depleted. I have a role to play, one I wish I didn't, but whatever... I didn't have enough energy to do it unless I saw you."

She sighed, her exhalation flipping up a lock of her hair. "So, if you're to be believed, you've been chosen to somehow help save the world, right? For the general public to remain unaware of this Dreamstate and that Winnowing you went on about, you have to...you have to do what, exactly?"

"You don't need to know all the details, but yes, that's about it."

"And even though you love me, you put me in danger anyway. For—how do I put it?—the greater good. Thanks for that." She laughed. "I mean, Sue's only one person. What's the loss of her life compared to the other millions in the world, eh?"

"When you put it like that, it sounds awful."

"Because it is."

A stony silence invaded the car then, wrapping around them, around Graham, as though it were a real thing, all cold and spiteful. He wanted to break it but didn't know what the hell to say. She was right, he was risking her life to save others, but that hadn't been his intention. He hadn't realized...

Yes, you did. You knew there was a risk of Karrick following, yet you went to Sue's anyway. Selfish bastard. She doesn't deserve this.

Which is why he had to do what he had to do.

"I'm sorry," he said, reaching out to touch her arm.

She flinched so he took his hand away. Dropped it to his lap where it rested, useless and still.

"But there's a way around this," he said. "A place I can take you, where you'll be safe."

"Oh, jolly good," she said, sarcasm coming through loud and clear. "So if you can take me to this safe place, why aren't we there already? And how come, if this Karrick man is so all-seeing, all-knowing, you can take me there without him finding out about it? Your story has so many holes, Graham. I don't know why I even pined for you. Why I even thought you'd come to your senses one day and we'd get back together. Why—"

He flashed his arm out and secured his hand to the base of her neck. He squeezed, hard, and registered the look of surprise she gave him—surprise liberally sprinkled with fear and hate. He pressed harder, willing her to go under quickly, to not flail her arms and fight him. She didn't. Her eyes fluttered closed, and she slumped in the seat, head flopping to one side.

"I love you," he said. "I've always loved you. And you'll understand soon why I did this."

He freed his arm then got out of the car, opening the trunk, shoving items aside to make some space. There was a blanket rolled up at the back, and he grabbed it, putting it to one side. He strode to the passenger door, opened it, then unfastened Sue's seatbelt. Once she was in his arms, he put her in the trunk, hating himself all the while but knowing, yet again, what he was doing was for the best. He tucked the blanket around her, stroked her hair away from her face, then leaned in to plant a soft kiss on her temple.

Easing out one corner of the brake light a bit, he was satisfied he'd created a big enough gap. At least she'd have a little fresh air coming in once he closed the lid. And when he closed it, heard the click of it locking, everything felt so final. So *The End.* What if his plan didn't work?

It has to. Bloody has to.

In the driver's seat, he pulled away from the side of the track then drove the car toward a stand of trees.

Once there, he shut the engine off, locked the doors so he could buy time if Karrick turned up, then settled back in the seat with his eyes closed.

He was heading to Rivald, to beg him a favor. To take Sue's essence into his cave and keep her safe – to the point that even if Karrick found then killed her, she would come back to life once this mess had been taken care of.

All Graham had to hope was that he could get into Dreamstate.

If he couldn't, fuck knows what he'd do.

* * * *

Jase watched everything playing out inside his head, frustrated to hell and back that he couldn't do a damn thing to help. Yes, he was in Dreamstate, had gotten there pretty easily, in fact, but he hadn't been able to pass any information on to the Team. They were oblivious to the potential horror that loomed ahead regarding the Team possibly losing Graham. If he could just finish getting information, maybe, when he woke up, he'd be able to free himself from those God-awful bindings and get to a phone, letting the Team know what was going on. He risked Karrick finding out, but if his purpose in this hideous play was to take the role of someone who might lose his life in trying to save others, so be it.

He'd miss Dan, though. Yes, he'd miss him and what they could have had.

Don't think like that. Be positive. You're here to do a job – so do it!

He felt someone else was there, got a whiff of Barry but couldn't for the life of him see where he was. So he concentrated on the cave, on getting himself to the pool. It was windy, so much so that it jostled his hair every which way, chilled his bare skin. But those were minor irritations, something he could endure. Letting the Team down wasn't. The shame and guilt he'd feel if he did that wasn't something he wanted to contemplate.

He pushed forward, finding it surprisingly easy to reach the pool. He stared down into the water, immediately arrested by the visuals playing out on the surface. Graham had stuffed Sue into the trunk of a car, and Karrick was driving around close to them, knowing they were around somewhere but not the exact location.

A shift of movement caught his attention, to his right, and he snapped his head to the side to catch what it was. Someone other than Barry was in Dreamstate with him, and instead of feeling relieved, it scared him. What if it was Karrick? What if Karrick had manipulated it so that his image jostled on the pool but he wasn't really trying to find Graham? What if...?

A shadowy figure darted into one of the caves, and Jase's breath caught in his throat. He hadn't been able to see who it had been, whether it was Barry or someone else from his Team. Something compelled him to find out, and he left the pool, floating toward the cave entrance. He went inside, carried—or pushed, rather—by the breeze. The figure rounded a corner and went out of sight. Jase continued in its wake, fear trying to make him turn back and get out, excitement and the knowledge that he had to do this spurring him on.

He came to a room cut out of the rock and saw a door, closed, but knew it was unlocked. He moved to stand before it then pressed his ear against the cool surface. Voices jangled around behind it, and he strained to work out if he recognized the speakers.

"Please, do this for me."

Graham?

"Just keep her safe. Bring her here. We don't have much time." Yes, it was Graham, a begging tone to his voice.

There was a sigh, long and loud, then, "This is becoming out of control. I cannot just do these things. I cannot influence what happens. You know that. And what would I be doing after all but holding a loved one in stasis until whatever happens, happens? You should not have visited her. Should have called upon her anchorage from far away, as you have done in the past. Yet you were impatient, were you not? Impatient to get your strength back."

"I knew time wasn't on our side. It was all I could think to do. Seeing her, it brought my energy back full force. Now I can do what has to be done."

"Yes, you can, but to what cost? I have to step in, to hold her essence here so you can get a job done — one that I am not meant to have any part of. If it is found out that I helped — and I have already done so by keeping you safe, holding you here — then, even if we win, we will lose."

"Who's going to know?" Graham asked. "I won't be telling anyone."

Laughter, raw and sharp. "Says you, who defected from the opposing Team."

"But I —"

"Yes, yes, I am well aware you are faithful to us now, that you will not waver in your allegiance. Oh, just go, would you? Go and do what needs to be done."

"Sue?"

"I will keep her. And if she does not come back to life afterwards—providing *he* finds then kills her, which I think he will—I do not want any blame delivered to my door. You must get rid of him before that happens. With him gone, the Winnowing will go much more smoothly. Another Killer will be appointed for their Team, one who has to get used to the role and might be unstable as he or she settles in. We might well win then things will go back to normal. Do you understand your task, Graham?"

"Yes, yes, I do."

"Then go. I do not want you coming back here until it is all over. The risk is too great."

There was a shuffling sound from the room, so Jase stepped away, keeping his footsteps quiet. Once he'd backed out of the cut-out space, he intended to run like the wind, back to the pool and the anonymity of the shadows there. Wait for Barry to appear. The shuffling grew closer, and if he didn't hurry, Graham would come out and see him standing there. More shuffles. Jase cocked his head, listening for them to sound again. They did. Right behind him.

He spun round, colliding into Karrick's chest, the tops of his arms gripped by the one man he didn't want gripping them. Jase opened his mouth to let out a shout of warning, but Karrick stared at him so intently Jase found himself mute.

"Shut that pretty, deceiving little mouth of yours before I shut it permanently," Karrick said. He shook him hard. "And to think I thought you believed in me, that you were on my side. I should have known..."

Jase wanted to lie, to tell Karrick that he'd gotten it all wrong, that Jase *was* on his side. No words formed, instead cluttering up his mouth, jostling with their need to come out.

Karrick turned Jase around so he faced the door.

"The man I'm after will come out of there in a minute," Karrick said, breath hot and nasty on Jase's ear. "And when he does, you're going to kill him."

"What?" Jase mouthed, the word a silent gust of breath. Goosebumps peppered his skin, and he had the urge to let his bladder go, to piss where he stood.

"Yes," Karrick said. "And then, once you've done that, we're going to find that Sue woman and you're going to kill her too."

Jase shook his head then cursed himself for it. He was supposed to make Karrick think he was with him, that he'd do his bidding. Quickly nodding, staring at the door handle as it was turned down, Jase rapidly tried to work out what to do. He prayed that Graham would take action, take matters out of Jase's hands. He prayed that he wouldn't have to kill anyone, even if that someone could be brought back to life later on. But most of all, he prayed for this to be over, a nightmare, a bad dream he'd wake up from to find himself in Dan's arms. Safe, nothing strange going on, the only thing they had to worry about being what they were going to have for breakfast.

Despite his situation, he grinned. Fear undoubtedly played a part in that smile coming into being, but he knew, deep down, that it had been borne of him not knowing what the fucking hell to do. How could he kill Graham when the man was clearly an important Team member and someone who was possibly needed for a successful Winnowing? How could he interfere with the way things were supposed to go, the way fate had planned them?

Please. If fate has got a hand in this, please, please show me the way. I can't do this alone. I'm not strong enough. I'm not —

The door swung open.

Jase stared wide-eyed at a man with horns and hooves. A man so terrifying to look at that Jase almost turned away. But his eyes, his presence, held Jase in place along with Karrick's arms.

"You," the horned man said, shifting his gaze from Jase to Karrick. "You are such an irritating thorn in my side."

Chapter Twenty-Eight

Leyton pulled up in Karrick's street, parking down the way a bit from his place in case Karrick was actually there. The last thing he needed was to be spotted. He sat in his van and erected a mindshield — whether it would work or not remained to be seen. If he couldn't enter Dreamstate, his other powers might also have been blocked. Still, it was best to be prepared.

He got out of his van, locked it, then walked along the sidewalk toward Karrick's place. He glanced at the windows. Lights were on and he sensed someone was inside but couldn't quite get a handle on who it was. If he believed his instincts he'd go ahead and just ring the doorbell, but the messages he'd received at Barry's had been indistinct and he wasn't sure whether he could trust them or not.

My tool pouch. I've forgotten my tools.

Annoyed with himself, he traced his steps back to his van. Inside the back, he reached under his little bed and felt for his pouch. There it was, the familiar and beloved feel of it beneath his fingers. He tugged it out, caressing it with one hand then hugging it to his chest. It hadn't let him down in the past and he had no doubt it wouldn't let him down now. The implements inside had done all manner of terrible things to people, resulting in their deaths. He just had to hope they'd result in Karrick's.

Am I strong enough to take him on?

"Yes," he whispered, the burn of what he loved doing best beginning to ignite inside him.

He took a moment for it to grow, to spread through him, giving him the energy he needed to fight this wicked, wicked man. His only issue was whether Karrick having a better state of mind, more power behind him because of it, would be a disadvantage to Leyton. Karrick might use his mind to get at Leyton, implant hideous images inside his head, throwing him off course, off his purpose.

Was it wise to face him now?

"I have to," he muttered. "The Team are relying on me."

He stood then strapped his pouch around his middle, ensuring the flap was open so he could easily grab any weapon he needed. He slipped on his gloves—never again would he make the mistake of not wearing them, especially if Rivald couldn't intervene and erase evidence. Outside, he relocked the van then went back to stand outside Karrick's place. He took a deep breath and a second or two to try to see inside the house.

He couldn't.

Still, the thrill of the chase, of the kill, was careening through his veins now, and he felt nothing would stop him from moving forward, doing what needed to be done. He approached the front door, nerves flickering, excitement skipping, and pressed the bell.

No one came to answer.

He pressed the bell again, rewarded by a muffled shout. So *was* Karrick in there, stopping Jase from speaking with a hand clamped over his mouth? Frustrated that he couldn't obtain the answer by going into Jase's mind, Leyton bent down to peer through the glass where a door curtain hadn't quite been pulled across properly. He saw a hallway, dark, but that darkness wasn't absolute owing to light spilling from what he could only assume was a living room. Was that the back of a sofa he could see there?

The muffled sound came again—and that's all it was, a sound, not words—and he decided that in order to get the job done, he'd have to break in. He glanced left then right, seeing no one in the street, only cars hugging the curbs and huge oak trees dotted intermittently along the pavement, their branches overhanging the road like the overprotective hands of a mother.

Leyton had no idea what that might be like, to have a mother who shielded him.

Stop it. Don't think about her now. She'll only distract you if you let her inside your mind.

He concentrated on the here and now.

This was a classy area, and he suspected that if he made a noise while breaking in, the police would be called in an instant. He needed to think this through, to get in then out as swiftly as possible.

He took off his sweater then draped it over his shoulder. Selecting a mallet from his pouch, he tested the weight of it in his hand. Satisfied it would do the trick, he wrapped his sweater around the end, tying the sleeve cuffs to keep it in place. After a deep breath and a moment to let the burn inside him get hotter, he swung the mallet. It crashed through the glass in the front door with a dull thud, the only other sounds the light tinkle of glass hitting the floor inside and his heavy breathing. Mallet in one hand, he reached through the hole he'd made with his other, unlatched the door, then pushed it open.

His heart pounded overly loud, his pulse a jack hammer of *whoomphs* in his ears. He sucked in a deep breath then stepped in, curious as to why no one inside had come into the hallway to investigate.

Perhaps they're waiting for me to appear. To catch me by surprise. Except they won't. I'm ready.

He walked down the hall, glass crunching beneath his boots, and came to a stop outside the door ahead. He peered through the crack near the hinges and spotted Jase naked on a sofa, his arms and legs pulled up behind him, wrists and ankles bound. Leyton admired the sight of him for a moment—not in a sexual way, but for the position he was in. A glorious position, one he could imagine using on future victims. All the easier to gut them...

Shaking his head and blinking, he checked as much of the room as he could, considering what range the crack afforded. No one else appeared to be in the room. Jase was asleep, making those strange sounds, and Leyton surmised he was having a nightmare. Poor boy.

Leyton searched the rest of the place, finding each room empty. So he'd been right. Karrick *had* gone, and he could only assume he'd gone to find Graham and Sue. The problem was, Leyton had no idea how long he'd been gone and what time he was likely to be back. He had to work fast.

Upon returning to the living room, he unbound Jase, wincing at the red raw skin on his ankles and wrists where the chain links had dug into his flesh. The young man's body was peppered with bruises and purple marks. Karrick would pay for those as well as everything else.

He shook Jase. "Wake up. Jason, it's me, Leyton. Please, wake up now."

Jase thrashed around, his arms and legs flailing now they were free. Leyton jumped back to save himself being caught by the limb weapons, frowning because Jase was still deep in slumber. Affording himself a longer reach, Leyton poked him with the mallet and again asked him in a strong and firm voice to wake up.

Jase's eyes flickered.

Leyton poked him again. "Wake *up*, damn you!"

Jase opened his eyes. Wide. His stare was strange, one that belonged to a madman, not some young snip of a thing. Leyton stepped back, the mallet tight in his fist, unnerved and a little confused by his emotions. Him, unnerved? That wasn't usual.

Something was going on, something Jase had no control over.

Karrick? Is he controlling him?

"Stop that," Leyton shouted, dropping the mallet then lunging forward.

He gripped Jase by the tops of his arms, startled when Jase struggled to such a degree that it was clear he hadn't really woken up. Making a snap decision, he let go one of an arm then slapped Jase hard across the face. Jase lurched to the side, and Leyton pushed against it, shoving him upright again. Jase panted, his breathing flow punctured by silent ellipses, his eyes glassy and obviously unfocussed.

"I need to get you out of here," he said, knowing, as he'd spoken, that taking a naked man out of here and being seen would possibly bring a shitload of hassle.

He pushed Jase backwards on the sofa so he rested against it then left the room in search of clothing. He couldn't find Jase's so opted for something of Karrick's instead—Nike sweats and a Superdry T-shirt—going back into the living room intending to dress him.

Jase was standing in the middle of the room. Leyton was ashamed to have noticed Jase's cock was shriveled, probably from the fear he'd been experiencing in his nightmare. Jase's mouth was moving but no sound emerged. It was a surreal moment, staring at him, wondering how the devil he could make Jase come out of whatever stupor he was in.

Jase jolted, as though he'd been pushed from behind, and the echo of a gunshot ricocheted through Leyton's mind. Jase ducked, making Leyton do the same, and the pair of them stared at one another on their haunches, Jase frowning, his expression one of bewilderment.

"Are you awake now?" Leyton asked.

Jase blinked. Nodded.

"Good. You need to get these on. I have to take you back to Barry's." He tossed the clothes at Jase.

"I just killed someone," Jase said, staring into space. "I just…killed someone."

"Yes, yes, it feels very real in a nightmare, doesn't it?" Leyton rose to his feet. "But I must say, it isn't half as thrilling as it is in real life. Killing someone is…beautiful."

Jase shook his head, remaining where he crouched. "It isn't," he said. "Not when it was a member of our Team."

"Don't be silly." Leyton took his arm and hauled him upright. "Our Team are all perfectly safe." *I hope.*

"They're not. None of us are. And Karrick, he'll be coming here for me soon." His gaze was unwavering. Odd. "I have to be here. I have to stay so he thinks I'll do whatever he wants, so I can find out what he plans to do next."

"No, you can't." He pulled the T-shirt over Jase's head. "You must leave now. None of us can seem to enter Dreamstate properly, and we haven't heard from you in quite some time, so it's clear you haven't been able to get through. It's too dangerous to leave you here without lines of communication. Barry would be very angry with me if I don't take you back now. Come along—lift that leg so I can get these bottoms on you."

Jase obeyed. "I was in Dreamstate."

Leyton snapped his head up. "Pardon?"

"I was in Dreamstate. Graham was there."

"Oh, thank goodness. And Sue?"

"She's in the trunk of a car."

Leyton frowned, trying to soak the information in. "I see."

"Karrick made me kill Graham. I shot one of our Team. He went down. He fell against a horned man."

"Right. Right. Lift your other leg, come along."

With Jase dressed, Leyton led him out into the street then down the pavement to his van. He helped Jase get in—a lethargy and heaviness seemed to have taken over Jase's body—then climbed inside himself. He chose not to engage Jase in conversation on the journey back to Barry's. The whole incident had left him feeling a little discombobulated and a lot annoyed that he hadn't been able to allow the *burn* to fully slice through him. Oh, how he'd wanted to kill Karrick, to rid them all of the pest that he was. It had been such a long time since he'd murdered someone.

He sighed. How he missed his little hobby.

* * * *

Karrick was livid. How dare that damn chit leave Dreamstate without his permission? He couldn't deal with that now, though. No, now he had a snarling Rivald standing in front of him. Graham was behind Rivald. The shot had gone wide—that bloody Jase hadn't even been able to get *that* right—and it would take all of Karrick's charm and persuasion to get out of this unharmed. Of course, Rivald wouldn't be able to do a damn thing, even if he wanted to, but Graham may well have a surge of new power sitting inside him since he'd made contact with his anchor.

Bloody woman.

Karrick wasn't prepared to take the chance of fighting a man with brand-new energy bubbling around inside him. Dangerous, that. Besides, he preferred to creep up behind his prey and stab them in the back, literally. And wouldn't that be justice? Graham had stabbed him in the back by going to the other side. Karma was such a bitch. He almost laughed at that but kept himself in check.

"Leave," Rivald said, "before Morland becomes aware of what you have done. You are not supposed to be in my cave."

Karrick did laugh then. "Morland won't mind. I'm just doing my job, after all. Killing members of the opposing Team."

"Not in here," Rivald said. "You are not allowed in my cave under any circumstances. I could contact Morland, tell him that you have broken the rules and it will ensure this…this fight comes to an end."

"So do that." Karrick smirked. "Tell him. Win by default."

"I will not." Rivald glared at him. "I prefer, much as it is possible suicide for my Team to do so, to play by the rules. Let things occur as they should. That is how it is supposed to be done. Now go."

Karrick couldn't believe that this man, this horned bastard, was prepared to lose by allowing Karrick to leave. Was he mad?

"As you wish," Karrick said. "But you'll regret this day."

Rivald didn't answer. Karrick looked at Graham, who appeared ready and willing to pounce.

"I'll see you outside," Karrick said. "*After* I've seen to your good lady."

* * * *

Jessica stood one step inside Dreamstate. Darkness surrounded her, cloying and as real as a quilt, cocooning her, pressing into her. She found it difficult to breathe so concentrated on taking air in then letting it out, regulating it so she wasn't bordering on panic. She thought she smelled a hint of Barry's aftershave, but the shadows around her were so deep she couldn't see him. She stared ahead, at the caves and the pool, knowing she wouldn't be able to reach them. Perhaps if she stayed here for long enough she'd pick something up. Any information was better than none.

Someone came out of Rivald's cave, a man by the look of it, judging by the height and breadth. She stopped herself from breathing rapidly, repeating over and over in her mind that if she just kept quiet, just kept it together, everything would be all right. The man walked toward her. Of course he would. This was the only exit into the real world. How would she manage to keep out of sight? He'd feel her here, even if she pushed into the deep shadows to her left. He'd sense it — any Team member would.

Oh, God, it's Karrick.

She swallowed the sudden lump in her throat and stepped left, trying to merge with the darkness, to be at one with it. Karrick came closer, then another person exited Rivald's cave. She strained to see who it was, relief sprouting inside her like unruly weeds when she realized it was Graham. Would Sue follow him out?

With Karrick only a few feet away, now that she knew Graham was alive, Jessica retreated, reversing out of Dreamstate and back to the sofa beside Daniel.

She opened her eyes, looked at him and said, "Graham... He's okay. Thank God he's okay."

"You got in again?" Daniel asked.

She nodded. "I think Barry was there. I smelled him. And Karrick was there too. He and Graham came out of Rivald's cave."

Then it hit her. What were they *both* doing in Rivald's cave? Karrick and Graham were on separate sides now.

Or were they?

Chapter Twenty-Nine

Barry grounded himself in the lethargy of release and extended his senses outwards. Fragments of motion and sound reached him.

Place is like fucking Grand Central Station.

Images drifted close to the surface of his mind then disappeared again before he could get a clear sense of them. It felt like people passing on a crowded street, or the vague press of suggestion and promise on a sweaty dance floor. He knew he was dredging up comparisons, but it all amounted to one truth. He wasn't the only one here. And it wasn't just another soul, perhaps Rivald, inhabiting this in-between state. There were many consciousnesses, many spirits floating in and out of his perception.

Rivald, of course, was easy. His foggy smugness permeated everything, though now it was underlain with the taint of uncertainty very unlike the master of his fate Barry was used to. He sensed weakness in the horned man, a vulnerability he would have given anything for just a few short months before. When the Dreams that had plagued him his entire life had come to a head and he'd discovered the underlying realm of terror he was forced to be a part of, he would have given anything for one small weakness in the creature he felt was to blame.

Now that very weakness he'd prayed so hard for was evident, and if he was smart, if he was the man worthy of Tag, he would take advantage. He would strike at the heart of the beast and gain his freedom from the horror his life had become.

The fog swirled around his feet, climbed his legs, gripping the denim of his jeans and clinging damply to his thighs. It crawled over him with sick suggestion, unnervingly like the slip of fresh dribbling down suddenly bare skin and he jerked back.

Get the fuck off!

To his horror, his dick apparently had no discernment between this creeping, horrific touch and Tag's loving caresses. Barry flailed, heard the faint but distinct creak of his office chair and the rattle of wheels over hardwood and the thud of the chair against the wall. He brushed at the foggy tendrils and managed, for the moment, to squirm away from the disturbing intimation.

Once more, he was standing in a place apart but linked to the cave and pool of Rivald's realm. The press of souls surrounded him again, but this time he could trace the foggy slips of connection to a glimpse of a blond, frightened being, a swath of unformed, untried but determined terror, and with that, a cold implacability covered in scale and a cracking crust of rotting flesh. The sense of that essence was all the more disturbing for being, at its core, human. Twisted, jealous, greedy human with so little connection to the virtues that Tag and Jessica and Daniel represented for Barry's own Team.

He knew, in that instant, he was sensing Karrick, a broken man, divided and without anchor to that which made him whole and redeemable. And the ball of burning fear he held in his grip was Jase. It had to be. There was no other explanation. There was a link between them. It was slick with an oily reed that flowed from Karrick and coated Jase in a thin layer of slime.

Barry shuddered and thought to reach out and touch Jase, sure his touch alone would clear that cruel coating from his precious skin, clean his soul of the taint Karrick was smothering him with. At the last instant, Barry thought better of the gesture and sank back into the mist. Jase had to clean his own soul of the disquiet and twisted desire Karrick awoke in him. He had to fight this demon on his own, because it was his demon, just as the bottle was Barry's.

Each of them had their own battles to fight and this strange, unhealthy desire for Karrick's violence was one Jase had to battle for himself. His reward would be the clean, trusted control Daniel could offer him, but Jase was the one who had to find the difference between the two and decide what he wanted. No one could do it for him.

Barry turned his attention to the faint, pale presence of a delicate nature that could only be Jessica. She was so ill suited to this life, and Barry mourned for her the losses she'd endured. But he knew she was so much stronger than she thought she was. She could put that tough, defensive face on because she had to, and she could protect herself, her heart and soul, in ways Leyton could only dream of doing for her. But it was that purity Leyton was drawn to, whether he knew it or not. It was her inner calm he needed, and Barry withdrew from her, his distance from her spirit being the protection she needed here.

That left the solid wall of fog that was Rivald and also, the confusion that lurked behind it. More of Karrick's twisted intent spoiled the honorable core of that consciousness. Barry sensed that this person, whoever it was, was not only terrified of Karrick, it was in thrall to him, so obsessed with the threat of Karrick that it clouded his judgment, caused him to make unbearably bad choices.

Graham. What have you done?

There was something very wrong with that soul, that person or thing directing Karrick. Something reaching, thin and fading. Barry cringed back from direct contact. It was wrong. Graham was wrong too, in a way that made Barry's skin crawl.

"Very good, Barry."

Rivald's thick fog crept over Barry's body, too intimate and unsettling, demanding his attention, and he shrank back from the wrongness of Graham's presence.

"I'm proud of you, Barry. You see so much more deeply than the others. When you wake, just remember what you saw here. I can't give you more than that."

Fog slid over Barry's skin, covering him, trailing over places Barry wasn't okay with and he tried to shrink away from that, too, but how did one avoid the air?

"Tag." His voice was small, uncertain in his own ears and he squirmed, twisting this way and that to free himself of the unwanted contact.

A hot, dry touch encircled both his wrists, holding him fast and he writhed harder, more frantic to get the cold fog off his skin. Once again, his cock ignored his brain, responding to the slippery coolness. His nipples hardened and he whimpered, begging for Tag, for the caress he knew and craved to override this creeping, sensual exploration.

Too far, Rivald! His mind screamed and his heart shriveled at the feel of what was happening to his body. *Stop. You can't have this. It's Tag's!*

A harsh, cold chuckle echoed in his head. *"In case you thought the only Tools at my disposal were to threaten your anchor, Barry, I can, in fact, take whatever I want."*

Something infinitely cold and implacable curled about his cock and balls. A pressure, disconcertingly hard, throbbed at the private entrance to his body, demanding entrance, and Barry screamed.

Was Rivald touching him? Or was it Graham? Or even Karrick? He was confused as to why Graham's soul seemed tainted here, when Graham had been so amenable in the real world. Did Graham carry some kind of passenger—did he own a double soul, one good, one bad? Was the bad side touching Barry in ways it shouldn't be?

Fuck.

"Barry!" Tag's face loomed out of the darkness.

Tag's familiar hands closed around his wrists, clamping painfully tight, holding Barry down, and his voice, hard and demanding, wedged its way into his consciousness.

"Tag?" Barry's breath betrayed him and stole the sound from his lips, leaving only the shape of his lover's name on the stale air in the room, unheard.

"I'm here," Tag assured him. "Barry, I'm here. I have you."

"He'll take me," Barry whispered. "God help me, Tag, he'll take anything."

"No." One of Tag's hands clamped over Barry's jaw, forcing Barry's head still. Tag's blue eyes bored into

Barry's, his gaze controlling and sharp. "He can't take what's mine, Barry, no matter what he says."

"He can. He...did?"

"No." Tag closed his mouth over Barry's and kissed him, hard and deep. "No. He didn't, and he can't. You belong to me."

Barry nodded, a miniscule motion allowed by Tag's grip on him.

"Now get up," Tag ordered, drawing Barry out of the office chair and pushing it out of the way. He turned them both, stood behind Barry and shoved him down so Barry's chest thudded hard against the desk, knocking the air out of him.

"No one fucks you but me. We've established this." Tag pulled the arm he held behind Barry and clamped it there against his back. "You Dreamers need a strong hand, it seems."

Barry whimpered again, the feel of cold wetness fresh over his skin, in his mind, crowding his heart.

"Spread your legs for me, Barry," Tag ordered, bringing Barry's attention back to his demands. "Spread. Now." He kicked Barry's ankle. "Wide."

Some faint but practical part of Barry knew this was foolish, fucking now, when the rest of their team was just down the hall, waiting for them. But the greater, needier part of him acquiesced to Tag's will, because Tag was safe. Tag was strong and sure. Stronger than Rivald, Barry was sure. More real than any dream could ever be.

He groaned when Tag pressed a cool, lubed finger against his hole then forced inside, followed quickly by another then a third.

"I'm not going to fuck you now, Barry," Tag whispered, leaning his hard, hot body over Barry's back and thrusting his three fingers deep, spreading and working Barry open. "I noticed you have a stash of toys in here. Brought them down from the bedroom when I was out of town, did you?"

Barry whimpered and managed an abbreviated nod.

"You're so needy."

Barry gulped down an undignified sound when Tag's fingers left his body, removing their punishing motion from him. He didn't want the sensations Tag was overwhelming him with to stop.

"But I like that about you. So this is perfect." Something else, cold and harder than a flesh-and-blood cock, pressed at Barry's opening, spreading him mercilessly as it entered him. He gasped into the stretch and concentrated hard on not flinching, not tightening himself further in protest at the brutal invasion.

It spread and spread him, seeming to get wider than he could accommodate before popping inside, then he felt the flange of a butt plug against his flesh and his hole closed around the thick shaft, holding the bulk of it inside his body.

"Needy and a greedy son of a bitch," Tag whispered into his ear. "I fucking love that about you." He hauled Barry up and turned him around, pushing him back to sit on the edge of the desk.

The feel of the plug inside him made Barry moan desperately.

Tag grinned at him, a hard, hungry light in his eyes. "Think about that for a while, Barry, and remember who owns you. Not that creepy horn-head."

Tag took a kiss, then, thrusting his tongue deep, leaned heavily on Barry and pushed his arse against the desk, letting the plug grind deep and his jeans rub painfully on Barry's leaking hard-on. When he finally drew back, Barry could only wish he'd been properly ravaged. As it was, Tag left him hanging, hard, desperate.

"Later," Tag promised. "When they're all gone." He nodded toward the partially open office door. "And this shit is all over. You'll be so thoroughly fucked, you won't know which way is up."

Barry could only nod his compliance. If he tried to make any sound at all, he knew it would be to beg.

"Sit there with that plug in your arse," Tag said. "Let the feel of it remind you who you belong to. Send the thoughts you come up with back to Rivald. Let him know he can't have you." Tag breathed heavily, as though fighting back anger at the fact he couldn't go to Dreamstate and kick ten rounds of shit out of Rivald. "Go on, tell him. If you got to Dreamstate, the portal must be working properly now, which means he'll hear your message loud and clear."

Barry shook his head. "I'm not so sure if it *was* Rivald. Something was fucking odd there. Like I had a glimpse into a very bad soul—there could have been three or four—and I didn't know which one belonged to which person. Karrick was there." Barry frowned, lifting his arse a little to alleviate the pressure. "Maybe he screwed with my mind, with how I interpreted things."

Rivald had dallied with Barry in that way before, hinting that he'd like more than servitude from Barry as a Team member, but never, ever had he been so rude as to push further than was decent. Much as Rivald was a strange beast, Barry couldn't believe he'd been the one to touch him. And as for Graham being bad—no, he reckoned that information had been planted in his head. It had to have been. And the voice being Rivald's, giving him the impression that Graham was bad...

Suddenly, all the coins dropped into the correct slots and he knew what had happened.

"That fucking *bastard!*" he said, launching himself off the desk. He reached around to remove the butt plug, tossing it into a partially open drawer. The cleaning of it could wait until later—Tag fucking Barry could definitely wait until later.

"What is it?" Tag asked, helping Barry fasten his pants.

"Karrick. Oh, he's good. So much craftier than we thought. He made me think…" Barry shivered. "He produced fog, as though it was Rivald, and made me think Rivald *touched* me like he wanted… He knew it would send me crazy, that I'd want to kill Rivald—and that would save Karrick the damn job. And as for Graham and me thinking he was bad—same result. I'd kill Graham for Karrick. Shit."

"You said there could have been four there. Explain."

"Six. I meant Six. Jessica, Karrick, Graham, Rivald, Jase and something else. Some kind of evil…*thing* that I assumed was a part of Graham, because that's what Karrick wanted me to think but—"

"It was the thing that drives Karrick?"

Barry nodded, finishing the task of making himself look decent. "So we need to find out where Karrick is and kill him, because if he goes back to Jase now with that *thing* inside him, Jase…isn't going to make it out of this alive."

"Fuck." Tag winced.

"Yeah, fuck."

Chapter Thirty

Karrick allowed himself a moment to chuckle. He sat in his Porsche on the roadside, letting the ripple of laughter flicker through him. Barry — what a complete and utter dick. The man had believed Rivald had touched him, that his master wanted him in *that* way. Of course, that was what Karrick had wanted Barry to think, but the fact that Barry had actually swallowed that line of bullshit... Well, it was something Karrick could have a good roar about afterwards, when the battle had been won and the Winnowing had taken place.

He sobered, telling himself that the time for giggling wasn't now. He couldn't afford to waste any more precious minutes. Quickly, he went through what he'd learned in Dreamstate.

One, Graham had ensured Sue was in stasis, safe in Dreamstate. The only way Karrick could change that was to find the woman, infiltrate her mind and convince her to return to her body. Once he'd done that, he could kill her properly.

Two, he had to deal with Graham. With the masters saying they couldn't intervene during the Winnowing, Karrick knew Rivald had lied about that. He must have had a hand in Graham's miraculous recovery, so the horned beast spouting that he was keeping out of things had been horse crap. And, much to Karrick's surprise, when it came right down to it, Graham wasn't a coward, he'd made that much clear. The man had opted to return to his body and continue his mission to help the other Team. Yes, Graham would also be dealt with, the defecting bastard.

Three. Jase. Seeing the cherub in Dreamstate had been a shock. Karrick had honestly thought Jase was on his side now, that the little twink had been telling the truth in that he wanted Karrick to master him in bed — that they would be lovers forever. How wrong Karrick had been — how skewed his senses had become, to the point he briefly wondered if he could trust them any longer. But who else did he have but himself to rely on? If his senses weren't working right, he'd just have to learn to adapt.

I'll continue as best I can. I'm determined to win. There's no question of me failing. I want Morland's position, and I'm going to get it.

So yes, Jase was third on his list.

A shame, because he did so enjoy fucking that tight arse. So enjoyed hurting him, making him bend to his will.

There will be others. Better arses. Better souls to crush.

Karrick smiled at that, feeling that after all was said and done, he could begin afresh, be the ruler of *one* Team — and he'd make sure there was only one — although he wouldn't reside in Dreamstate like Morland and Rivald did. Oh no, Karrick belonged in this world, and he'd damn well rule from here. After all, there wasn't anyone but Him to answer to, whoever He was. And surely, if Karrick showed Him how efficient he had been in winning, surely He would allow Karrick to live where he chose.

If he doesn't? I'll kill Him too, then become Him. I'll create a new master for the Team and reign as their king.

He laughed demonically, realizing, with only a bit of discomfort that he sounded as if he were going mad.

Am I? Does it matter if I am, so long as I achieve what I want?

He shrugged, wanting to get everything clear in his mind. After he'd thought things through, his next steps were crucial in pulling the win off.

Four. After Jase, he'd go to visit Barry. Lure him outside. It was just a shame he didn't have Maggie anymore to do that for him. No matter, he'd climbed inside many a mind in the past and would do so again. Enticing Barry out into the street, then Tag, then that Daniel person and Jessica... Yes, he'd kill them one by one, leaving Leyton until last.

He relished the thought of killing a Killer.

With everything clear now, he settled the back of his head against the seat and closed his eyes. When in Dreamstate, he'd picked up a peck of fear from Graham, had glimpsed a rapid visual of Sue in the trunk of a car. So, if he were Graham, where would he have parked that car?

Karrick tuned all his senses into the same frequency and concentrated. He saw trees and...there! He snapped his eyes open, started the engine, then pulled out onto the road. He didn't have a conscious idea where he was headed so let his body take over, watching as he steered right then left, then another right, which brought him out onto an empty road. A flurry of excitement wiggled in his belly when he saw some trees ahead and he just knew, knew that car and his quarry were hidden by them. For a second he contemplated his car being heard by Graham, but really, Graham surely had other plans, other places he needed to be, and Karrick guessed the man was scrabbling around in some Dream or other, trying to connect with the members of Rivald's Team to let them know what was going on.

That was okay. More than okay. It meant Graham would be so immersed, sitting in that car, that he wouldn't hear Karrick's approach.

Karrick checked his rear-view mirror. The road was void except for him.

Excellent.

He drove on then parked up. Out of the car, he breathed deeply, catching a shade of Graham's scent on the swift breeze.

Yes, you're here, you interfering bastard, but not for much longer.

He realized, as he walked toward a thicker bunch of trees, that he would have to dispose of Graham before Sue. Coaxing the woman back into her body might take some considerable time and needed all of Karrick's concentration. Worrying that Graham might wake from wherever he was and catch Karrick at work just wouldn't do. He shrugged again. It didn't much matter what order he got rid of them, just so long as he did.

He glimpsed a spot of color between two tree trunks and made his way closer. A car was parked, and someone sat in the driver's seat. At the moment it presented itself as a silhouette, the head bent to one side, as though Graham was asleep. Did Karrick want to wake him before the kill? Yes, he did, but on the other hand, it might be better just to eradicate him quickly.

But what if Rivald pulls Graham into stasis again and keeps him safe?

"I won't give him the fucking chance," he whispered, creeping up alongside the car.

Taking a deep breath, tamping down his excitement, he edged closer to the driver's window. Peered inside.

What the hell?

Someone was sitting in the seat, but it wasn't Graham or Sue.

A doll. *A man-sized fucking doll?*

Rage swamped him, threatening to render him blind and take over his whole being. He breathed in then out of his nose, willing the force that drove him to take a step back. If he allowed it to overcome him, he wasn't sure what he'd do—and he'd have no recollection of it later. And he wanted to *know* what he was doing, to love every second of his kills, revel in them, adore them, so he calmed himself just enough so the force was kept at bay.

"The trunk. Check the trunk," he muttered, his voice coming out as one not belonging to him. He giggled maniacally as he strode to the back of the car. He kicked at the lock, surprised the lid creaked open a little but pleased that fate was on his side.

As it was supposed to be.

He felt it in his bones that he would become the victor, the one to rule.

He lifted the lid.

No one was inside.

"You bloody motherfucker," he said through gritted teeth, feeling that force encroaching and pushing against it again. But what had Karrick expected? Graham has learned from the best, after all. "I've got to hand it to you, Mr. Green, you really have thought this through properly, haven't you?"

He turned, surveyed his surroundings, and inhaled deeply to see if he could smell Graham and his woman lurking, hiding out behind the trees. There was a faint whiff of Graham, and a skimp of perfume that must be the woman, but nothing strong enough to indicate they were still around. It was better to make sure, though.

He scudded through the area, his pace hurried, him intent on spotting anything out of the ordinary. There was nothing but trees, trees, and more fucking trees.

Back in his car, he took a moment to regroup.

Where would he go if he were Graham?

"Barry's. I'd go to Barry's."

He stared at himself in the rear-view mirror, lifting his eyebrows as though questioning his answer. And, as if he were someone else entirely, he replied to himself.

"So then go there after seeing to Jase. Go to Barry's and kill the rest of them in one fell swoop."

Graham held his breath as he watched Karrick talking to himself inside his Porsche. The man was clearly crazy — or crazier than he had been — and that threw a huge spanner in the works. Dealing with Karrick in the past had been difficult at the best of times, but now? Now that he was clearly losing it?

Fuck.

Sue's weight against him was literally dead — a body with no life, the muscles and bones heavy with the loss of it. He couldn't move without her toppling to one side, though. No yet. Not until Karrick had driven away. Their hiding place, on the opposite side of the road to the trees, in a ditch, kept their presence a secret well enough, as did Graham smearing their clothes with cows' shit from the field behind him. They reeked of it, and it had been the only thing he could think of to mask their usual smell from Karrick.

Karrick nodded, like he had come to some kind of decision, and the sound of him starting his car made Graham lower his head so he was staring through strands of high, dry ratty grass instead of over them. He allowed himself a second or two of relief, but he couldn't let his guard down, not completely, and tensed as the Porsche sped past.

After counting to one hundred, he shifted Sue away from him, propping her against the back of the ditch. She looked like an obscene human doll, similar to the one Karrick would have seen in Sue's driver's seat – or at least Graham assumed Karrick had seen it. Graham had tried something he'd been practicing for a while now – projecting an image from his mind and placing it where he wanted it to be. Whether Karrick had laid eyes on it or not, it didn't matter – Karrick was gone, objective met.

Praying to whoever might be out there and on his side in this madness, Graham hauled himself out of the ditch, paranoid that Karrick would come steaming along again in that damned car and ruin everything. Before he could change his mind, he sped across the road then raced to the trees and Sue's car, his chest burning with the effort of running. He got in, drove back to the ditch then left the engine idling while he got out. Dragging Sue from the ditch was harder than it had been to put her in it, but he managed eventually, placing her back in the trunk and hating himself for it. The risk of someone seeing her limp form in the passenger seat once he got to a built-up area wasn't a risk he was prepared to take.

"I'm so sorry," he said to her as he covered her with the blanket, gently tucking it around her. "But it has to be this way if we're to have a life together once all this is over."

He closed the lid then made sure the brake light was still loose, even though she didn't need the fresh air, didn't need to breathe. But she was alive somewhere in Dreamstate, so affording her the decency of comfort, even though technically her body was dead, seemed the right thing to do.

Once he was in the car, he thought of the other 'right' thing to do.

He needed to close his eyes for a while, try to get into contact with the Team and warn them that Karrick was most probably hunting them down. He didn't have much time, for what if Karrick came back?

His attempt at connecting failed. He hadn't expected that at all. Was that because he was now a proper member of their Team? Had his abilities been limited like theirs were?

They can't be. I made Karrick see the doll.

But did I?

"A phone," he mumbled, opening his eyes. "I'll call one of them. Barry — yeah, I'll call him."

It was then he realized he didn't have any of their phone numbers.

He felt sick, and it wasn't just the stench of cow manure that contributed to that. Panic assailed him. How the fucking hell was he going to get to Barry's quickly in Sue's clapped out Ford when Karrick had a high-speed Porsche?

"Shit. Aww, fucking shit!"

He shook his head, took a deep breath then started the car up. He'd give it his best shot. Maybe get back to the town where Sue lived and ring the operator for Barry's number.

But Barry's surname, he didn't know it, and his address became elusive, dancing on the recesses of Graham's mind, just out of reach. Was Karrick messing with his head? Was someone else?

He didn't know, but he had no choice but to hope he could get to Barry's before Karrick did—or at least before Karrick did any damage.

Graham pulled away from the ditch, his heart heavy.

"Come on," he told himself. "You can do this. You have to. The world's population depends on it."

Chapter Thirty-One

Leyton hammered on Barry's door then rushed back to his van parked on the drive. He opened the side door, staring inside at Jase, who looked incoherent slumped on Leyton's little bed.

"Come on," he said, tone brisker than he'd meant, "let's get you where you're safe."

"None of us are safe, not anymore," Jase said, his sentence slurred, as though the young man had imbibed in far too much alcohol. "Wherever we go, he'll find us. Karrick. He'll get us all."

Leyton was well aware that what Jase had said was true, but the burn was growing inside him and he knew — hoped — it would reach such heated proportions he'd have no trouble killing Karrick when he crossed his path. And he had to believe that. If he didn't, what was the point? If Morland won, if that man had sole control over every Dreamer in every corner of the world, he suspected the planet would go to ruin.

As he helped Jase out of the van and onto the drive, he contemplated the Winnowing. What was it, and why was it happening? Something came to him then, another dump of information where he just *knew* it was the truth. Every so often, things shifted in the world. Wars broke out, changing life forever. Technology evolved, also changing life forever. These days, communication was so easy that people had become lost in it—it had taken over day-to-day living, like a great human presence that guided people to bend to its will.

The Internet, how it had served a brilliant purpose in educating the masses but at the same time had dumbed them down, turning people into robots, slaves to Facebook, Twitter, and whatever else floated in that strange ether that existed, yet it did not. Leyton had lost count of how many times he'd seen people glued to their cell phones, walking down the street as they typed messages on forums and lost themselves in…in what? A real yet make-believe realm? Had that been engineered somehow? Had Morland had a hand in infiltrating innocent people's minds, steering them toward being dependent on their cells so they didn't notice what was really happening around them, giving him the ability to work mainly undetected?

Yes, that was what had happened, he was sure of it.

"Oh, God, Jase!"

Daniel's startled voice dragged Leyton from his thoughts and he allowed Daniel to guide Jase inside, past Barry and Tag, who looked a little disheveled, as though they'd been tussling or arguing, their faces flushed. What had been going on while he'd been out collecting Jase? He was determined to find out. He had to. Rivald had said much rested on Leyton's shoulders, but he also needed to relay the latest information he'd been given.

He went inside, closing the door behind him then following the others into the living room. Everyone sat staring at him expectantly, and at one time he would have loved the elevated position he'd taken on, but now? Good Lord, it felt like nothing but a huge burden. Killing Karrick—that was something he looked forward to with relish—but everything else that went with it? Could he handle taking charge when he hadn't really done so before? Oh, he'd been the link between Rivald and the rest of the Team, but since their powers had evolved and each member had been able to contact Rivald in their own way, Leyton had been somewhat defunct, if you didn't count him killing.

"What's happened?" he asked Barry, refusing to dwell on his emotions now. If all went well he could examine them later when he parked up in the seclusion of some trees and got into his bed.

"We managed to get into Dreamstate while you were gone," Barry said, giving Tag a sidelong look that spoke of a secret between them.

Leyton didn't care much for secrets or knowing what the two men harbored between them—unless it had something to do with the Team's mission. He sensed it wasn't so refused to press the issue. "Yes?"

Barry explained what Karrick had done there.

"So he's evolved some more." Leyton wasn't sure whether to feel jealous of Karrick's obvious rise in power, how he was able to mess with minds and cause such unrest.

How can I defeat a man like that?

He stopped himself going any further with that. Self-doubt was Leyton's best friend but it had no place here. Not now. Not when the Team—who still had their attention on him—clearly looked to him for answers.

"Right, well, we can expect him soon then," Leyton said. "Angrier than he would normally be once he discovers Jase isn't at his house."

Leyton glanced at Jase, who was curled up on the sofa next to Daniel, pressed so close to his side it appeared they were one person with two heads. He shook that thought away and concentrated on the more important things, the main one being that they had limited time to make plans for how he was going to kill Karrick.

"But I've killed angrier people," Leyton assured them—or was he trying to reassure himself? Whatever, he had their rapt attention and that was all that mattered. Now was as good a time as any to reveal what he'd discovered.

Just tell them. Blurt it right out.

"I know what the Winnowing is," he said, noting Tag's raised eyebrows and Barry's slack jaw.

"You do?" Jessica sat more upright and leaned forward on the sofa beside Jase, propping her elbows on her knees. "What is it? Why is it happening—and why are we so important to it?"

He related what he knew, then, "Everyone, for the most part, has been so locked in cyberspace they've failed to notice what's going on around them. Crime rate is up, wars are raging, people are being maimed and slain in the name of religion time and time again, and even though people know it's going on, their perception seems to have been dulled. Conversing on forums and such is more important to them, hiding away in this almost creepy cyberland that's been created—on purpose, I feel, by Morland—where they're safe from the harsh realities of life."

"But Facebook and the like are full of news items in the feeds," Barry said. "People *are* seeing it. People *do* know about it."

"Yet many of them are desensitized. They scroll past it because it's too much. In a way, it's boring to them. And those who *do* recognize that the world is going to ruin and who try to get others to really see it...they're fighting a losing battle. People have had enough. They just want peace, and if that means ignoring the world's troubles, then that's what they'll do. It's a perfect scenario for Morland."

"So what the hell has that got to do with the Winnowing?" Daniel asked, stroking Jase's hair. "People have always either taken news on board or ignored it."

"The Winnowing," Leyton said, "is a new wave of change. Like I explained, look at the waves that have gone before. This one is the mother of them all and we should be very afraid if Morland wins. I know now what he's been doing."

"What?" Jessica asked.

"He's somehow got inside people's heads," Leyton went on. "Those with their noses firmly pressed to their cell screens are the ones who will be taken over first."

"Taken over?" Tag said, sounding like he didn't believe a single thing Leyton had said. "Come on now..."

"He could be right," Barry said, shoving a hand through his hair. "We've seen how minds can be altered. Look at how I attacked Leyton. What if Morland's been giving cryptic, seemingly innocent-looking information online for years and no one's aware of it yet until he does something to the text in emails or on forums—you know, puts in some kind of secret code that will trigger people into blindly following his will. Fuck, that sounds—"

"That's exactly what he's been doing," Leyton said, knowing the frightening truth of it, knowing it sounded crazy but that it really was the goddamned truth.

Oh, God. This is worse than we thought.

"Morland can't win," he said, his alarm coming through so bright in those words he'd swear the Team had been blinded.

They blinked at him, digesting the implications of what they'd been discussing, and their expressions were mirror images of each other.

Dread. Horror. Absolute fear.

"Christ Almighty," Tag said. "And this Him, this overall master—do you think he's aware of this?"

Leyton thought about that for a moment. A crash of data crammed into his head, so much so he thought it might burst from the pressure. He bent over, crying out, grabbing his temples in an attempt to soothe the pain.

"What the fuck?" Barry said, kneeling in front of Leyton and taking hold of his wrists. "Deep breaths. That's it. Calm down. This isn't all on you, Leyton. It seems like it's all on your shoulders but it isn't. We're here. You're going to have to kill the bastard—"

Leyton snapped his head up, peering at Barry's fuzzy countenance. "I know that. You think I don't know that? Karrick is my mirror. I have to get rid of him."

Barry caught his lower lip under his teeth and grimaced. "Morland, too, I think."

Leyton ground out a pained sound and dropped his gaze. He knew Barry was right. He didn't have the faintest clue how he was going to do that, but he knew Barry was right.

"Not on your own," Barry assured him in a low, soothing voice. "We'll help in any way we can. We're a Team. There has got to be a reason we *are* a Team, right?"

That made sense, made Leyton feel better, and he nodded, lowering his hands to his sides. Barry let go of his wrists and rose to stand beside Leyton and rest an arm across Leyton's shoulders.

"We've all been placed together to stop this," Leyton said, clarity coming hard and fast, the data stream slowing so he could read the images carousing in his head. "If Morland is stopped before he releases his online code, things might settle down. He can't release it yet because of the stipulation stopping him and Rivald from doing anything to affect the change, but I have a feeling Morland will do it anyway at the last minute. Yes, Morland and Rivald have been placed on a ban of sorts and He has ordered that they can't get involved or alert their Teams as to what is really going on, but if you were Morland, would you obey that order when you'd spent years working toward taking over the world?" He stared at everyone in turn. "And we thought—stupidly, I see that now—that we were only here to stop killers. I know now that there are so many other Dreamers, all either on Rivald's or Morland's Teams, who work in different departments, so to speak."

"What, like some secret network of jobs or something?" Daniel asked.

"Something like that." Leyton smiled sadly, unable to believe he was coping so well with giving out such bad news. Maybe he was a leader after all. "Rivald is the one engineering the good things, trying to make the world a better place. Hard to believe when he is so weird and sometimes acts sinister, but there you have it. Looks can be deceiving." He nodded as more information presented itself. "And Morland is the warmonger, the bad fellow, the one who ensures evil people do evil things in every facet of life."

"Like angels and demons," Jessica said quietly, lowering her gaze to the floor and frowning.

"Yes," Leyton said. "All those myths... I thought they were fairy tales. Turns out they were true all along." He sighed before continuing. "The Winnowing occurs every hundred or so years to prevent the likes of Morland completely controlling the world with hate, and for the past few hundred, he's succeeded in remaining in power." He took a deep breath, finally understanding why this Winnowing was so important. "He's convinced Him that nothing should change, that since the dawn of time there has been good and evil, so why alter that now? Himself has declared that evil is gaining such an upper hand that the world's good is in danger of dying out. That people will turn on one another if Morland's code gets out, until there are nothing but bad people left on the planet."

"Fucking hell," Barry breathed. "This is seriously freaky shit. Is it insane that I absolutely *know* it's true?"

He glanced around, as did Leyton, who was relieved to find the others shaking their heads, agreeing that as impossible as it was to believe, the truth embedded as deeply as DNA, couldn't be denied.

"Didn't want to believe people really were getting nastier," Barry went on. "I tried to tell myself it was the job. That I was a cop. I got to see the worst side of human nature, but even so... Compassion and empathy" — he glanced around the room at their companions — "people still have those, right?"

Silence. Leyton wanted, uncharacteristically, to reach over, pat his shoulder or something, reassure him that yes, the world — people — were inherently good. Instead, he found himself fiddling idly with his shirt buttons.

"So what the fuck?" Barry exploded. "Did He wait until Morland was on the verge of giving out his code before He stepped in?"

Leyton frowned as he searched for the answer to that. "He presides over good and evil. He thought — he hoped — that evil wouldn't *get* so evil. But it has and he had to put a stop to Morland being able to do what he's good at — destroying mankind."

"I see." Tag slid a hand down his cheek then back up to rub at the nape of his neck. "So what, did He announce this latest Winnowing? I mean, are they set at certain times or can He just declare one is in progress? What? I don't understand."

Leyton shifted his stance, instinctively squaring off, although he knew Tag wasn't a threat. The cop was still a man who didn't like not having answers. It made him edgy.

"Explain," Tag snarled. "Please."

Leyton swallowed. "Yes, He can bring about the Winnowing whenever He likes. This is the one hundredth. It's special, which is why He has declared that there can only be one winner this go-round. Since time began, He has given evil a chance to live alongside good, to have a decent balance, but lately that hasn't been the case."

Barry chuckled wryly. "Not just lately. You look at all the wars. It's bloody obvious evil gets the upper hand far too often. He has allowed him to get away with it too fucking much, if you ask me."

"He has, I agree." Leyton closed his eyes for a second then opened them again. "Good or bad — only one winner. If Morland wins, people will gradually get worse, the awful things occurring will get worse, as they have been even just this past five years or so. If Rivald wins — if we win — we have one hell of a job on our hands."

"How so?" Jessica asked. "Won't good just fix it all?"

"You'd think so, wouldn't you?" Leyton said gently. "But there are Dreamers out there programmed by Morland. Even if good wins, those Dreamers will continue to do bad things in Morland's name. Of course, there are good Dreamers on his Team, those who have no idea they've been used — like Maggie and Graham."

Jase shot forward in his seat, away from Daniel, staring into space. "I see it."

"See what?" Dan asked, moving forward so he could hold Jase close to him again. "See what, babe?"

"If we win," Jase said, eyes bugging, hands shaking, "our job is to seek out all Morland's Dreamers and bring them in, to Rivald, so they can be tested to see if they're bad or good."

"What, us?" Jessica asked, snapping her head up to stare at Jase. "Just our little Team? How the hell can we manage that? The world is massive!" Her voice took on an edge of hysteria. "I can't go roaming around the planet chasing bad Dreamers. I'm not equipped for that crap. None of us are. What the hell?" She rose and began pacing, gnawing at the inside of her cheek so that her skin kinked.

She stopped walking. Paled. Hugged herself.

"What?" Barry asked, getting to her before Leyton could. "What's the matter?"

Her mouth opened and closed. She shook her head rapidly.

"Tell me what's wrong!" Barry demanded.

"Karrick," she whispered, her whole body shaking. "I felt him inside me. He's coming. He's coming for us right now."

Chapter Thirty-Two

Karrick blasted along his street, uncaring that his engine made a horrendous racket. He'd gunned it back here like the devil was on his heels, and somehow he knew that was the case. He'd never questioned what or who he was, why he did the things he did, why he'd become a Dreamer, a Killer. It had suited him to be paid for murdering people and being a part of something so fantastical it wouldn't be believed by the dim-witted humans. Those humans roamed the planet thinking the meaning of life was climbing the ladder of success or, on the other end of the scale, walking miles to find clean water then walking back to their shacks only to find the sun had evaporated the majority of that very water they had gone to collect. Whatever their goals, humans — and he realized now that he wasn't human, that he was something very *other*, more so than he'd believed before — strove to better themselves and that was about it.

Greed, their desire to outdo their neighbor — whether it was by material or monetary gain, by growing crops so they didn't starve, trekking for that goddamn water so they didn't die from thirst—was their driving force. Karrick was no different, except his greed was to rule...something—something he wasn't too sure of but knew he was destined to rule it.

"Good and evil," he muttered absently as he drew up to the curb then cut the engine.

Where had that come from? What had made him think that?

"I am evil."

He chuckled and exited his car, lighter of spirit since he'd entertained those last, deep thoughts of his. Rushing up to his house so he could play out some particularly nasty evil with Jase, he was stunned into halting by a jagged hole in the glass of his front door.

"That little fuck has got away..."

Why had he not anticipated this? Why hadn't he *known*?

His spirit darkened then, went so black it threatened to swallow him whole.

No, don't swallow me. Don't make me forget what I'm about to do. I want to see, to know, to feel...

He took a deep breath to erase some of that darkness, raising the hue to a mid-gray, something a lot more manageable. He kicked the door, watching as it swung open, the handle bashing into the wall. He went inside, anger burning a hole in his gut as he spied the broken shards on the floor. On the *floor*, not the ground outside.

Someone had broken *in*.

"They've rescued him. Fuck it. Fuck, fuck, fuck it!"

Why had he thought they wouldn't? Or, more to the point, why hadn't he thought about this scenario at all? He'd been so intent on getting to Sue he hadn't figured Jase would be collected and taken back into their fold. He'd been so sure of himself, so sure that he could kill Sue and return to Jase within a couple of hours, that Jase was safe trussed up in his living room. Yet Jase had escaped him in Dreamstate. He hadn't waited for Karrick to give him specific orders once Jase had fired a shot at Graham.

"I should have known the little brat would somehow manage to go back to them, that he wasn't safe here, even though I'd tied him up."

Of course whoever had collected him would have smashed the glass to get in. Of course they'd have cut his chains. Of course they'd have fucking well escorted him back to that bastard Barry's place and secreted him there.

Karrick smacked his head against the wall, the absurd thought that the door handle had done exactly the same thing making him laugh like he hadn't laughed in years. Fuck, his stomach muscles were hurting from the force of it, and somewhere deep inside he acknowledged that he was losing control again. He didn't want to believe it—couldn't believe it—so pasted over the cracks in his unstable mind and strode into the living room.

He'd expected Jase to still be there, even though the evidence so far indicated otherwise. He'd *hoped* Jase would still be there. Why? Because, he admitted, hating himself for doing so, he cared for the little fucker. He'd seen a future, them together, Jase taking the pain and Karrick giving it. Jase by his side as his queen, Karrick the king of…whatever he was striving to be the king of.

He wanted to be Him, and although he didn't know what being Him entailed, he honest to goodness believed he *could* be Him.

Who is He? Why do I think I can be Him?

He didn't bloody know and he had no time to ponder those questions now. He had a job to do—one that had changed since he'd sat in his car going through the points on his kill list.

Jase was no longer on it. He'd keep that cherub alive if it was the last thing he did, forcing him to stay with him, to love him, to rule with him. Karrick prided himself in being a master manipulator, a man who could bend anyone to his way of thinking. If he killed Jase, he'd never know if he would have succeeded in convincing the twink to idolize him the way he wanted.

"You're mine, cherub, and whether you like it or not, you're going to stay mine." He smiled, visualizing Jase on his knees, begging Karrick to shove that whip handle up his arse. "You loved it," he whispered. "And you'll love me."

He left his house, not giving a shit that someone could walk in there and steal his belongings. They didn't matter. His mission did.

* * * *

Graham pulled onto Barry's drive, cutting the engine behind Leyton's van. He thought for a second about whether to hide his car elsewhere in the street so Karrick didn't know Graham was there, but how would he get Sue's body inside without someone seeing him carrying her down the road?

"Stupid," he muttered. "Get her inside the house now *then* move the damn car."

But did he have time, though?

Before he had a chance to ponder that, Jessica came out of the house, rushing toward him. Her eyes seemed recessed, and dark shadows surrounded them, as though she'd applied make up that had smeared. Her cheeks were whiter than their usual rosy hue, and he immediately knew something had happened.

"Thank God you're okay," she said, gripping his elbow then snapping her hand away in disgust. "Is that shit all over you?" She didn't give him time to respond. "Quickly, get inside. Karrick's coming."

"I know, that's why I'm here, to warn you—and thank fuck I got here before him. He tried to find Sue—hell, I'll explain it all soon. I need help carrying her."

Jessica frowned as she looked across at Sue's car. "Where is she?"

"In the trunk."

"Um, I don't want to know... I'll go and get Barry."

She walked toward the front door, but Barry was already on the threshold, Tag close behind.

"Sue's in stasis," Graham said. "Can you help me carry her? She's literally dead weight."

Barry grimaced, and Graham guessed it was at the stench emanating off him. Tag's eyebrows went up.

"Literally?" Tag asked.

Graham nodded.

"Damn, this puts me in an awkward position," Tag said, scooting around Barry then jogging to Graham. "Christ, you stink. Right. So she's dead—I'm a cop. I'm duty bound to call this in. You know that, right?" He rubbed circles over his temples.

Barry came up behind him. "But she isn't dead, not really. To anyone but us she'd appear to be, but she's still there somewhere. Come on, we need to get her out of sight. She can go in the other spare room, the one Dan and Jase aren't in."

Graham moved to unlock the trunk. "I have to move this car. Hide it so Karrick doesn't think I'm here. When he arrives, if he's in the kind of rage I think he'll be in because he couldn't kill Sue properly, he'll be so intent on getting everyone else he'll maybe forget about me for a while." He glanced down the street, thankful that no Porsche was in sight, that no rumble of a car engine could be heard. He lifted the lid, ashamed once again that Sue was in such a confined space, covered by a blanket that made her look like a murder victim. And he *had* murdered her, in a way.

He closed his eyes for a moment, opening them to find Barry and Tag already hauling her out. Tag took sole control of her and disappeared into the house. Barry stared down the street, obviously having the same thought Graham had, then placed a hand on Graham's shoulder.

Barry grimaced and screwed up his nose. "Man... Go and park in the next street. I'll leave the key for the back door wedged into the soil of the pot plant beside it. There's a shed out there. Get inside it in case Karrick thinks to surprise us from the rear. He won't see you. I have a venetian blind up in there. The shed's angled so you can see right into the living room from it. Stay awake! And make sure no one gets in here." He tapped the side of Graham's head. "You would not believe the shit that's going on. Make sure you stay...yourself. Fuck, that doesn't make any sense." He squinted down the street and curled his lip. "There are mind games going on. A shitload of...stuff. Just try to keep your head—keep the crazies, enemies—out. And the enemy is more than just Karrick. It could be anyone, any other Dreamer from your old Team."

Graham nodded. "Do I need to know what that shitload of *stuff* is?"

Barry shook his head, eyeing the street again. "Not yet. You need to focus on making sure Karrick is killed, if none of us does it first. Then get to Dreamstate and get rid of Morland."

"What the fuck?" Graham knew things had taken a turn for the worse, but *killing* Morland?

"Too much to explain, no time to explain it in. Now go." Barry gave Graham a slight shove then went back into the house.

Graham drove the car to a decent hiding place, wondering what on earth had been going on while he'd been up north. Did Karrick know the latest 'shitload'? How did it change things? And did any of them know what the hell the Winnowing was yet? Not knowing the answers to his questions proved a bind, made him think too much when he should be concentrating on his task.

Sighing, the exhalation ragged with his fear, he exited the car then made his way to Barry's street, keeping his head low and his wits about him. He shoved his hands into his pockets, trying to appear inconspicuous, but he doubted he would, given that he was covered in dried shit. He stopped between two parked cars at the curb, checking the street to make sure it was clear for him to cross. It was, so he darted over, then scooted down the side of Barry's house and into the back garden.

He went straight to the back door, digging inside the plant pot to find the key. He slipped it into his pocket, smoothed the dirt back in place, then headed for the shed, entering to find a neatly kept space with tools hanging from hooks and a work bench pushed against the back wall. It could serve as a seat if his legs got tired and he'd still get a clear visual into the living room.

From where he stood by the window, he could see Jessica, Daniel, Jase, Barry, Tag and Leyton all gathered, sensibly standing against the walls so their silhouettes weren't seen from the street side by Karrick. The living room spanned the depth of the house, so Graham had a good view right through to the front window. He'd see Karrick coming, as would the others, but the net curtain slightly obscured the clarity. Not good—it might hinder them spotting Karrick immediately, but it was great in that Karrick wouldn't be able to see in very well unless he went right up close to the glass.

So the crazy man might choose to surprise them from the back way after all. There was no net curtain on the rear window, so everyone was in plain sight. Graham knew he didn't have what it took to confront Karrick in the garden by himself without using any tricks, but he did have a plan.

He'd try conjuring up an image again and place it in front of Karrick. While Karrick was occupied with it, Graham would creep up behind him, using one of those tools on the wall to bash his head in. It wasn't something he ever thought he'd contemplate doing, ever thought he'd get pleasure from doing, but if it meant saving Sue, he'd do it.

To save her he'd do absolutely anything.

Chapter Thirty-Three

Leyton stared at Barry across the room. The man's question had thrown him a little. He wasn't used to telling people how the burn worked, how killing made him feel so alive, so energized, so...happy. If he wasn't a Killer Dreamer he'd be labeled a psychopath, except that term wouldn't be correct. He was more a sociopath, his condition thus because his childhood had shaped who he had become, and that he could feel empathy and emotions. He did feel remorse at times, and could become attached to groups or certain people.

Neither of those terms were really who he was, though. All he wanted was to please, and if being a Killer meant he made people happy, then that was what he would do. That was why he felt pleasure when killing.

And it all made sense now, why he was who he was, why he was on the Team he was on. He wasn't evil or bad—he was good, on the good side, and—odd though it might be in such a situation as this—he felt relief that what he'd thought he was—a terrible, terrible person—wasn't the case at all.

He cleared his throat. "It's there all the time, the burn. It never goes away. But it grows hotter when I know a kill is imminent. Before I got this latest information, I used to think the burn was in me, a part of me, just me wanting to kill, wanting the thrill of it, but I do believe it burns because someone is about to commit murder and my senses are warning me of it. When it grows hotter it means I'm close to the potential kill site so I can perhaps prevent it. When it burns lower, I'm simply just too far away to get there in time to make a difference."

How had he known this? Why was this only being made apparent to him now?

"Which is why murders still happen," Tag said, who stood beside Barry and stared through the front window.

"Exactly." Leyton nodded. "And because there aren't enough Killers in each town or city. I thought I was the only one here until I learned of Karrick, but if there are only the two of us operating these parts, both for different reasons, there simply isn't enough manpower to prevent all murders."

"And Dreamers have to come into being," Jessica said from her place nearest the window next to Tag, "and clearly there isn't a specific order in which they're created. Some will be Killers, some Mind Sweepers and whatever. It's a shame Dreamers can't be made on tap."

Leyton could only agree to that. Then there would be no murder at all if each murderer could be caught before they played out their acts. But with bad Killer Dreamers on the scene, maybe there would still be homicides. It was all too confusing for Leyton to think about in any great depth at the moment.

"Do you have the burn now?" Barry asked, leaning against the doorjamb.

Leyton forced himself not to sigh. Hadn't he just said the burn was there all the time?

Barry must have realized what he'd said, because he went on with, "I mean, is it hot right now? Really hot?"

"The temperature is rising as we speak."

"So someone is going to get killed near you," Barry said.

That stunned Leyton. He'd thought…he'd thought the burn meant *he* had to kill someone, but he realized now that it really meant the opposite. Someone was going to be killed. He glanced around at the group, wondering who it would be and hoping to God it wouldn't be any of them—that it meant Karrick was the one who would die, not the Team, not his Jessica…

"Yes," Leyton said, "but I'll try my best to make sure it isn't one of us."

Tag fingered his gun, which hung from a holster on his belt. He still studied the front window. "As will I."

"We all will," Barry said, glancing at Jase on the other side of the closed living room door. "Although I think our little Visioner isn't quite on the ball at the moment—and Daniel." He studied the dark-haired young man. "No powers. You shouldn't have been dragged into all this. Maybe you two should go upstairs, hide out in the room with Sue."

Beside Jase, Daniel widened his eyes in alarm, briefly taking his attention from the back window to give them all a look in turn. "No offense, but I'm not sharing airspace with a dead woman."

"She isn't dead," Jase said quietly, eyes closed, like he was trying to catch hold of a vision. "She's just empty, for the time being."

That was a good way of putting it, Leyton thought.

Something prodded his thoughts in another direction. "Listen, much as this topic is taking our minds off what's to come, we ought to be concentrating on Karrick's arrival. We have no solid plan save for me going for him as soon as he comes in. What if I can't get to him and he lunges for one of you first? I should stand by the door that leads out to the hallway so I'm the first one he sees."

"But that won't be the case," Barry said. "Think about it. When you come to a doorway, where do you look first? Beside the door? No, you look directly into the room. You're standing exactly where you need to be."

"I'm too far away from the door, though. I'm opposite on the other side of the room." Leyton gritted his dentures. "I need to be closer. Everyone else is too near to his entry point. You're all on the wall where the door is."

"Trust me," Barry said. "He'll see you at first. You all by yourself against that wall. And he'll get angry, dart forward, his focus on you. That's where we come in. Behind him. I'll get him in a chokehold, everyone else can grab his arms and legs, and you..." He paused. Swallowed. "Can gut him or whatever the hell it is you do."

Leyton's burn grew hotter. "He's closer."

"Oh, God..." Jessica leaned her head back against the wall and closed her eyes. Then she snapped them open, as if what she'd seen inside her head was too much to cope with.

She stared over at Leyton, and he admitted that what she saw now probably wasn't much better. His face. The stuff of nightmares.

"Plus there's Graham," Barry continued, jerking his head toward the rear of the house. "He's got our backs."

"What if Karrick brings someone with him?" Jessica asked, shifting her gaze from Leyton to stare through the nets at the front window. "Like the other people from his Team, the ones we don't know about."

"Then I'll kill them all," Leyton said, convinced he could manage that.

With Jessica so close, he could manage anything.

* * * *

Karrick wasn't stupid. As he zoomed through the streets on his way to Barry's, he knew damn well they'd all be waiting for him. Even without probing into Barry's house via his mind, he knew. Anyone would, even the dimwit humans of this world. He wasn't worried about anyone but Leyton, and even then he thought he could take him down. Going inside their heads would be his approach, pitting them against one another, making them argue and fight so they were busy when he lunged at their Killer.

He laughed, tapping his hand on the steering wheel in time to the music blasting from the radio. Aretha Franklin gushed on about respect, and it tied in exactly with what he expected from people. A bit of bloody respect. He'd show them. They'd see what they should be in awe of.

At the end of Barry's street, he parked up and sat for a moment to gather his senses. He cast his gaze about, pleased to see no one around. Barry's house sat as lonely as it always did down at the bottom there. Barry's car was on the drive, as was Leyton's van, but he couldn't see any sign of that Sue woman's car.

"Not surprising," he muttered. "The fucking thing's probably still chugging along somewhere with Graham frantic that he isn't going to get here in time. And he won't."

He closed his eyes, content that no one would ambush him, and projected his thoughts and his *self* inside Barry's house. He frowned. It was empty—he hadn't expected that at all—and as he roamed the rooms, anger brewed inside him. He floated out into the back garden, coming to an abrupt stop as he spied a body facing away from him on the path. Who was that? It looked like Maggie with that tousled reddish bob, but that wasn't possible—unless Rivald had butted in once again and held her in stasis. That was all he needed, a bitch of a Mind Sweeper on Barry's Team.

He moved closer, tilting his head to hear for any sounds that someone else was near. There was nothing except the twitter of birds and the rush of air tickling the leaves of bordering bushes.

She was on her side, legs bent, arms up by her face, hands in prayer. She appeared to be asleep, but with her not moving with the rise and fall of breath, he knew she was as dead as a doornail.

The breeze wafted a tress of her hair, making it seem like an unseen hand played with it.

Unnerving.

He took another step, then another, and caught a glimpse of her cheek and the dark lashes resting on it.

Sue?

Elation swept through him at the idea it was her. With the house empty, he could go into the garden for real and kill that witch once and for all. He moved nearer still, until he stooped over her and checked her face to see if it matched the one he'd seen in his mind when he'd visited her house.

Oh, yes, it was Sue all right.

After another sweep of the house, Karrick opened his eyes and checked the street again. All seemed clear, so he reached into his glovebox to pick up his flick knife. He inserted it into his jacket pocket and, convinced he had a free run, he got out of his car and prepared himself for one hell of a satisfying kill.

* * * *

Graham held his breath. Someone was at the back gate. Unfortunately, there was only one window in the shed and he wouldn't be able to see who might come into the garden until they walked down the path. He blinked, slightly nauseated from the stress of making it seem like no one occupied Barry's house and that Sue was sprawled out on the ground. It wasn't difficult to envisage her there—she was in the same pose as when he'd left her in the trunk, minus the blanket. He wondered if Tag had left her on the bed in the same position.

Emotions, the caring kind, threatened to overtake him, so he shifted his gaze and thoughts from her, only holding her close in his mind so he could continue to create the illusion she was on the path.

The gate slammed, the sound giving Graham a jolt. His heart jolted too, and he swallowed down bile that had crept up his throat. Footsteps—he recognized them as belonging to Karrick—then the man himself appeared.

Karrick jabbed the toe of his pointed boot at Sue's midsection. Although she couldn't feel it, Graham still winced and gritted his teeth to avoid shouting an obscenity. He curled his hands into fists, ensuring he didn't shove open the shed door and barge outside to confront that evil motherfucker.

Not yet. Wait until he's thoroughly occupied.

Karrick stopped what he was doing and stared at the shed—at the window. Graham swallowed again. Could Karrick see him, even though Graham had shrouded himself? Karrick came right up to the window and pressed his nose to the glass. It misted with his hot breath, and Graham held his, swearing that Karrick looked him right in the eyes.

Fuck off. Go on, fuck right off.

Karrick obeyed, and Graham wondered if that was from him ordering it in his thoughts or from Karrick finding the shed empty. If it were the former, Graham couldn't chance experimenting with a new power now. It was hard enough maintaining three separate illusions as it was.

He glanced through the back window of the house. The room still appeared empty, so he switched his attention to the garden again. Karrick knelt beside Sue and stroked her hair. Graham wondered why the fuck the man was doing that and fought the urge to go out there and warn the man that if he touched her again he'd kill him.

But you're going to kill him anyway, so why bother with a warning?

Why bother indeed.

Graham launched himself out of the shed.

Chapter Thirty-Four

"Graham's on the move," Jase said.

Leyton stared at the back window, spotting Graham flying out of the shed toward the garden path then going out of view.

"Stay where you all are," Leyton said, amazed when everyone obeyed.

He shifted along the wall so he could get a better look. Graham had wrestled Karrick to the ground and they writhed on the path. The burn boiled Leyton's stomach acid until it became so hot he clutched his belly in agony, bending double. Never before had he felt such a wicked burn, and he figured it was because the one he had to kill — or the kill being attempted out there — was so fueled with high-octane anger that it out rivalled any other.

"Do not follow me," Leyton said, running across the room then out into the hallway.

He went into the kitchen, the image of the men fighting a blurred mesh of shapes on the other side of the mottled, opaque glass. He wrenched at the handle but the damn door was locked. He spied a set of keys on the counter so grabbed them then fumbled the one he thought would work into the lock. Fate was on his side as the keeper slid back with a clunk. He snatched up a carving knife from the drainer then flung himself out onto the path.

Graham and Karrick were tussling, wedged together from the hold each had on the other, rolling over and over as they fought for dominance. Leyton had no clear moment to plunge the knife into Karrick without hurting Graham at the same time, and an unholy thought lodged itself in the forefront of his mind.

Then kill them both.

The burn's intensity increased and he almost doubled over again, the strength needed to keep himself upright threatening to elude him. He managed it by the skin of his dentures and rushed toward them, knife held up and steady, his other hand outstretched so he could grab hold of Graham and toss him aside.

"Stop!" Leyton shouted as the men reached the bottom of the path.

Karrick faltered and, as he pushed Graham upwards and off him, he glanced across at Leyton. Graham's face, pinched, the skin drawn tight with high spots of color on his cheeks, was a terrible mask of fury and if Leyton didn't hurry, Graham would beat him to the kill.

A surge of kill energy raged through Leyton, and he dove forward, yanking Graham away with such force he threw him to the other side of the garden. Karrick scrabbled to his feet, keeping his attention on Leyton, then drew a weapon from his pocket. He flicked a blade out, poking at the air in front of him. Leyton's was far superior, but he'd killed many a man with a small knife like Karrick's so knew the size and length mattered not one jot. It was the sharpness that counted.

"You!" Karrick said.

"Me," Leyton replied.

They circled one another, and Leyton could taste Karrick's burn. It was different to his own, less happy, less good, more angry, more evil. He drew on it, pulled the essence of it into his body, gratified to see Karrick blink in surprise. Leyton did it again, one massive, hefty pull, reveling in the rush of nastiness that scoured his veins and corrupted his thoughts. All he could see was himself. All he wanted to do was kill himself. All he wanted to do was...

Leyton stared at the knife he held, widening his eyes as he drew it toward his face, the point gleaming in a quick burst of the waning sun. Karrick's burn infected him, an acidic cruelty that seemed to shrivel his internal organs, its next destination to melt his brain. He realized too late the implications of him inhaling Karrick's wickedness, every last drop of it, and that there was possibly no turning back, no getting it out of his system. Leyton's innocence in what he was and how he really didn't know how himself or Dreamers worked barreled into him with mean, unrelenting force. Taunting him. Bullying him. Trying to reduce him into a shivering, compliant little wreck.

The knife point got closer.

Time slowed.

Karrick laughed weakly, leaning back against the fence, his knife falling from his hand. The man had no energy, Leyton had stolen it all, but it didn't matter because Karrick's objective was going to be met regardless. Leyton was going to kill himself, Karrick would be the only remaining Killer, and if the vile bastard managed to claw his burn back, plus Leyton's, he have enough power to wipe the others out within seconds.

Morland's Team was going to win.

Evil would rule the world.

"No," Leyton roared, his neck tendons straining against his skin. "No!"

"We are depending on you," Rivald said from somewhere in the recesses of Leyton's mind. *"Use his burn against him. Use your own. You are strong. You can do this."*

The boost of support had Leyton frantically searching for his burn. He felt it cowering away in a corner of his heart, heard it whimpering that the end was nigh and he would soon plunge that carver right into his eye socket.

"Come to me," Leyton wailed at his burn. "Please, come to me."

Karrick pushed himself off the fence then staggered forward, obeying what he thought was a command aimed at him.

"Be careful, Leyton!" Jessica shrieked. "Move out of the way. There's a gun!"

And oh, that was what he'd needed. His anchor. His precious, precious anchor.

An awful, loud bang erupted, echoing through Leyton's head, making his knife arm jerk away from his face. A red bloom of blood flounced onto Karrick's shirt just below the collar, and Leyton literally saw red.

"No," he said, "this is my kill, my duty."

Whoever had shot Karrick had a poor aim, but Karrick's cry of pain and widening eyes showed he was injured enough that he was momentarily stunned. The reverberating noise from the gun spurred Leyton's burn out of hiding and had Karrick's scurrying away. Good heat gushed into him, and the familiar feel of it brought intense relief and the severe need to finish Karrick off. Karrick's burn had fled elsewhere. It clearly hadn't returned to its host. Karrick slumped against the fence again, bringing one hand up to cover the flower of blood on his shirt.

"What an anticlimax," Karrick said, his breathing short, crisp, labored. "What an absolute shit of a finale."

Leyton disagreed. "It isn't over until the fat lady sings. Come on, fight for your life. Fight for evil. Fight for what you were born to do."

Karrick stumbled forward, keeling over onto the path. He reached out for his flick knife, fingers playing the concrete like imaginary piano keys.

"That's it, reach for it," Leyton said. "Now get up. Get up and fight me." He sneered, his burn devouring his body and mind. "Or are you that weak you can't even find the energy to pick up your knife? You are not pure evil. If you were, you would be able to attack me even with your burn gone."

Leyton knew that wasn't true but he enjoyed seeing Karrick suffer as he digested that taunt. Leyton's own burn had let him down once Karrick's had strong-armed it into hiding, and he'd had a small taste of what it would be like not to have it. Leyton could no more kill Karrick without it than Karrick could kill without his. With no burn, they were just men, plain and simple, and that frightened him. Who would he be minus his burn? What would he be like?

He realized he would never know, for his burn was back, proud and roaring, ready to help him end this madness, there to carry him through the days ahead once the Winnowing was over.

Karrick got hold of his flick knife. He struggled to stand then stared at Leyton, his eyes showing his confusion, his apprehension and the devastation that he wasn't who he thought he was. They had both taken their burns for granted, but Leyton would never forget this day, never forget how precious his was.

"That's it," Leyton said. "Now kill me."

"What the fuck are you doing, man?" Barry yelled from somewhere behind him. "End this—or I'll fucking end it for you!"

That was all Leyton needed. The impetus to take that final step. He wanted the glory—and it belonged to him. Rivald had hinted at as much. He took one step forward then plunged his knife into Karrick's belly, swiftly lifting it upwards, smiling broadly as that white shirt was decorated with more than just a small blossom of claret. Karrick screamed, his head hanging back, blood filling his mouth then seeping out, two rivers of red flowing down his chin. Karrick gargled, raised his hands to clutch at his belly, seemingly trying to tug the edges of his wound back together.

Leyton pulled the knife out then wedged the handle between his teeth so he could rip open Karrick's shirt and see the damage he'd done. Intestines and innards spewed out, smacking onto the path and the tips of Karrick's boots. Leyton grasped his knife again, hearing the sound of retching behind him, the groans of horror and one hissed "*yes*". He lifted the blade, resting it against Karrick's neck, pushing the wicked man until his back hit the fence.

"This ends now," Leyton said. "For all your threats, for all your posturing, you are the weaker man. How does that feel?"

Karrick couldn't answer, but his response was to spit a gush of blood into Leyton's face. The heat of it warmed Leyton's heart, warmed his skin and he swiped his knife across Karrick's throat, gaze fixed there so he could watch the skin part, the blood rush forth, and hear one final, tragically pathetic moan from his adversary. Leyton let him drop to the ground. Karrick landed on his front and Leyton lost no time in stabbing the man in the back. He had to be sure he was dead, couldn't contemplate Morland saving him by whisking him into stasis.

A God-awful rumble shook the ground, and Leyton stepped back, knowing by instinct what was happening. Morland was on his way, and if he showed himself in fog form, Leyton would be no more. He couldn't fight insubstantial matter. Couldn't stab mist and cause any kind of damage.

The back gate flew off its hinges, and a man appeared, a hideous, wide-as-hell man with eyes that had clouds for the whites and fire for the irises. That small detail was quickly tossed from Leyton's mind as he worked out what to do next. He retreated a few steps, gripping his knife handle, knowing he needed to pick his moment and pick it well — or the rest of his Team were as good as dead.

The man advanced, naked, his hair flowing in a sudden gust of wind. The sky darkened, as though he'd brought sheer evil with him and had scattered it into the air. Leyton's heart rate accelerated, the thuds painful, his throat promising to close up as fear built there.

"Morland," Leyton said.

For an answer, Morland opened his mouth and roared. A swarm of hornets came out, thickening the air with their black-and-yellow jackets, creating a giant buzz that hurt Leyton's ears and drowned out his voice when he goaded Morland to kill him.

Leyton's body seemed to fill with power as each hornet stung him—power that was Morland's, rich with malevolence, heavy with immorality. Leyton was ready this time. He harnessed it all and tagged it onto his burn, enriching his own supremacy instead of his burn scurrying away.

Leyton roared back, and a plague of locusts left his mouth, their fat bodies almost choking him, scratching his lips as they fought their way out. The insects landed on Morland, seeming to eat him, spitting out chunks of his flesh before going back for another taste. Morland's scream drowned out the click of the locusts' frantic wings, and twisted in the air to form thunder that rumbled into Leyton's body and rippled through the gray, swollen clouds.

Rain burst from them, and as the first acidic drops fell, burning Leyton's skin, he darted forward, giving Morland the same treatment he'd given Karrick. The hornets flew off Leyton and into the wound in Morland's stomach, the creatures crawling, burrowing until each and every one of them packed out his insides. Again Morland screamed, another clout of thunder boomed, and Leyton whipped his blade across that evil man's throat, cutting off his dreadful sound.

Morland toppled forward. Leyton scooted back, knife held at his side then, as Morland whacked onto the path face first, Leyton launched a frenzied attack. He sliced, he stabbed, he gouged. The locusts crawled out of the new wounds on Morland's back, chomping at his flesh, scuttling to untouched parts and devouring them until there was nothing left. They launched themselves into the air, bodies fat, wings flapping slower, then landed on Karrick, a dessert for already over-stuffed bellies.

Leyton remembered to breathe. He took a huge breath before stepping back and kept going until his backside met with the wall of the house. He turned his head and saw his Team clustered in the doorway, spotting Graham there too. But he wasn't interested in Graham. Or Barry, Tag, Jase and Daniel.

No. Jessica was the one he sought.

She stood leaning against the counter, her arms across her middle, eyes wide and full of the dreadfulness she'd witnessed. He thought that perhaps she found him hideous to look upon too, but it didn't matter. She was safe. She was alive.

"Oh, my God," she said, pushing through the small crowd.

She came outside and pressed herself to him, holding him tight and crying so hard her body shuddered. He could have told himself that there was still a chance for him with her as he stared up at the sky growing lighter, at the clouds switching from gray to white, the air ridding itself of evil's taint and bringing instead the goodness, the sharp tang of a beautiful autumn day.

But he didn't.

She cared for him enough to touch him without revulsion scudding through her. She cared enough to have been worried for his safety.

And that was all that mattered right then. That was all.

Chapter Thirty-Five

Jessica hitched in a shuddering breath, and Barry found himself holding his own, waiting for her to release it.

Silence settled like fog over their shoulders. It spread out from them, the deep, protective kind of quiet when nature curled in on herself and held all things still. Finally, Jessica sniffed and her breath bubbled out, the only sound. Then Leyton moved, rubbing small, awkward circles on her back, and the scratch of his calloused fingers on the cotton of her shirt broke the tension.

"I've got...you." Leyton said, his tone hushed and hesitant. "You're safe."

"For now," Tag muttered.

"We're all safe." Barry shot Tag a quelling look, as though admonishing him not to frighten the children.

Jessica shook herself and squared her shoulders before taking a tiny step away from Leyton. She didn't look up at him, but she didn't move far from him, either.

"You...you did...it." She wrapped an arm around her middle and played with the collar of her shirt with her other hand. "You did...something." Finally, she looked Leyton in the eye. "What did you do?" Her voice was barely a whisper and it trembled.

Leyton looked down at her, his eyes sad. "What I had to do to protect you."

The words were a reverent promise, and for once, Barry watched as Jessica gave the big, scarred center of their Team a tremulous smile and nod.

"Yeah." She shuffled around to look over the yard with the rest of them, but still, she stayed close to Leyton.

"Now what?" Dan asked. His voice, too, trembled, but he kept an arm firmly around Jase.

"Inside," Barry said. "Everyone. In the house and — Fuck. I need a drink."

Tag grabbed him, fingers of his left hand digging into the flesh of Barry's arm just below his left elbow.

Barry bristled at the contact. "Not literally," he mumbled.

"We aren't done," Tag said.

"Yes." Barry waved a hand over the yard. "We are. You saw."

"You're an ex-cop, Barry. You know this isn't the end. There will be bodies. Missing persons. Explanations."

"Not tonight," Barry said firmly. He sounded a lot stronger than he felt. He knew he did. He also knew Tag would see his inner shaking any minute. He glanced around at his yard. "This house." He shuddered. "It's a fucking lodestone for bad karma."

Leyton smiled at him, and it was not exactly a pleasant expression. "I think that depends on your perspective."

The man was fucking messed up. Barry eyed the place where Karrick had gone down. The ground there was dark and oily and seemed to writhe slightly. He half expected it to burst upwards in a swarm of locusts at any moment, but instead, inky black smoke bubbled from the ground, staying only inches above it, and roiling over the spot.

The same darkness hovered where Morland had fallen. It clung to the spot, as though it might put the fearsome creature back together from the rapidly decaying flesh and disintegrating bone.

Barry vaguely thought such a putrid mess should stink to high heaven, but it didn't. The only real smells in the air were that of vomit, impending rain and Graham's stench.

"Inside," Tag said quietly, releasing Barry only long enough to turn back to the house and herd everyone ahead of them.

Barry glanced back to see the rolling fog-like substance begin to writhe more frantically and send out flopping, flailing tendrils, as though searching for something real and alive to latch on to.

"You need to contact Rivald," Tag whispered at him. "Find out how to deal with this mess."

"Right. Because that'll be a piece of ca—"

"Barry!"

Jessica's shout caught his attention, and he hurried into the kitchen. She was there, struggling with Leyton's weight as he slumped into her. She tried to guide him to the counter and Graham rushed to help her steady him, but Leyton was rapidly wilting as they dragged him inside.

"What's going on?" Barry asked.

"So tired," Leyton whispered. "Oh...dear." He slumped against the counter, then they were forced to lower him to the floor as he passed out.

"What the fuck!" Barry knelt beside him. "Leyton!" He slapped the man's thickly scarred cheek. "Don't you fucking dare, you bastard. Leyton!"

Tag touched two fingers to the slumped man's neck. "Pulse is strong," he said, a note of relief in his voice. "I think he just passed out."

"He has never passed out before," Barry said, trepidation tightening his gut.

"He's never vomited bees before, either," Tag reminded him.

"They were locusts," Dan said.

Everyone turned to look at the young man and he shrugged. "They were. Locusts. Meat-eating...locusts. Oh, God."

He rushed from the room and Barry heard the bathroom door slam and the faint sounds of yet more vomiting.

Barry couldn't blame the kid. Barry was an ex-cop. He was used to the ugly, shitty, disgusting things people did to one another. Still. Tonight, he understood the impulse to empty his stomach.

Jase sighed tiredly. "I'll go see if he's okay." He wandered from the room, even now dazed and looking battered and confused. Nevertheless, he did stumble unerringly to the bathroom and let himself inside, as though even mostly lost in that haze, he would be able to find his anchor. His other half.

Barry looked to Tag, grateful beyond thought to see Tag's blue gaze fixed on him. His stomach settled. His breathing calmed, and for the moment, at least, he felt grounded and whole.

"Get him to the couch," Barry said at last. "I'm going to try to contact Rivald."

Tag nodded, motioned to Graham, and together, they hefted Leyton off the floor.

Jessica trailed them, seemingly unwilling to let Leyton out of her sight. It was weird, the way she was acting. Worrisome.

She turned at the doorway and gazed at Barry. "You have to call Ross," she said. Her voice was low and husky and her face pale.

"Why?"

She shrugged, looking confused. "He's a cop, isn't he? He'll fix...." Her attention wandered to the living room, where Barry heard Tag grunt as Leyton was dumped a little roughly onto the couch. "There are missing pieces," she mumbled and left the kitchen for the chair next to Leyton.

Barry blinked after her.

Missing pieces. Ya think?

"She might be right," Tag admitted. "I'll try to get hold of him. See if anything has come across his desk other than Graham. And the dead kid."

Barry nodded. "Okay." He studied Tag's face, the fine lines around his eyes, and wished to hell they had been put there with laughter instead of stress. "Tag..."

"I'll be quick. You do your thing and I'll do mine. Go."

"Right." *Best to get it over with.*

Steeling himself, Barry headed for his office. It seemed like as good a place as any to get some quiet and try to reach Rivald. Not that he knew what to expect if he did manage to enter the Dreamstate. He hoped for answers but braced himself for disappointment.

Seating himself at his desk, he laid both hands flat on the top and closed his eyes. Truthfully, he didn't really know how this even worked. He simply focused on what he remembered of the path to the cave, as dream-like and surreal as that trail always seemed.

A breeze dusted around his ankles and he looked down. His bare feet were pale against blackened stone and the detritus of the city streets dragged desultorily along the ground, passing him as the slight wind tugged at the short hairs on his legs, arms and chest.

Naked? Oh hells no!

He tried to think himself clothed, stepping back, reaching behind him for something — anything — to ground him. Darkness surrounded him, and the trail, thin and rocky, wound away before him. It seemed longer than usual, the air thinner, the fog curling around his calves colder.

"Fuck." Barry rubbed at his legs — still bare — and shuddered, tripping backwards, keeping his eyes on the path ahead. There was a wall at his back, and his momentum, meek as it was, halted. Darkness closed in before him, the path disappearing into the shadows. His bare arse fetched up against hard stone. No. Brick. He glanced down and saw concrete beneath his feet.

Dread seeped into his bones. This was so not happening. Not now. Not after everything.

A dry chuckle wafted out of the darkness beyond the bright light that bloomed to blind him.

"Oh." A male voice, deep and slick, slithered out of that blank space. "It's happening. Did you think you'd escape?"

A cold, silvery *snick* sounded and Barry felt icy chills stripe his chest. He looked down, unsurprised to see beads of blood weeping out of a cut across his pecs.

"Don't do this," he whispered. "Please don't —"

Another slash, this one across his thighs, and another, slashing his biceps almost to the bone. His wrists were tied now, arms stretched out to either side, his ankles fastened by rope to something he couldn't see that dug into his calves.

"Who are you?" He peered, trying to see beyond the light. God, he'd thought...hoped...he was beyond these dreams. How he wished he was beyond them.

"What do you—ah!" Another slash cut across his abdomen, not deep, but painful. "Fuck!"

Out of the darkness came a laugh, cold, heartless.

"Who I am doesn't matter," the voice said. "What you did to get here is what matters. Hope you had a nice goodbye smooch with the wife and kiddies. Because you ain't going back."

The bite of steel dug into Barry's side and he moaned. Whoever he was, whatever this person had done, his killer was taking his time. The knife came out with a wet *shlock* and trailed over his stomach. He flinched when it dug into the cut there and he realized this was going to be torture, never knowing when the next cut would come. Not knowing if it would kill him or just hurt.

There was nothing in the world as frightening as knowing you were going to die. Slowly. Painfully. Helplessly. Terror washed through him, and his bladder released.

Laughter. Cruel and satisfied as another slice trailed down his inner thigh. The agony of piss in the cut made him scream until he was hoarse.

"Please..." He shivered as the flat of the blade slid down his cheek. Barry closed his eyes and gritted his teeth, willing the arsehole to do it already. Slit his throat. Get it the fuck over with. Let him wake up.

"Tag." He clung to the name, its meaning blurred in his mind between *boss* and *lover*. "Find me. Fucking hell, just find me."

More laughter. Then a door slammed somewhere in the distance. The light grew warm, the wind died down. Denim clung wetly to his legs and crotch.

"Barry!"

He was shaking, hard, and realized it wasn't the cold or the fear. There were hands on him, gripping his shoulders, shaking him.

"Barry, wake up!"

He blinked, pushed at the hands and scrambled away, kicking his feet to move him away from the confinement of the desk. His wheeled office chair skittered back, and he found himself staring at Tag, into his stormy blue eyes, the scent of piss filling his nostrils.

"What happened?" Tag asked.

Barry shook his head. "I—"

"Think, Barry."

Tag crouched in front of him, and Barry squeezed his legs together, embarrassed by the wetness in the front of his jeans.

"It's okay," Tag soothed, stroking his cheek. "Just think. What did you see?"

Barry shook his head. "I thought…" He closed his eyes, and the pain surged back, an echo of the dream. "Fuck!"

"I know." Tag gripped both his biceps. "I know. But you have to think. You have to see it again. Tell me what you saw."

A small sound in the doorway had Barry looking up to find Jessica standing there, arms wrapped around herself.

"Ross," she said quietly.

"Oh. No." Barry felt the blood drain from his face. "No. It couldn't have been. He's not married. No kids."

"Divorced," Tag snapped. "Two kids. Why does it matter?"

"No." Barry swallowed bile. "Did you talk to him? Did you find him?" He glanced up at Jessica. "Is he...?"

"I spoke to him," Tag said soothingly. "He's fine. What is going on?"

"We have to warn him."

Tag lifted both eyebrows. "About?"

"Someone wants to hurt him, Tag. Very badly."

"Who?"

Barry shrugged. "I have no idea."

"How do you know? You've never known before."

"There's never been a Winnowing before. Who the hell knows how that's going to affect things!" Barry knew shouting wasn't going to help matters but he couldn't help it. The Dream had blindsided him. Without even realizing it, he had expected them to taper off, maybe go away altogether. He had thought their Team had won. That their job was done.

He'd hoped.

"How do you know it was Ross?" Tag asked again. "Are you sure?"

He wasn't. Not completely. The difference this time was knowing what the victim was thinking outside the panic. Understanding thoughts that weren't his. Tag as 'boss' in a way Tag had never been Barry's boss, at arm's length, professionally detached, if friendly, and older by decades instead of years. Tag as an assignment, rather than a partner, someone to observe and catalog.

Which was a revelation. Someone had been assigned to their precinct to keep an eye on their captain? It could only be Ross. Anyone else close enough to really make any pertinent observations had been there for years, and Barry got a sense that whoever he'd *been* in that dream hadn't known Tag all that long. So only Ross could have been sent into their midst to keep an eye on Tag. But why? Because Internal Investigations was still gunning for him?

"Fuck." Barry drew in a deep breath and dug his teeth into his bottom lip. "I'm going to try again." If Ross was there to report on Tag, Barry had to know why.

"No." Tag's gaze turned fierce.

"I have to."

Tag glared at him a long time. "Not here." He glanced at Barry's crotch. "Come upstairs and get cleaned up. Then maybe—"

"We've talked about this, Tag. You don't get to call these shots."

Tag growled at him. "There are some I do get to call." He reached into the bottom desk drawer and pulled out a thick silver cock ring. Holding it up, he pinned Barry with a look. "I'm calling them now. Upstairs. Shower. Bed."

"Tag—" Barry swallowed his protests as Tag leaned over his piss-soaked lap and kissed him. Hard.

God, the man had to love him.

"Enough argument," Tag said when he pulled away, and Barry could only nod.

In the doorway, Jessica shuffled back and lowered her gaze. "I'll find Ross," she promised. "Warn him."

Tag nodded curtly, and she disappeared.

Barry followed Tag up the stairs and into their bedroom. The door was closed and locked behind him, and before he had any more time to protest, Tag was peeling him out of his clothing.

"We have to contact him," Barry tried, one last time.

"And we will. He's a cop. A good one, and a grown man. He can look after himself." He stepped back and nodded for Barry to remove his shorts. "And there is no chance he'll ignore a call from Jessica. If anyone can convince him to be careful, she can."

"What makes you think that?"

Tag grinned a short-lived grin. "You really don't get straight men at all, do you?"

Barry shrugged.

"Shower," Tag ordered, effectively putting an end to the discussion. "Now. Go."

Barry obeyed, because if he didn't get straight men, or even really, other gay men, he got Tag, and he knew that voice. There was no compromise in it, so he went. The shower was short, hot and thorough. Less than fifteen minutes after Tag had shaken him out of the terror, he was on the bed, stretched out on his stomach with Tag straddling him, kneading at his shoulders.

"Tell me the dream," Tag ordered.

"Now?"

"Now. Details."

"Tag—"

Tag swatted his arse—hard—and Barry snarled. "Fuck!"

"Do as you're told."

"Why tell you now? Just fuck me. Make me forget."

"Details," Tag insisted, laying the flat of his hand over Barry's arse. "Quickly."

Barry hesitated. The spank that earned him was not the pleasurable kind, and he twisted half onto his side.

Tag straightened him back out and laid his hand flat on his arse again. "Don't make me wait, Barry."

So Barry told him every detail that he could remember. How it had begun on the path to the cave, how the familiar landscape had morphed and twisted, and how he had gradually realized he was not in some random stranger's skin.

"If that sick fuck gets his hands on Ross, Tag, it's going to be ugly. Really ugly. And you know Ross. He won't die nicely."

"He won't die at all. We'll make sure."

"When have we ever been able to make sure of any of it?"

"You didn't die in the dream," Tag reminded him. "So Ross isn't fated to die either. It's the one consistent thing, Barry. Whether you've noticed it or not, I have."

"Noticed what?"

"When we're going to find a body, you die in those dreams. You know you died. You remember that. When there's a chance we might stop it, you dream horrible dreams, but not death dreams."

"That's not true."

"It is true." Tag got off him and rolled him over so they were sprawled, Barry naked on his back and Tag stretched out facing him. "I keep track. I know when to rush an investigation to stop a murder, and when to start searching for a body."

Barry stared up at him. "You never said…"

For the first time in a very long time, Tag looked uncomfortable. "Sometimes I can't make the investigation go fast enough. Sometimes you dream the same dream over and over and eventually, it ends in death when it didn't before. Sometimes, I want to tell you it's not too late, but then…what if it ends up taking too long? What if I tell you we have time, and time runs out? It's hard enough on you to Dream like this in the first place. I never wanted to give you hope when I couldn't be sure it was real hope."

Barry didn't know what to think about that. The Dreams tortured him, and Tag had withheld this vital bit of information? Why? To keep him from hoping? That was cruel.

Tag touched his cheek.

Barry was so deep in shock he didn't think to move, and so Tag's fingers drifted down and closed gently around his chin.

"Maybe I should have said something before now," Tag said. "I didn't because all I saw for our lives was more of this — constant struggling to stay balanced — and I've seen you when you lost faith. I couldn't endure putting you there again. I couldn't be the one to give you that chance at saving someone and then take it away. I suppose that was selfish of me — "

Barry surged up and rolled Tag onto his back, pinning him there and glaring down at him. "You — " He fought to hold on to his temper. "Should have told me. You should have said."

Tag nodded agreement. "I know that now," he said quietly. "And I'm sorry. I can't go back."

"But from now on. This is important, Tag. It's another piece of the puzzle. Do you see?"

Tag's blank stare said he didn't see at all.

"It means there's more to this. To the Team. To you being part of it. If you know how to tell a death Dream from one that matters, even if that's just in my case… Don't you see?"

"We can concentrate on the living. On saving people and not running down dead leads?"

"More than that." Barry rolled off Tag again and spread out on his back. He watched as Tag sat up and pulled the cock ring from his pocket. "You are my anchor. You keep me sane. That will never change. But if what you say is true, then you are so much more. You can see more clearly than I can. Maybe more than any of us—and maybe because you're the only one who's never seen beyond the veil."

"Daniel hasn't either."

"Then you'll talk to him. See if he can predict Jase's Dreams, like you can mine."

Tag looked at him thoughtfully for a long time before eventually nodding. "Fine. But not tonight. Tonight"—he held up the cock ring—"I have different plans."

Barry rumbled out a sigh and nodded.

The cock ring fitted snugly, leaving Barry feeling tightly bound, even though it was the only nod to bondage or control Tag used.

"That's all?" Barry asked. "All I get?"

Tag's hand, cupped around his chin to keep Barry from turning his face away in disappointment, slid gently down his jaw until fingertips caressed his throat. "All you need tonight, Barry."

"Says you." Barry glared a mutinous glare.

"Of course says me. I'm in charge."

"Says you," Barry repeated, and knocked Tag's hand from him.

He sat up and would have heaved Tag off his lap, but Tag surprised him with a hand clasped, palm against his collarbone, long, calloused fingers curling up the nape of his neck, thumb circling at the base of his throat.

"Enough of that, lover." Tag leaned forward and planted a kiss that stole Barry's breath away.

He fought the flutter of his lids as Tag pushed his tongue past Barry's lips, invading his mouth, surging past the vague memories and residual fears. Tag had wanted him to recap the Dream and now it wouldn't leave him alone. The thought faded under Tag's assault, and Barry found himself on his back, struggling faintly against the kiss and the feather-light hand still clasped like a suggestion just under his Adam's apple.

Oh, God. Fuck. Too much.

He curled his fingers under Tag's. All that accomplished was that he now felt his own knuckles pressed to the side of his neck inside that grip, crowding out a little more air, closing in a little more of Tag's control. He lost the battle to keep his eyes open.

Tag pressed that advantage, and the sharp tug of pulled hair made Barry groan. He was fast losing control, not just of the kiss, but of everything. His whole body was sliding into Tag's sphere of domination. His legs parted and fell open. His cock had long since hardened to near pain in the constriction of the ring around its base.

A desperate whine left his throat, and Barry cringed inwardly at the weak, pathetic sound.

"That's it," Tag soothed, moving his mouth and tongue from Barry's lips to his chin, then his throat, where suction and teeth left marks of ownership.

Barry squirmed under him, aware that the hands, recently at his neck, were now far out to one side, Tag's long fingers wrapped tightly around his wrist to hold him spread open. He pushed at Tag's shoulder with his free hand, trying to get him far enough away to see into his eyes, to see where this was going.

The hand doing the pushing was quickly moved, as though he had no strength at all. Spread and pinned, Barry blinked his eyes open to find a view of the ceiling then every sense was quickly overtaken by the sensation of Tag's mouth as he made his way down Barry's body.

Collarbone…the little divot in the center, just at the base of his throat…his left shoulder…down his biceps and back to his shoulder…

"Oh! Fuck!"

Tag's teeth came out as his lips closed around a nipple, and Barry bucked under the sharp pain. It drew all his attention. The Dream faded from thought, from memory from existence. Pain seared his mind, shot white sparks behind lids once more tightly shut, banishing everything dark and uncertain to the deepest corners where it all cowered, but, miraculously, stayed as Tag eased off.

Barry heaved in a breath and let it out again in a cutting, bright sob. "Again!" he pleaded, writhing and lifting his chest for another such encounter. "Tag…"

His begging garnered results as Tag's lips closed over his other nipple, and before Barry managed to haul in another breath, it was forced out of him by the pain. He ground his teeth and bucked, twisted his hips, and finally, let go of a shouted curse that bounced off the walls.

Tag rose up to hover and leer, thoroughly pleased with the reaction.

Barry wheezed and watched, too dazzled by the bright lights still spangling in his vision to manage more.

"Lift the small of your back," Tag said quietly, guiding Barry's body to follow the instruction by pushing a hand under his spine and lifting.

Barry arched for him and panted as Tag instructed him to place both his hands in the resulting hollow under his body. Barry fumbled, tangling his fingers in the sheets, but Tag was there still, to steer him then place a palm on his stomach, indicating that he should relax.

He lay that way, hands pinned under his own weight, and finally got his breathing under control just as Tag grinned and bent back over him. His mouth quickly took over all Barry's attention again while Tag lapped and kissed his way over Barry's torso.

It was the waiting that kept Barry in the very physical realm where Tag wanted him. The anticipation of those teeth digging into flesh, nipping a pinch of his skin or closing with more bruising force on larger areas. Every time he almost got his breathing back under control, Tag knocked him off balance until he was panting and gasping, and when the wet heat of Tag's mouth finally, *finally* found his cock, he had no breath left to even sob his relief.

Tag sucked and licked at him, manipulating his body so his legs were spread wide. The invasion of thick, slicked fingers in his body was almost no surprise at all. He was so overloaded with sensation, he barely noticed his hips beginning to lift to the rhythm of Tag's sucking. It was the stretch of another finger, the depth of their plunge into his body that banished the foggy haze of over-stimulation and focused his attention on his arse.

Tag withdrew from his cock with a last, loud and heated suck, and Barry once more released his tension in a brash, uninhibited curse.

"Look at me," Tag ordered, and Barry did, immediately obeying the command, needing to see the familiar gaze of blue on his face.

Tag pumped his fingers mercilessly into Barry, commanding his attention with a stern but deeply loving gaze.

"Release yourself," Tag said gently.

Barry furrowed his brow. "What?"

"Do it. Take the ring off. Come. Do it."

"You—"

"You don't need me, Barry. You know you don't. You're strong enough to do this without me." Tag leaned in and kissed him with the same demanding, all-consuming attention as he had at the very beginning. It was a short kiss, though, then he was leaning back on his heels, watching, thrusting his fingers deep and nodding. "Do it."

Confused, but trained to follow Tag's direction, Barry liberated his arms so he could reach between his legs to deliver his dick from the restriction of the heavy ring. The freedom was cock-pulsingly good, and he dropped his head back with a groan.

"Stroke yourself."

Barry dragged his head in a sluggish, negative gesture and ground his hips down on Tag's fingers, letting his release rage through him without needing to touch himself. It surged up from his soul, turning physical as it coated his stomach. Satisfied heat rolled through his loins. He groaned and pulled his knees up and out, giving Tag unfettered access to his arse.

Tag growled at him and even as the last of Barry's orgasm shuddered through his system, he heard the jingle of Tag's belt and the rasp of his zipper.

Tag pressed Barry's knees hard against his chest, curling his spine to its limit, then Tag's fat cock nudged at Barry's opening for a breath before Tag took him.

The burn and stretch was phenomenal, opening Barry up when his body wanted to close in around itself in satiation. Tag claimed him when he normally would have soothed him, took his pleasure when he might otherwise have given Barry comfort. It was a different kind of domination this time.

Normally, Tag grounded and centered him. Tonight, Tag took what he wanted, giving Barry no chance to refuse. Tonight, Tag demanded Barry give of himself, that Barry be strong enough to satisfy Tag's need. The idea that Tag assumed he had the strength to give so much astounded Barry.

"Tag..." Barry's near-breathless voice barely overrode Tag's grunts. "Tag."

He reached a hand down and pressed his palm to Tag's cheek. Sweat slicked between his palm and Tag's face. "Tag!" Barry forced the word out and finally, Tag met his eye.

The look was haunted. Uncertain.

Barry caressed his sweaty face and curled his lips into a grim smile. "You can fuck harder than that, Tag. I know you can."

Tag stilled, jolted off his rhythm. "I—"

Barry lifted his back off the bed, groaning under the pressure of forcing his spine to bend even more so he could reach Tag's lips with his own. "You're right," Barry promised between kisses. "I can do this." He closed his mouth securely over Tag's for as long as he could hold the awkward position, then fell back and gripped the backs of his knees. "For you, babe. Anything."

Tag's eyes glimmered, the rims reddening as Barry watched. "I—"

"Do it," Barry echoed Tag's earlier command.

Tag thrust hard once, then again, but stilled, hesitated.

"Anything," Barry repeated.

Thankfully, Tag didn't need further prompting. He fucked, more determinedly than he ever had, claiming every ounce of Barry's body and attention.

As Barry watched his lover's face, Tag's finely crafted control disintegrated. He thrust wildly, without finesse or thought, like every time his hips crashed into Barry's arse, he thought it could be the last time, his last chance. Barry couldn't soothe away the wild. He couldn't tame the desperation. He could do nothing but offer himself as the vessel for all of Tag's fears and frustration. He could only take in the broken bits so they had a place to dwell when Tag needed to be stronger than Barry could manage. He could be Tag's home, his safe place. He could hold the broken, he realized, in ways Tag never could. He could *be* broken so Tag didn't have to be.

The fucking—because there was no other, no gentler word for what they were doing—grew more heated with every thrust. Tag no longer consciously controlled anything. His hips pistoned. He held Barry in a bruising, painful grip, bent in half in a way Barry was going to regret in the morning. But Tag had no idea of the discomfort he caused. He pumped his hips, chased his orgasm, and relentlessly pursued release that was far more than physical. His soul needed purging, and Barry was going to be his means of emptying the darkness that had dogged them for longer than Barry wanted to admit.

The physical pounding was beside the point. When Barry gazed up into Tag's eyes—darker now, a deep, hungering blue that was physically impossible—Barry knew what he must look like when Tag had no choice but to hold him down for his own good. It was a little terrifying to see the demons there, inhabiting his normally controlled and stern lover. This was Tag beyond hope of control or reach.

Barry cupped his lover's face, rubbing both thumbs through the wetness on his lined, stubbled cheeks. "I can do this for you," Barry whispered, making promises he wasn't sure Tag heard. "I can take this from you. Let me."

Tag gasped, ragged and harsh, and pounded harder. Barry winced but shifted his hips to accept the increased thrust.

Tag curled a lip, growled and hammered hard, snatching Barry's hand from his face and pinning it to the mattress, growling out his domination. Barry accepted the censure, but maintained eye contact, even as Tag's eyes darkened to nearly black, like a threat spoken between their hearts. Barry did not flinch away from that look. If Tag had this inside him, it needed to come out. Barry knew how to be in darkness, how to survive there, even how to live when the shadows took over. Tag should know only light. He willed Tag to let go of whatever it was staining the moment.

"Barry?"

"I'm here."

Tag's hand moved from the burning grip around his wrist to lace, fingers intertwined, with Barry's.

"I'm here," Barry said again. "It's okay."

Abruptly, Tag's eyes lightened, widened in shock, and his body stilled, cock buried deep.

Tag's release came with a shout and a curse, gritted teeth and tense muscles. Barry waited out the storm of heavy breathing, shuttered eyes, and stuttering whimpers until Tag collapsed on top of him.

The motion pulled Tag free of his body. Wet, sticky heat flowed out of Barry, but he ignored it, wrapping arms and legs around Tag, holding him tight to his chest.

"I'm sorry," Tag breathed. "So sorry." He buried his face in Barry's neck and there was more heat there, more dampness, more stuttering and broken breaths.

"It's okay," Barry assured him.

"That wasn't fair."

Barry shushed him, petted his hair, rocked him until Tag's breathing eased and he snuck his hands under Barry's body to clutch at his back.

"We're a team, right?" Barry whispered. "You and me. From the beginning, before anyone else ever showed up. You and me, Tag."

"It's too much to expect you to take my anarchy like that. I should have stayed in control."

Barry pushed at him until Tag reluctantly lifted his head. His eyes were puffy and red, his nose runny. He looked miserable and defeated.

Barry kissed him, tender, offering nothing but the love overtaking his every thought. It should have terrified him to see Tag so lost. It only reminded him he was man enough to carry them some of the time. Hadn't he remained sane while Tag was away? It also reminded him he had not once asked Tag if he was okay during all that time. Clearly, he hadn't been.

"I was worried sick," Tag said, gruff finding its way back into his voice. "I was crazy with not knowing, not being able to see your face, look into your eyes, be next to you at night. It was killing me."

Barry nodded. "I should have asked." He remembered the vision when Tag had come home, the images warping and shifting until it was his own hand plunging a knife into Tag's breast. He gasped.

"What?" A tight line appeared between Tag's eyebrows and his lips turned down at the corners.

"The vision I had. Of...hurting you." He couldn't say 'killing'. That was too...final. "It was never Karrick or Morland. It was *me*."

"What?"

"I...did that. That was my own mind trying to get my attention. Or my heart, maybe. I was hurting you, in truth. Not like that. Not physically. But I put so much on you when you could do nothing for me. And I knew, in the back of my head, that it was too much to expect of you. I wanted you to be the strong one. I didn't pick up the ball when I should have. That vision was my own conscience trying to get my attention — to fix it. Fix us."

"We were never broken," Tag protested.

"We were too far apart."

"Well, I was hundreds —"

"No. I mean here." He placed one hand over his heart and one over Tag's. "I dropped the ball, Tag. I didn't check in with you. I let it all go one way, you supporting me. This, tonight?" He cupped Tag's cheek again, lifted his head so he could kiss him, gentle, giving in ways he hadn't in years. "This was a long time coming."

Tag stared into his eyes, neither agreeing nor arguing.

"It was."

"I shouldn't lose it like that, Barry. Not in bed. Not when we're —"

"Shh. You didn't do anything wrong. You released me before you lost it. I was okay. You knew that I was okay, or you wouldn't have let yourself go. It's fine. Tag."

He kissed him again, taking long minutes to explore his lover's mouth with his tongue, pluck at Tag's lips with his own, nibbling when Tag began aggressing and demanding control over the contact. It turned playful, and, Barry thought, serene. Not building to another release, but lazy and comfortable. It lasted until Barry lost track of anything but the kissing and the touching, and when Tag declared an end to it by pulling back, his gaze was once more level, calm and pure blue.

"You amaze me," Tag rasped. His voice was low and spent. The fucking, the cursing, the crying had done him nearly into sleep, and his eyelids drooped. "When you fall apart, you get stronger."

Barry snorted. "If you say so." He pushed his chest out in an attempt to draw a full lung's worth of air into his body.

Tag grinned and slid off him, curling so their legs intertwined and they were facing one another. "You in the wet spot?" he asked, pushing a dark curl out of Barry's eyes.

Barry shrugged. "Who cares?"

He kissed Tag's forehead, his nose, his lips, and Tag sleepily kissed back. He was still lost in the gentle blue of Tag's serene smile when he fell asleep.

Chapter Thirty-Six

Jase crouched and ran his hand in circles over Dan's back, waiting out the dry heaves. How many times did this make, he wondered? Dan's queasy stomach continued to prove his lover's greatest weakness.

"You would think I'd be getting used to this by now," Dan said, his voice wobbling around the last few quivers of his throat. He leaned his elbow on the toilet seat and rested his head in his palm. His bangs scrunched up between his clenched fingers to stick out in all directions.

Jase felt a distant twinge of something that told him seeing Dan like this should affect him somehow.

"There is no getting used to this," he said finally. Even to his own ears, Jase thought his voice sounded flat.

It must have to Dan, too, because he lifted his dark head, squared his shoulders and swiveled to plunk his arse onto the bath mat. "Come here."

He held out a hand and Jase didn't think twice. He took it and knelt between Dan's legs, facing him.

"Talk to me," Dan ordered.

Instead, Jase stretched up and used his free hand to run the sink and warm a cloth, which he used to wipe Dan's mouth and face.

"Jase." Dan took the cloth from him and tossed it into the sink. "Stop."

"Let me—"

"Stop." Dan pushed him gently back so he had room to get to his feet.

"I want to...take care of you." Jase's voice softened. His gaze drifted to fix on Dan's crotch, now at eye level.

"Get up."

Dan pulled on his hand, and Jase rose, reluctant, to stand before him.

"Don't treat me like glass, Dan, please." Jase's eyes sparked, hot with tears. He clung to the sting, to Dan's hand, to reality, unwilling to slip back into the fog where Karrick had left him. "Please. I need—"

"Babe, I know what you need." Dan cupped his face. "But you have to trust me."

"I do."

"Then stop."

Jase clamped his mouth shut, but he moved, closing the space between them and wrapping himself around Dan. He rubbed his groin against Dan's, eager to feel his lover's interest. Not waiting for Dan to respond, he began kissing Dan's neck, squirming into him, making it impossible for Dan to pretend he didn't know what Jase was asking for.

"Stop!" Dan pushed him back, a grip on each arm. "No, Jase. Stop this."

"I need!"

"Talk first."

Jase shook his head, devastated by the rejection. "I...can't. I—" The agony overtook him, but he couldn't cry in front of Dan. Not now. Not when he had been so sure they were back and solid. He couldn't look at him.

Spinning, he fled.

"Jase!" Dan's voice was loud, hard, and the sound of his pursuit was close.

Jase ignored him. All he had to do was make it to the end of the hallway, and the front door was right there. He'd be free. Alone.

He gripped the doorknob and Dan's footsteps halted.

"You stop, Jase," he growled. "You stop and you come back here."

Jase shook, tightening his fingers on the handle, but he didn't turn it.

"Come back here."

Jase couldn't move. His feet were cemented to the floor, his spine fused to immobility. He couldn't face Dan, couldn't see anyone else who might be in the room witnessing his flight. He didn't know what to do.

"Jase." Dan's voice had lowered, but the edge remained. The utter command.

Had Karrick's voice had that edge? It had. But not so keen and focused a point. Karrick's had been...hysterical at times. Frightening, a saw-toothed blade used to hurt him. Dan could never be frightening in his command. Only in his absence.

Jase whirled, desperate suddenly to see his lover there, to know he was present and waiting.

Dan's lips turned up slightly in a grim smile. "Come to our room." He held out a hand.

Any trace of the queasy, unsteady man of a few moments ago was gone. Before Jase was the man he'd met so very long ago, who had taken him home and splayed him out that first time, cajoling Jase's cooperation and surrender with words and touch, not needing restraint of any kind to achieve his will. Jase had submitted willingly because Dan had looked at him with such certainty that Jase was his. There had never been a question.

Dan looked at him the same way now. He knew. Jase belonged to him. The uncertainty, the hesitation, had all been Jase's.

Dan took a step closer, still out of reach, but closer.

"Don't doubt us, Jase. Not anymore." He smiled gently. "It wasn't all you, babe. I questioned. I shouldn't have, but I did, and that sent you to Karrick. I know better now. I see enough of this world, fucked up as it is, to see that you and me are right. Right enough to make up for all the other shit. Come upstairs. I'll show you."

Jase shook his head. "I can't." In his gut, he knew those two little words were more truth than he'd spoken in weeks. Karrick had broken parts of him, and he couldn't let Dan near those cracks and crevices. He had to protect his lover from that darkness Karrick had released.

"The beauty of it," Dan said, being the one to close the distance between them this time, "is that you don't have to. Leave it to me. I will do whatever is needed. Whatever you need."

"Leave me alone?" Jase asked. "Can you leave me alone?"

Even as he'd said it, he felt the cold of the fog creeping back around his heart, shrouding his brain, making it hard to think and feel. It was a sensation he'd almost grown used to around Karrick. The brilliant spots of sheer pain had alleviated it, and he'd reveled in Karrick's ability to peel back the veil so he could see normally again. He'd needed those moments of clarity so badly. He'd needed Karrick.

Darkness shouldered in on him, and he sank back, pressing his frame against the door just to feel something outside himself. That darkness could be so seductive, shielding him from the confusion of real life, from the hurt of Dan leaving him, from the Dreams. But it was smothering as well. He would lose himself in it. Like falling asleep in the snow, it was both sweet comfort and deadly release.

"Karrick liked the dark," he murmured. "He liked to keep me there."

Dan's smile never wavered. "You don't belong alone in the dark, Jase. Karrick was wrong to let you think that."

"He never would have left me."

Karrick had wanted to rule. Not just Jase, but everything, and he'd meant to keep Jase at his side as he did, the ultimate symbol of his control.

"He never would have left me," Jase repeated in a whisper.

"And to prove I'm not like him, I should?"

"I don't know." Jase gazed into Dan's eyes, truly lost and confused. He had so little idea what he needed or wanted. But closed in the pocket of protection between the door and Dan's body, he felt safe, at least. Alone? Maybe. But not abandoned. Karrick had abandoned him in the most vulnerable state imaginable. Left him in pain and helpless, proof that he controlled not only Jase's body, but his very life. Jase couldn't abide the possibility of that ever happening again.

"Then let me help you figure it out." Dan was warm. Present. Comforting. Familiar.

Were those reasons to trust him?

Jase looked up into his eyes and saw clarity there. There were no shadows and not an ounce of uncertainty. He might have a weak stomach, but he had a stout heart, and strong hands, and Jase craved both those things.

He pitched forward, and Dan caught him, held him tight. There was nothing sexual in the embrace, only the promise of a future.

"I'm going to take you upstairs now," Dan whispered into his hair. "I'm going to help you shower and get clean, and I am going to inspect every inch of you." He leaned Jase away from him just enough to see into his face. "*Every* inch. You understand?"

Jase swallowed and nodded.

"I need to see what he did to you. I need to understand why you let him."

Again, Jase nodded.

"And every bit of what he did will be washed away before I'm done with you tonight. Do you understand that?"

Jase wanted to believe him. He wanted what Dan said to be true.

"Come on."

He wanted so badly, he allowed Dan to lead him back up the stairs to the room Barry had offered them. They went inside and closed the door. Jase expected the instructions to begin at that point. He waited for the order to strip but it never came. Dan stood in front of him, watching him, considering him, but silent.

"What are we waiting for?" Jase asked at last.

Dan smiled. "Don't move." He went to the closet then pulled out the candle box.

As he set it on the table next to the bed, Jase watched him. Dan paid little heed to his scrutiny as he shoved the bed up against the wall and spread first the plastic, then the cotton drop cloth on the floor next to it. He arranged a candle holder with a red candle and a variety of other candles in the center of the drop cloth. The red candle and one of the tapers were partially burnt and Jase frowned.

"It's fine, babe," Dan assured him, following his troubled gaze. He picked up the red candle and lit it. "This is just for the flame. To make it easy to light the others." He held it up a moment then gently blew it out to set it back in its holder. "The other one is because I wanted to know what it feels like."

Jase raised one eyebrow.

"If I'm going to do this with you, I have to know."

"We've done it before."

Dan smiled, the expression a little chagrined. "And I was very, very lucky I didn't hurt you. This time, I'm doing it right." He set the lighter down and turned to Jase. "I've read up and asked someone who knows what she's doing. I took the time to make sure I can keep you safe. Now. About your clothes…"

Unexpectedly, a flash of fear jolted Jase, and he clutched at the front of his shirt. He should not be afraid. Not of Dan.

"It's okay, babe. We'll go at your pace." Dan approached, hands out, until his fingers touched Jase's hands twined in the front of his shirt. Gently, slowly, Dan loosened Jase's fingers.

Jase let him, allowing Dan's touch as they stared at one another. The cold fear inside him wasn't about Dan. His head knew this. His heart didn't need to be told. It was his body that remembered the pain and the desertion, even the threats Karrick had visited on him. It was his body that had to relearn the trust he'd once shared with Dan.

He let his hands fall to his sides and drew in a deep breath as Dan lifted the hem of his shirt, drawing it slowly up his torso until Jase had to raise his arms and allow it to be removed or refuse.

He lifted his arms.

The shirt made his hair stand on end with static electricity as Dan pulled it off him, but Dan tossed it aside and carefully smoothed his hair back against his skull with a soft smile.

"Pants?" he asked.

Jase nodded and let Dan remove his pants and underwear.

He had been naked in front of Dan hundreds of times so he wasn't sure why it surprised him to feel no additional discomfort to be so now.

"My turn," Dan said, keeping his voice low and calm.

Jase watched him strip then accepted his outstretched hand. Dan led him to the bathroom adjoining their room, and inside, where Jase waited for Dan to adjust the water temperature.

In the shower, Dan did as he'd promised, beginning with Jase's hair and scrubbing and examining every square inch of his body. When Dan reached Jase's arse, Jase flinched. He couldn't help it. The memory of the brutality of Karrick's use of that whip made him first blush, then shake.

Dan gathered him into his embrace and took long minutes soothing him. When Jase finally had the shaking under control, Dan stepped back enough to look at him. "I'm going to try again. I have to look and be sure you're okay. Nothing more."

Jase clenched his jaw. "I don't mind," he said.

"It's fine if you do. We have our whole lives. We'll figure this out."

"Why would you?" It made little sense to Jase that Dan was suddenly willing to take on all this additional baggage when he had left him over only the Dreams before.

Faintly, through the walls, Barry's voice raised in curses made them both stop to listen.

Finally, when the excitement seemed to die down again, Dan smiled. "That's why. Because what they have is what we need. I made a mistake throwing it away, but I will do everything you need me to do to repair that damage I did."

"Why?" Jase asked again.

"Easy."

Dan gathered him into his arms, and Jase gratefully rested his cheek against his lover's shoulder. Water streamed over and between them, warming his skin while Dan's embrace soothed his soul.

"Because I love you," Dan said. "I want you in my life and I want to take care of you. I want to protect you because your life is all about protecting people you'll never know. You deserve the best care I can give for that."

Jase made a grunt of acceptance.

"Now let me look at your arse. Let me be sure there's no lasting damage."

Jase hated doing it, not because he was frightened any longer, but because doing so was confession that he had put himself in harm's way. He had deliberately allowed the possibility of damage being done to Dan's property.

"It's okay," Dan soothed, running a hand over Jase's flank as Jase bent to allow the inspection.

His hands were gentle as he parted Jase's cheeks. The examination was thankfully only visual and very swift. A look satisfied Dan that Jase was bruised, but not otherwise hurt. He was quick to right Jase then pull him into his arms, Jase's back pressed to Dan's front. He cradled him there, murmuring sweet words in his ear until Jase relaxed again.

"I'm okay?" Jase asked finally, his voice shakier than he might have liked.

"You are." Dan kissed the side of his head.

"It hurts," Jase told him, surprised that the confession had blurted out of him. He'd been ignoring the aches and pains, focusing on everything else Karrick had nearly destroyed. His body had been the least of his concerns until now.

Now he understood that as much as Dan wanted this chance to keep him, it meant Jase had to surrender not just his heart, and the Dreams — two things he hadn't even hesitated over in the past — but everything.

He'd always suspected he was broken. His heart was of no great consequence. He was defective. If anyone wanted such a questionable thing, he'd give it. The Dreams, he'd willingly give away if he could, or share the burden if that was all he was allowed. But his body? His body was the only thing he had any real claim or control over. If he wanted what Dan offered, he had to give that up, too.

"Let's finish up here," Dan said, tenderly setting him firmly on his own feet. "And I will take that hurt from your mind, okay?"

Jase faced him. "You can do that?"

"I can certainly try." He cupped Jase's face. "I know this is more terrifying for you than anything, Jase, letting me have this." He dropped his hands to Jase's shoulders. "I'm asking you to give me the only thing you can call truly yours."

Jase stared at him.

"I swear to you, I will take what you give me and make it better."

"You promise?"

Jase knew it was an impossible promise to make. He stared into Dan's eyes and waited.

Dan leaned in and kissed him, long and firmly, but with so much love Jase's toes curled. He pulled back and Jase saw the promise in his lover's eyes. He also saw the truth.

"You and I will make the best of what we have," Dan said. "Make everything better?" He smiled and kissed Jase's forehead. "I won't make you a promise I might have to break. That would only make it worse when bad things happen, and you know they will."

Jase nodded.

"So I won't lie to make you feel better now."

"But you'll cover my body in hot wax so I can forget for a little while that I let that monster use me in ways that—"

Dan put a finger over Jase's lips and shushed him. "Tomorrow, you and I will sit down and you will tell me everything. Tonight, it's about a small flame and some melted wax and the chance to cleanse your body. That first."

"You think it will work?"

Once more, Dan pecked his forehead, and this time, he left his lips in contact with Jase's wet skin for several heartbeats. Finally, he moved to look into Jase's eyes. "I hope, babe. I sincerely hope. But I have only one way to find out, and I hope you trust me enough to let me try."

Jase sighed and leaned into him. "All I want is your hands and your heart, Dan."

"In that order?"

Jase felt Dan's chin on the top of his head and relaxed into the arms that surrounded him.

"Tonight, yeah."

"Yours," Dan whispered. "All of me."

"And the order?"

Dan kissed the top of his head. "Trust me."

For the next little while, there were only quiet commands and Dan's hands as he turned and manipulated Jase, gently shaving the fine hairs from his forearm and his legs. He felt strangely silky and bare as Dan toweled him dry.

"What about this?" Jase ran both hands over his chest, not hairy, but not completely bare, either.

Dan smiled. "You and I are both a little too shaky to manage shaving the rest."

He cupped Jase's cheek and leaned in to claim a kiss. It was tender and time-consuming and left Jase slightly breathless.

"For tonight, this is enough." Dan trailed his fingers along Jase's arm, shoulder to wrist, and Jase shivered.

"Okay."

"Come with me." Dan took his hand and led him to bedroom. Together, they sat in the center of the drop sheet.

They faced one another, legs crossed, knees touching, and Jase watched in silence as Dan lit the red candle then a white taper and a white pillar.

"Questions?" Dan asked as he worked.

"Why two?"

"One for dripping from a height," Dan said, picking up the taper. "Here." He wrapped Jase's fingers around the slim candle then his own right hand around Jase's left to hold the candle with him. "Like this. Hold my hand." He offered his left hand, palm up.

Hesitant at first, Jase looked into his lover's eyes and saw only patience and calm. Dan placed the back of his left hand in Jase's palm.

"We're limited to arm span like this, but it's okay, because I've tested it on myself already. I know how it feels." He lifted their hands, clasping the candle so it hovered in the air above and between them, and guided Jase to tip the taper until a drop of wax plopped onto Dan's upturned palm. He hissed through his teeth but didn't flinch as drop after drop landed on his skin.

Jase watched in fascination. "How does it feel?" He sounded breathless and excited. His heart skipped and stuttered as another drop landed on Dan's palm and the near-cool wax splashed his fingers.

Dan smiled at him as he straightened the candle and rearranged their lower hands so Jase's was on top. "Ready?"

Jase nodded, holding his breath.

"No, no." Dan let go of his hand long enough to press his palm to Jase's chest. "Breathe. Don't hold your breath."

Jase licked his lips and drew in a deep suck of air. He let it out then drew another, gazing into Dan's sweet, enduring brown eyes until he could see Dan was satisfied he was under control.

"Good," Dan praised.

Jase smiled, deeply, from his heart, for what felt like the first time in years.

"Oh, babe." Dan answered his smile with a sigh of contentment and took Jase's hand in his again. "Ready?"

"I am," Jase said, and was pleased his voice sounded stronger now.

Dan's hand under his was warm and he felt the hard patches of wax against the back of his own hand, interrupting the soft sensation of skin on skin. Even that was interesting and exciting, and Jase's stomach dipped a bit, like maybe his cock could, eventually, take interest in something again.

"Look at me," Dan said. "Not your hand."

Jase obeyed, gazing once more into Dan's eyes.

He knew the drip was coming because Dan tilted their hands, and an instant later came the splat of heat on the meat of his palm. He gasped.

"Too hot?"

"N-no." Jase let out a breath then pulled in another.

Dan tipped the candle again and another drop landed on top of the first. The heat was less, and Jase breathed through it. It was interesting, being a part of the process, but he longed, as the next drop fell, to give the control of it over to Dan. He didn't want to know when it was coming. He wanted Dan to create the rest of the world around him, sink him into sensation and warmth.

"What are you thinking?" Dan asked.

Jase shook his head.

"I can see into you, Jase. You know that. Just as you can see into me."

And he was right. Jase could see the patience and the love in Dan's eyes. He could see the determination. And, behind all of that, he could see the desire in Dan for the time Jase would be willing to trust him again.

"So what's on your mind?"

"I understand," Jase said finally. "How it works." His fingers on the shaft of the candle twitched under Dan's.

Dan nodded. "Okay. Put the candle back in the holder." He released his own grip, and Jase did as instructed, fitting the candle back in its stand. "Good."

Dan caressed the side of Jase's face and neck, kissed him again, and smiled. "I need you to sit very still, yeah?"

Jase nodded.

"Good." Dan retrieved the taper and held it aloft again, instructing Jase to keep his gaze on Dan's face.

The drips came at random intervals, sometimes landing on previous wax splotches, sometimes on bare skin. The sharp jolts of heat flashed right through Jase, stripping away the last of Karrick's foggy haze, brightening all his dark corners. With each drip, Jase came nearer the surface of his own being, and by the time Dan was instructing him to lay down on his back, he was floating in a bright cloud of compliance where every beat of his heart was strong, thudding through him like a drum.

"Very good," Dan whispered, rising up on his knees to hover over Jase. "Close your eyes now."

Jase did.

"The pillar candle has pools of wax," Dan said, his voice steady and conversational. "It isn't any hotter than the taper, but there is more of it." He arranged Jase's arms so he was lying on his back, palms up and arms out at angles from his body. "You might feel some splash on your sides, but it won't be too bad. You tell me if anything is too much."

"Yes," Jase whispered from the pure dark behind his lids. He could sense Dan next to him, his lover's calm presence a balm.

"Good."

A moment later, a searing trail of blissful heat ran from Jase's palm up the inside of his forearm to the inside of his elbow.

"Ah! God!" He groaned as the heat dug into his body and warmed his soul, sparkling through him, up his spine and making the hair on the back of his neck stand on end. The heat flushed him and traveled from the roots of his hair down his body and stirred his sex. "Oh." He moaned, much more softly.

"Very nice," Dan whispered.

After that, the wax was interspersed with soft touch, caressing fingers, and Dan's wet, hungry mouth. Jase never knew what to expect, and the temptation to open his eyes and watch his lover was so strong at points, he had to screw up his face to keep them closed.

The torture was exquisite. Divine. He had almost believed Karrick had ruined him for the feeling coursing through his blood now, warming his body, stiffening his cock.

"Dan..."

He couldn't keep track any more of the last sensation. Pain and pleasure blended, the heat all one, his skin tight from cooled wax and goosebumps all at once.

When Dan's hot, wet mouth closed over his cock, he bucked, thrusting into the perfect suction. His swears and breath burst from him along with his orgasm and he was left puddled on the drop sheet as Dan drew back.

"Open your eyes."

Jase did, to stare up at Dan, sitting back on his heels between Jase's legs. The room was lit only with candlelight. Dan's eyes were deep, dark and satisfied as they flickered in the glow.

The creeping fear of unsafe sex shivered through Jase as he gazed at his beloved.

"Calm yourself."

Jase started.

"What is it?" Dan leaned forward, bracing a hand on either side of Jase's head to peer down on him. "Your eyes." His voice crept toward awed and gruff, but he didn't look away or indicate that he wanted to.

Jase knew his eyes had gone black. He wasn't alone in his own head, and although they had all longed for contact with their Master, the sensation of having Rivald in his head at such a time made Jase whimper.

There was a dry chuckle behind the presence making itself known. *"You humans and your scruples."* Rivald affected a deep, put-upon sigh. *"I'm tired, child. I apologize for the invasion at such a...delicate...time. But you have always been the most receptive, and you are most open to me now. I wanted you to know all is well."*

"Well?" Jase asked. "No STDs? Because you can control that?"

"Our investment in you is substantial, child. Do you think something as mundane as a virus will hinder our use of you? I think not."

"Well. Bully for us, then," Jase muttered.

That dry, sardonic chuckle came again. *"It is as well that I am pleased with you. I can ignore such attitude in my good humor."*

"You're pleased with me?" Jase wondered if he should be surprised by that. He wasn't sure he'd added anything at all to the success of their bid.

"You may feel you contributed nothing, but in fact, your bravery in facing Karrick was the thing that allowed the others to get to him. You were his weakness, while facing him was your strength. You should be proud. You and your Team did well. The Winnowing will proceed under our guidance, as it always should have been. Enjoy these next

few days of true rest. When I call on you all again, your work will be tenfold what it was."

Jase shivered. "Why?" he whispered to the voice. "Why so much? We've already done what you wanted."

"And there is more to do."

"More death," Jase sighed, despairing. He hated that part of their job very much.

Dan petted his face, watching him with concern.

"And more life. Have faith, child. Not all those you encounter deserve to die. It will be your partners' jobs — Tag, Daniel, Sue, Ross — to sort out who lives and who is left to Leyton. A task I do not envy them."

"What?" Jase would have sat up, but Dan was in his way, still running soothing hands over him. "Why? Why them? That isn't fair!"

"Because those of us who see beyond the veil dwell too much in darkness to be impartial. Let those who live in the light seek it out in your targets. It won't be easy."

Jase had the distinct impression Rivald was looking out of his eyes as he gazed up at Dan's concerned but loving face.

"I truly feel you have all chosen your other halves wisely. I have faith, child, and so must you."

"Faith," Jase breathed.

But there was no response. Rivald was gone.

"What happened?" Dan asked. "More Dreams?"

Jase shook his head and held out his arms. "Not tonight, love. Not tonight."

Epilogue

What Rivald had promised Jase would be days of rest were anything but for most of them, Daniel included. Perhaps in the realm beyond the veil, there was little to do until Morland and his errant Tool had been dealt with there. Barry's explanation that the defeat of the two in the earthly realm had bound them to the other side permanently seemed simple enough. Over there, Rivald could dispose of them as he saw fit. If Barry knew what the Tool Master planned for the traitors, he didn't say. Daniel thought it was probably just as well. He didn't think he wanted to know.

He was content to pack up every last stitch of clothing and stick of furniture he owned and move it all to a small house across the street from where Barry and Tag lived. The place was a one-story, miniscule little brick house with a single bath and two tiny bedrooms. It was all he and Jase would need for their new life together. Unlike the others, he didn't question the money they were supplied to live on. They deserved it, after everything they had already been through and everything they were still likely to endure. For however long this little vacation lasted, though, he was more than ready to ensconce himself and Jase in that house and remember exactly how well they fitted together, bodies, minds, souls.

Deep down, he knew this time was best spent binding Jase to him, and himself to his lover. They would need the ties, and Jase required that Dan do anything and everything to erase Karrick from his psyche. Sure, occasionally, they crossed the street for a meal, or to help clean up the mess left behind by evil meeting its demise in Barry's and Tag's back garden, but for the most part, they kept to themselves.

* * * *

The dream of Ross didn't come again. Tag wasn't sure if that was a relief or a worry. Barry spent more than a few nights tossing and turning in anticipation of it. The suspense of not having that particular Dream was almost as bad as the nightmare itself. All Tag could do was resort to fucking him into oblivion and hope the physical exertions were enough to let Barry get the restful sleep he so needed.

He took some time off to help his lover purge their yard of the tainted soil where Morland and Karrick had died. They shipped it out by the truck load, commissioning Ross's pick-up for the task, and Ross himself to man a shovel.

Putting the man to an inquisition about how and why he had been assigned to Tag's precinct would wait until Tag was back in the office. For now, he observed the younger cop and bided his time.

* * * *

"I feel it," Ross said quietly.

Jessica studied him, a frown on her pretty face. Her blonde hair was pulled back in a bouncing ponytail, and she wore a set of sweats far too big for her. The pants and sleeves were rolled up at ankles and wrists, and the knees of the pants were ground through with soil. They had both been in Barry's back garden, Ross shoveling foul-smelling soil into the back of his truck, and Jessica transplanting new flowers along the power-washed walkway leading from the back door.

The heavy slabs had been pulled up and the soil around them removed, as well, and now the area was ready for new life. Ross could think of no one better to implement that plan than the pert young woman gazing at him with such intensity now.

"But why would he?" she asked. "You've known about us from the beginning. Why would he start to suspect you now?"

"I have no idea."

"It doesn't make any sense," she said, sipping from the glass of water in her hand and wrapping her free arm around her middle. She leaned on the counter opposite him in the little kitchen and rested her elbow on her forearm. "He's trusted you with everything, and you have done nothing but help us clean up mess after mess. There is no reason for him to suddenly stop trusting you."

Ross studied her troubled face.

"Unless there's something we don't know about..."

She was talking to herself, Ross knew. Not even looking at him, but the words sent a shiver down his spine. She did that more and more lately. Everyone on the team had a confidant. Graham, the new guy, had his girlfriend, Sue. Barry, of course had Tag, and Jase was practically glued to his very possessive boyfriend, Daniel. Even Leyton confided in Jessica, and while Ross was sure the big man still scared her, she had softened somewhat toward him since he'd so definitively defeated their enemies. If she didn't like him, she at least trusted him, and was kind enough to him to hide her disgust.

"Jess." He touched her biceps, but she grimaced and brushed his hand away.

"Cal would know what to do," she muttered.

Ross managed, barely, to stifle a growl. He had no right to be jealous of a dead man. It was no fault of anyone's that Jessica's boyfriend — or fiancé, or whatever he had been to her — had died so brutally, and should be no surprise that she missed him. She'd seen him killed. She had to live with the memory and the misplaced guilt that he was dead and she wasn't.

She'd once told Ross that as much as she hated the whole business, she wished she had known what she was in time to save him. She felt she had been a lure, even then. Only not knowing what she was, not knowing the rest of the Team even existed, there had been no way to protect her or save Cal. Still, she felt responsible in retrospect.

"What do you mean, 'Cal would know what to do'?" he asked.

"Well, he was a reporter, wasn't he? A crime reporter. He knew what questions to ask. Where to look when things felt fishy."

She gazed up at Ross, and he was caught off guard by the bright, watery glint in her big blue eyes.

"He was good at his job," she went on. "If there was something to the way you think Tag is treating you now, he would know what pile of red tape to dig under to find out why. If there even is a why."

Ross's gut clenched, a cold fist tightening around his innards. Cal *had* been very good at his job. He'd been a right nuisance, as so many reporters were. If there were answers to find, he had been the type to find them. Ross didn't like to be glad the man was dead, but he figured it was just as well Cal wasn't around to do any digging. He was fairly sure the secrets the reporter would uncover were not all that deeply buried.

Which was why Tag's sudden and inexplicable scrutiny made Ross nervous.

"Maybe you're right," Ross said. "Maybe I'm imagining it."

Jessica sighed. "I just wish..."

Her breath hitched, and this time, when Ross reached to touch her, instead of pulling away, she leaned toward him.

He took the glass from her grip, set it on the counter, then pulled her against his chest. She didn't resist as he wrapped an arm lightly over her shoulders. "Shhh." He rested his chin on the top of her head. "I know, Jess. I know."

She didn't sniffle or sob, but pulled in one wobbling breath after another while he rubbed her back. Movement from the corner of his eye caught his attention and he looked up, unsurprised to see Leyton hovering in the shadows, watching them.

The big man's eyes glittered from the depths of his scars. His fingers wandered listlessly over the buttons of his shirt. His lips were a straight, hard line as he stared at Ross.

The look didn't feel threatening, just...sad. Resigned. Leyton said nothing as he watched them, and soon, Jessica was pulling herself upright. She wiped a hand over her face, grabbed her water then gulped it all back. She hurried past Leyton, who melted back into the shadows against the hallway wall to let her pass.

The front door opened and closed quietly, and Ross was left alone with the lurking Killer.

"Something is not right," rumbled Leyton's voice from out of those shadows.

"What do you mean?" The cold feeling in Ross's gut intensified.

"There are pieces missing."

Ross had heard that said a few times now, since what they all referred to lately as 'That Night'. "So people keep saying, but what does that mean?"

Leyton took a few steps forward, bringing his bulk and his ragged face, into the light. "I had a mother once," Leyton said. "She made me." He indicated his face. "But Rivald raised me. I see more than most people think. If it takes me some time to understand what I see, make no mistake, I see it. And you"—he jabbed a finger in Ross's direction—"I see. You know what I am. You know what I do." He took another step forward. "I will protect her. I will protect them all."

"Meaning?" Ross crossed both arms over his chest and widened his stance as Leyton took one more, small step toward him.

"When I was young, I saw black, and I saw white. I never understood gray. I knew I lived in the black." He cocked his head. "I think I was wrong about that, but I still see shadow far better than I do light."

Ross stared at the man. He talked in riddles and that was not like the Leyton he had known. "Are you saying you see me as a shadow on your Team?"

"They want to trust you," Leyton said. "I don't have to. I answer only to the burn."

And that was clear as day. Ross gave a curt nod, which was answered only by a grunt from Leyton, who turned and left the room without another word.

About the Authors

Jaime Samms

Jaime writes, romance, fantasy, urban fantasy, shifter stories about men, about life, about love. Her work is populated with mostly men, most of whom are into each other, and yes, we do mean into each other. You can find plenty of free reading on her website.

She also reviews for Dark Diva Reviews, mostly the same types of stories, and will happily spout her opinion on the books she reads to her kids, who she home schools. Finally, she's occasionally gainfully employed. She writes for the love it, and hopes to pass on that love to her readers, her kids, and anyone else who comes along.

Sarah Masters

Sarah Masters is a multi-published author in three pen names writing several genres. She lives with her husband, children, and three cats in an English village. She writes full time and is also a cover artist and blog designer. In another life she was an editor. Her other pen names are Natalie Dae and Charley Oweson.

Sarah is busy co-authoring with Jaime Samms. They have several books in mind so will be writing for a couple of years to come! She also needs to finish her M/M novel, the tale she's dubbed The Book That Doesn't Want To End. She's at the last chapter but is afraid to open it in case that last chapter isn't really the last chapter...

Jaime and Sarah love to hear from readers. You can find their contact information, website and author biography at http://www.totallybound.com

Totally Bound Publishing